beyond this point

beyond this point

HOLLEY
RUBINSKY

McCLELLAND & STEWART

Library and Archives Canada Cataloguing in Publication

Rubinsky, Holley, 1943-
Beyond this point / Holley Rubinsky.

ISBN 0-7710-7854-4

I. Title.

PS8585.U265B49 2006   C813'.54   C2005-906876-0

We acknowledge the financial support of the Government of Canada through the Book Publishing Industry Development Program and that of the Government of Ontario through the Ontario Media Development Corporation's Ontario Book Initiative. We further acknowledge the support of the Canada Council for the Arts and the Ontario Arts Council for our publishing program.

The excerpt that appears on page v is from the poem "Two Words: A Wedding" from the collection *Selected Writing: As Elected*, by bpNichol, edited by Jack David. Published by Talonbooks, 1980. Copyright © bpNichol. Reprinted with permission of the publisher.

The epigraph that appears on page vii is an excerpt from the poem "The Loneliness of the Military Historian" from the collection *Morning in the Burned House*, by Margaret Atwood. Published by McClelland & Stewart, 1995. Copyright © Margaret Atwood. Reprinted with permission.

Typeset in Sabon by M&S, Toronto
Printed and bound in Canada

This book is printed on acid-free paper that is 100% recycled, ancient-forest friendly (100% post-consumer recycled).

McClelland & Stewart Ltd.
75 Sherbourne Street
Toronto, Ontario
M5A 2P9
www.mcclelland.com

1 2 3 4 5   10 09 08 07 06

For Yuri Rubinsky
1952–1996

"There are things you have words for, things you do not
have words for. There are words that encompass all your
feelings & words that encompass none. There are feelings
you have that are like things to you, picked up & placed in
the pocket, worn like the cloth the pocket is attached to, like
a skin you live inside of. There is a body of feeling, of
language, of friends; the body politic, the body we are
carried inside of till birth, the body we carry our self inside
of till death, a body of knowledge that tells of an afterlife, a
heaven, an unknown everything we have many words for
but cannot encompass. There are relationships between
words & concepts, between things, between life & death,
between friends & family, between each other & some other
other."

– bpNichol, from "Two Words: A Wedding"

". . . I tell
what I hope will pass as truth.
A blunt thing, not lovely.
The truth is seldom welcome,
especially at dinner,
though I am good at what I do.
My trade is courage and atrocities.
I look at them and do not condemn.
I write things down the way they happened,
as near as can be remembered."

– Margaret Atwood, from
"The Loneliness of the Military Historian"

beyond this point

1

The voice on the phone had its own idea about what Kathleen Elliot should be doing. And it was immediately obvious to Kathleen that the woman behind the voice didn't know her, didn't know that her emergencies were internal, her turmoil inside and based upon – who knew? – probably a chemical imbalance. The 911 voice seemed to have no idea of the impact of her tone. The fear it set going. Either the woman hadn't a clue or didn't care that her brusque, efficient manner was making things worse, making Kathleen more frantic and further committing James to being, truly, *on the floor unable to move or get up* and unable, as far as Kathleen could tell, to hear her. Or maybe the woman was unaware that her bossiness was prodding Kathleen toward a disturbing notion, along the lines of *maybe there is something*. Maybe James really was –. It was unthinkable that an ambulance was already on the way. Possibly Kathleen had been too quick to judge, too quick to reach for the phone. Now there was the unflappable voice, the telephone wire connecting the clipped, rehearsed words to James's prone silence, the fact that he had projects and papers and his computer on of no significance. The change in their circumstance, James's and hers, inched forward. Kathleen lost her balance, nearly tripped over him. The voice wanted to know if she had done CPR. James was face down and everyone knew it was not a good idea – moving the body. All right, so she would do it, make-believe a real-life emergency *as though* –

I'm sorry to bother you – she had not said that. She dialed and said, James is on the floor and – *My husband is on the floor and he won't get up. He's not moving. I'm afraid to touch him in case –*

An ambulance was on the way. *Stroke*, she was thinking.

The galvanizing monotone ticked through a checklist, causing a dizzying rush: She must do something, must do it now! She dropped the receiver on the bed, kneeled again to him. She slid her hands under his chest and lifted. He came up an inch, solid as stone. She tried again, heaved and manoeuvred him onto his back. When she opened her eyes, she saw that he did not look like himself. He had put on a mask, slightly garish. Dark circles lay under the eyes, dark circles purplish-blue. She placed her mouth atop his. His lips were cold. She forced breath in. His mouth was dank, his beard – she puffed, she blew, she pressed on his stiff chest. *It's not working*, she shouted into the room and bent again and pressed on his hardening chest as – *What is he doing? Why is he doing this?* – something irrevocable rippled past. She whipped round to catch it, heard a sound from the phone, and scooted across the floor on her knees to pull at the receiver. "It's not working. I think he might be –"

"The ambulance is outside your building, go open the door or they will kick it in."

"I think he's had a stroke." Kathleen shouted, not meaning to shout.

"Go and open the door or they will kick it in."

"– but I can't leave him alone!"

"Go now and open the door or they will kick it in." The woman was implacable. "They're on the elevator now, almost to your floor. *Go now.*" How did the woman on the phone know where anybody was? Incredible! Kathleen reeled, staggered to her feet. She said to James, "I'll be right back," and skittered down the hall, perplexed by how much that woman knew. She opened the door to a fist poised and was pleased at the timing.

She had no choice but to step aside to let them in – they were already moving, they were large and disguised by complicated uniforms, and she bumped against the old leather suitcase from James's French grandfather, which was kept in the hall. Remembering her manners she called to their backs: "Come in. Please, he's – he's on the floor – bedroom," and "Oh come in" to the last man, pushing a machine on wheels off the elevator, adding helpfully, "They've all gone to the bedroom, down that way." Giddy that the unfathomable was taking place on this Sunday night. *There's before and there's after.*

The thing was, seconds after James's fall, or collapse, it must have been more like a collapse – she'd had no thoughts and was working on a giggle. *I mean, What is this?* They were in another passing moment in their lives together; he would rise, cough, shake his head, apologize for the scare. They would pull back the duvet and go to bed, just like any ordinary night. Except for the insistent voice on the phone: "The ambulance is at your building now, they are crossing the lobby. Go open the door. Now!" And then she'd snapped her hand away from him, worried that she was yielding to an unthinkable notion, too soon breaking a bond between them, letting go of him too soon. "I'll be right back," she'd said. She had scrambled to her feet, run down the hall, frantic with dread, *there is something terrible happening,* turned into the entry hall, *a realness to this moment.*

She was out of breath.

Two police officers had appeared in the living room and seemed to be keeping an eye on her, blocking her way to James. "Don't go in there, ma'am," the younger man said. To contain her heartbeat she meandered around the room, touching the glass table and on it, the violet in the little pot, the leaf prickly as though it had forgotten to shave. They were given the plant when James's grandmother died; it had been hers. To the officers Kathleen responded reasonably, telling them in some detail what happened from the time she came home, assuming they would be interested, they were in the apartment, weren't they, and if she got the details together correctly then all of what merely seemed to be happening would stop and something else, something more likely, would take its place.

"He was on the phone with his doctor, his kidney specialist, and he told her the numbers of his blood pressure and she told him it was sort of high and her husband, a cardiologist, was at home too, listening to the radio, and he said the pressure was on the high side – the husband and wife were talking back and forth to each other while James hung on the line – and, though it didn't seem urgent, they said if James wanted to go to the hospital, he could. I told him not to get on the exercise bicycle, I told him before I left, don't do it at night – and when I got back, I changed into my nightgown." Kathleen looked at the nightgown. "As you see," she said, descending into childishness, slightly lifting the long skirt. The nightgown was the green flannel one. "He's only forty-three," she added, a reassurance in the face of his relative youth.

The men surveyed the middle distance. They were big and tall, that was all she could tell about them. One said, "You should call someone."

She had to think a moment what he meant and had the idea he meant for her to raise her voice. She knew the person she would call was in the bedroom on the floor and would be embarrassed if he found out that she had shouted. *Oh* – the officer meant she should use the phone.

"To meet you at the hospital."

"Oh." She held the receiver in the air, listened to the dial tone. Who to call? The only person she could think of her oldest friend, Davida Adrianna, who lived out west, in Ruth, British Columbia.

Davida answered and Kathleen spoke rapidly, confidentially. "Listen. It's James. The ambulance people are here and things don't look good. We're going to – where are we going?"

"Toronto General, probably," one of the men said.

"Toronto General, probably," Kathleen said into the phone, over Davida who was shouting questions, calling her name: "Kathleen, Kathleen, what is it?" Kathleen moved the phone to her chest, so she could hear what the younger officer was saying.

"Sometimes they go to Mount Sinai."

The older one shook his head. "Toronto General, probably."

All this mundane conferring seemed encouraging. She lifted the phone again. "We think Toronto General. Oh, Davida, I – I have to hang up." Kathleen hung up and started toward the bedroom.

"I wouldn't go in there, ma'am." The officer spoke patiently, as though he'd used these words on other occasions.

The phone rang. Kathleen picked it up. It was Davida's husband, Boris Malenko, and he said, "We can't be there to help you. Call someone in your building, a neighbour, a friend. Someone you know in Toronto. Kathleen! Call someone now." He hung up. Kathleen looked at the phone. More people telling her what to do. She thought of someone James knew, and the phone number worked its way out her fingers and they said, "We'll find you," and she hung up again and went, anyway, toward the bedroom but lost ground – the hall was so long, so dark – until her bare feet were making pitter-patters, the un-obtrusive, sweet pitter-patter of a child's feet scurrying along a hallway. As she neared the open bedroom door, she noticed the large back of someone kneeling – she couldn't see James, would see him, in fact, only one last time – and turned her gaze and ducked past the kneeling group toward the closet. Again her thought was to be polite. "Don't mind me. I won't look." She didn't have a clue where she was. Or where she imagined she was.

It was like this: Kathleen was home from a classical concert. New music. New composers. She was home long enough to talk to him, change clothes, massage his upper body. Then she had heard him fall in the bedroom, a heavy, single-syllable thud. Not a crumpling, she didn't think it was so slow as that, the sound she heard was full – weighty and forceful and final. Did he lose his footing, try to catch himself? Did he reach out, grasp at something to keep himself from falling, did his fingers graze the edge of the bed on his way down? Did he try to take a step, try to cry out? She didn't know. She'd heard nothing, had had her back turned. When the muffled sound came, she'd whirled and looked and frowned to see him face down on the floor. The sound of him meeting the floor, colliding with it, had jolted her from her search in the medicine cabinet for a muscle relaxant. Or an Aspirin.

Moments before she started looking, she'd left him on the massage table, left him quickly, because – suddenly – her hands had come to a halt, sensing something that caused in her an unreasonable rush of adrenalin-driven alarm, and she had fled, perplexed. Moments after, he had passed behind her along the short hall outside the bathroom door. She'd heard him moving in the bedroom.

As he passed, she'd been undergoing a paralyzing moment at the open medicine cabinet. Looking back, she would see herself as rooted to the spot, helpless and despairing. But waiting? Would one call it waiting, that kind of stuckness she'd been in, that enervating powerlessness? Waiting for something in itself implies foreknowledge. When later she had time to think about it (and she would have plenty of time), she would come to realize they'd had forewarnings, forebodings even, they'd had a whole cornucopia of signs. The horseshoe – the lucky horseshoe – propped over the lintel of the front hall closet had fallen off with a clank, they'd both been home, both too absorbed, too apathetic, too unwary to bother to put it back in place. She had picked it up, to get it out of the way, and placed it on the suitcase that belonged to James's grandfather. Someone always going somewhere, someone always just about to leave. She had wondered, casually, in passing, in and out of the apartment, how the horseshoe had stayed balanced so long, why it hadn't taken a dive sooner, the door opening, closing, banging in the draft; the changes in temperature, the heat in winter, the air conditioning in summer, those inconstant temperatures unsettling. Then there were the slight shifts in the building itself caused by the jangling of the elevator beyond their bedroom closet wall or the metallic banging of the garbage disposal hatch beside their door, the drilling into concrete in the parking lot out back – naturally she would assume all or some of this would have caused the horseshoe to destabilize. Just once it fell and just once neither of them – James nor Kathleen – put it back. That was a sign. They were too exhausted, perhaps from their life together, disappointed by the grind and drill of busy living, phone calls interrupting any flow, trips out of town, the packing and unpacking.

Suspended on the brink of panic at the medicine cabinet, her fingers searched among bottles of capsules and remedies, occupied briefly until the sound came, the sound of his body resolutely encountering the bare floor. She looked over her shoulder, a fluttering in her chest holding her feet to the tiles. Her neck rotating, slow as a tortoise, chin to right shoulder, and then the looking, her shoulder leading, body turning, all breath gone. The stare, the blink, the thrust of the neck. The frown, the confusion, the falling forward into action against her will.

Leave time. Stop there.

The blood-pressure gauge she'd given him at Christmas was half wrapped around his arm. She saw the figure of him on the floor and knelt at his side. His head was turned to the right. But she would never be able to recall the particulars. Sometimes she would see his forehead pressed directly to the parquet and envision a large bruise resulting from striking the wood, but hadn't noticed a bruise when – she would have to get to this – she'd slid her hands under his inert body and heaved him over onto his back. What she'd seen when she turned to respond to the sound was – what she saw was, he was face down and rigid. His head was skewed, his left cheek pressed to the floor, his lips crushed against it. He was silent; he made no sound, no movement nor twitch – except – her heart had skipped a beat – an exhalation bubbled from between his lips, a passage of air that issued from his throat like a sigh of immense relief.

She knew exactly what was going on.

Touching his arm, she spoke calmly enough: "Don't do this to me."

Oh, let's not do this.

She said, "Please don't do this to me."

Wait a minute here. James wasn't getting it.

Indignation rising, she said – *She cried, she cried out*: "You *are* doing this to me."

Her hand grappled for the phone on the table beside the bed. The room slowly, very slowly, rose in its own exhalation and James was going, he was on his own road, he broke easily as a bubble and was gone without a sigh or whimper or word of farewell. His second exhalation led him outbound toward the horizon.

The future sidled in. 911 was on the line.

In the walk-in closet, arms wrapped round her knees, she didn't know which way to pray – that James would come back or stay gone. If he were paralyzed but his brain was working, he would want to stay alive. What good would it do, she'd wondered aloud, to have a great brain but be unable to blink or signal? They were having one of those married conversations, teeth crunching peaceably on toast.

She had scampered down the hall and ducked into the bedroom closet to change out of her nightgown, the rationale being that something would happen next, after the immense quiet, after the muffled immensity of whatever was going on in the bedroom had resolved itself. They were in it together, waiting: the two police officers in the living room, the three – she thought it was three – paramedics with James, she herself in the closet. She was apologetic to the officers, that she was leaving them alone, and with perfect courtesy – obsequiously, superstitiously polite – she had promised not to peek at what the paramedics were doing with James. The ambulance, too, was waiting under the canopy outside the lobby. Then they would tear off somewhere, head down University Avenue a dozen blocks, to Toronto General or to Mount Sinai. She'd come into the closet for a reason. She couldn't think why. She was in an uproar! She had to change into the clothes she'd had on earlier, when James was in a different mood, perplexed and slightly breathless. She had been out and he was just off the exercise bicycle. She had come home and said whatever she'd said and reassured him and calmed him down, her action (her inaction) either getting the point or missing it entirely. She would never know.

She'd got away from them, scooted down the hall. She was in the walk-in closet in the semi-dark, arms wrapped round her knees, when something physical grabbed her and took her breath away. *Something is wrong with James.* From where she sat, her clothes hung to the left and James's to the right, and there was the smell of the insides of his shoes and the odour of the sweetish powder he would tap into the pair he would wear in the morning.

She lost more ground, aware that her heart was expanding with exhilaration, lifting out of her chest, because it knew that *James was all right.* Her eyes streamed, tears flowed. She wondered what she would do – not what she would do without the man, she hadn't got that far. She wasn't *without him.* She was on the journey *with him*, not yet realizing that he, in fact, had left her behind.

She drifted. Came to. She had been in the closet too long, they had gone. *Something is wrong.* She hurt all over. The ambulance was outside the building, the engine was running, the doorman on duty was a man named Alvin – she didn't know Alvin was on tonight, but she had a remarkable (and passing) ability to see where she physically was not – and saw the flipping red light of the ambulance. She knew the idle curiosity that led to stepping onto the balcony, resting palms on the iron rail atop the concrete slab that kept lightweight furniture and plants in plastic pots from world view, casually hoping to see the body on a stretcher. Noting the solid ka-chunking of the various ambulance doors, turning back inside, shrugging: I wonder who. I suppose we'll find out soon enough.

The flashing light like a wail minus the sound.

Someone called her name, and she intended to get up off the floor, but was curled onto her side, her hands folded as though in prayer against her cheek, and she thought it best to stay that way.

Someone said, "Ma'am?"

And: "Oh, sure," she answered brightly, she couldn't help it, training from girlhood. As she scrambled up, her fingers caught at a dust bunny. *It was not like she didn't own a dust mop.* She stared at the dust bunnies on the floor by James's shoes, pierced with regret.

No evidence in the bedroom that anything had taken place. No spills, no wrappers, no tubing. "Hello? Is anyone here?" No reply. She felt a ragged surge of hope – help might be out there! Her agonizing premature, a bad dream, *a mistake*! James would not believe what she'd been conjecturing.

Someone stepped into the light at the end of the hall. "This way, ma'am, you come with us." The two officers hovered near her as though she were a criminal, which, esoterically, spiritually, karmically – realistically – she was, surely at fault somewhere in this scenario. A big mitt of a hand clasped her shoulder, a quick, sympathetic touch, and it was over, then, she knew. Tears chunky as lava rock clustered behind her eyeballs.

They led her down the hall.

They waited for the elevator in the spot where James in the morning tied his shoelaces, one of his straight-faced time-saving manoeuvres, one that amused her, her head angled out the open door. She smiled and the tears dribbled down her cheeks as the elevator pinged.

2

On the West Coast, two ferry rides north of Vancouver, Lenore Carmichael – back to using her maiden name – wasn't sure what she should do with herself. About her life, about the polyps, about whatever was causing her intestinal trials. The bowel disease, the diverticular disease or ulcerative colitis – symptoms, then no symptoms. The aberrant intestinal trouble was back or it never left or it never was in the first place; the truth was somewhere deep inside (one of her private jokes). Despite repeated slogs to the health-food store for the bottles and capsules and powders and despite a whole dizzy winter of swallowing cancer-preventive remedies – Essiac and shark cartilage – and various brans and bowel cleansers, her bowels remained alternately bound or loose: cryptic.

Last fall she'd seen a specialist on Vancouver's Hastings Street, waiting seven weeks to get the appointment. The reason she'd managed to get the referral in the first place was because there wasn't a permanent doctor in Perpetual Rain, Lenore's name for her northern coastal town. No one was keeping track of her medical history. Locums were coming and going. The newly minted doctors and the humming retired doctors landed a while and then were gone; and why take a chance when a patient continued to complain that something was wrong? The Chamber of Commerce was endeavouring to lure a permanent physician with gifts – ski passes to Whistler, weekend salmon fishing. They were considering throwing a house into the offer. "Strange," Lenore had mused aloud at a meeting of Kinsmen wives, "to give the most to the one who has the most already." Thinking of doctors' salaries. Though she could understand a doctor's hesitation – golf in the rain.

Two days before that appointment in Vancouver, she wound down the coast, floated across inlets, arrived at their condo in West Van. Their son, Gary, nineteen years old, was staying in the condo until he pulled himself together. She had left a message on his voice mail saying she was coming, but had he cleaned up? No. Pop cans. Crumpled food bags from McDonald's – he worked at McDonald's – left behind the sofa in front of the TV. She took in the clutter. Why was he like this? He had been a docile baby, a careful little boy, eager to please. The four months Jack was in Ecuador saving the teeth of the Third World, she and Gary had spent hours in the kitchen together. Mother – his grandmother – resentful of old age, had moved into assisted living at last. Cooking with her son had been solace for Lenore. At the age of twelve, Gary was borrowing library books on bread-making, and he had his own sourdough starter. The house had smelled like heaven back then. She had signed him up for a culinary college after high school, but he refused to go. He'd imploded, became snarly and hostile.

The bed in the guest bedroom hadn't been ready for her either. She'd had to locate a set of sheets at the back of the linen closet (his laundry hamper, based on the stinky socks that fell out when she opened the doors). She sniffed the sheets and found them untrustworthy and ran them through the washer and dryer. When Gary showed up the next morning, he looked terrible: pimply and pale. He played guitar in a garage band or something like it. What they thought they were playing didn't matter to her; they made dissonant unmusical racket. She said, "Are you deaf yet?" He didn't answer. He locked his bedroom door. How could someone be that age and still have acne? Greasy hair, what was left of it. He was like Jack, his hairline had begun to recede in his teens; but to have shaved it and left a ratty-looking tail? That and the earring cried for attention.

The oncologist's office had set a better tone than the doctor himself. The massive room and the walnut panelling obviously suited him; he, too, was so well groomed he gleamed. He'd seemed vaguely unsettled by her appearance – perhaps the wiry strands of salt-and-pepper hair that had got loose from her bun, the film of moisture on her wide upper lip, the snug fit of her bottom in his petite leather chair. Whatever the reason, he hustled her through his opening gambit, a simplified spiel about what could be going on regarding her intestinal symptoms, quick peeks at his wristwatch, expecting her, she thought, to be grateful for his time. Whole minutes passed, her silence broken by numerous ruminating clocks: a bookshelf clock, a grandfather clock, the bronze travel clock on his desk. She'd found it unbearable that she hadn't been able to just say Yes to exploratory surgery. She'd wrestled with her stubbornness, the pros and cons dipping in and out of consciousness, her brain overboard, her thoughts eluding the net. "Something dedifferentiated," he'd said, "but the tissue is unambiguously vulnerable; we could catch it if we act now." She'd held up the X-ray to the lamp on his desk and peered at her clouded interior. "The surgery is a wise precaution and might, just might, save your life in the long run." He'd sounded exasperated.

Where did they teach them these shallow, disheartening lines? He didn't care about her one way or the other – he couldn't be bothered to look her in the eye. Inexplicably, the omission, that particular omission on his part, drained her of will.

Now, as anyone could plainly see, she'd made it through the winter and was alive and kicking, sitting at the kitchen table by the window, the space heater warming her feet, playing solitaire. There had been developments on the home front, however. It wasn't colon inflammation that had her upset now. It was Jack. Jack, who had become fit and healthier looking. Jack the comelately hiker, jogger, backpacker. Jack the dentist with his new "ultimate white" smile. He wanted out of their marriage, a turn of events ironic to the point of pain. Despite all the times she'd compromised to keep the marriage going, despite all she had put up with – all she had taken for granted! "My husband, the dentist" – said proudly, spitefully, angrily – how often she had said it in their life together, a tacit understanding between them, so she had assumed: husband, wife. Wife, husband. Yet, the man was leaving her or was in the process of leaving her – really, in the daylight it was hard to take the whole thing seriously despite the fact of his absence. And despite the rendezvous he'd arranged for them in a bar called, appropriately enough, Desolation, during which he'd made it clear where he stood. He was leaving her for his assistant, a girl named Mandi, with an "i." Where was the man's pride? Frankly embarrassed at having lived so long with a man exhibiting such a paltry imagination (*who else* would a dentist leave his wife for?), she spoke up about it, beating the other Kinsmen wives to the punch; their knowing glances at each other had not escaped her. The women, however, had no sense of humour, and worse, they seemed to think that she – Lenore Carmichael, teaching specialist! – was a person who needed handling; she'd felt in her thighs the skanky pudding of their pity. After a prolonged silence, the psychologist in the bunch murmured, "We understand." Lenore laughed, a bray of sound, and why not? What could they possibly understand? Her whole life was shot to hell. The husband she'd taken for granted was gone, her son was a mess, she was intestinally disturbed – or not – who could she trust in the end. And she was stuck – mired, more like it – in an environment she would never get used to: this rockbound coast, the cold salty sea, the rain, conifers constantly dripping.

Who can I trust in the end? No pun intended. She slapped down a card. Who said she was stuck? That was the question. There were ways out. For one thing, she could kill herself. Others in Perpetual Rain had. The miserable town was used to people getting out of town the easy way. *Easy way out, indeed. I should be a stand-up comedian.* It was this constant internal ridicule that was so exhausting. The voice in her head, badgering. Did other people judge everything that crossed their minds, turn everything into a joke against themselves? *Ha, ha, ha.* Syllables for her tombstone.

The joke, however, was always on her. She was the one trying too hard, struggling with her booming personality, her lack of finesse – aware too late, when the backlash hit – and then the endless apologies, running around sheepishly picking up after herself. Her life was at the point of being so irreparable that maybe she should just kill herself and be done with it. No overdose of laxatives – though, if you pictured it, what a revenge. No razors, no bathtub. She didn't like baths, she got goosebumps on her arms as the water cooled. Bathtubs were out. There was the car, the garage, carbon monoxide, simple, quiet. Her suicide would fix him. Or – she bit her lip – would it? Hardly; her demise might play right into his hands. And why give him the satisfaction of thinking she cared? She would not. She laid a jack of spades on the queen of hearts. There was the image of her marriage: she, the queen, distant and tolerant, he currying her favour. On another stack she laid a black queen on a red king. No, *here* was the image of her marriage: he controlling and she quashed by him, aggrieved by his power over their lives and where they lived it: always *his* job, *his* career. She set the deck down, stared out the window at the rain. She was going crazy trying to make meaning out of random cards. A long-time marriage falling apart could do that to you. Make you doubt everything. Make you a prisoner in a mudhole of a place. She tapped her blunt fingers on the table.

There was a point beyond which living was intolerable, the point beyond which it was impossible, for instance, to tolerate being a person no one liked, beyond which tolerating your pity for yourself and keeping a stiff upper lip were simply not doable. It was not like she didn't know. People right and left disliked her: her husband, her son, nearly everyone she worked with at school. It was terrible to realize – she did *know* – that there weren't many sympathetic qualities about her; she was abrasive, she was defensive, she was overbearing. Personality defects out the yin-yang. What if you knew yourself to be always out of the loop, the one at the wood's edge, far from the fire, laughing your big laugh, always hopeful?

For a minute the game had been going well, but now it was obviously lost: a buried nine of clubs. She could start cheating – switching a card from the ace pile back to a playing pile just to lay down that two she'd turned up. Her fingers could slip and she could pull the second card instead of the third and pretend to herself that she didn't know she'd done it. There were so many ways to make a solitary game go better. This afternoon, however, she wouldn't play that way. Game lost, that was that. She shuffled the cards and wrapped a rubber band around them and placed them where they belonged on the windowsill. As of last Saturday – face it, kiddo, she said to herself – the man was out of the house. His jockey shorts packed, the drawer empty. She had driven to the office, rifled through personnel files, found the girl's address – Mandi with an "i" lived in her mother's big house – spotted his car out front. The woman would be surprised to find an old satyr in her daughter's bed when she returned from sunny Spain, but that juicy surmise didn't matter to Lenore. He did not come home. She went into school on Monday and took sick leave for the remaining five weeks of the term; she had enough days owed her to stay away forever. Newer, younger teachers were rushing into the breach.

He dumped you. The whole damn town already knows.

The rain eased and a blue patch appeared in the sky, beyond the fence in the next yard. A bluer, purer patch of sky than she'd seen for weeks. Maybe the blue sky was a sign, a big, obvious, unsubtle sign, so that someone equally obvious and unsubtle would realize it. A lesson of some kind waiting. *Think about it.* An upbeat ending might be feasible, even for her, if she could get beyond this mess here and now. She wiped the tears from the corners of her eyes. She doubted if she believed in lessons – too cynical to believe in lessons – but she could imagine deliberately, intentionally – *prudently* – changing herself into someone who was childish in just such a crucial way, changing herself into someone who believed in lessons, signs, and omens. A person needed goals, after all, and sometimes a person needed to believe in something – anything, she thought, her spirits rising – in order to keep going. She thought of the town of Ruth, in the Judith Lake Valley. She had had some youthful good times, or almost good times, in Ruth. She could take a trip, visit her brother, Larry, and his wife, Nan, and possibly stay with them or someone else she knew way-back-when. Lenore pictured herself in Larry's stainless-steel kitchen, baking cookies with her nieces and showing them how to chop the onions for her famous Boeuf Bourguignonne. An old-fashioned recipe but good. Why the hell not go to Ruth? She picked up the phone and dialed her brother.

She heard him pouring a drink in the background, probably Scotch. "I want to come back home," she said. She wasn't just asking for a visit, was she, she was asking for a stay.

"Hamilton is a far piece," he said, using the hokey voice he used while thinking fast. He was referring to Hamilton, Ontario, where their father's family originated. She and Larry, along with their mother, hadn't lived in Ruth until they were older.

"Duh," she said but didn't give him time to enjoy himself at her expense. "I'm leaving Jack."

Larry didn't reply. She heard ice cubes tinkling.

"He's a bully, he never spends any time with me. A psychological bully. Inconsiderate too. Other reasons." She felt light-headed. The idea that she could be the initiator, the one leaving – "leaving Jack," she'd said – hadn't occurred to her until she heard herself say it. Surely that was a good sign. She'd taken that first step and called Larry and already her brain was bubbling with ideas.

Then, excited by the idea of leaving Jack, she began to repeat herself, and she was aware of the repeating, and aware that her voice sounded alarmingly schoolmarmish, a lot like their mother.

She raced on until Larry interrupted, "Whoa, sis. Get hold of yourself, think about it."

Her mood plummeted, and she was assaulted by the usual doubts: He didn't want her to visit. Who would want her? Her breathing had become noisy and rapid, and an old, old anger stuck in her gut like a chunk of gobbled cheese, indigestible. She considered hiding her hurt feelings behind a blistering attack on him; he would expect her to blast him. Instead, she would behave rationally, calmly, like the mature adult she was. She said, "I don't have any place else to go." She sounded calm but also hysterical, which she realized she was – she was calmly hysterical, heading toward fretful.

She heard him sigh. "Why are women nuts?"

"Women do not accept the *fait accompli*," she said. The outlandish words made her feel better. Let him figure them out.

"Guys can't keep up," he said. "The female persuasion has mysterious urges, they send out mixed signals."

Larry had experience with girls and women; he and Nan had four girls, the oldest a teenager away at boarding school. He was a large, unkempt man, handsome in a soft way. He had dark lashes and an ingratiating smile. He had always been Mother's favourite. She pictured him in the new kitchen, sneaking an early drink. He would go to seed all at once, she realized. "Don't apologize for Jack," she warned. "Don't you toast his escape either. I know you, Larry Carmichael."

A brief silence followed, the sound of her brother giving in. "Okey-dokey," he said. "Drive careful. I got a million-dollar view of the lake you don't want to miss."

She was in a sweat when she hung up the phone. She dabbed her forehead with a paper napkin she found crumpled on the table. Larry's mission in life was to impress people. In their need for attention, the two of them were similar, but Larry had gone all out in his bid. He wanted to bowl people over. His building-supply store the biggest in Ruth. His big house, his thin wife, his four pretty daughters, his lake view. Lenore knew about Judith Lake. Fifteen thousand years ago it was a tongue of ice. Sheets of ice covered everything except the peaks of the tallest of the mountains, Mounts Jasper and Sebastian. Three thousand years later the ice retreated, leaving the lake that Larry was so proud of, as though it had bobbed into existence the moment he had a view of it. As she was recalling high-school geography lessons, thinking about glaciers and ice and trenches and wedges of sediment, the sky gave in and fell over her bright yellow house – she was targeting cheeriness when she chose the colour – and the rain was sloppy and heavy, the sort of coastal rain that could take the whole day, or the rest of her life, as far as she was concerned, to wear itself out.

She had to do something. Take matters into her own hands. Beat Jack to the punch. Get going, get righteous. *Leave me, will he?* She would see about that. She trotted into the living room and paused at the coffee table and picked up a little box inlaid with mother-of-pearl. She would have this trinket from their Malaysian holiday, and he would not have it. She found a cardboard box and put it in; it was a beginning. She looked around their living room, furnished in shades of taupe and beige – *his* colours. Boring, boring, boring! She began grabbing things in earnest. She was not walking out with nothing, not after all these years. She galloped around the house, packing things into red and blue milk crates she'd pilfered from grocery stores and into three of Jack's best suitcases, each with a discreet numbered label attached to the handle, Jack organizing the world. "We'll take Six and Eleven," he would announce and she wouldn't argue because, as he was pleased to remind her, he had a gift for spatial relationships. "We'll take Two and Five," and she'd hurry to the garage and find the cases lined up in the right order, the way they belonged.

Soon she realized there were quite a number of things she didn't want Jack to have. Most of them wouldn't fit into her Honda Accord. She phoned the storage people and scheduled a pickup time. Now she was free to pack the pots and pans and the everyday dishes. Let him eat off paper plates. The arrangements were so easy it seemed possible that destiny was lending a hand. The next day she went out and bought more boxes and packing supplies and packed her mother's Limoges. The teapot, sugar bowl, and cups she packed separately, rolling and wrapping the dainty platinum-rimmed porcelain into the *National Post* – a paper, she thought, not worth doing much else with – because she'd owed them to Larry for years. Actually to her sister-in-law, Nan. A promise she'd made to Nan under duress. Mother had just died, and it had been a terrible death, anger radiating from Mother's eyes and from her pores. The body aflame with anger. The disinfected room filled with Mother's wrath, and Lenore, awake in a vinyl-covered chair by the bedside, endured, fearful that Mother would guess – would *know* in that shrewd way she had – that her daughter was fervently aching for her to die. Shaken after the experience – the guilt – she had promised Nan the tea set because she herself no longer deserved it.

The house soon attained a friendly, disorderly appearance, something, for a change, going on – linens and papers and creams and bottles strewn chaotically about, as though someone was up to something. As though there was a larger purpose in the house beyond tidy survival, her urge to endlessly neaten overcome for the moment. She stuck office labels – red, blue – onto the furniture, the lamps and chests and knick-knacks she wanted in storage. When she'd run out of red and blue, she found a box of yellow and carried on. When hungry, she stood at the opened refrigerator and nibbled on the good stuff. She defrosted the filet mignon and broiled it and enjoyed every morsel. When the rain stopped, she was in and out of the house – mud on the carpet and did she care? No, she didn't! – hauling boxes and cases. There was a lot of back-breaking sorting to do, to fit things in the hatch. She drove down the driveway to the street with the Honda not quite full, to see if she could do it, leave so much behind, and she could not; the thought of the wasted space and leaving anything important made her woozy. She headed back into the house and collected more: her cookbooks with the detailed notes, the best issues of *Gourmet* magazine, her soup ladle from Italy, Jack's steak knives. *Ha, ha, you bastard.* She crammed things into the car – the need to cram things was third on her list of self-hatreds. The plan, however, the forward-moving plan, had begun to design itself. She would recuperate in Vancouver at the condo for a day or two – she would bring a box of Hostess Ho Hos for Gary, as a peace offering – and then she would hit the road *and keep on going.*

3

Mory Zimmerman, on tiny Lasqueti Island off the West Coast, had been feeling feverish and unwell. The feeling of being tired came and went, and one day she and her eleven-year-old, BB, took the tugboat-ferry from Lasqueti to Vancouver Island and then she hitchhiked to the clinic in Nanaimo to get tests for everything, HIV and the anemia that her little boy was known for, and for syphilis and gonorrhea. She was a slight-framed girl with a sprinkle of freckles across a flat nose and springy black hair and large breasts. The nurses in the clinic spoke slowly to her. They asked, "How do you make your living? What do you do?" And she answered that she let men touch her. Invariably the nurses' brows came together. Mory thought, They think I'm dumb. It's something to do with telling the truth.

"Do you sleep with many men?"

"No, I don't sleep with them, I sleep with BB. But the men, they find me."

Her life was like that. She waited beside a road, and some man would find her in the nick of time.

"I have limits," she added. To escape from the university boy that time on Texada Island, she and BB swam out to a rock in the cove and perched, stark naked, while he was kicking stones, feet bleeding, on the shore. He had chased them down the bank. When she got back to the yurt, her clothes were ripped and the walls of the yurt were damaged too. It had taken her days and errands into the village for help to get the yurt back in shape. Later she had the miscarriage and she thought it was him wanting too much from her. She did not feel hurt about the bleeding and the clots despite BB's screaming. That was BB's nature, to lose his head. He had nerves, he had come about wrongly, she wasn't so dumb as to be oblivious. One of her papa's words.

"I have limits," she said again to the brown-haired woman, trying the word on her tongue, working on the *s* and the *v*. I hab limut. I hab lim-mutz. *Have* limutz. In school, a lady made her look in a hand mirror and watch her lips and tongue. The men knew about the limits. "They know" came out clearly and she was pleased, even though frowns filled the air. Brows down, the woman's fingers moved a pen. They were always writing when she was in the room. It seemed insensitive, her mummy might say. *Insensitive.*

"You are insensitive," she said to the nurse, her voice sounding fine.

The writing stopped. A look came her way. "Yes. I'm sorry. It's my job."

Silence then until the refrigerator behind the desk clicked on.

"What do they do, the men you . . . find?"

Mory touched her breasts, caressed them with the knob of a thumb. "Like this," she said as clearly as she could, and the fridge stopped and the lady did also and BB smiled because, despite appearances, he had a few clues.

She caught what he'd had, the Camaro man, she felt sure he was the one. It was the mention of "whores." He got it from one of them and then gave it to her. So there it was, HIV. The Nanaimo nurse was saying, "You have done it too often, you have not protected yourself, don't you know any better?" And Mory said, Why, what. And the nurse rolled her eyes and made her own sigh and said, "For heaven's sake. Don't you at least watch the news?"

They asked her who she had been with and the name almost came into her head. He had a Camaro. He was the one, she told them.

"Yes, but since, Mory. Who have you been with since?"

Nobody spoke while Mory regarded a trash can near the door.

"Can you remember a name, Mory? Where have you been living?"

Mory and BB had been up and down the coast, on and off the islands, housecleaning sometimes, picking cherries in the Okanagan. Then she went to Gabriola to help clear a bad weed and stayed for a while, helping a man pour the foundation for his house. She went to Salt Spring to clean rooms in a hotel one summer. It was only lately she'd begun to feel homesick for Neon Bar, though there was no sensible reason why she should.

The story was too long to start telling. She shook her head at the nurse. "Maybe nobody," she said. "I think nobody."

"We can't make her talk," the nurse muttered to someone in the hall. "We can't give her a lie detector."

She wasn't sick yet, they said, but she had it. The virus was in her and not acting up and so she wouldn't think she was sick, but she would be wrong. She was supposed not to have sex ever again because what she had was catching, like measles, they explained; or if she did ever have intercourse again, she was to ask the man to wear a condom. A rubber, they said. They gave her a packet of six condoms. The nurse took her into an examining room and showed her how to unroll the condom on a model that made Mory blush.

"Oh, honestly, come off it," the nurse said. "Look here."

Mory watched the condom roll down the erect penis. It was pink, pinker than any man she had seen. She thought maybe she hadn't seen many in such bright light. The tips were pink, she thought, in general they were.

After the visit to the clinic, it was drizzling rain. A local man gave her a lift to the Lasqueti ferry. Even though she sort of knew him, she and BB went through their routine: he went limp so she could hoist him, as though he were a cripple, and slide him across the seat, between the man and herself. BB was like a sprouting green bean with legs, she often thought, now that the words had arranged themselves in that order. Once inside the car, she moved fast; the man wouldn't get rid of them so easily if she was belted in and he'd heard the click that meant Go.

Back on the island, she lay down on the mattress. BB got hold of her new condom stash and rubbed himself against the chair that had her overalls thrown over it. He was naked and his pecker was hard, big as a bobbling wiener. He was hopping about and giggling, a wet condom in his hand. He had the beginnings of hair down there, and suddenly he frightened her. She had not thought of her boy as ever growing into a man.

"Be safe," he said and tried to unroll the thing while he was shivering and his legs were spiking about. This display – the giggling, the condom – was spooky. He was only eleven. The laugh was not nice. The expression on his face – wild – like he might not be able to stop himself, like he might get rough. He had seen men be rough before. For a moment while he danced over her, she felt helpless to stop him. She heard her breathing and it sounded scared to her own ears. He could not cross that line with her, though, that would not be right. This she knew. It was one thing she did know. She would not take this behaviour from him. When he danced closer again, she attempted to slap him. He escaped the slap and made a face at her. There was menace in his behaviour, she could feel the ugliness in her belly. This time her hand connected to his cheek and she meant that smack. When he ran to her, crying, she said, "Get back. Stay back."

It was the way with boys and men. They just were crazy about their things. BB was four when he'd discovered his, while watching her get dressed after a sponge bath. Only four and too little to know better. He couldn't hide his feelings, his tongue had slipped between his lips as he reached for her breasts, and then he touched himself. She had kissed him, leaning over into him the way she might with a lover she needed to keep for a time. She was sad for him and she reached her hand down and cupped her palm over his little hand. Then she kissed him on the cheek, and she said into his hot baby breath, "BB, what Mummy has is what we *eat from*. It is not for fun." Which made her understand it herself. She said, "This is food for us," tapping her breasts. "It is not for you to get your rocks off."

Now he was a near-grown boy who had seen too much. It was her fault. All the times she'd let the men come into wherever they were living – a room, a yurt on a summer property, someone's house they were borrowing – and BB a boy watching her as the flames from a fire changed what a man looked like. In firelight the faces that had no bones grew bones. The faces that were fat and old became plump, the skin sweet, nice enough to touch; a worried face that chewed on itself like a marmot in a trap glowed and the reflective glasses hiding the craving made the face seem smart. She felt smart herself when they so plainly needed something from her, even the ones who scorned her for what they wanted. Sorry for them, she would undo the clasp on the bib of her overalls and say to BB, "Go behind the curtain now, go now. Take the dog." They had a little black dog in those days, but it had got lost. And then whatever the man wanted, to suck on her or say quiet swear words to her, she would let him do because it made her feel better.

She gazed at the timbered ceiling with the patch of water stain and thought about BB turning into a horny boy. Still a boy but at an age when bad things could happen. He was skinny and small for his age, except down there he was not small. And he was growing stronger through his arms and back, she had noticed. She had to be responsible for him or else find someone who would. If you were sick, as the nurses said she was, and you had to take care of someone – he was her baby – then you should go back to the one place – Neon Bar – where there was someone who would help. She thought of the lake, Judith Lake, and the two creeks that met north of it and the cabin that BB had never seen and the mountains that he had never smelled. She rolled off the mattress and said to him, "We're going home. You don't know that place, but I do."

She packed their sleeping bags into a mesh sack and a change of clothes and BB's stuffed toy sheep into a backpack and tidied up the cabin, sweeping everything out and straightening the canned goods and burying the crackers and flour to keep mice and squirrels from ransacking the place and maybe pack rats too, which were so smelly. She did not leave a note for the people whose land it was, they wouldn't care anyway and she didn't write very well.

They crossed from the island and again hitched into Nanaimo, this time to a pawnshop to sell a ring someone had given Mory. She would use the money for the big ferry to Vancouver, and the pawnshop man gave her extra money, and she said, "Thank you" and BB also said, "Thank you."

They were just walking off the ferry at Horseshoe Bay, buses rumbling behind them, when a Ford Explorer found them. It was early, but already BB had taken her hand as he did when he was tired. This man, wearing dark glasses, checked out her profile, then dropped his eyes to her breasts; he couldn't help but look.

"Hi," she said, but he didn't answer. Just drove.

On the Trans-Canada, the man didn't say anything to her, didn't even look at her after his first look, and she began to feel uneasy in the pit of her stomach. When she said she wanted to stop somewhere, his eyes passed right through her. "Yeah, sure. And you need money for food for the kid." He drove fast, jaw twitching. Near the first mountains he stopped for gas and locked the car with the remote when he went to the restroom. As though he was locking them in. BB was asleep. Her heart was racing, the blood was gathering in her throat; she was afraid for a reason she couldn't name. She squeezed the handle and opened the door. The theft alarm sounded – waa, waa, waa – announcing troubles. She lugged BB out. They stumbled into the bushes in back of the station. The car was still telling everyone that someone had escaped. She smelled gasoline and melted cheese from the nachos they sold in the station. Her stomach growled, too bad. She pushed BB onto the ground, rested his head on his little stuffed sheep, his eyes on her wide, and lay beside him, petting his hair. They would be dirty, but sometimes dirt did not matter.

The Camaro man, that other time, had seemed nice. He was just the sort of man who tended to find her, a nice man with a family, wife and children; he mentioned the children right away to show that he did not mean her any harm. And she talked about BB, how he was not a normal boy. Her talking about BB made it easier for the man to come on to her after a while, as though he was special because she talked about her son with him. This helped the man to feel good, she understood, and that particular man, the one in the Camaro, touched his crotch without knowing he was moving his fingers in that direction and she watched his fingers flick himself down there, the man having feelings and getting tense and hard in his body and uneasy in his heart like he had to do something right away to help out. She felt her nipples stirring as they drove. And she knew she and BB would have a place to stay that night. In a deserted area with trees alongside a dribble of a creek, he said he had to go pee and she should come with him. They locked BB inside the car so he wouldn't follow. The man was puffing and his cheeks were rosy. He was big in the belly with thin legs. She gazed at him and waited. He said, "I haven't fucked anybody outside. Like in raw nature. I always think about it. Probably get my ass bit by bugs." He said, "Turn around." Later he said, "I usually pop whores and they won't do it outside. This was A-OK. I was really going to town there."

At the door of her motel room he said, Leave your door unlocked, get the kid to sleep. She told him they would need money for breakfast. He let out a long breath. "I thought you were different," he said. "I thought you liked me. You are just like the others."

"I thought you liked *me*," she'd said.

Be quiet, she said now to BB, the warm, oily smell of nachos making him want some. She placed her arm over his fluttering little heart. The Explorer had stopped its wailing.

4

From deep in a nest of bedding in a cabin set close to where Glacier Creek joined the Enterprise, Oscar Zimmerman coughed, a nagging, wearisome cough. His beard and awful breath as he coughed were mostly what his wife, Frieda, was aware of, concerning him. Beard, breath, and scraps of gummed bread, his too many books dusty on floor-to-ceiling shelves, buckets of vile slops. In her life of being married to Oscar Zimmerman, she had seen and heard more than she signed on for. The two of them were principled and against war, and his decision to move north to Canada was supposed to have brought them consolation. The surface of the terrain that they came to, the aspects easily reached, had been scraped of trees in the boom era nearly a century before. The word she and Oscar had used back then was *desecrated*, the land skimmed of what was reachable to prospectors with pickaxes and mules, to men with traps, bandsaws, barges, and determination. Logs and timber, high-grade silver galena, pelts of martin, muskrat, mink, weasel, and grizzly bear were borne away on tugboats with names like *Valhalla* and *Hercules*, loaded into narrow-gauge railroad cars or paddle-wheelers heading west or south. Some of the more enterprising made it to Neon Bar and beyond, and a few stayed and took up smallholder farming, generated electricity from creeks, built a four-room school, and grew the loveliest sweet peas, according to all reports. Then, in a more peaceful wave they had come, Frieda and Oscar Zimmerman, at a time when the land was catching its breath, restocking, replenishing.

Late in their forties they were surprised to have conceived a child, a girl. On the puny side, they would have said back home, but their own dear infant. The child grew into daddy's little girl, then something else besides innocence and light. On that particular point, Frieda's mind had given up. She never had anything to say about it to anyone. The prolonged absence of their daughter, however, and the child she bore (whom they had never seen), sent Oscar shockingly off – unbalanced, insane at times. Angry at the rancid odour left from a passing bear. "My place, *my* territory, you bastard! *Mine.*" Fists raised against a nibbling doe. That had been him in the years before the last fall and a hip that wouldn't heal.

Nothing to be done, she believed, in the end; all was as it was meant to be. No sense in railing at fate and what you couldn't change. The body too old to do anything but stay put. Understanding coming too late.

She stood at the open back door squinting her eyes against the light. She wondered if the white mushrooms were sprouting in the green grass. From above, they looked like faded petals of wild roses, scattered far from the bush. But Frieda could not see well; everything was stored in her imagination. Her ears picked up crackles in the woods beneath the constant rushing of the two creeks. She heard breathing when there should have been none. Someone out there. Spying on them. She said hello but received no answer. She tossed a rock from her bucket beside the door, but her arm was weak and the rock thudded nearby. In her day she'd had good aim, she'd had a keen eye with a slingshot. She had loaded it with dried soybeans – and then watch those critters scatter! Thumped a bear once, stunned a raccoon, zinged a few deer too, eating beet tops. One time there had been a yelp and some cursing. The angry voice of a boy. But there had been no boy living anywhere about. Not then, not now. There was no one. There was only herself and the nasty old man, hardly breathing, nearly gone.

Above the hamlet of Neon Bar – Poppy's Convenience & Gas at the crossroads and the Centre for Light Awareness hidden along a lane – a bear awoke. All winter the old bear had been out of touch, nestled deeply inside himself. Now he was well rested and soothed by dreams. The confusing moments of establishing his whereabouts were over: he had sniffed the air, extended his claws, slowly rolled on his wrinkled pads, then rubbed his back into the cold earth and stretched his legs. His fur was scruffy; in his youth he had glistened. His rump was wet from the crushed slush of snow almost gone. He smelled skunky and felt hunger. He shook himself and moved out.

Down the mountain from where the bear had wintered, eighteen-year-old Miles Logan – called Milee – finished digging a hole to shove his mother's possessions into. He was short and lean overall, but his arms were sinewy and strong. He wore logger's boots with metal on the toes. He kicked at the pile of his mother's clothing, separating bras and blouses with his boot, and took a last look. His mother had been a Sonemayer, a pioneer family in the Judith Lake Valley. Her ancestors had started the

Silver Bell mine, they had been prospectors and then merchants. She'd not listened to her grandmother and married badly – Milee's father, who died in a car accident when Milee was fifteen, hadn't worked a full day after the local mill closed – and consequently, she did not inherit the family house in Ruth. Instead, she'd inherited a tendency toward drunkenness. She had given birth to one child, a boy who had two voices talking back and forth in his head instead of the usual one, a voice that fooled around, interrupted him, made rhymes. She knew about the boy's two voices, and she'd coyly made the most of it: Which little man wants to give Mummy a kiss tonight? His mum had liked his reluctant little kisses. She had liked the bedtime stroking she called "pets." Come and pet Mummy, love. Come on now. He hadn't done that for her in a long time, but it was there, between them, that history.

The family had always lived in a single-wide trailer on another man's land, paid a minimal rent. After his mother's burial (she'd wanted a church service led by the local pastor; she'd converted at the end), Milee threw her personal items out the door – her nail polishes, her pairs of strap sandals, the leather ancient, cracked, and peeling, the bright ill-fitting sweaters she knitted that no one wanted, her clothes. It was a drizzly day when he was satisfied by the depth of the hole. His sweat was cold on his brow as he kicked and pitched and shovelled every single thing of hers into the opened ground and added a splash of kerosene from the can by his side and struck the match. Her belongings made a good blaze. And then an old half-dead birch that had never recovered from a lightning strike spontaneously combusted, a crackling poof the sound he recalled when he came back to himself. In the greasy stink of the residue, all that was left of his mother, he could see the symbols of her being a particular kind of female: the unburned spiked heel of a shoe. Lipstick cases oozing red. Black nylon panties, melted in among skeins of nylon yarns in pinks and purples.

Around Neon Bar it was common knowledge that Milee Logan talked to himself; everyone at one time or another had heard him. The ladies at bingo down at the Church of the Redeemer agreed, however, that he was a young man who minded his own business, and it was wise to leave well enough alone. He was a willing worker whenever, that is, he could be lured out of the bush.

5

At the Centre for Light Awareness, Gabriel Markovice left the meditation room to make a phone call. His partner, Lucinda, knew this fact because she was fixed on him, and particularly mindful of his every move. He bypassed the phone in the office, where, she thought, he suspected she might be, and quietly entered his bedroom. The door shut behind him. Working on the book in the meditation room first thing in the morning was his routine in the month since they had arrived home from a winter away. He was writing what was intended to be a sequel, a book to ride the heels of the first, which already had a following. He'd tried writing the manuscript by hand and tried word-processing and now was talking it into a Dictaphone, gathering more words, as he put it, which could be progress should they turn out not to be merely repetitious. Writing a second book, he'd told Lucinda – the office phone lit as he picked up his extension – was like picking grit from your teeth in a dust storm. He smiled as he spoke because it was not an expression he normally used. His real gift, she thought, was as an intuitive. He worked best with groups because he was receptive to psychic emanations. In a group he appeared relaxed, waiting and listening through the opening chatter and introductions, collecting their psychological tensions, culling their personal histories out of the communal ether. When he had by this mysterious means grasped what the individuals in the group needed and why they were together, the workshop would begin. The teaching could last one afternoon or one week. What he said in one seminar was never repeated, in the same words, in another.

Part of the problem with the manuscript – the phone must have been ringing on the other end, Lucinda heard the squeak of the chair as he sat – was that true stories about healing sounded unhinged. Or the people were belittled or made trite, like those case studies in psychology texts. They had talked about this obstacle. Due to the pressure to get the manuscript done – his San Francisco publisher wanted it *now* – they made changes in the winter program, the getaway to Arizona, California, Texas. No long retreats, they decided. Fewer distractions, he said, would aid the writing. By then Lucinda knew he was lying through omission, but she didn't know what the omission was and kept her silence. He asked her to put together a cycle of three-day weekends that they named Intensities. They toked in the fireplace room and came up with names for these new, focused workshops: "Accessing the Light Within," "Mapping Your Inner Landscape," "Soul Embodied."

His voice speaking into the phone was low, and he didn't talk for long. He hung up – tenderly, it seemed to her, listening – the click of the receiver restrained. He slipped barefoot down the hall and back into the meditation room and in a moment came the scratch of a match – he was lighting candles. She was able, then, to spy on him through the crack in the door; her stealthiness had become slightly alarming even to her. He placed himself on his cushions, entwined his legs. Then he smiled. He was not smiling at her; he was unaware of her. He was smiling to himself about something she was not supposed to know.

This was it then, this was it then. You spent fifteen years with a man expecting this was it, then, this was it, and then, it was.

The waking up hurt, like hell must feel to those who believed they would be cast down into it.

She had been in a state of despair when she signed up for her first workshop with the word *transformational* in it. She was separated from her husband, frail after a miscarriage, considered herself despicable. She'd been a dancer in a small troupe, and when she hurt her ankle, she'd married a guitar player from Guadalajara, for no reason other than it flew in the face of her strict upbringing, and consequently she was outrageous and unthinkingly cruel to him. When the miscarriage came – a few cramps, hardly a warning, her husband's pyjamas scooped from the bottom dresser drawer to stem the tide – her life suddenly became real. The blood made it real. She thought that losing her baby was due to irredeemable transgressions on her part, a weakness in her character. Despite her reading and study of nature and human nature and, maybe, simply, the bad luck of the draw, she saw herself as tainted, incapable of right judgment in a spiritual sense, someone with a karmic imbalance. She was in that mood when she met Gabriel.

At her first workshop, a shy, straight-haired girl had introduced herself by saying of herself and Gabriel, "We travel together." At one point the girl was on her knees, collating fourteen copies, five pages each – Lucinda watching, as though learning a job – the girl apologizing because she'd forgotten to make the copies before the session, though (Lucinda was to find out how it went) Gabriel probably changed his mind at the last minute about what he needed.

The women in the circle on pillows were watching the girl, some envious and flirting with Gabriel behind her back, some toying with fantasies of being with him because he was *so masculine, so beautiful and full of wisdom*, imagining themselves in her place, and some sad already for her. Knowing the ending. You just had to look at him to realize he would never stay faithful to that wispy creature. For one thing, while she was talking, he didn't glance her way even once, his eyes always resting on the cloudy windowpane. You knew – Lucinda certainly knew – that the straight-haired girl's time was coming to an end.

He was different from any man most women in his groups had ever met. All his women felt that way about him; Lucinda was not so untested. Gabriel, well, he had charisma and he was stunning to look at and he took her flying, literally swooping her over the foothills in his plane – he had an American Yankee then, a two-seater with a canopy – and later he ordered champagne brought to the table and it was good champagne and the glasses the right ones. She went with him to his bed and then with him into his life, a pattern of women, she had come to understand over the years. At first she didn't like living in the Judith Lake Valley, because it was remote, usually wet, everything grew – too much green too fast. That changed as her heart slowed down and her anxiety moved off and she began to gain respect for weather and amenities. She began to see that in the mountains you couldn't take running water or electricity for granted. Surges in rural electricity could melt your computer in an instant, blow the element on your hot-water tank; heavy rain could knock out the dam built to capture water from the creek and you would be hauling buckets just to flush the toilet. She became appreciative of the old outhouse and the utility of candles and began to take pride in understanding how things worked, how to use tools and fix things.

At the turn of the century, a pioneer named Nell Sonemayer wrote that she had been brought such a long way, "out to the end of nowhere." Initially, Lucinda, too, felt the isolation imposed by the mountains. Nell wrote to her cousin in Seattle – Lucinda had found a few letters in a yard-sale chest of drawers – that she'd been brought to the end of civilization, the "godawful & Mosquitoes" line Lucinda kept on the bulletin board in the kitchen. Nell had written: *We ordered a nice line of harness and saddles, etc., which were to come by freight but as winter set in early that year, the shipment was frozen in the river. This was a great setback. But, just at this time it was discovered that they must have shelter for all the goods being sent to the various mines. Thousands of bolts of canvas were in the stores but they had to get made into sheets. Here is where I stepped in, for they found that I had brought my new Singer machine with me . . . and at 10 cents for every running yard sewn, it meant a fine profit.* Nell Sonemayer sounded so pleased by this outcome that Lucinda thought that she, too, could find a way to be happy and productive in this remote place. She set out to help Gabriel use his talents. They built up the Centre. Things happened, as things did in a relationship; she was proud of her adaptability.

She was not a small-plane enthusiast – rough air made her nervous – but she did love takeoff, she'd always loved takeoff – his bare forearm on the stick, adding power, his left hand pulling back on the wheel, lifting the two of them smoothly off the earth. To celebrate the beginning of the winter cycle, they usually put down in Ashland, Oregon, a town that hosted a Shakespeare festival and had good hotels and B&Bs and nice restaurants. They usually stayed at the old hotel downtown, had a meal in a French bistro, ordered a bottle of decent red wine. Instead, this past November, he landed in Medford and chose a motel close to the airport, and they'd eaten in a shack called the Luv-U Chicken. They didn't speak except to pass the salt, and he paid for separate rooms.

The window in her room turned out to be stuck. She'd noticed that the door to his room was ajar, left that way on purpose for her, she'd assumed, feeling smug, on the chance that she would visit. Aroused, she thought they might have a quickie – clothes on or off, it didn't matter to her; it was the rush she was after. A gush of warmth, not hormonally driven for a change – menopause a hound on her heels – poured down her spine, and she padded complacently down the hall and tapped on the door. He said, "Sorry, I'm on the phone." She peeked in anyway. The phone cord was curling across his chest and he was wearing a white undershirt and red jockeys.

"Obviously you can't be calling your girlfriend when your old one is farting familiarly in your bed," she mumbled, stumbling over the pronunciation of *familiarly*, as she usually did. She chastised herself about trying that word, and added, "I suppose here we go again." Being hard-nosed and worldly. It had been a while since his last dalliance. She backed into the curry odours of the corridor and ambled up and down outside the rooms, examining the red-flocked wallpaper and the intricate pattern in the paisley carpet. She sauntered past his room again – the door closed now – and out the back, walked around the parking lot, gazing at the hazy night, came in the front entrance, said hello to the fellow at the desk and still, no phone light blinking in her room. By the time she had her door double-locked, she'd convinced herself that her remarks to him were amusing, along the lines of a domestic joke. As though any amount of her making light of it would get them through this again. As though they would ever find peace with the need he had.

Her divorce from her Mexican husband wasn't officially final, though for at least nineteen years she hadn't had occasion to speak to him. She was faintly conscious of her motivation for getting free of her dead marriage, fleetingly aware that her need was based on her uneasiness about Gabriel, but it didn't matter; being legally free to marry became a personal imperative. In January, while on a break, hosted by friends on a ranch in the hills behind Malibu, she phoned the records bureau in Los Angeles and tracked down the problem with her divorce – a missing signature. She drove the rented convertible – she had asked Gabriel to order a convertible – north up Sunset Boulevard, hair flying, to the courthouse and the signature was added and that was that. She began plotting her marriage. She did not inform the groom.

By the time they were in Dallas she had it in mind to buy material for her wedding attire and headed for Richard Brooks.

She had long bones, *enviable structure*, the consultant said. Lucinda considered ideas for suits – pictured herself married in a suit of charmeuse and Italian wool in an untamed garden ready for harvest and wild grasses up to your knees, the garden nestled in a clearing, the layers of oversized mountains rising up behind. The idea was too absurd, she thought, though she was reluctant to give it up. She went instead with a cotton from France, a print of flowers on a field of cream.

At the end of March, her inner monologue took a brief downward turn due to an incident during a tea break at a house in the Catalina Mountains of Tucson. A thousand stars were visible from the deck. A woman with a handwoven cape draped over her shoulders followed Lucinda outside and wanted to know if she and Gabriel were married. Lucinda answered quickly, sounding oracular to herself. She said, "We have been married a long time." It *seemed* true but didn't *sound* true; she herself didn't believe it. For a minute, fingering the lipstick-pink flower of a Christmas cactus, the woman seemed satisfied and then she resettled the cape with both hands and asked again – perhaps, Lucinda thought, because her ring finger was lacking. The woman said, "What *is* your relationship to him?" The words that rose to Lucinda's lips were *flunky*, *drone*, *lackey* – she was hard on herself – the organizer, the scheduler, the secretary, the banker, the shopper, the reluctant cook. The one who lit candles, ladled out tea. The mistress. The utilitarian female. Like pulling out of a dive, she levelled herself and kept quiet and smiled benignly. The next day she drove to the shops at River and Campbell and bought herself a simple, expensive gold band that she tucked away.

Now, the time of year when the garden was newly planted – the "three sisters" her favourites, squash, beans, corn – and her hands strong from her hard work, she waited in the kitchen, giving him twenty minutes in the meditation room after his phone call, and then went downstairs, along the hall, carrying a remnant of a feeling that the outcome depended wholly upon her and if she was really, really attentive, everything would work out fine. She ducked her head in the doorway and apologized for the interruption. She took off her shoes and bowed slightly to honour the space. "Good morning," she said.

By then he was in the willow-green wingback chair in the centre of the room that faced the altar and its alternating objects. Yesterday there had been a bud from a pear tree. That day the abalone shell was back, its inner lustre like the throats of hummingbirds that wintered in Arizona. An aroma of cedar incense issued from the burner. The room had one chair and the other seats were pillows. She chose a big blue velvet one from the pile and pressed the skirt under her bottom and sat cross-legged at his feet, her hands resting on her knees. "Good morning," he said.

"Is there anything I can do?" This asking also an old habit of hers. His eyelids were puckery, in him, she knew, usually a sign of fatigue. Yet he appeared to be in robust health, tanned and wearing on his pinkie finger his new Navajo ring, a bear carved in silver, inlaid with gold. He said, "I'm going to have the work transcribed. I have someone lined up. You remember her from last year. Idaho."

"Yes, oh yes." *Of course.*

They called her Idaho, she and Gabriel – Lucinda liked saying "Gabriel and I," she liked saying "we" and "us," she liked saying "between ourselves" – she could hardly stop herself from it. The woman they called Idaho had a complicated history. She'd gone so far as a Catholic to become a novitiate and worked for the Mother Superior in the abbey office and then had begun to realize she desperately wanted to have a child. The man she'd then married – an older man who owned a large orchard, plums and pears – couldn't father children and he'd known it but kept the secret from her. When she first came to see Gabriel, she'd had bruises.

Lucinda, recalling Idaho, breathed in, tongue behind her teeth, made herself aware of her nostrils and the air moving in and out. She visualized a stone falling into a pool. "Yes," she said, emerging. "Of course. Idaho." She blinked. She waited. He peaked his fingers and squinted across their tips. The roof of her mouth went dry as a bubble of heat broke softly inward, flowing into her belly in waves. She patted her forehead on the sleeve of the shirt she was wearing that belonged to him, conscious that she wanted him to notice she was wearing it. He smiled and said, "Didn't that used to be mine?" She bowed from the waist, awkwardly. He nodded, acknowledging, she supposed – *at least it was something* – that she willed the question from him.

He said, "You can't help it." He said, "Lucinda, I'm sorry."

Lucinda lowered her gaze, stubbornness rising like an unexpected tide. She accessed only the surface of what he meant – that she was wearing his shirt or taking pride from willing a question from him, or that she was running hot and cold or that someone was in love with him again. He touched his fingers on her crown chakra. His touch was firm yet gentle, so exquisitely masculine a touch in her experience that she never tired of it. Heat radiated from his palm down her spine.

"I'm sorry," he said again and his fingers played with her auburn hair, coiling the smooth strands of it. His hand slid along the side of her face, and he lifted her chin.

Her lips kissed his fingers. She wanted to make everything up to him – their winter of distraction, her resentfully glancing just at the reassuring whole of him in the habit of long-married people. Her running off to the apartment they kept in Phoenix to get away from the demands of everyone needing him. He said, "Umm," as though her kisses felt lovely. Her tongue played over the nails. She opened her eyes. He tweaked her chin and smiled and withdrew his hand. "You'll be all right. You know that." Again she declined to follow his meaning. She was taking no chances that cognizance might rear its unwelcome head, and on getting up she put her wrist on the small of her back in the way that pregnant women do. She had been thinking of pregnancy and babies and juice and she wanted to make love to him, she wanted to feel him inside her.

"You're all right," he said again.

"I won't be right about anything," she said – suddenly festering about domestic demands – "if we're not ready for the summer picnic and if the carpet layers don't get here before the first workshop." She was reminding him of the picnic the Centre hosted, together with Pastor Fred Worthy and the Church of the Redeemer, started by the pastor and Lucinda to make peace between the "hippie place" and the "Bible thumpers," since the two groups shared adjoining land. She was reminding him of the new rug she'd ordered for the sleeping loft where Centre guests stayed. She was reminding him of his house and home and of what was important when you came down to it.

She tossed the pillow onto the pile and gathered her skirt. She tossed the pillow, she gathered her skirt, she was filled with righteous virtue, she would think moments later in the kitchen. She went back to the meditation room, stepped inside wearing her shoes. He opened his eyes and she saw him return to the room, not entirely pleased at the disturbance. She said, "I need you to be present. Really present." She sounded stilted and strained, politely overwrought. She hated this attitude she fell into so easily, and she shrugged, groaning, and she did get a smile from him, and she let the familiar thought come, Maybe we can get through this.

6

On the Trans-Canada, west of Hope – the chainsaw carving capital of Canada, she'd read on a sign as she'd flashed past – was Lenore Carmichael. She came pell-mell around a curve in the road and hit a shadow, a patch of crunchy leftover ice that turned out to be slick beneath. The Honda lost its grip, swung tailwards, ignored the solid yellow lines. It slid slowly into the oncoming lane and was barely missed by an SUV, honking as it tore past. The Honda catapulted into a ditch like a frightened rabbit, nose down, on the wrong side of the road, and Lenore's forehead slapped the steering wheel. Her car squatted, panting, a fan spinning in syncopation with the drum beating in her ears.

It had been a mistake to stop at the Vancouver condo after packing the Honda and leaving Jack. She and Gary had had words over her walking out on his dad and she'd been rattled ever since. "I'm leaving your father," she'd announced over a breakfast of her vegetable frittata – she'd had to go to the grocery store for some decent food – experimenting with saying the words out loud – the word *I*, the word *leaving*. There was so much more dignity to the *I-leaving* combination compared to *I was left* that she expected Gary to be pleased for her: "Way to go, Mum." Something like that, whatever it was overaged teenagers said these days. She was merely practising, for Lord's sake, she didn't mean for him to get upset. He had, however, sat rigid in his chair as though struck. His pudgy face with acne scars struggled to keep back tears. In the end he'd cried, "I'm not moving, if that's what you think!" Then pelted into his bedroom and locked the door. She hadn't asked him to move out. Hadn't thought of it. Attributed the remark to his having been stoned, or wiped, or drugged out of his mind.

Now, in the ditch, she felt the jostle of tailwinds of other vehicles speeding happily along in the bright day. Then an older model Cadillac drew to a stop and backed up, on the shoulder, toward her. A man with a skimpy moustache stepped out and called: "Are you all right?" Her heartbeat was still in her ears, and she could only nod. He walked over and opened her door and asked her to step out. The ribs on her left side hurt and she could feel her forehead busy building a lump. It was chilly in this spot in the shadow of the mountains; she shivered. The man's voice sounded official, like a police officer, someone interested only in the facts as he began asking questions: "Can you stand, touch your index finger to your nose? Good. Bend forward and back, stand upright, turn your head to either side. Do you feel dizzy? Have you been drinking?"

She performed the tests to the best of her ability and didn't complain about her bruised ribs or the goosebumps on her arms or the ache in her head. Her heart had softened because someone cared enough to bother. Her eyes teared up. She had a question of her own: "Do you have children?"

He glanced furtively toward his own vehicle. A woman had emerged and stood with her back against the open passenger door, staring at Lenore, her expression full of hatred or loathing. *As though she knows me,* Lenore thought. *As though I owe her an apology.* She almost called over that she was sorry. For whatever the lapse might be, she was sure to be guilty of it. The man spoke, his voice lowered: "The wife and I weren't blessed with children."

"Ha! It sure wasn't a blessing for me," Lenore said. "I had just the one. I think he's into drugs."

The man shook his head, perhaps commiserating with her about the deficient younger generation. Or perhaps he felt sympathy for her, personally, or for himself. Lenore couldn't keep the words in. "I'm sorry," she said.

The door of the Cadillac slammed and the wife was back in her seat. The man apologized with opened hands. "Permit me," he said, "to get your car out." He returned to being businesslike; they were merely strangers who'd met on the road instead of the lifelong friends Lenore thought it possible they could become because he seemed so understanding. He adjusted the driver's seat for his longer legs and in the next minute the Honda erupted backwards and landed with a bounce on the highway. His face out the window, the man was chuckling despite the buffeting of a bus tearing by too close. He parked her car in front of his, facing in the direction of Vancouver. She would have to do a U-turn across the lanes to face east, toward the interior where she'd been headed, unless she trusted that the near-accident, and his placement of her car, meant something. A sign – yes, she thought, signs were needed when you didn't know what you were doing! – and maybe the universe was telling her she should turn back. While she was pondering the significance of her car pointing in the direction she'd just come from, she scrutinized the man and noticed that he kept his lips pressed close to his teeth, as though his lips weren't like everyone else's, the stretchable kind. Why it mattered about his lips she didn't know. He said, "I hadn't intended it to be so dramatic. Japanese cars are . . . My wife . . ." He ran a thumb quickly along his moustache, gave Lenore a wry, complicit look as though she would understand, and backed away, step by step, toward his own car with the unhappy wife in it.

Geese skeined eastward across the sky, high overhead. She heard their distant muttering. She smelled gasoline and tar and juiced weeds and her own unflattering sweat. She tasted blood. She got back in the car, squinted into the rear-view mirror, opened her mouth, and peered in. Lots of silver. Jack the dentist did not believe silver amalgams caused immune disorders. He believed *Homo sapiens* had become a species of wimps. What we needed was to pull a little rope, haul a little water. Yadda-yadda. Hearing his voice in her head made her strangely sad. Despite it she lurched away from the ditch and, pedal to the metal, sprinted back across the yellow line. She settled in the slow lane, going toward Ruth again, feeling slightly out of breath. The steering was looser, but maybe that was good. To be looser.

She moved along slowly. The geese had become dots in the distance. The road was like a trough, the slopes ascending from it rugged with sharp grey stones. She could hear running water though not see it, everywhere intricate networks of rivers and creeks, glacial meltwater, trickles. Though she was east of the Cascades, heading to the uplands – toward the interior forest, in her case – the sound of water would remain a constant. *Of course it would*, she thought. *The rain if nothing else, dummy*. Now she was nearing the Hope Slide, where one pre-dawn morning half a mountain gave way, spreading tons of debris across the highway. The weighty southwestern section had heaved the equivalent of a deep sigh, Lenore thought, and let itself go – *whoosh*. If you couldn't trust a mountain, what could you trust? She accelerated, as she always did at this point; more people were killed in B.C. due to rock fall than to earthquakes or floods, she'd heard that fact enough times to respect it. Which mountain in this chain would give way next? When would another ordinary, weary mountain collapse, revealing its dried-up, rubbly insides? Like her marriage: the misery out in the open now, everybody knowing. *He. She. Her. And then he –.* The tongues would be flapping in Perpetual Rain; everyone would have a say.

Change, so fast in coming, appeared when you least expected it. The thought made her pull a tissue from the box on the passenger seat and dab her eyes. When she glanced up, there were two people beside the highway up ahead, a girl and a child. As though they were nymphs just materialized into sunlight from the dark bush near the ruin of the mountain. The girl grew into a woman, a young woman overlarge in the chest, Lenore couldn't help but notice as she drew closer. They were not thumbing. Their eyes didn't try to catch hers, they didn't smile at her approach. They were simply hand in hand beside the road. She drove past and then appraised them again in the rear-view mirror. Beyond her own straight eyebrows set in a frown, she saw that the child's head was shaved. That detail made her wonder. Was he sick? Were they travelling home after some wretched treatment?

She put her blinker on and braked. If this was, in truth, the first day of the rest of her life – a cliché that might have something to it, the way the day was going – then she should pay attention. Everything might be a sign in a day so wrought with perilous adventures. Helping someone in trouble was good for the soul. Probably good for karma too. For the second time in twenty minutes she did a U-turn, whipping the car purposefully across the centre lines; she was familiar with the manoeuvre now. Her shilly-shallying on the Trans-Canada might mean, conceivably, that she wasn't committed to leaving Jack. A bird's-eye view of the Honda and its cavorting on this particular section of highway could indicate some confusion – Ruth, Vancouver, Ruth. Lenore was not a quitter, however, and since she'd gone to the trouble to go back for the ill child – a good Samaritan – she would follow through. "Get in!" she called, lowering the windows as she drew abreast. "Anything can happen to you out here, take my word for it!"

The Honda rattled a new rattle when she put it into neutral. Her foot tapped the pedal impatiently. Why didn't they open the door? About to swear, she realized – Lord – there wasn't room. On the passenger side alone was a pile of necessities and last-minute grabs – maps, a Thermos, a portable radio, her purse, a basket of socks, and a jumble of audio-book cassettes, a sweater, a coat, and underneath, barely visible, a twenty-four-pack of chocolate Slim-Fast. What was she thinking, taking passengers? She should slam on the gas and drive away, yet her foot did not move to the accelerator. She was asking herself questions: *What about the new beginning? What about the first-day business, the signs, all that?* She shifted into park, pulled on the handbrake. She leaned across the seat. "Where are you going?"

"Neon Bar," the girl said. "Up the lake from Ruth."

Ruth. Neon Bar.

Lenore felt a tap on her head, a moment demanding attention. *Fate.* She understood, then, that Fate was here, in the forms of a girl with odd speech and the scrawny boy by her side. In high school, Lenore had gone to parties in Neon Bar, reeled around under the stars in the dewy, clean grass, the music from the open door of the community hall – the pulsing music, the fluorescent lights on so late – markers of their rowdy, young presence, no matter that she wasn't asked to dance, she'd got over that. She was *there*. Enough to have survived the rides in the crowded cars, a mickey of rye passed around hand to sweaty hand, the boys driving in the dark like maniacs on the narrow curving road *up the lake, up the lake*. Anything possible, up the lake.

"What's your name?"

"Mory Zimmerman. He is BB."

Lenore grunted. Mory Zimmerman wasn't the daughter of anyone she'd known, too bad; might have been useful in finding a place to stay. She looked again at the girl. Flat-faced and sleepy looking, not too bright, and the child, close up, was no victim of illness, just a runt, clutching a tattered stuffed animal of some kind. The girl had an unhurried, implacable expression that could be interpreted as trusting, Lenore thought. Maybe the girl was trusting her, confident even, that Lenore would figure out how to fit them in the overcrowded little car. Mory Zimmerman wasn't going anywhere unless it was with Lenore Carmichael. Coming to that conclusion, Lenore was touched and felt a rush of fondness. She started grabbing things from the seat and handing them out the window. "Here. Take these around to the hatch. Go ahead. Open the door. Clear a space."

Out of the car, she trotted around to the back and, without thinking, yanked open the hatch with a pop. Shoes dropped, followed by a whole basket of sundries – B6, selenium, folic acid, tubes of cellulite cream, bars of deodorant, a purse-sized can of Static Guard. The plastic vitamin bottles wearing their bright, energetic labels rolled toward the ditch. "Oh, for Lord's sakes," said Lenore, attempting to grab a few things but stopped in her downward bend by her aching ribs. At that angle, she could feel the throb in her forehead. She straightened. "I may be battered, but I'm not beaten," she said. "Let's get this stuff back in the basket." The boy began scampering around, picking up things, and Lenore turned her attention to the hatch. She peered inside. About two inches' clearance in all directions. Not a chance in the world of cramming the rest in without unloading the works, taking half the day, wearing herself to a frazzle beside a damn highway. She reached in and chose a suitcase at random, one in the middle, and then she leaned in with her shoulder so that nothing else would escape and slowly pulled on the suitcase, and a spatula got past her, a carving fork, a pair of underwear, a towel, some rocks.

She looked at the rocks. Rocks? Jack's. From his hike last year up Willard Peak. Attainment of the summit a real accomplishment, she admitted it. Yet she recalled how satisfyingly spiteful it had felt ransacking Jack's rock collection. He was so proud of his rocks because he had sweated to find them, toiled to bring them down. How hateful can you get? she asked herself. "Don't anybody move," she said to the hitchhikers, her voice raised. "I'm to the point of cracking."

Mory Zimmerman and the boy stopped, still as statues. Lenore looked at the pair of pink satin underwear – unworn, a surprise for Jack before she found out he had someone else's underwear on his mind – on the wet gravel, along with the spatula, the fork, the rocks, the towel. On the highway, two semis came up behind them, came too close, and thundered past, horns blasting. Lenore jumped; adrenalin surged. The girl and the boy merely stood together and did not, Lenore supposed, think of giving those truckers the finger, as she herself did. They were alert for her cue, their attitude respectful, and suddenly Lenore saw herself as someone urgently in need of respect. She rolled the underwear into the towel, along with the fork and the spatula, and shoved the towel under the driver's seat. She brushed the palms of her hands together; done. She said to the boy, "Do you like rocks?"

"He's a danger around rocks," the girl said. *He'd a danger 'round rock.*

Lenore laughed, loud, grateful for the humour – a danger around rocks. She herself might become, any second now – any second! – a danger around rocks. To her ears her laughter sounded forced, her attempt to make the journey so far – east, west, west, east – an amusing story to be told after dinner in a room full of couples. She could almost see Jack at the head of the table and hear herself from the other end, striving for hilarity: I was in a state, let me tell you! There I was – ha, ha – beside the road again, that time trying to be a good Samaritan.

She extricated two more suitcases, set them on the ground in line with the first. "Eenie, meenie, miny mo," she said. By *mo* it was in her sites, at the end of her right index finger: Number Eleven. It keeled over with a gravelly thump, as though it knew it was doomed. Another sign. "This is Number Eleven," she said to the girl. "Don't ever marry a man who numbers his suitcases!" Everything she said exploded out of her mouth, sounding raucous.

"Give me a hand." There was no going back. She intended to hide the suitcase in the woods, why hide it she did not yet know. The girl took the handle and Lenore pushed from behind, and down into the ditch and up the bank and into the woods they went, while the boy stayed with the car. It was surprisingly dark among the densely planted trees, and the air was sodden and heavy. Cold drops plunked onto their heads and noses and eyelashes as they walked, bumping the suitcase between them. Goosebumps rose on Lenore's upper arms from the cold and the creepy damp of the moss-laden trees and she herself – a maniac – in running shoes that were absorbing water like sponges.

They propped Number Eleven against an old stump covered in lichen and a strange orange mushroomlike growth protruding out of a crack along its side. The stump was well out of sight from the road. "Good luck," Lenore said to the suitcase. She couldn't recall what was in it, the decision to leave it behind and take these people at least as far as Ruth becoming more irrevocable with every breath. She wiped her palms, slapped at her slacks, marched down the bank, shoes squishing, and out of the woods toward the car.

"We better get a move on," she announced once back on the edge of the highway, and then, as though stricken, she didn't move. She stood looking at the rock cliff-face across the way and at the sky, clouding up. She watched the clouds assemble and didn't move to collect the odds and ends strewn around the car like confetti after a wedding. Traffic passed and then no one was in sight and it was almost silent except for occasional splashes and kerplunks from the limbs of trees as the last of the winter burden, the grainy ice, slid onto the wet ground. Lenore wondered if a breakdown felt like this – silence and the inability to act. Then a thought occurred to her. "Oh!" she said. "We have to *mark* this place."

The marker would be a good use for Jack's rocks. They would be off her conscience and back outdoors, surely their hearts' desire. She chose a smooth boulder from the side of the road for a base and the three of them rolled it into place – rib pain by this time Lenore's accomplice – and then Mory and BB piled various rocks on top, Jack's too, and by the time Lenore had packed what was left and changed out of her wet shoes and socks, they had created a squat, man-shaped marker that no one would disturb, an inukshuk, marking a place someone might need to return to.

On the road, giddy and gratified and dry, the car heater on for good measure, Lenore began to talk. "Mother's dishes may be in Number Eleven, you know, I can't remember everything. Mother's teacups might be there in the woods. '*Limoges*,'" she said, imitating her mother's nasal tone. "'*Limoges, my dears*' – Mother said this to her bridge ladies every single time they came to the house, as though telling them something new. The ladies parroted behind her back – they'd whisper, '*Limoges*,' pinkies raised."

The girl listened politely, the long-legged child asleep, his head in her lap, his body draped under the dashboard. The road curved and opened to rolling farmland, blossoms on cherry trees pink and fragrant. Lenore said, "I've misplaced the list of what's in each case, so I could be wrong about the china. Oh, dear. I'm losing everything lately."

In Grand Forks, she pulled into a hotel parking lot. The café with the Doukhobor food was situated in the downstairs of a hotel that appeared derelict due to grime on the stone edifice and small bleak windows. The food was good, though, and Lenore knew exactly what to order. Soon plates swimming in butter appeared – perogi, vareniki, cabbage rolls. "BB doesn't like cabbage rolls," the girl said. Lenore again noticed the girl's speech: Not an s to be heard, the ls swallowed. The work that should have gone into her – speech therapy out the wazoo!

A family of four occupied a table on the far side, across the wide aisle. A little girl was turning five and there was a new baby that everyone wanted to hold. Cupcake wrappers and blown-out candles littered the table. Lenore noticed that BB was intent on them. The cook came out of the kitchen to admire the baby. Evidently the mother worked at the café and it was her day off. A waitress, a friend of the birthday child's mother, emerged from the kitchen carrying a gift, a big box with a red bow on it. The table clapped and the little girl squealed while her father helped unwrap the package. Inside the box was a giant red Elmo.

"Good Lord!" Lenore said. "Elmo reaching this far into the wilderness!"

The child at her table stared hungrily at it.

"You have your sheepie-sheep," his mother said.

The girl spoke slowly. The two of them, thought Lenore, were altogether low-reward sort of people, the type she'd worked with for years in her special classes. People who took forever to accomplish anything. Having to remind herself, day after day, Patience, patience, while mentally intoning, Lift the pencil. You can do it. Then saying out loud, "I think you can do it," fooling neither the child or herself. Then her mind butting in: Get on with it before the sun sets! And then placing her hand – large compared to his, her nails painted red, his bitten – and saying, sounding – she knew, she knew – like a monster from his nightmare: "Let me help you. An 'A' goes like this," and grasping the little hand, feeling the muscles twitch.

Her eyes flicked from one to the other. Though the child wasn't obviously sick he might be a carrier of some dread bacteria, he might be *communicably* diseased. What had she got herself into? She thought of the child's filthy stuffed animal on the passenger seat, probably polluting her car. She hadn't thought about germs enough on this trip; she'd just been winging it, trying to be a good person. She could picture filthy sheepie-sheep micro-organisms crawling – did micro-organisms crawl? – onto her own seat. There had been a bad smell too. A distinctly bad body odour. The child with snot oozing from his nose – she hadn't paid attention to the snot! – the mother's thin arms – scabbed elbow, scratches, she saw now as the girl wiped the child's face with a wad of toilet paper taken from her backpack, he wiggling away, as boys always did – Gary certainly had.

Lenore picked up a serving spoon and licked butter off the back and put the spoon back on the platter. People like this girl and her scrawny boy were everywhere. Nothing to do now, she thought, but to press on. She stood and paid the bill.

They drove on, kilometres slipping past. She didn't intend to arrive at Larry's with her nerves still humming, however, and she chose to overnight in a town approximately three hours from Ruth. "We could go the entire way," she said to her hitchhikers, "but it's wise to stop while you're still ahead." Whatever that meant. "You could use a shower," she said pointedly to the girl.

"We have friends." *We hab briens.* "What time do you leave." A statement.

Lenore considered. "Friends to stay with? I could drive you."

"No, it's close here. Their house. What time do you leave."

A surge of her old self and Lenore was ready to dump them and *hasta luego*. "Oh, make it seven, seven-thirty. I won't wait, though. I really hate waiting for people."

In her room she pulled the bedspread off the bed, touching it as little as possible. According to a magazine article, motel bedspreads were crawling with germs and invisible vermin from naked bottoms sitting on it and drunken lovemaking between strangers, disgusting to think about. It was bad enough that she'd taken on hitchhikers. She settled into the bed, tried to snuggle into an ungiving foam pillow and the thin layer of blanket. Her rib ached. She woke at first light and pulled the drape aside. Parking lot empty except for her car and one Wal-Mart truck taking up the rest of the space. An orange street light. A scene that appeared devastated, she thought, and then, with the word *devastated*, Number Eleven came to mind, and for a while she couldn't make herself move from the edge of the bed, hands clasped, worrying. About leaving the house in the mess she left it in, admittedly, at first, half proud that she was capable of such irresponsible behaviour. But Number Eleven? Her mind remained paralyzed about what the abandoned suitcase contained.

They hadn't spent the night at anyone's house, it was apparent when she laid eyes on them. They were sitting on the ground, leaning against the motel building in a location that couldn't be seen from the office, not that the office was open so early. Lenore had a remorseful second – she'd had extra towels and she'd had hot water – but she couldn't be expected to save every indigent on the planet, could she? "Good morning!" she called, making a stab at sounding cheery.

On closer inspection, she saw that though their faces were clean, the underlying odour remained, an odour – she'd figured it out – of woodsmoke and garlic that would be a trial for the rest of the trip. She would drive with the windows down. She took them to a café and bought breakfast – plates of eggs, bacon, pancakes, the works. Anxiety made her hungry. They too ate ravenously, their faces set on the food. From a safe distance across the table, she was drawn to analyzing them again. A tightly knit pair – something odd about them, however, something not right – she must stop her mind from that track. Stop it now, she said to herself. Focus on something else, she said to herself, and filled the interior of her mouth with the comforting fat of bacon and let her teeth and tongue enjoy it.

On the road again, she asked, "Why are you going to Neon Bar?"

It took the girl half a mile to form an answer. "A healer lives there. Everybody on the coast knows about him. Talks about him. His name is Gabriel. He will help me."

As the girl struggled with the speech, Lenore envisioned the fellow named Gabriel. He would be older than Gary, in his mid-twenties or early thirties. An intense youth with good hair gel and charisma and a lazy streak. In Vancouver they littered the landscape, those thin, handsome young men with a calling, a gift of astrology or tarot cards or knowing what the vulnerable wanted to hear. Their voices were pitched sweetly, they zeroed in on their targets, they had girlfriends, and slept anywhere in exchange for a reading or a toke or whatever else those people did.

A healer, indeed.

The road turned northward, at last, and climbed into the mountains. It began to rain. Stacks of snow lay, hard and unyielding, on both sides of the road where a plow had scraped it and Lenore slowed, worried about the temperature along this ridge, nothing to see but tree trunks and the rain as it splattered the windshield. She turned on her wipers, listened to them squeak, Fix me, fix me. She thought, If it isn't one damn thing, it's another. She began to worry that the rain would turn to ice and that the tires would slip on the surface of the narrow road and slide into the embankment; the car might be in that sort of destructive mood.

The road descended, and they began the curves tracking the river and then the lake, Judith Lake herself, opened and there were vistas again, the clouds able to spread out, the air warmer.

Entering Ruth, Lenore had a plan, knew what she was going to do. She pulled up in front of the post office. Everyone in the valley stopped at the post office for something – mail, a chat, a ride – and her hitchhikers would have no trouble getting to wherever they were going; it was early in the day. "Right. A healer," she said, as though the conversation had just ended. They got out and solemnly thanked her. Lenore nodded, waved, pulled away from the curb. *Save us, Lord.*

Winding down the driveway to Larry's house in her exhausted, flustered little Honda, she felt drained, as though she had been travelling for days and days. She felt like a pathetic beggar. She might as well *be* a pathetic beggar, she thought: The car a jumble, her eyes red-rimmed from a rotten sleep, the unclean smell of her hitchhikers permeating the air. And now, before her, rose Larry's big house. Rectangular in shape, an imposing three storeys and very Cape Cod blue. Crisp, white trim. (That influence would be Nan's; the square wooden planters on either side of the door, packed with forced red tulips, Nan too.) In the house would be a British Navy flag somewhere discreet but in your line of sight, Nan making sure you knew her ancestry; she'd been stuck-up even in high school. Lenore caught her breath. You did not have to see people regularly to know them very well.

It was a house built to make a statement, she thought. It did not blend in with the woods or the water beyond it, visible through the branches of the firs; the house was too big, too abrupt, the pruned land around it barely recovered from the bulldozer. But the place was Larry, vintage Larry, Larry manifested – the size, the views, the deck that she did not doubt was on the lakeview side, the deck that would make you feel privileged just to sit there.

She had to hand it to him: Larry's enterprises did pay off. At the age of ten he resold newspapers to old people, charging fifty cents a delivery; he'd get the papers by raiding entire newspaper boxes in their neighbourhood. Or he'd buy one paper and take two or three and ride his bike onto the next so vendors wouldn't catch on. He'd moved fast in the early days, trading cars for boats for derelict buildings, got grants, renovated, bought and sold, made good.

She came to a stop in front of the two-car garage and stayed put. He damn well knew she was there; he would have an alarm or a motion detector inside the house, Larry keeping track, covering himself. He would make her wait whether she politely rang the bell or beat her fists on the door; he had been a power-tripper as a boy and she knew he hadn't changed. She bided her time, listened to the crows cawing. The front door opened, and she sprang into action. "Darling boy!" She rumbled toward him. She called him "darling boy" because their mother had called him "darling boy" and jovial banality had become their manner of dealing with each other. She resented that he had been the favourite.

He was bulkier, larger, puffier head to toe, than when she'd last seen him. He quickly kissed the air beside her cheeks, one side and the other. "We does it like that these days." Chuckling over his little joke. "Us types." She laughed appreciatively – people let their guard down around him, thinking him stupid.

Inside, he had to point out the chandelier that hung in the entry hall. She had to change into house shoes. "The rules," Larry said. He led her into the living room, pointed out the stone fireplace and the burgundy leather furniture grouped around it, to where Nan was posed on the arm of the loveseat, dressed in black stretch shirt and jeans, one hand resting delicately on the wrist of the other. She cried, "Oh!" as though surprised by Lenore's arrival. She leapt up gracefully and danced, arms out, toward her sister-in-law. "Dear Lenore! How sorry I am about *bad Jack. Shame* on him. And I'm *so glad* you've come home to the family. We're here for you."

Nan's attitude – the pretentious caring, the feigned sympathy, the bad acting – was so expected, so *familiar* that Lenore found herself touched. The warmth of Larry's hand in the crook of her back was comforting too, after the frenzy of the last few days, the decisions, the packing, the leaving. She was caught off guard and suddenly teary. She murmured, "What a lovely room, and the pillows match your lipstick." Then, shifting her weight, she teetered and said, "Oh, my." She felt herself sag, and Larry, damn him – it nicked her pride – was holding her up.

7

Tuesdays and Fridays Estelee Chapman drove down from Neon Bar to Ruth in her van that had *E. Chapman, Unlimited* painted on its side. She made her living, she said, by being diversified. She picked up mail, delivered breads and pies, drove people to and from the airport, tourists mostly who came to the valley for powder skiing in winter and spiritual retreats in summer. Spring to fall, she worked primarily for Lucinda and Gabriel at the Centre for Light Awareness, running errands, seeing to people. A lot of coming and going, suckers after miracles, in her opinion, but – she would be the first to admit it – she had a soft spot for the two who ran the Centre. Lucinda was a bit of a stickler – "Our guests are not 'marks,' Estelee. Always call them guests!" – and Gabriel. Special, that one. He looked at you, you know he *saw* you. Made you believe he'd never met anybody so fascinating.

She spotted Mory Zimmerman and a kid – he must be the one – on the bench in front of the post office. She didn't hesitate, leaned across the seat, and called over, "Oh, it's you. Bus north, leaving on time. Come along now, hop in."

They drove for ten minutes or so and when the boy, clutching a tattered stuffed sheep, fell asleep on the bench seat in the back, Estelee said to her passenger, "Your father is ill. Terminal, I'd say. He will, I expect, be glad to see you."

Mory lowered her gaze to her hands in her lap. Her thumbs began tap-tapping. "I don't think so."

"Ah. You have something else in mind."

"We are looking for Gabriel."

Estelee hummed to herself and then after a while she said, "Oh, some things are just bad-ass terrible."

She stopped at the entrance to the Centre for Light Awareness and came round to slide open the door for BB. The boy was a sight, mostly bones and not handsome. But here he was, willing to smile. She rubbed her hand over his prickly scalp and turned to shake Mory's hand. And here was a girl, she thought, in need of a good meal. She explained, "I have deliveries – prescriptions – or I would take you inside and introduce you. You'll be fine here. These are good people. You may remember them."

Mory followed the boot trail through the wet grass, BB tagging behind, up onto the porch. She considered knocking, but the house felt closed up, like people did not want to be bothered. They settled on the steps to wait for someone. In the meadow that sloped toward the stands of cottonwood, beyond which lay the head of the lake, there were lilac bushes, uncultivated and tall, the lavender and purple and white buds beginning to fill out, the field itself a yellow carpet of dandelions. The air was soft in a way that Mory recalled. Small birds flitted in the poplars, a raven called, there was the sound of water. She followed the sound to a creek bubbling over rocks a, deadfall across it. She would not let BB drink because of beaver fever, which she explained to him would make him go from both ends. They sat on small boulders and washed their hands. She opened her pack and took out a

Coffee Crisp that she had been saving. It was crushed, but it didn't matter; BB was hungry, his tongue would be grateful. They walked back to the house and Mory opened the outside tap so they could drink. They went back to the porch. BB gave her a bouquet of wilted dandelions.

Lucinda stepped onto the porch and found two travellers hunched together on the bottom step. At least once a season someone wandered through the open gate needing help; when you gained the reputation the Centre had, you were bound to attract people in extremity. About these two Lucinda sensed worry, a little cloud of worry especially around the girl. No doubt they needed a place to sleep and wanted to work. She stood quietly with them for a few minutes to determine if they carried with them an energy she should know about – negative, depleting to others – and felt clear about them, but did understand that they themselves would require a lot of work, including the need for a bath right away.

"We are looking for Gabriel." The girl had to say it twice.

"Of course you are," Lucinda said, aware she was clasping her hands so that the knuckles showed.

"Sleeping place?"

Lucinda nodded. She reached out and took BB's hand, squinted at his fingernails. "He needs minerals," she said. "Do you give him supplements?" She laughed, in apology, and shook her head. "Oh, dear. Rude of me. Of course. I am –" She shook her head again and composed her face. Then she cocked her head and said to the child, "Are you a good helper?"

They both nodded: yes and yes.

"You need showers and food."

They nodded again.

She found out their names and led them into the mudroom, where bundles of garlic and ears of dried corn hung from hooks on the wood-planked walls. They removed their shoes and put their socks in a laundry basket. She picked out short cotton robes and said, explaining the robes, "Gabriel likes Japanese things," and led them through the kitchen into a small room with a toilet and a shower. "This used to be an outside shower. But times have changed. We don't do that sort of thing any more." She laughed again. "It's rustic" – there was daylight through the warps in the wood encasing the shower, and the pipes were wrapped with a fitted charcoal-coloured material.

"I didn't introduce myself, I'm sorry. I'm Lucinda. Lucinda" – she paused – "You can call me Lucinda." Then she demonstrated the turning on of the water. Hot and cold were opposite from what they usually were. "Do you understand?"

Mory nodded. Lucinda handed her shampoo and washcloths and towels and soap. She said, "I can't put you inside. The loft is a mess, because I'm replacing the carpeting. I can put you in the tepee out back. It's good-sized."

"Thank you," Mory said.

"Leave your robes on when you come out, so I can wash your clothes, all right?"

"Thank you," Mory said.

Finished with the shower, BB came into the kitchen wearing the robe, the sash tied twice around his waist. Lucinda poured him a glass of milk and he thanked her. Mory came out, fluffing her hair, and Lucinda picked up their clothes from the bathroom chair and went to the utility room to put them in the machine. BB barked, "Bow-wow," and Mory kissed his scalp. Gabriel stepped into the kitchen and smiled. "No fleas on that head." Mory blushed because he knew about fleas and lice. He knew the reason she had shaved BB's head in the first place.

While Gabriel was walking with the mother, BB played outside as Lucinda sorted through the drawers of the desk in the kitchen. She'd set the child up in the front garden, with a wheelbarrow and a trowel. He was an odd-looking, stringy sort of child, teeth nearly as small as barley pearls. After a little while she couldn't ignore him bobbing up and down outside the kitchen windows, peeking at her, a boy in no need of a pogo stick, she thought. She went out. He was shy but willing to help arrange the tepee where she'd decided they would sleep. The tepee was used primarily for couples who needed some time alone or, more so in the past than now, for one of Gabriel's sweat lodges. She took BB along the boot trail to the storage shed to collect the foamies he and his mother would need for sleeping on. The bedding she'd already aired, as though expecting someone.

Carrying a pillow, he followed her up the trail to the benchland behind the house. It was pretty up there, she always liked it, a good view of Judith Lake. She showed him the outhouse and where the extra toilet paper was kept, in a can with a lid on it so the rodents wouldn't eat it. Inside the tepee there was a smell of mildew that even Lysol, she knew from experience, wouldn't much help. Sun come, she thought, in the simple way the child's mother spoke. BB helped her shake blankets and fold them. They went back for cushions to sit on and some kindling and split wood for the firepit.

On the last trip, they met up with Gabriel and Mory emerging from the lake trail. He was nodding at something the girl was saying. A ray of sunlight caught his hair, the silver-white hair that the male New Jersey Markovices had; Lucinda'd seen the photos of his father and uncle in *Business Week*. In the next while, as she bustled about showing Mory and BB the garden and the bear-proof garbage can and where the lawn mower was – self-propelled, so she would have to wear shoes and the boy was not to try it on his own – Gabriel's slow smile followed her. Like the girl she knew she definitely was not, Lucinda nevertheless allowed herself to bask in the attention and pretended their trouble was due only to the long and distancing winter between them. She did not think of the woman whose name he'd mentioned or why, she, Idaho suddenly knew how to transcribe, if indeed she did. The white shirt rolled to the elbows and the jeans fitting his lean body so very nicely distracted her and caused little electrical currents of lust to course through her belly and hips, along with adolescent optimism: Marko-vee-chay. *Lucinda Markovice.*

Gabriel's acceptance of the newcomers, his attention to their settling in, had nothing to do with her womanly ministrations, nor did it seem to have anything to do with her, she thought later, because when she was done showing them around and was expecting acknowledgment from him – a peck on the cheek, a word – he tossed a nonchalant wave her way and went on foot toward Lightning Cairn Road, hiking to the airstrip to check up on the new plane. Lucinda stood in the field and watched until he was out of sight. Examining the plane was an obsession with him, she thought – the manner in which he touched it, could hardly keep his hands off it, how before every flight, during the walkaround, his left palm followed the right as he pressed skin, tapped fingers on bolts and struts, flicked a finger at a tidbit of dirt. He sniffed her vents, her fluid leaks, he peered into her crevices and joints, twirled her prop. Lucinda stood watching him go, hands on hips, jealous of the new plane, the expensive Nav-II equipped Cessna Skyhawk. All his attention to the settling in of Mory Zimmerman and the boy meant only that the summer – hers – would have them in it.

She went back inside to attend to e-mail. Ann-Marie, the Cincinnati psychologist – a retreat-only booking for the last week of July – had sent eight overwritten, flagged e-mails. She impressed upon Lucinda, again, that she needed just the environment, not Gabriel (wonderful as he no doubt was). She was bringing *her own people* (italicized), cancer survivors, which

Lucinda already knew. She informed Lucinda that she intended to arrive a day earlier than Lucinda had suggested in her last e-mail, and while she supposed it would be an inconvenience, she knew Lucinda would understand, smiley, smiley – parenthetic happy faces. As well, she had a grateful student who insisted she bring his homemade tofu and she was acceding to his wishes, so if the driver picking her up at the airport would please bring a cooler. It was necessary that she arrive early in order to make arrangements for her special, special people. One of them was afraid of heights and required a ground-floor room. She wrote: *The woman fell off a horse at the age of three and besides her ovarian cancer had been grappling with the terrors of inner space ever since.*

Lucinda tapped out, *Dear Ann-Marie: Everyone sleeps in a communal setting in the spacious loft. There are well-made, safe stairs from which to access the room. The experience . . . well, I will leave it to you to help her through what may possibly be a watershed experience and a release from her pain. I regret having no other options. Please let us know what you decide. Sincerely, etc.*

She sent it off, already disliking Ann-Marie, and perhaps the whole city of Cincinnati. A new message popped in, Ann-Marie wanting to bring her dog, a chihuahua. Lucinda fired back: *P.S. No dogs.*

8

That evening in Ruth, the Carmichaels were dining on the deck, the three youngest daughters, the ones still living at home, away at summer camp. It was chilly outside – there had been a brief, hard downpour – but Larry set up the umbrella and turned on the heat lamp and then he began barbecuing thick sirloin steaks.

Lenore was glad for the sizzle of the meat and the spacious, peaceful view, the flanks of the mountains wreathed in white wisps of floating cloud. Lenore wore a jacket of Larry's, shiny and zippered, a Molson's beer ad on the back. She and Nan were well into a bottle of Australian shiraz. Nan tried lighting candles, but they guttered out, and she left and came back with a hurricane lamp. She snipped off the end of the wick with a pair of small scissors she carried in her pocket.

"How's Karen?" Lenore said. Her oldest niece was at boarding school in Calgary and had stayed for summer session.

"Oh, fine, just fine, fine, fine," Nan said.

Larry cleared his throat. "So now. Tell my kid sister how you were saved from cancer," Larry said. Lenore did not know that Nan had had cancer. She hadn't heard that news.

"Why didn't you tell me?" She hadn't mentioned her colon troubles to them either, but that was different.

"Oh, it was such a minuscule thing, no big deal," Nan said, lowering her gaze.

"How could it not be a big deal?" Lenore was thinking of her own run-in with the oncologist. Thinking about her bowels caused her body to break into a sweat. She had to go to the bathroom and she needed to get there fast. "Excuse me," she said.

She applied a perfume spray that she found on the counter next to the heart-shaped guest soaps. She hadn't peeked into the medicine cabinet, mostly because – she took her seat outside again – there wouldn't be anything revealing in a guest bathroom anyway. She moved her glass closer to the bottle. Nan poured another glass of wine for each of them and gave Lenore a look Lenore couldn't quite interpret – keen or coquettish or a combination of both. Larry rattled the ice in his glass. Nan reached for the Scotch and poured him another drink. "Glenfiddich," Larry said to Lenore. "You noticed, eh?" He lifted the steaks off the grill and placed them on the plates. Nan ground fresh pepper over them. They passed the food around. Lenore was famished.

Nan said, "I *was* saved from cancer. Don't let him fool you." And then over knives grinding on the china, blood from the perfectly medium rare steaks oozing into the baked potato, she told the story of the biopsy on her breast and about the miracles of modern medicine, thanks to Larry for bypassing a wait list and sending her to Calgary to a specialist who'd had a cancellation. "An angel was watching over me, because the timing was perfect. I am so blessed." Lenore had never heard Nan use such language. Nan pointed to her perky breasts. "A true miracle." Lenore and Larry looked. "The scar is right here somewhere. A tiddly-widdly, teeny-weeny scar where the bad cells were lifted out and flushed away. Lar, show your sister exactly where the knife cut. Oh, come on, Lar, it's not like you're not *interested*."

Larry pointed: "Eenie, meenie, miny mo." He reached across the table and lay a finger on Nan's right breast above the nipple. When he started the *eenie, meenie* business, Lenore remembered Number Eleven and felt a stab of regret.

"Now, dear, you've heard the whole story again. That's what you wanted, isn't it?" She laughed, a short laugh, and brushed his hand away. "But you are my hero," she murmured and, turning to Lenore, blinked away tears. "He really is."

After dinner Lenore untangled herself from Larry's schnapps and Nan's easy-listening jazz, pleading a headache, and slipped downstairs to the room they'd given her. She was intoxicated and bloated with food. The headache was a convincing excuse, because headaches ran in their family; their mother had been the headache queen. Their world stopped whenever her migraines came on, real or convenient; eventually she and Larry saw patterns to the headaches – a working day, house needing cleaning – and couldn't trust her. She was a whiner. She made them feel guilty. She and Larry took turns applying washcloths soaked in cold water, folded neatly, across their mother's forehead. Her wispy voice, eager to shoo them out of the darkened room: "Be grateful you don't have to endure this pain." Mother's eyes closing. It was hard for Larry to be quiet. He was a lumpy boy, tears often trickling down his grubby cheeks, lips warping across his face in the attempt to beat back tears. Mother had a way of making him cry. Boys hated you to see them crying. Gary had been the same.

Lenore patted her distended belly. Too much meat not chewed enough and on top of it, Nan's homemade chocolate mousse with enough caffeine in it to keep her awake until dawn. Dark and dawn reminded her of the suitcase in the woods. Poor Number Eleven, alone. Similar to her own situation, alone in these particular woods, in a room that smelled of carpet glue. She thought of Jack. How stupid she was not to have realized! Had she been more on top of it, literally, she would have twigged to Jack's intentions sooner. His laptop gone from his den one day. A very bad sign. And when the clerk at school said to Lenore: "Oh, I hear it's just an affair," Lenore was oblivious enough not to know what she was talking about. How could you be so blind? She'd scrambled fast, retorted like a good sport: "Oh, yeah, middle-aged men! Worse than menopause. *Oh, Lord*," exaggerating, using big gestures. Then she'd ducked into the teachers' washroom and stared into the mirror. The whites of her eyes were showing around the irises; she looked crazy, beyond help.

Upstairs, the music. They might be dancing. Touching. Gazing into one another's eyes. Initiating sex. On the burgundy couch, under the mahogany table in the dining room, their bodies nestled on the plush living-room rug. *Her brother? Nan?* Since when did long-married couples have an evening of music, cognac, and candlelight? What about favourite TV programs? What were she and Jack doing all those years? She believed that not much made her cry, but this, the idea of couples and cognac and candles did.

Within a few days, Lenore began to think that Nan was watching every morsel of food she ate. "Are you sure?" she would say when Lenore reached for the maple syrup a second time. "Lots of fat in cheese," she would say when Lenore's cubes were cut bigger than Nan's. "Oh, but," she said, reaching into the utensil tray of the dishwasher, "we always put the flatware eating-ends down. The reason why is obvious." It wasn't the correction Lenore thought she minded so much as the sense of being watched and evaluated, which increased her awareness of her own precarious situation as a guest.

Lenore looked in the phone book for familiar names, classmates from school who might still live in Ruth. She asked around. Some quick research established that her home-ec buddy, Gail, now owned a shop with "boutique" in its name. The fact of the shop made Lenore hope that Gail just might have a big house and, maybe, a spare bedroom for an old pal. Driving across the bridge into the new section of Ruth, Lenore envisioned staying at Gail's place for two or three weeks until she could figure out what to do next. There were so many decisions. Stay in Ruth, look for a place to rent? Throw darts at a map, travel, go somewhere outlandish where no one knew her?

Gail's shop featured a line of animal prints and casual clothing for all ages – babies, teens, and the mature woman, as well as maternity wear. She wore big gold earrings and several bracelets on each wrist. Someone came out from the back to look after the register when Gail invited Lenore next door for coffee. "You have to be versatile if you want to stay in business in this town. Women," Gail said, "have become my area of expertise." They ordered two decaf lattes, non-fat. When the cups and plate of almond biscotti arrived, Gail asked Lenore how she was keeping.

Lenore hardly knew where to begin, partly because she was analyzing whether it was possible for her to be friends with someone so tanned and toned and perfectly groomed, someone so at home with herself, someone who had also had – this an area of Lenore's expertise – her teeth so subtly, professionally whitened.

"I'm divorcing my husband," Lenore said. The words just tumbled out.

"Oh, you poor dear! I've been there myself." Gail said she had no children. She and her partner were avid day hikers. Their hobby was cresting ridges, the more vertical the challenge the better.

Lenore saw that Gail was interested in her and the interest could be the chance she needed to remake their friendship. She decided to talk about Jack, to tell Gail the story she hadn't told to anyone else. She tried to be humorous, emphasizing key words, like *true love*. She launched in. "His relationship with the girl-friend is – so he says – his one and only foray into True Love. Can you imagine? After I put in thirty years? Him saying such a thing to my face?" She'd agreed to meet him in a bar with a view of Howe Sound, pinball machines in the background and a jukebox in a corner, Jack into his new look: black sweatshirt, hair pulled into a ponytail. Sipping the latte, Lenore confessed to Gail that she'd had mistakenly inflated ideas: "I secretly thought he wanted to ask my forgiveness. The place was sort of romantic."

Gail's eyes widened.

"How was I to know? It was humiliating." Lenore didn't mention precisely how humiliating the experience had been: She'd dressed carefully and worn foundation and lipstick and black mascara and she'd bought a body-slimmer though she couldn't get into it at the last minute. He had shaken hands with her and when they were seated on stools at a round table and had ordered drinks, he began by clarifying that he didn't want to hurt her feelings. The more he'd thought about it, however, he said, the more he simply couldn't resist sharing his joy with her. He said, "The feeling I have for this girl is the first real love I've experienced in my entire life." Lenore was into a pint pitcher of beer – he was drinking Diet Coke – and looking out past the flickering candle at the desultory, rain-soaked view – gulls in grey and white bobbing on grey and white. He wanted her to understand that he hadn't known before what loving someone – really loving someone – was like. "It's awesome," he said. "Wild." He hoped, for her sake, that she would find the same thing someday. Lenore spun her glass in its little puddle and thought about hanging herself from the rafters of the garage of the suburban house he'd bought over her dead body when they left Vancouver.

"You poor kid." Gail laughed. "You should try swing-hitting. I've moved into a whole different world. You saw the gal with me in the store? My partner, Jo?"

Lenore said she had.

"Her."

Lenore let her jaw drop in girly amazement; she'd seen the look, the "oh-my-god" look, on the *Oprah* show. "Ohmigod," she said, getting it almost right, "Isn't that fabulous! Well! Hey! All right!" She was very, very sorry that she'd blabbed the story. Not because Gail's partner was a woman, but because Gail had laughed so comfortably, obviously happy – so heartily happy – while Lenore had made herself sound so truthfully, woefully pathetic. She was stricken by shame and cleared her throat in order to hear what would come out. "Oh, girlfriend, I am *so* afraid of climbing. The altitude, my knees." And then she was up there and panting, nervous already about getting back down.

At Larry's she was becoming more cagey and defensive – no, she thought, more *puerile*. Secretive and furtive. She started hoarding bits of food – a cookie Nan wouldn't miss, a peanut breakfast bar from Larry's stash in a back drawer, chocolate chips from an open bag. These she found under her pillow, smeared like fecal matter; it was creepy what was happening to her in Larry's house. She had to wash the sheets and remake the bed at a time when Nan was out, because if Nan was in the house, she would take notice, she noticed everything and she wanted to know precisely what was going on. So that by the time Nan invited Lenore to join her for lunch at the Judith Lake Golf Resort, Lenore was, as she would tell people later, pretty far into a kind of paranoia.

They sat under an umbrella, the sun surprisingly warm for June. Nan said, "We can't even enjoy the sun these days. We have to worry about it not raining. All you hear on the news is low snowpack."

"I don't care if it never rains," Lenore said. She looked out over the putting green. "It's hard to imagine *a golf resort* in Ruth. Nine holes were here in my day, I think, but no food to speak of. Potato chips maybe." Her burger arrived and she bit into it with gusto, grateful for the gobs of mayonnaise. Breakfast at Nan's house had become toast and tea, after which Lenore would swallow a senna stool softener, hoping for the best.

The waitress placed a pitcher of iced tea on the table. It wasn't icy enough, according to Nan, didn't have enough ice cubes to suit her. She pressed her fingers briefly to the pitcher's side and shook her head. "Sometimes I can't wait until Larry sells the store and we can go to an area with decent restaurants, enjoy *nice* food." She cocked her head, indicating, so Lenore assumed, that she would understand, having lived in Vancouver for so long. Lenore considered this gambit a trick on Nan's part. If you agreed with her it was like saying you didn't love the mayonnaise burger. And she did. Or that she hadn't had a decent bite to eat since she arrived.

She said, "Going somewhere nice was not where Jack wanted to go." As soon as his name was out of her mouth, she was sorry. So far she'd avoided revealing details.

"I don't want to pry." Nan set her hands side by side on the table.

Nan did want to pry, she certainly did, Lenore thought, blinking. Nan's nails were manicured. Squared off. White tips. Intimidating. Lenore said, "Oh, it's – no big deal, really. Middle-aged crisis, the usual." She felt herself pinned and sputtering.

"Who is she?"

"Um, she's young. See, Jack liked the rugged life on the coast –"

"– other things, from the sound of it –"

"– well, yes. He's taken up fishing, hiking, even hunting. But it's – I was happy in Vancouver. I didn't want to leave. I don't like fishing or hunting."

Nan rallied with a little laugh, a bell-like titter that Lenore figured was at her expense. The idea of Lenore fishing or hunting, even walking very far, woods or no woods, was comical, she knew. She herself laughed. Anybody seeing her knew she would never be found hiking along a mountain ridge or kayaking a river. Not even on her worst day.

Nan said, "If only relationships were that pat." She leaned in confidentially. "And how is my dear nephew?"

"Gary and some friends are working on a movie."

"Oh?"

Nan's pinkie finger was raised, its nail poised to break Lenore's little bubble. Like Lenore's own mother had been, Nan was impossible to lie to, not that Lenore wouldn't try. "Yes, they've – uh – got a camera, the works. An Internet project," she added, inspired. "He's still working at McDonald's, just a part-time gig, until – you know." It was sounding pretty good. Pretty much as Gary told it to her last year. He did own a lot of DVDs. Lenore took a big bite. The mayonnaise oozed out. Just disgusting enough so that Nan turned away. Fine. Nan had everything: figure, looks, a man. And girls. Lenore envied Nan her daughters. A daughter would phone, check up on you, let you visit, set you up in the spare bedroom, feed you chicken soup if you needed it.

"I've just had a thought." Nan handed Lenore another napkin. "Did you bring the tea set? You haven't said anything about it this whole time, and I didn't want to upset you more than you already were – you are feeling better, aren't you? – but my fingers are crossed."

Lenore wiped her mouth. She picked an overmicrowaved bun from the basket, hard as a brick. She bit into it anyway and inhaled some dry flakes. She choked. Nan watched for a second before passing a glass of water. Lenore wondered if she should lie and tell Nan that the china was in storage. (She had an idea about what Number Eleven contained.) Or should she tell the truth that she'd abandoned a suitcase in the woods . . . Maybe not. Lenore coughed again and patted her chest. Mumbling, she said, "I forgot."

"Pardon?"

"The china. I forgot."

"*Porcelain.* And you distinctly said you'd packed the set separately from the things that went to storage. You said you wrapped them individually in proper dish-packing material, and put them in a suitcase that had a number. You were quite firm about it. Write down this number, you said. I believe you were drunk."

"I wasn't drunk."

"You were drinking."

"I wasn't. If anything – it was sleeping pills. I take sleeping pills since Jack, well, since Jack reconsidered. He reconsidered, I reconsidered."

Nan cocked her head. "Reconsidered?"

"Did you – uh – did you write down the number?"

"What?"

"The suitcase number. Did you write it down?"

"No."

"Well, there you go," said Lenore.

"Pardon? Excuse me? I don't quite understand. You promised the tea set to me. I know it's missing a cup and I think the creamer shattered that Thanksgiving when the girls were – oh, never mind. The point is, it's baby-blue platinum *Limoges.*"

She sounded just like Mother. Lenore gaped. She covered her mouth to suppress a nervous giggle that was working its way up her esophagus. She said, "I was the one who spent hours and days and days in the institution –"

"The nursing home. The very expensive nursing home. I should know since Larry –"

"Right, so he paid – a few extras, right, but is that what *really* matters? I was *with* her. For years. At the end. The very end. You were nowhere in sight." It was disconcertingly effortless for Lenore to recapture the picture of her mother picking at her quilted coverlet, her mother's fingers compulsively going pick, pick. Lenore had bought the coverlet at Wal-Mart, to replace her mother's old, stained one. Her mother was angry and wordless – it had been a debilitating stroke – possibly about the coverlet coming from Wal-Mart, Lenore had reasoned. Who could tell? But the nurses said the elder Mrs. Carmichael probably wasn't aware enough to be specific about being mad at any particular thing, but Lenore pointed out that they didn't know her mother. Gary was twelve and hanging back, still hiding behind Lenore, watching his grandma's fingers. Lenore had started taking him for visits when his grandma first came to the coast to move into the assisted-living complex; he'd always tagged along. He worked on a puzzle or wandered the halls while Lenore sat in the chair and talked, earnestly, as though, in her last months, her mother could understand a word she said. Lenore complained about Jack. She gave Gary money for doughnuts and soft drinks. After the visit it was invariably dark. They would head straight to the bright lights of McDonald's. She never gave Gary much thought. She had to get things off her chest and therefore she talked to her insensible mother. Lenore said things like, "My husband had to leave *his wife and child* in order to find meaning in life." This was when Jack was in Ecuador. She was snide and dismissive and went into some detail regarding Jack's marital flaws. The other ladies were paying attention, peering her way. Often she believed that, at last, she was being understood, though hers was a nailed-down audience: Six ladies in wheelchairs and not one of them certain what year it was. It hadn't occurred to her that Gary would be upset by anything he saw or heard. She hadn't meant to scare him. She hadn't considered how scary elderly people could be to a child used to television. The smells. The soiled bibs. He started having nightmares. She should have had her head examined for taking a child to that place.

Suddenly she was in a sweat, overpowered by the heat and the light reflecting off the flat lake below. She nearly fainted from a craving: She had to have ice cream right away, a luscious pile of cold, rich ice cream with chopped nuts and fudge chunks, and she needed it – absolutely required cold ice cream to paralyze the roof of her mouth immediately.

Nan tapped a nail. She lowered her eyes. "Other things were going on in my life," she said, "at that time. Karen and – well."

For a second Lenore wasn't sure what they'd been talking about, then it came back. Mother. Larry and Nan staying away. Her thoughts turned to the tea set. She said, "I reconsidered. That's all I'm at liberty to say. By the way, do they have Ben & Jerry's here?"

Nan looked up. "It's not like I *need* any more things. It's simply that I had my heart set." She placed her napkin on the table and asked for the bill.

"Chubby Hubby? Chunky Monkey?"

Lenore knew she'd earned Nan's scathing look.

She didn't know where to go after the lunch, or what to do; at least they would say hi to her at Gail's shop. The outfit she ended up buying was a departure, but one that Gail said was essential at a time of personal crisis: Lenore should let herself live big. In a moment of inspiration, watching Gail's bangly wrists, Lenore pictured herself as predatory, not a depression-leaning bone left in her body. Now, coming into Larry's house through the utility room, she felt a little abashed. Gail made her boom with confident laughter and then she'd put her credit card on the counter. The other woman, Jo, had nudged a bowl of chewy caramels her way. Remnants of caramels were still stuck in Lenore's molars as she entered the kitchen, toting a new fuchsia pink linen jacket and leopard-print pants that they had assured her would go great with her salt-and-pepper hair. Larry was at the counter, pouring a drink. He raised his glass in a toast.

"You seem tired," she said, setting her bag down.

"Aye, gill, it's always in ya to criticize." He swigged back the contents of his glass and poured another.

"I wasn't being critical."

"There's a bundle you don't know about relationships, kid. Keeping them together. Coddling them along. It's better you stay out of it."

"I just meant to be nice."

"That's all right, forget it."

"Oh, for Lord's sake." Larry was *forgiving* her.

9

The cabin Kathleen was in was set at the far end of the field, a miner's cabin, not too dilapidated to be made habitable despite its age. The cabin was primitive, restful compared to the continuing chaos in the Toronto apartment. Silence lay all around outside and the cabin had nothing of James's in it. While exploring his new property, Davida's husband, Boris, had discovered a seam of galena behind the ridge as well as a shaft that someone had prospected by hand and timbered up and never finished. Kathleen imagined the crazed, hard work of the digging and the mood of the lone man driven to go farther in, to press deeper with his tools, no matter the reports about the galena in this region not yielding much silver; he was not leaving. He had come this far west and he had tramped this far north, he had taken himself away from wherever it was he started, that particular place with its unalterable facts. Veins of silver and, so he'd heard, gold, still cropped up everywhere; you had to know how to find it. Her imagined man turned off the main trail, not a follower, and hiked up the mountain, exploring the ridges, and came back to the flat land where he struck a camp, felled trees, and set a fire and subdued it and created a clearing, deer moving through the following spring, their long teeth looking for saplings, their lips longing to nibble on something tender for a change. The man she imagined liked the smell of the place. Crusts of dirt and blood in the beds of his nails – caused by the killing, the cooking, the handling of wood – he cut a huge tree, sliced it, notched it, did whatever they did to make a tight, tidy place. He had no dreams, and he wrote in pencil by the light of the kerosene lamp. He was asking, Kathleen thought, for a little yielding from the mountain; it seemed to her that back then, as now, forgiveness is what we most need.

They had been laughing after dinner and he had touched the small of her back. They were standing close like that when Davida, nearing the staircase landing, rolled her eyes and went on up to bed; she'd had a headache most of the evening. Boris and Kathleen then kissed, a family sort of kiss that left her tingling. Afterwards, Kathleen bumped into him, curious, readying herself to be complicit, oddly complicit – Davida was, after all, her closest friend – but looking forward, with a mixture of curiosity and illicit desire, to what he might do next. He picked up the sugar bowl and the creamer she and James had given them for their wedding shower and set them on the counter in the kitchen near the blue vase, holding the array of irises Davida had picked in the garden – the first, lushly purple with mauve beards. Then he turned to her.

The day after Kathleen arrived, the three of them had gone out in his new sports boat, a sixteen-foot fibreglass bowsitter, a bargain, according to Boris. He had discovered how much its owner owed the local bank because he knew the banker, Ruth being a small town and Boris a big man in it. (This was how Davida told it to Kathleen.) He paid cash and quoted to the women, as he parked the car at the dock, the exact figure he had saved. The seller, who owned a failing little deli in the next town, was not happy to be rescued by Boris Malenko, so Davida informed Kathleen as they descended the ramp. They were tagging along behind Boris, who was carrying the picnic basket. "Boris doesn't have a good reputation," Davida said, "in part because he can be a bully." She hadn't seemed to care that he heard.

He had bought a boathouse, one that was dressed in weather-worn shingles and adorned by rusting sheet metal, that belonged to an old-timer living at the Frances Hill, the retirement home Boris owned and Davida managed. The lock that Boris inserted his key into at the boathouse door was large and shiny gold. "A lock like that is a beacon," Davida said to Kathleen. "It shouts 'something of value' over here. I told him that, but he doesn't listen." They stepped from the unsteady dock over a little patch of slimy water to the threshold, Boris taking Kathleen's hand to help her with balance. Inside, despite the heat of the day, the boathouse was cool and cavernous, the sound of rocking water echoing against the walls. The sleek boat with blue trim gleamed in its bay like a live thing; you could almost hear it growl with anticipation, its bright white fibreglass coating tinged with green due to the intense reflection from the shallow water. When they smiled at each other, their teeth were especially white. She liked the soothing underwater feeling created by the dim, glowing colour; she felt calmed.

Boris, wearing brand-new boating sneakers, knew what he wanted the women to do and in what order it was to be done. Davida and Kathleen came to mock attention. The boathouse door on the lakeside had to be ratched open through a compli-cated system of pulleys and levers, and then it had to be locked in place on both sides. The boat had to be started just so, after securing the buoys and collecting the life jackets from hooks on the wall and tucking them under the bulkhead. The pole had to be ready, in case anything untoward happened in the backing out – "In case it bolts," Davida said – and the boat were to scoot against the timber frame of the door, risking a scratch; it had to be pushed back into slightly deeper water and the outboard motor let down, after the bow was untied, of course.

Instantly Kathleen loved the sound of the engine inside the boathouse, deep-throated rumbles followed by splashing caused by the propeller. The noise filled her heart. Boris backed out as she guided the bow outwards, using the pole against the carpeted edges of the boat bay. Davida, who would rather be on a horse any day, tied a scarf around her head and put on the dark glasses she'd ordered from the Eddie Bauer catalogue. (Her little conceit, Kathleen knew, was her relationship with nicer catalogues.) While they were in the bay, heading for open water, Boris complained about the engine. "Eighty-horse is okay. But you should see the four-stroke babies – wow." He planned to buy a big inboard next.

"He suffers from terminal disappointment," Davida had said. She was small boned and wiry, wore her hair pulled back into a bun, and thrived, Kathleen liked to tell her, on adversity, which was why she'd married someone as difficult for her as Boris Malenko, a man whose name said it all. Because he'd accepted the job in Ruth, they'd moved from Vancouver, where Davida had been happy working as a legal secretary for a Children's Aid law firm, into the interior where she made no secret that she was working hard to make herself fit in. Kathleen cast a quick look at her friend hunkered on the bench at the stern, prepared to endure the outing. The "terminal disappointment" remark was similar to one she'd made a few years before – that Boris was among the chronically disgruntled. At the time, she and Davida were taking a walk along the shore while the men – Davida's new husband

(Boris) and Kathleen's husband, James – the boys, they called them, not believing either had ever really been a boy – were occupied with lighting a bonfire. Neither of the men the friends had chosen had earned woodcraft badges and neither had been a Boy Scout. James came from European intellectuals, via Scotland and France, and Boris from older parents, carpet merchants – not a camper in the group. When Davida made the remark about Boris, Kathleen smiled because she thought that she, too, was burdened by an ingrained assumption that things should be finer, or more perfect, or larger than life. In those halcyon days, she craved anything extraordinary.

By the time the two women had wended their way back through the spindly cottonwood, the fire was going and they were grateful, hands and feet cold. The fellows, both bearded, one black and one red, were looking pleased with themselves. They grunted as their wives took seats on the logs they had rolled into place. "Mountain men," Kathleen said to Davida, and they'd laughed, feeling silly, and James – Kathleen did notice that James hid a smile. The fire glinted through the fine red hairs of his beard.

The house the Malenkos had then was on a hill in the old part of town, a house you could see from practically everywhere. It had turrets and three storeys and was drafty. The renovation that had sold them in the first place turned out to be shoddy; pieces of plaster fell without warning in the upstairs hallway. The electrical service was substandard – turning on a hair dryer upstairs while the clothes dryer was on in the basement caused the whole house to drop dead. Boris had wanted the showiest house in town and had got it. Davida phoned Kathleen to cry. The power had gone out for three days (they had worn snowsuits day and night, she said, and played Monopoly by candlelight. No one invited them for dinner). She would leave him if they didn't find a new place. The house had a potential buyer, and though Boris would lose money, he did not suffer from his losses. That was the celebratory reason for the bonfire and the chocolate cake and the homemade rhubarb wine.

James had seemed fond of Boris; he found him enterprising as well as something of an idealist. As an example, he used the Frances Hill Retirement Home: "The elderly don't have to move out of the area. How long had this town been needing such a facility?"

"But he used government funds and he took advantage of an old man to get the land for next to nothing and he exceeded the budget."

"Kathleen. It got done."

"Most people think he profited. You know, money under the table."

"His heart is in the right place," James said. "You'll see." She'd snickered at that idea – she had just become a certified counsellor and was proud of her now-honed intuition, which did not leap to "good-hearted" when applied to Boris. They were upstairs, in the guest bedroom on the third floor, talking, packing for the continuation of their trip west, because James was speaking at a Pacific Rim conference in Vancouver. He held his ground, peering at himself in the ancient wavering glass above the dresser, knotting his tie. "Yes, he will take what he can get, I know, I know. He keeps people stirred up, yes. But that piece of land where the Frances Hill is wasn't being used, so he went after it. And did something worthwhile. He knows what's worth saving; look at it that way. For some, whether they admit it or not, he was a saving grace."

Kathleen supposed, looking at Boris at the wheel of the boat, pleased as a boy, that for some he had been a knight in shining armour, though she wasn't so sure if that was the case for Davida any longer. Davida's expression remained impassive, her scarf fluttering behind her. Kathleen knew she didn't like speed or noise, which was always the way, wasn't it – that having chosen the fastest man around to marry, you spent half your life coping with motion sickness. He said, "We can't give you a thrill until we're clear of all the runoff debris." Kathleen looked and saw that the surface of the lake had a film on it, pollen, cottonwood mostly, he said, and dead woody stuff from the edges of creeks, now beginning to run into the lake in earnest, as the ice was melting fast since the weather had turned so warm so suddenly. "Look up," he said. "There is hardly enough snow up there to get us safely through this summer." There was snow on the peaks, as far as she could tell; she didn't know the difference and she said so. "It should be down to there," he said, pointing to a line midway down the chain of mountains. "You should feel cold now," he said, "even at this speed." She leaned in to hear him over the motor. "What you have to watch out for," he said, "is the big stuff underneath. It lurks. You might see just a twig, but under it a whole log is waiting to rip a hole in your hull."

Out at last from the bay, he seemed to frame a clear run, and his hand, firmly grasping the speed control, continued forward and the boat leapt and plowed, picking up speed until the bow began to fall and the lake, Kathleen thought, allowed them to plunge into it and then rose everywhere to greet them. She whooped with joy: The view in all directions was vast – water, mountain, sky. An orange haze lay to the south, from the fires in eastern Washington, Davida said; she'd seen it on the news. Otherwise, to the north, pallets of blue, green, blue, the hues varying from solid to airy. From town she hadn't realized the distances – the immensity of the lake and the vast seriousness of the mountains. They were whipping along, closing in on the far shore. Kathleen whooped again and Davida turned away. She would know when Kathleen was trying too hard – overfunctioning, they called it in Psych 300 – yet it felt good to be in the mood to try. She wanted out of her own tight skin. Wanted to feel her hair blowing, snapping against her neck, and she stood, holding the edge of the windshield. The wind struck her upper body, sent chills up her arms. Her ears ached from the cold, winter holding on under the superficial layer of warm air.

"Thirty-seven miles an hour," Boris yelled her way. He was playing with pitch, trying to get another mile of speed. He gestured for Kathleen to move up front, into the bow. She was laughing and nearly lost her balance as she lurched forward to fall onto the passenger-side bench, in front of the windshield. There were no hand railings, the boat wasn't that big, so she put her feet up on the vinyl cushions and wrapped her hands over the gunwales in an effort to stay put. The boat bucked over the swells and roared forward. Cold water splashed her arms and hands. As her hands went numb she felt better; it was a relief not to feel anything. "Time for a lesson," he shouted and lowered the speed. They lurched forward, sliding over swells of water. He dodged a floating log that bumped against the stern, missed them, missed the propeller. He sat her in the skipper's seat. She couldn't see over the windshield, so he passed her two float cushions to sit on. "Fearlessness," he said, "is key to manoeuvring." He showed her how to give the engine full throttle, let it rear up, how to whip the wheel sharply port or starboard. A gleaming white glacier, normally hidden from view, began to appear from between two peaks, moving forward as though coming toward them.

"Enough!" Davida said at last and they coasted to a stop in a shallow cove. Boris cut the engine, and they drifted into the shadow of a cliff, rust and chartreuse-coloured lichens climbing its granite face. The boat bobbled, the lake lapping placidly against its sides. Clouds of gnats swirled over the shiny expanse of water. In the cracks and fissures of the cliff, wildflowers grew, pink and purple, leaves a vivid green. There was a tree that appeared to be growing upside down, its roots plunging down the face of the rock, its boughs – Davida said it was a cedar – turned up at the tips.

The sun sparkled on the wine-bottle seal as Boris peeled it off. He tossed the seal overboard.

"Boris!" Davida said.

He appeared to be abashed, which must be tricky for him, Kathleen supposed, resembling as he did someone's idea of a Russian gangster: black hair, beard, small, sharp eyes that missed nothing. He was also big and clumsy in the way some men are when they know they don't have to be careful. Davida fished out the net from under the back bench and captured the torn seal while Boris patiently held the wine bottle and Kathleen leaned over the side to keep them balanced, thinking that Davida's fastidiousness could be a little exasperating.

Eventually they were settled and he poured the Carneros Chardonnay into plastic wineglasses that had purple grapes at their bases. A shrill cry broke the silence, and Boris said it was an osprey hunting. He had an old pair of binoculars, which she could not focus in time. She put them down. She said, "I like your new place," speaking of the thirty-eight acres with its house and the cabin. There was a spring on the property and a stream that ran through it. They planned to tear the house down – "Seventies-style ranch," Davida explained dismissively – and possibly build on the ridge where there was a view. "But it's steep, and it will be damned expensive to get a road up there," Boris pointed out. "No lake view, the way it is, bad for resale." He tipped the edge of his glass against Kathleen's and then against Davida's. "But, hey. Now that we can be out on the water, we're not in such a hurry."

"I could see buying a house here in Ruth," Kathleen said. "You know, something small, Victorian, that I could fix up. Something mine. A project."

"I might happen to know a few places." Boris grinned in her direction and accepted a pastrami sandwich on a paper plate that Davida handed him.

"She wouldn't want to live in the middle of nowhere," Davida said, passing him a napkin.

"At least I'd know where I was."

"The Judith Lake Valley definitely has potential." Boris held his wineglass up and inhaled. "Good stuff," he said to Kathleen. "Ordered it from Vancouver."

"My point exactly," Davida said. "All the good things are on the coast."

"But there's the Internet, now, baby."

"Don't call me that."

Kathleen took a big sip, let the wine open in her mouth, and found it delicious. She settled snugly in the bow, her feet up, enjoying the view of the mosses and lichens embedded in the cliff face and the big tree at the top wearing a conical hat, so high above them and so close to the edge. She had been worrying about what to do with herself. She was working, part-time, as a counsellor at a resource centre for people with life-threatening illnesses, and the work was rewarding, but the rest of her life in Toronto was coming apart – people she and James had known, helpful in the beginning, began to fade away, and whenever she was invited out, she was so rigid inside that she couldn't be sociable. She made everyone uncomfortable, including herself. And she begrudged any common couplelike gesture – the casual way a husband touched his wife's shoulder, the way the wife ran her fingers along his collar as she spoke. Seeing, close up, natural behaviour between two married people created such intense longing in her that, although everyone wanted to be kind and empathetic, it was hard for them; she made it hard for them. Sometimes, during what was supposed to be light conversational sparring, she came out punching. She went around with a chip on her shoulder, one she couldn't feel most of the time. Nearly every day she worked with people who were ill, recovering from radiation or chemotherapy or making decisions about whether, following surgery, they should choose chemo. They had to weigh and balance everything: their own exhaustion, the needs of the children at home. Some were dying or fighting dying, waging a battle with their bodies; some needed help with acceptance. It seemed terrible to Kathleen – a deep, personal flaw – that the suffering of others did not make hers any less. But because of these experiences, so close to the bone, she thought she might have something to offer, a book of some kind. Taking the last sip of wine from her glass, she said in a confiding tone, "I've been thinking of writing a widow book. What it's like, in the first days, in the first year."

Boris popped the last of his sandwich into his mouth. "Is a publisher interested?"

Kathleen crooked her neck to glower in disbelief. "What did you say?"

Davida said, "That is so like you, to think of the payoff before the project is even off the ground."

A shrewd look crossed his face. "Have you actually started writing?"

Kathleen swished her hand in the water. "A book isn't like renovating a house," she said.

Davida sat forward. "All right, so you haven't actually *done* anything. What's the point of view?"

"Who are you people? The point of view is *me*."

"That might not be enough," he said, pouring more wine into Kathleen's glass. The alcohol molecules streaming up her nose made her eyes water.

"I think we've upset her," Davida said.

"We're being realistic."

"It's realistic, oh, really. *No one* would want to know the experiences of mere *Kathleen Elliot*. I mean, who do I –"

"– but they would, of course," Davida said. "If you have –"

"– the right concept, the right outlet," Boris finished.

"– Right! Me and millions of other widows moaning into the wind. The next best thing to a blank-paged journal, let's face it. *My* book won't have any sentiment, period. It will be ruthless and brutal, the way I feel." She stood up and brushed bread-crumbs off her lap. The boat rocked.

"Hey," Boris said.

Davida let her breath out in a way that made Kathleen look at her. Davida peered up over the rims of her glasses. "I don't think you feel ruthless and brutal, as you put it."

"I am. I do," Kathleen cried.

"You don't," said Davida. "You feel left out of the inner circle, dropped by God."

Kathleen did not have a clue what she was talking about. No quick retort came to mind, and she knew she would end up sputtering something she would be sorry for. If she was "dropped by God" – what a preposterous thing for someone to say! – what did it mean? And what was Kathleen supposed to do about it? Her preoccupation with missing James, her emotional chaos, was driving her outwards, leading to behaviour that a counsellor – she herself – could see as indicative of someone nearing a breaking point. In Toronto, she impulsively ran out of the apartment and into department stores or boutiques, examined things, asked to see this or that, hoped to chat with a salesclerk – about anything, the weather, she didn't care. She pursued moments that were time-consuming, normal-seeming. In front of a movie theatre just letting out, there she was, zipping into a crowd of strangers to discuss a movie she hadn't seen. Or hanging around in a coffee shop, hoping to find someone willing to exchange views on Italian roast versus French. She had become the hand touching your sleeve in the subway, the eye trying to catch yours in the lobby of anywhere. All the pouncing, half gasping, out of the apartment and into the streets had led her to become hopelessly entangled in the doings of strangers, other people's business so compelling and mystifying. If they – out there – were not aware that James Georges Elliot died – how could they be unaware of such a breathtakingly unbelievable fact? – but, if they were not, then what were they doing the livelong day, what were they thinking about?

And, in the next moment, she would be back in the apartment, lying on the parquet floor, surprised and heartbroken to have been stood up by James again. As though James had another life to live and something more important to do than take her for Chinese on an ordinary Wednesday, or maybe he was tired of corn-and-quinoa soup, fed up with the chicken she was serving because he wouldn't eat fish and she was cutting down on red meat. She lay looking at the legs of things: the curved wingtips of the glass table, the stained pine knots on the legs of the Peruvian table his uncle gave them for an anniversary, the golden-brown piano legs, tapered and solid, holding the piano his grandmother used to play. There were the chrome legs of the Corb chair, perfect for short people and they both were. There were dust balls, and there was her heart knocking against wood.

A kingfisher flew parallel to the boat, guarding the shoreline. Davida started to speak. "I didn't mean it the way it sounded –"

"Hush," Kathleen said. She set down the untasted half of her sandwich and stepped onto the seat and launched herself over the side. Her landing was a churning of arms and legs. Water shot up her nose, a searing, penetrating cold that caused the membranes to ache. She gasped to the surface and pushed the hair out of her face, shocked into a shriek of laughter.

Boris escorted her across the field, the beam of his flashlight leading. Kathleen was shivering and couldn't seem to stop. At the bottom of the steps he wrapped her in his arms. "I'm sorry," he said. Her head rested under his chin; she could feel the slight, cushiony pressure of his bearded chin on her crown – and it felt to her as though someone, at last, had put a cap on her craziness and there would be no more acting-out for a while.

A raccoon waddled past the cabin, heading toward the house, paying no attention to them.

"They're nervy," Boris said, easing his grip. "Similar to your old buddy, with her philosophical big mouth."

"I just didn't get it."

He paused. "You might say it's a spiritual crisis, a phase. She's been seeing a fellow, a guru, up the lake. Her new pal, Miriam, has something to do with it."

"What?"

"Shh." He ran his fingers over Kathleen's lips. "Sleep well."

Inside, after watching his flashlight weave across the field of tufted grass, she picked up the Judith Lake historical booklet that Davida had left on the nightstand. Davida mentioned that Kathleen should take a look at the photographs, because when cleaning out the cabin, she'd come across glass plates taken at the turn of the century, stored in collapsing cardboard boxes. She gave them to the Judith Lake Historical Society, which printed the ones that weren't cracked or ruined. Kathleen curled on top of the blanket and studied the black-and-white photographs of women in high-collared blouses and bustled skirts and high-topped laced-up boots, on outings in various woodland places, the men with them slender and straight-backed, carrying hats.

Her original miner could not have taken photographs of cultivated people. Her original miner, according to the book, was probably a "side-hill gouger," which meant a man with big dreams. Kathleen saw him as small and sinewy, possibly a runt, pushed out of somewhere and pitted against it all – against a mountain – at the end of his options and at the end of the century, his stubborn digging, his lone digging-in the proof of his intensity. Now that she knew the photos had been found right here in the cabin, her man required transformation – he had to become more robust, educated, and he had to own a bowler hat. Besides the axe and the saw and his picks and his leather satchel on the cart, besides the mule – there had to be a mule – to pull it, the man had to cart in the camera, the glass plates, the lenses, the polishing cloth, the tiny tools necessary to such a complicated mechanism and its wee screws and hand-crafted parts. Perhaps, she thought, there had been a personal loss, a harrowing sense of failure, that compelled him to move his precious objects to a cabin in a clearing, the mountain at its back, the mist curling on the lake in mornings. Maybe his messages out said, "Soon." Maybe his solitary endeavour with the secreted mine was an excuse to deflect whatever he needed to stay away from: a woman's expectations, a death.

Women with perky hats angled on their heads were shown stepping out of canoes or posing picturesquely on rocks above the lake at a place that was recognizably across from Ruth, the caption read; she thought they'd raced past it today, she thought she recognized the crescent shape of the beach, the creek running through it, and that particular granite outcropping. So her man had not been so solo as she first assumed, and in her mind the miner and the photographer divided and became two men, the one isolated by choice, the other a respected citizen living in town, taking outings on Sundays. But she didn't like that idea. She wanted her man to have everything, the private and the public, and bagpipes too, as she and Davida used to say, and she imagined him as being, literally, a man with more than one hat: he had the little cabin as a hobby and picked away at the claim above it whenever he was moody. She looked at the women again. Judith Lake, she knew now, was deep and cold and wide. She wondered how they had climbed so high in those shoes and whether if it rained, they had cared. She wondered if they had done anything to protect their voluminous clothing, and if they worried, when the lake blew up into ruffled waves, whether they would make it back across. Their boats were so small. She worried about that. She envied the bravery of those women on the far shore.

10

The wood cookstove that had belonged to the pioneer Nell Sonemayer provided Lucinda a cheering warmth at such an early hour in the morning, when the clouds were drifting over. Then it tended to warm up suddenly, no rain, and the trees would look sorry for themselves by late afternoon; this had been the pattern so far. Not so bad, however, as Phoenix. Lucinda had checked Phoenix weather on-line and it was already 36°C. Outside the window the new leaves were *grabber green*, a term that meant you could hardly keep your hands off them. Lucinda was at the sink, a Norland potato from last year's crop in her hand. She looked up. Clusters of straight-backed pink and purple lupines and lilacs, and among them, there was BB, scabbed knees and barefoot, looking very much like a character from Hawthorne, throwing his legs and arms about in a strange dance. The struggling morning light, the bluish colour of mother's milk, was the shade of his pale skin. He must be cold, but she thought he seemed the sort who might not be able to tell.

Like the sizzle of water meeting flame, there came a damnable hot flash. Bubbles gathered on her forehead and her armpits tickled and dripped and the corduroy skirt she was wearing gave off whiffs of must and last year's woodsmoke. Shaking her hands dry, she thought, *No wonder the man isn't in my bed.* Trying for wry humour. She slipped into garden mocs and practically leapt off the porch to plunge into the warm humid air, flapping the long purple skirt, undoing the buttons on her shirt. The boy gaped. She wasn't thinking, had already forgotten him, and began to flush, in part because her breasts weren't what they were. She fixed herself, fingers fondling the pearly buttons, working them care-fully through the neatly stitched slits: everything, these days, had connotations of sex. "Good morning, BB," she waved. He blinked and bobbed his head. She raised her voice slightly and spoke slowly, "Will you remember to bring in the kindling from the woodshed, do you think you might remember that?"

Soon he brought the small pieces of wood into the mudroom, his jeans unzipped, blades of juicy grass clinging to his feet. His eyes avoided her chest, not wanting her to know that he was thinking about her in the way, of course, she supposed he was. She cleared her throat. "When our guests come, you must check your zipper more often, BB. Some people will be upset. We have guests who come all the way from the city." She emphasized the word *city* and sounded liked such a prig, it made her snort. "I'm not laughing at you," she added.

His head dipped to inspect his fly, and the odds and ends of kindling still remaining in his arms fell to the floor; he seemed oblivious to the racket. His chin dropped, exposing his tongue as he tried to speak. "Hi, hi –" On the floor between them were cedar sticks and split shingles, bits of fungal and woody matter, curling sowbugs and clods of dirt.

"Mummy said –"

"Yes? What does Mum say?"

He turned his back and tugged at the zipper. "Boys know things." This was the first string of words she'd heard from him. His earnestness made her stifle a giggle.

Mory was sweeping the summer kitchen, vacuuming the screens, snagging cobwebs from the corners, standing on a kitchen stool swiping at the ceiling, for when Milee Logan came back to work at the Centre, this time to paint. Lucinda wanted the screen-enclosed outdoor eating room painted; she planned on mixing the cans of leftover paint stored in the tool shed. Mory knew Milee, of course, remembered him as a toddler in saggy diapers when his father used to come up to the cabin to tinker around with her papa's cars. When her papa was still letting people come up. The room had to be clean before painting, Lucinda had explained to her, and after the sweeping they would get the ladder and cloths and a bucket and scrub the walls with TSP. Willamina was supposed to be the one working at the Centre for the summer, but she couldn't. Or wouldn't. Mory didn't catch everything Lucinda was saying on the phone to Mary Populakis, over at Poppy's Convenience & Gas. Mory had known Willamina Populakis since she was a crawling baby. The two years Mory's papa let her go to school with the other kids, she would walk from school to the store to wait for Papa to pick her up. Whenever Willamina's poppy was angry – he was very angry once at Mary for ordering kalamata olives when nobody in Neon Bar or entire Western Canada, for that matter, knew what they were, or wanted them – Mory remembered the oddest things – Poppy's bawling voice made Willamina cry. Babies did not like shouting, Mory knew. When Mory would come angling into Mary's kitchen after school, Mary would tell her the news: Willamina was cranky that day, Willamina was funny that day. She'd laugh and beam at Willamina, who would crinkle up her face and then Mary would laugh again.

Mory remembered the back-and-forth between the mother and the baby, and she tried to use it with BB when he was a baby. A baby wanted very much to be independent, which Mory herself understood. Where she was raised, up by the meeting of the creeks, too far to walk in the winter or when it was raining hard in the spring, she was not independent of her parents, no matter how often she hid from them and let them call her name and promise her Hershey Kisses.

Lucinda said she could go to see Willamina and phoned to say Mory was coming. Mary said she would drive her back. She left BB with Milee, the two of them moving tables and chairs in readiness to wash the walls, walked over to visit Willamina. She passed a companionable dog, a black Lab who wagged his tail, a dog she did not know. There was lots different now. Short, furry, puzzled-looking Highland cattle and two llamas – new – a trailer in a messy field, Volvos in abundance along a driveway – old – and a parts-only rusted tractor, past the new house. After a long walk past nothing, she was into Neon Bar itself. Black Angus cattle the same, in the field across from Poppy's store. She went past Miriam's No-Videos, past the gas station, into Poppy's Convenience. Mary was stacking loaves of her French bread in a basket on the table next to the deli.

"Would you care for a hunk of bread still warm?"

Mory thought a moment and said no. "It looks good, though." If she took a hunk, a whole loaf would be wasted and the chickens out back would have it.

Mary folded her arms and studied her. Mory stood and waited until the inspection was over. "Eleven years," Mary said. "I still recognize you."

"Same here."

Mary laughed. "You're the funniest girl. Your father is at the end of his life. You know that?"

"I do."

They both glanced then at the bread, and Mary said, "Take some up to Willamina and keep the loaf for yourself. She's waiting for you." Her brows knitted. Mory thought there was something so nice about Mary's eyes even with the dark circles under them. She took the bread. Mary said, "It works out in the end, I guess, if you believe in God's will."

Mory went upstairs and walked down the hall, past the guest room, a single bed in it that used to be Ja-Ja's, the room painted a rosy pink. Ja-Ja was Mary Populakis's mother, Willamina's granny from Greece who lived with them until she died. Mory came to Willamina's room, lavender and blue. Willamina was propped against pillows in the king-size bed that took up most of the space. The spread was a floral pattern in blues and purples and blacks that made her look bruised in the shade-drawn light.

This big bed was hers because Poppy, who ordered it for himself and Mary, changed his mind. He wanted the old double bed back because, he said, he missed his wife in the new one. Everyone around Neon Bar had heard the remark, and everyone still liked it. So Poppy said.

Willamina said to Mory, "God, you just are so cute. I would recognize you anywhere. What have you been up to all this time? I know, I know, I don't have to be in bed any more, I should only have been in bed for, like, ten hours, the public health nurse was here yesterday, she forced me to walk up and down the hall and up and down the stairs, she said I should move, that I was doing damage to my internal organs by lying around. I know, I know." Willamina started to cry. "I'm just totally scalloped, my insides skewered, scooped out, and trashed."

Mory sat down in a rocker chair and tried it out, rocking quietly. She carefully pulled the bread so that the top came off. She put it in her mouth and chewed. Mary baked very good bread.

Willamina was in a talking mood. She had been the same when she was nine years old, the last time Mory had seen her. Willamina was always thinking out loud, talking and asking questions. She told Mory about her female trouble. She sneered when she said, "*Female* trouble," like it was something to hate.

The trouble started with pain during her erratic periods – too much blood, not enough blood – and pain during sex. Then there were lumps she could feel, pressing fingers on the plain of her tight belly, growing where her ovaries were. Her feet up in a gyn's stirrups the first time, she had her fingers crossed. Her boyfriend – her *man friend* – Conrad, fourteen years her senior, wanted a baby; he would not marry her until she was pregnant. She wasn't sure she wanted to be married, much less to him, but there was an implied challenge. "Women," Willamina said, "go out of their minds because of babies, either having them or not having them."

In the apartment building where she'd lived in Toronto, her neighbour was a tall woman who wore monk's robes. A schizophrenic, the boyfriend said. The woman talked about "sinful evillers." It was a crime against God to bury in sand a baby, she'd said to Willamina (cornered in the hall), can you imagine the sinful evillers who bury? Willamina couldn't, though she was in her second year of journalism at Ryerson and interested in offbeat news. Conrad enjoyed her young body as his personal fertile ground. During sex, he was plowing his field, sowing his seed. Then her body began to have its emergency. At the bad news, Conrad stamped his foot. His child would have been a foot-stamper too. Would have been one of those cute, serious, fussy kids, given to temper tantrums. Conrad wanted a special, gifted child, but Willamina would have settled for the ordinary kind. The gynecologist did her best. "The moon pulls babies out of you, Ja-Ja always said. But the moon will never pull a baby out of me. Have you heard that? About the moon and babies?"

"The moon is good for lots of things," Mory said.

Willamina laughed but clamped her hand on her belly as though it hurt. She said, "I told her to stop calling me Willa-myna, she always does that, she's British or something, like she doesn't get my name. And I said, 'You just call me Willie. I want everybody to call me Willie.' My name is now Willie."

Mory realized Willamina was talking about the public health nurse.

This new person named Willie said, "Would you mind getting under the covers? I am so cold, it's like my bones are freezing."

Mory kicked off her shoes.

"Can you tell who I am? Sometimes I don't know who I am."

"I known you since little," Mory said.

"Would you mind? Be careful of my stitches. They're stapled."

She lifted the covers and Mory lifted them on her side and wiggled herself in. Willamina was very thin and wearing an old flannel nightgown that was rucked up her thighs.

They lay together quietly, then Willamina said, "I need you closer. Would you move closer? Would you mind? You have the sweetest face and your boobs are something else." Willamina wrapped a leg over Mory's hip and pressed her small, tight breasts against Mory's full ones. "I wish I was a lesbian. If I were one, I swear I would kiss you. Have you ever kissed a girl?"

Mory's neck was cricked but that wasn't the moment to say anything. She smelled Willamina's egg-shampoo hair and her stale breath.

"Oh, God. I just wish I were into women. A woman would be gentle, you know, instead of macho like that stupid Conrad. Thrusting. Penetrating. *Plowing his field, sowing his seed.* I must have been out of my mind."

"Men can make you sick."

Willamina swallowed a giggle. She struggled with air for a moment before she recovered. "Oh, I want to kiss your mouth. You have a very sexy mouth. May I kiss you? I promise I won't tongue you. God, guys just love tongue."

Mory lay still and felt cold little fingers touching her through her T-shirt.

"It's okay," Mory let her lips part. They breathed together and felt and smelled each other. Willie put her tongue on Mory's lips. Mory could tell, though, when Willie left and Willamina returned because Willamina took her tongue back and gave Mory a peck. She said, "I just couldn't go the whole way, though it was cool. I am just too distracted by misery. Oh, I have been the Christ crying for a solid week and I can't stop." She rolled onto her side. "Ouch, goddammit." She cried some more, her head in a pillow.

Mory slid out of bed and pulled tissues from the box on the headboard shelf. She tapped Willamina on the arm and handed her a wad of tissues.

"That goddamn Conrad just figured I couldn't be the vine upon which he could grow the fruit of his goddamn loins and that's why, that's why –"

"He left," Mory said.

"Well, it wasn't like we had a real commitment. I mean, we were never engaged. I'll never forgive him, though. It was so horribly demeaning. I had this fantasy of escape, eh, and I went around bragging to everyone, and now I've messed up a whole semester – I went to live with him off and on and it's a long way from Mississauga to T.O., and we'd be in bed instead of my going to class, the traffic would be bad. Conrad fucked with my brains, and my self-esteem is just a pile of dog dirt."

Mory handed her another tissue.

After a while, she went downstairs to the kitchen. Mary gave her apple juice they made up the mountain on Lightning Cairn Road, defrosted from last year's crop. "I have missed this," Mory said. And Mary had a surprised look on her face and then she laughed at the joke.

11

Kathleen sat up, gasping, and flung back the sheet. She didn't know where she was, didn't recognize where she was. James on the floor was as clear as though it had just happened and worse, she knew the ending. She did not know what she'd done wrong or why she had lost him.

She leapt out of bed, knees trembling, the light through the cabin window a watercolour of faded blues and greys. She threw on some clothes. It was cool out, a relief from the heat, and mist lay on the field. She turned back for her jacket and then tiptoed down the porch steps, already guilty, because she had a glimmer that she was going to be reckless: the drive to get away, somewhere, anywhere, was paramount. She saw something odd on the ground, a piece of burnt wood, round and slightly shiny. She searched the sky, wondering how it got here. The news from just south of the border was that people were being evacuated and houses were burning. She placed the wood back where she found it. She crept up to Davida's Toyota 4Runner. Davida always left a set of her keys in the car, on the mat in front of the driver's seat. Kathleen glanced at the house to see if anyone was awake, if they were taking any notice. The blinds were down, the drapes closed; she might have smiled as she turned into the road that led from their part of the mountain, might have smiled had she not been so frantic – brain numbed as though stunned by a hundred spotlights. She drove around town in circles – Ruth had more streets than she had imagined, short streets that ended at the base of mountains or the banks of creeks – and then she found her way to the marina and parked and watched the ducks lined up on moorings, their heads tucked into their wings. She contemplated the boathouses, quaint, painted little peaked-roof houses in a row. She breathed into her hands to bring her gulping breaths under control. And then she realized she knew where Boris kept his spare key. She remembered it hanging on its hidden hook. When she had the thought, the internal pressure eased.

In the boathouse, heart beating fast, she began to feel awake and excited, because the order in which he'd done things came back – that the boat had to be pushed back a little in its bay so the prop wouldn't touch bottom and to press the gas bulb three times and to push in the key before turning it. The burst of the engine made her jump. Adrenalin poured in. The sound was immense and baffling because the engine hadn't seemed so throbbingly *loud* – and at that instant she realized the exit door wasn't open. She thought she would faint. The boathouse was filled with blue smoke.

Out on the water, though, it was different story. All around was the dawn, the immensity of the mountains; there was even the call of a loon. She sat on the float cushions and pressed her thumb on the button to bring the motor up just a little, just as Boris had done. She let 'er rip. With the focus of a terrier after a rat, that little boat flared the water, digging deep curls on both her sides, and surged forward, half in flight. Kathleen could hardly catch her breath but stood up and leaned forward as Boris had done, to bring the nose down. She swerved around a floating log – its appearance sending a spike of heat through her – and she tore for the far shore that got farther away as she left the safety of the bay. She changed her mind, turned back, began, instead, to practise turns.

It was during the second or third sharp turn to port that the canvas tarp billowed. Even inside the boathouse, Boris snapped the tarp to keep dust and dirt from the inside of the boat. She had left it snapped only at the back and rolled loosely on the bench, instead of tucked and stowed under it as Boris had done. She caught the flicking movement out of the corner of her eye and when she jerked her head around, the wheel, held by only one hand, slipped out of her grasp and the boat skewed in the water, veering hard into the tight turn. Water blew onto the aft seat, the splash it produced hard-edged as a slap, and the canvas snapped away and hovered for a second until it began fluttering down. She tried to get the boat under control, coaching herself by then – "Slow down, slow down, slow down" – but the canvas, crumpled in a tent-shape on the surface of the water, was behind her and receding. She turned back – erratically, as she was shaking – and, bouncing on the swells caused by the wake, tried to aim for the canvas without nudging it, but coming close enough to it so as to be able to – do what? – she didn't know. She could jump into the water, she had proven that, but would she be able to get back aboard, hauling canvas? What if the boat left without her? She looked around – Ruth and the bridge and the point, the cliffs of the east shore – to gauge her location. Too far from anywhere to swim if she had to. While considering the options, the boat had bobbled near the canvas and she stretched herself over the side, tucking her feet under a seat, fingers twitching, so close, so close – and not close enough. Floating past it. It was getting smaller. She knew it was getting smaller. It was swamping, its edges seemed darker, wetter, and its centre seams were caving.

In the end, she allowed the canvas, specially made for the boat – she knew that, he had made a point of it – to slide into the lake. She didn't jump in after it and was inept at turning around to get it, her will paralyzed. The cover was new and whoever crafted it had worked hard to customize it, to cut the shapes exactly and sew the snaps precisely. Boris was proud of it, proud of its tight, perfect fit.

She was disbelieving as it sank from sight, and she circled around with an almost humorous eagerness, convinced that it would surface so she could try again. She would have a second chance. When it was obviously going down, she still wasn't persuaded, and then it was gone. She hadn't tried hard enough to save it. She didn't jump in, she didn't shut off the engine – uncertain it would start again, aware that she didn't know what she was doing. She was giggling by then, flummoxed and panicked, both. Through her heedless behaviour – speeding! testing fate! – she had challenged the gods, dared something to happen, and it had. She had circled at high speeds, aware of the canvas, only partially snapped, bumping around on the bench, unwrapping, until a flap caught the wind and she let it go and she lost it.

She managed to tuck the boat back in the boathouse where it belonged. Shivering, she drove around on the back roads and along the highway, halfway to Tucker, chiding herself, beating her fist on the dashboard. She didn't want to go to Tucker, a town she knew only because Boris and Davida had picked her up at the airport there. Everything she knew about this part of the world depended upon them. She turned around and roared back up the highway, feeling very sorry for the physical loss of the canvas, for being so passive in the face of near loss, for not being heroic in any way, for being cautious; for asking for pain and getting it. Sorry for her foolish, arrogant behaviour, for not believing anything could hurt her again – not even Davida's expected airy annoyance that she had taken her vehicle – for setting herself up, for fearing she wouldn't have the strength to climb back into the boat, for fearing the motor would get entangled in the canvas, and, finally, for trying to make light of what was happening, as though she was an observer rather than participant. She could not believe her luck, she could not believe her loss. She did not know what she had and she had let it go as though it were God's will. She was so daring at first, so useless at the crux.

They were having a morning at home, it seemed, and were still upstairs. They came down in their nightclothes, Boris first, hands shaping his beard, Davida after, tying her robe. Her hair was out of its bun and flowed around her shoulders. She crossed to Kathleen and squinted, reaching in her pocket for her glasses. "What is it?" She peered beyond Kathleen as though someone else would be present soon. She sounded alarmed.

"I lost it," Kathleen said and started to cry. Davida put an arm around her and led her to the red chair. Kathleen sat on the edge and told them what had happened, the whole story: "I've been driving around in circles, talking to myself, and then I realized what it was I was feeling. Like I had lost James again." She put her face in her hands and sobbed. She felt Davida's small hand touch her shoulder.

They were quiet. Kathleen raised her head and studied their faces.

Boris said, "You took the boat?"

Kathleen blew her nose. "What?"

"You are saying you took the boat?"

She frowned at him, the hand dabbing her nose motionless.

"Leave her alone," Davida said.

"She took the boat. She took the Toyota and she took the boat. That's what I'm hearing."

"I'm glad you're all right," Davida said haltingly. "You are all right?"

Kathleen studied her hands. The fingertips were bluish as though they were freezing. She picked up the wadded tissues on the floor. She didn't know what to do with them. Davida put out her palm.

Boris, pacing, seemed to be deliberately misunderstanding everything she had said. "You woke up, you went straight to her car, and you sneaked off with it. You then went to the marina and took someone else's personal property. You rode around outside the bay way too fast without a life jacket on. Oh, it wasn't dark, eh? Oh, well, that makes it just fine. That canvas was specially made and not cheap. A perfect fit. But that's neither here nor there. What matter are the moral and ethical implications."

"Oh, get off it!" Davida said. "You are such an ass." She took Kathleen's hand and tugged her to her feet.

They started toward the kitchen. Stopping midway through the dining room, Kathleen pulled back to say one thing more to Boris. She said, "You don't get it. You just don't get it."

Davida let go of Kathleen's hand. "Doesn't get what?"

Kathleen whirled to her. "What this was about. I wanted you to see the parallel."

Davida made a face. "I do see it. Nevertheless, you behaved stupidly and were lucky the damage wasn't worse."

Kathleen glanced from one to the other, bewildered.

"You *took* the boat," Boris said, as though the emphasis would get through. "It was theft. You *took* the boat and you lost something that wasn't yours."

Kathleen reached for Davida's hand and squeezed it and began backing out, gibbering. "I'll go straight to bed and get some rest, I promise. I'll bring a cheque over to cover the – well, you know. Sorry, so sorry." When she reached the cabin she looked back. Davida was on the back stoop, the skirt of her robe open, the sun shining in her glasses.

Kathleen sat on the porch, holding the portable CD player and wearing her earphones. She sat and watched the clouds form themselves into James's profile. When she grasped what she was seeing, a rush of excitement tingled through her clear to her toes. She gaped. Yes. Clouds were bunching in from the west, gathering overhead. There was his good nose, his beard, the crown of his golden-red head, drifting toward the Rockies, which made sense; he'd always loved the mountains. She pushed *Play* and the voice began by asking her to wait, to hold on over distance and time, and if she did, he would come for her.

James was sending her a message, it was clear, and that he would ask *her* to wait for *him* was confounding and possibly brilliant, because, it was obvious, was she or was she not the one waiting – the one still alive, in a body – while he was off being a cloud? It astounded her that she had come outside when she had, in time to see him. His presentation – choosing a popular song along with a cloud visual – these two factors created the necessary element of wit to be truly James. He had chosen this manner, these means – the sky and the song – to keep in touch. She thought, What if help *is* out there, what if help is everywhere?

The voice sang of the promise to come for her as long as she saved a place for him in her heart.

"Okay," Kathleen said and went inside to blow her nose.

She waited until Davida's car was gone. She wrote a blank cheque made out to Boris. From her suitcase she took the tie in its flat little box that she planned to give him – the tie was one of James's – and walked over to the house, bearing the gift, to apologize. Crossing the field, she saw a big-antlered stag drinking from the stream. He noticed her and wasn't worried, his gaze steady and opaque. Stopping, she watched him watching her and took a deep breath. The air was fresh and smelled of grass, and the earth was exuding a little heat, even this early; it would be a hot day. A yellowish haze hung over the mountains.

The tie she'd chosen for Boris was one that James often wore for a day of negotiation. That would suit Boris, she thought, and if James were paying attention from somewhere, he would appreciate her choice. The whole tie idea – giving James's friends or colleagues a tie, or letting them choose one themselves – came from James one night a few months back – the idea was so his that she was sure he had put it in her head. One rainy afternoon she had tilted her head into his suits, still hanging in his part of the closet, and sniffed them. They smelled good, a hint of dust, an undertone of leather. They smelled like good suits, slightly warm as though his body had just exited for the evening and planned to return. The silk ties, intelligent and occasionally savvy complements to the suits, hung in their places. She hadn't much noticed them. She touched each one as she counted – forty-four ties. Thirty-nine were silk, a small fortune when she added it up. On the twice-a-year shopping expeditions for James's business clothing, the salesman always offered her the posh and comfy chair with a view of the tailor's three-way mirrors – the *wife's chair* – where she sat holding James's wallet. She didn't need to see inside to know he wouldn't have enough cash for even a short taxi ride. He was always asking her for a dollar or two or five. It drove her crazy, but that was James: wandering around the world with a credit card and not two cents in his pocket and a St. Christopher's medal tucked behind a plastic window. The wallet was fat with business cards and tiny, handwritten notes for projects and Chinese cookie fortunes: SUCCESS IS AROUND THE CORNER, YOU WILL HAVE A LONG LIFE WITH MANY REWARDS. Then James and the tailor would emerge from behind the curtains, and James would step up to the platform and the mirrors, the tailor patting James's shoulders and pulling the jacket between two fingers at the back, James placing his thumbs on the lapels, regarding himself with satisfaction, and begin, slowly, to turn to her. The suits chosen, she and the salesman would gather ties, making a case for each one as though James were reluctant and the ties had to be forced on him. She laughed. The man had a tie *collection*.

In the morning she'd draped the ties over the backs of the chairs and the piano seat and hung the whimsical ones – an elephant, an orchid – from the standing lamps. She held back half a dozen (including the one that would eventually be for Boris). She got on the phone and sent e-mail.

The knocking on the door from the men who came to choose a tie was generally shy and hesitant. Each had given the idea of dropping by the apartment a great deal of thought, she imagined, rearranging their day to fit a trip by cab or a long car ride through traffic, rescheduling a meeting or postponing an appointment. They were dazzled by the array, the colours, the quality. Many of the ties were businesslike – confident stripes heading upward like the graph lines on a good quarterly sales report – and the stripes themselves were thin or wide or pencil-point, and there were ties in solid colours, as well, for the get-ahead days – the crimsons and scarlets, the navy blues, a gold. The men, diffident toward her, ducked into the apartment. They shook her hand, took in the proliferating ties. An uneasy thought crossed some minds, she was sure: perhaps they had erred into a scene of eccentric, unbefitting mourning and shouldn't be abetting it. Yet, like shoppers everywhere, they were drawn to particular colours and wanted to inspect and touch and wonder. "I remember James wearing this tie," they would say. We were in Chicago. Or New York. Or Budapest. They said, He wore this when we signed the contract; or, Didn't he wear this to my wedding? And Kathleen knew the answers. No, Yes, Remember when. Will my wife like it? the married ones mused. What would my wife pick? A question asked twice that at last she understood to be a cue for assistance from the helpless or the colour-blind. She pitched in: This one goes with your brown eyes, she said, or this would be very nice with the suit you're wearing, that one larky for those special summer nights. Take your time, she told them. There's no hurry. They moved around the room like boys, watching their elbows and their clumsy feet. When she closed the door on the last man, she was reluctant to do anything with the leftovers, attached to their colourful presence, did not want them to feel badly about not being chosen. She thought she and the ties had something in common; the bottom-line was that they were the remainders. She and the left-behind ties hung out together for another day or two until she started dropping them off, one or two at a time into Goodwill bins, or handing them to working men in mediocre suits who seemed like they could use a good tie. The strangers took them. The bins accepted them. She gave two, a rose pink and green stripe and the last of the red backgrounds, to her favourite doormen.

Now she stood at the back door of the house and wanted Boris to be surprised and pleased to see her bearing a gift from James. She knocked at the door, instead of walking in as she had been doing, and Boris, barefoot, eventually came to open it. He didn't glance her way or say good morning. He just led her through the kitchen and dining room and down the hall to his office, a room with dark wood panelling, the computer monitor bright. He sat down and continued tapping. "What is it?" he said.

"I could come back another time." She was still standing.

"Give me a minute."

She fixed her gaze on the books in piles on a second desk.

"Sit down," he said.

She sat in the wingback chair and studied the back of his head. His hair was black and curly and though his beard was nicely shaped, he needed a neck trim. His ears, the slivered tops, were sunburnt. He needed to be reminded to use sunscreen on them. His shoulders were broad and his legs long. His calves and ankles were defined, handsome and tanned.

He closed the laptop and swivelled his chair so that they were facing each other. "Yes?"

"I wrote you a cheque."

"Good."

"It's blank."

"Even better," he said and laughed.

"Ha," she said, suppressing a smile. "How much should I make it for?"

"You don't trust me?" This made him laugh again.

She ignored him. "I'm trying to do the right thing. I'm embarrassed at how stupid I was. I shouldn't have taken the boat, none of it."

"I agree," he said.

He was steely and gave nothing. "I told you I was sorry. I told you I'm embarrassed. I told you I was a fool –"

"No, you didn't mention that part," he said.

She smiled, acknowledging his wit, but went on doggedly, "I told you I was a – I told you I was sorry. What more do you want? What do you want me to do?"

He glanced down at his hands and began snapping the fingernails, one at a time, using his thumbnails for leverage. She watched his large hands curl and snap, curl and snap, the little popping sound distracting.

"You have long nails," she said, feeling idiotic. "A whole orchestra," she added, trying for humour.

"So I do." He smiled broadly, rubbed his palms together. Placing his hands on his knees, he leaned toward her. He was wearing bermuda-length shorts and his knees were nicely sculpted.

She shifted her gaze. The photo of a moose in the middle of a lake caught her eye. "Did you take it?"

"I don't take things that belong to other people."

Her face coloured, cheeks burning. She stood – determined that he would not get anything of James's – and the slim box with the tie in it dropped onto the carpet. Boris smoothly picked it up and handed it back. "Thank you." She felt her bottom lip begin to tremble. She sat back into the chair. He touched her arm with his right hand. His hand, despite callouses, felt soft and warm. "No problem," he said. "Sit down. I'll bring some coffee."

She waited, heart pounding.

He handed her the coffee, the way she liked it, dark and black. He raised the blinds. When he was seated, she set down her cup and picked up the box and awkwardly, shyly (which surprised her), lifted the tie out of its tissue and lay it over her hand as a salesman might. She let him inspect it. "I thought you would like this one," she said. "I thought it would suit you."

"In what way?"

This time she gave him a look, narrowing her eyes. "Are we going to do this again?"

"Sorry." He shrugged, folding his hands.

"I think he wore it to your wedding."

"Which one?"

The largeness of his body and its stillness against the light coming from the window gave her pause. A ray of light slanted onto the back of his hand, revealing it with such clarity she could see the roots of the curling black hairs on his skin. His face was nearly hidden, but she could see the pinkness inside his mouth as he opened his lips and repeated, "Which one? Were you there?"

As reasonably as she could, holding herself in check, she said, "James said some nice things in his speech about Davida's marriage to you even though he didn't know how obnoxious you were. Are." She rolled the tie quickly around her fingers and tossed it toward the box and missed. It was hanging partway off the desk.

Suddenly, startlingly, his index finger was in her face. "You're trying to make moments, you are inventing moments." The finger disappeared; he had stepped away.

She frowned. "What on earth do you mean?"

"All this ceremony. The ties that bind. Soppy, sentimental stuff. Do I appear to be a man who needs another tie?" He snapped his fingers. "Actually I *am* a man who needs another tie. How about

I wear James's tie for just the sort of business, a zoning decision, he wouldn't care for: more condominiums in the bay."

"Give it to me."

"No. You're the one who created this loving moment to honour James, a man who is" – he stopped himself from saying *dead*, she could feel the word on his lips – "who is no longer with us. You will say next, if I give you the chance, that he would want me to have it. I don't believe in life after death, and as far as I'm concerned, when the brain is dead, it's dead, finished, kaput. I do not intend to have you witness my tears over James. Tears are *your* specialty."

"It's only been a year."

"A year, six years, yesterday, I cannot help you," he said.

She slammed out the back door and stomped across the field. The cabin in the distance was so small against the mountain looming behind it and the cold, angry man behind her.

She heard a tapping that sounded like the pileated woodpecker that lived in the spruce tree. It took a minute to realize where the sound was coming from. Davida was at the door. "Awake?" She came in balancing a big bag and a portable coffee mug. She set the bag in the corner. She shook her head at Kathleen. "I'm sorry," she said. "I have some coffee and a cinnamon roll." She set the mug on the nightstand next to the bed.

"Why should you be sorry?"

"That you're unhappy. I'm sad for you."

"You're going to make me cry."

"I brought you a supply of tissues." Davida cleared away a pillow and sat on the bed. "Do you want to talk?"

"No." Kathleen said, "A counsellor isn't supposed to give me that yes-no opportunity, remember? Oh, I can't get it right in my head. Did I call you that night? The night James –? Did someone call you?"

"You called. It was the middle of the night here. Boris was still up with his stupid satellite system. He was obsessed. Trying to make it work. We couldn't sleep, and I had that horrible cold, my ears plugged up solid. Which is why I couldn't be with you, you know, in the first days. You told me what had happened at the hospital and I said, 'He always liked my chicken curry,' and you wondered what that had to do with anything. It didn't, it just came out."

"I hadn't bothered to get your recipe to make it at home. Guilt."

"A little unproductive," Davida said.

"His eyes changed colour, you know. At the end. They turned to a sea-foam green. It took weeks before I remembered."

"They do."

Kathleen frowned in puzzlement.

Davida said, "The Frances Hill is a place where people sometimes die. Eyes do change. To that colour." Davida's tone was gentle. Kathleen began to cry.

Davida touched Kathleen's head, taking strands of her hair in her fingers and pulling gently.

"I just keep bashing around, doing everything wrong. I can't ask him anything, that's the thing I'll never get used to. He won't ever be on the other end of the line, phoning from the airport. Or phoning to say he didn't call last night because there was an unexpected meeting that lasted late. *I didn't notice*, I might say, a lie – I was like that, pride-filled: *Who, me? Miss you? Ha ha, as though there aren't movie theatres galore on every street corner.* My God, if he crossed my threshold just one more time, I would show him love and affection. He would have to say *not now* and I would just be there, grinning like a fool, my love a constant, vibrant, piercing flame that would *keep him alive*." She blew her nose.

For a week the apartment had been filled with people, on the phones, on the computer, letting everyone know. For the order of service, someone told her she should find something James had written, and she'd recalled a particular prayer – he had started writing prayers for modern life, one of his many projects – and, sleepless, she had drifted barefoot along the hall, past the rustling and sputtering and through the swarming dreams and nocturnal sorrows. The door to her office was ajar and someone lay on the floor, a mound in a sleeping bag. She padded to James's office and paused and listened. Someone was snoring behind the closed door, and, feeling shrewd, she knew it wasn't he.

"Finding that prayer so easily led me astray, I think," she said to Davida. She hadn't turned on the lights in the living room, where the filing cabinet was, so there must have been a moon. On the glass dining-room table, the neat lists of who should phone whom, who had been told, who had not. Two phones, two fax machines, a laptop, a plate of blond brownies, sugar bits on the table. A crumpled tissue. She faced the living-room windows. In the imperfect dark outside, leafy branches shone, lit by street-lights around the perimeter of the small park below the building. In her mind, she spoke loud enough for James to hear: "Where is your prayer about prayer?" She floated past the potted violets and the sprays of gladioli and the mounds of moss-based designer arrangements to the oak filing cabinet and halted in front of it. Then she opened the drawer and slipped her fingers in, and there it was. A sheaf of papers, the prayer she wanted on top. Finding it so easily she took to mean that he was still around, taking care of things, somewhere ethereal but close by. "You remember it: *I am starting to understand that it matters less to whom I pray than that I pray.* James was feeling grateful for a lot of things."

"It wouldn't occur to Boris to be grateful for anything, much less write a prayer. He is totally unconscious. Which is why I can put up with him," she added. "He's so unconscious that even when he's being intimate, he doesn't intrude on my privacy." Davida stood and went into the bathroom. The water ran. She came back with a warmed washcloth and handed it to Kathleen. Kathleen put it over her face, the steam feeling good.

"We have some helpful people up the lake. To talk to. If you want."

Kathleen lifted a corner of the cloth. "The idea of explaining again what happened is exhausting." She inhaled the cooling cloth to her nostrils and puffed out the air through her mouth.

Davida laughed and lifted the cloth off her face. "Hey. See what I've got."

In the cloth bag she had red-checkered curtains for the windows and dowels, sanded on each end, and screw hooks and other tools. "I was in a gingham mood when I ordered these from the catalogue. Yes, Sears this time."

Kathleen had a bite of the bun, and then they pulled the bed out from the wall and Davida stood on a chair and screwed in the hooks using a drill and the wrench, and when she was finished, they moved the bed back. Kathleen splashed her face and combed her hair. When she went out onto the porch, Davida said, "Don't let him intimidate you. He will just go and go until he wears you down, until he gets you. It's a pit-bull characteristic."

Kathleen felt a flush of pleasure.

They drove north of Ruth, on a narrow, winding road that climbed, and then the land began to spread out into meadows and in that area, on someone's farm, was where Davida was keeping a little mare she'd bought. Davida said, "If you keep going on this road, you'll come to Neon Bar where the Centre for Light Awareness is. Heard of it?"

Kathleen didn't think of either one of them as New Age. "Light awareness? As opposed to heavy awareness?"

"It's an interesting place." Davida put both hands on the wheel. Her manner told Kathleen she didn't think she was funny.

"Okay." Trees went by, a log house. Kathleen waited.

"I went up to the Centre for a workshop once. Just to see. Boris was giving me headaches and I thought, Why not?"

"Why not?" Kathleen said. They called it echoing.

"It was interesting," Davida said again.

"Because?"

"I met Miriam there – have I mentioned her? – Miriam Fauquier, the friend we're going to see. It's how I got Blaze. My horse," Davida said. "Miriam's mare, a sweet old girl named Babe, and mine hang out together in Miriam's fields and I go and ride whenever. You'll like Miriam," she added. "She's from Quebec. She bought the old Silverbell Farm and turned it into a herb-growing business. She ships all across B.C."

Kathleen had more questions about the workshop but didn't ask them. She knew Davida. Two "interestings" in a row meant she wasn't going to reveal anything. After a few more miles, they turned down a gravel road in the direction of the lake. Davida talked about her friend. Miriam had never married but had three children, a four-year-old boy and a three-year-old girl and an eleven-month-old that she was nursing. She loved children. She had been a mortgage broker and had invested well, and now, besides the herbs, she was raising a variety of chickens and had invested in a few goats for cheese production.

"Her kids are so positive, they're fun to be around. Unlike Esme," Davida said, rolling her eyes. Boris's teenaged daughter was a pill and pest, in that order, according to Davida. It seemed true. Kathleen thought Esme had been snotty to James, that time on the beach, letting him know that picking up shells and sticks to build a fort was dorky. Until her remark, James had been immodestly proud of his fort.

They parked and walked down a lane and found Miriam in the packing barn. The motto over the door read, *Herbs do not do the healing. The herbs bring the body into balance, and the body does the healing.* The barn was fragrant with mint and thyme. Davida pointed out the drying peppermint hanging from the rafters and the old screen windows hanging from the ceiling joists with rosehips drying on them. Miriam was laughing with two of the workers as they walked in. Kathleen shook her free hand. The blond-haired baby on her hip had been eating berries from the purplish stains around his mouth. "Pie, if you can believe it. It's his fault," Miriam said, nodding at a young man, who smiled and went back to the plastic containers. Davida introduced them, and Miriam said to Davida, "We're not doing sprouts any more, did I tell you why?" She placed her hand on Davida's narrow hip and propelled her back into the sunlight.

Miriam was attractive, her eyes a very light green that was similar in tone to the fair olive of her skin. Her hair was long, ash blond, held in a loose ponytail. With the baby on her hip, she was like a figure in a mural promoting natural health and hard work on the land. Her hands were brown and calloused, Kathleen saw, the nails sensibly short, but on her wrist she wore a bracelet with a garnet set in it. Miriam noticed Kathleen's interest, and she smiled, showing fine, straight teeth. With a slight Quebec accent, she said, "A present to myself."

Kathleen followed the two women down the lane toward a house with three bay windows opening to the lake, listening to them talking about sprouts and the problems with storage in most grocery lockers and the various moulds that took hold despite the care with which they were packed and grown. "I just sell sprouts locally," Miriam explained to Kathleen in the kitchen, putting the baby down. He made a crawling beeline for the table legs and began working himself to standing. "I've tried telling him. He'll hit his head in a minute," she said, turning on the kettle. "Boys are not quick learners, as a rule." Davida laughed and the corner of Miriam's mouth turned up and then she reached for a tea ball from the drainer. "Have you tried birch-leaf tea?" The baby hit his head and shrieked.

During tea and homemade banana bread, Miriam brought in a carton of eggs. Davida paid her three dollars and opened the carton so that Kathleen could see inside. "They're satiny green, all shades," she said. "From Arucana chickens. Amazingly good.

Miriam has turned me on to the whole idea of biological diversity. I don't know how I could have lived this long and not have been more aware." She shook her head. "Boris won't eat them. He won't eat eggs or bread that aren't white." Miriam laughed. She bent and kissed Davida quickly on the lips.

"It is not funny," Davida said, colouring slightly. "He is such a dinosaur, such a *capitalist*. Oh, let me tell you what he did. Talk about absolutely no forethought. The floor of the cabin, right?" She went on to tell the story of when, one Saturday, Boris rented a sander and after vacuuming with a shop vac (borrowed), he poured half a gallon of Varathane onto the floor with the intention of spreading it evenly with a device of his own invention, a sponge mop rolled in Saran Wrap; he thought the texture would be interesting. Unfortunately, as he was getting started, wearing gumboots and wading through the powerful chemicals, he had an allergic reaction and his eyes and nasal passages began to swell. He could hardly breathe. "He came flying out, gasping and flapping his arms. He was wearing a yellow rain slicker – slicker, yes – and if I hadn't happened to be working in the garden, he could have been in real trouble." The floor, when they returned from the hospital where he was treated with an antihistamine, had thickened in the dippy places. Despite paper masks and then – "if you can believe it," she said, smiling at Miriam – a gas mask that he borrowed from an old-timer, he could not undo the damage of the Varathane having set, and it remained tacky along the south wall, which is why they'd placed the bed where it was. She threw an old Persian rug over the floor when it had got to the point where it wouldn't grab things. Boris's family used to deal in Persian rugs, and many weren't as precious as the name suggested or as fine as the family encouraged viewers to believe in the TV ads for their flagship store in Winnipeg. *Flagship* a term the Malenko family respected.

Davida seemed to enjoy telling the story. She was wearing a long skirt and a new black, trim-fitting V-neck sweater that emphasized her lean body. She was not wearing a bra. Her nipples, hard little nubs, showed as she lay back in the chair, laughing.

Kathleen thought about the Boris in her story, a large man in a yellow slicker panicking on the cabin's porch, and felt sorry for him. A few days back, he had come into the kitchen, his knuckles and palms scraped. He had been working on a woodlot up the mountain, having firewood cut in order to sell it to the Frances Hill. While Davida was in the garden, Kathleen made him put his hand in hers, and she examined it. She tweezed out splinters from the mound of Venus. His was relatively flat and James's had been fleshy. James had compact hands and Boris's were big and loose. On the outer edge of the palm there were small cuts and flecks of dried blood. She cleaned his wounds and insisted on putting a bandage over the worst one. He laughed and let her do it. "I am taking no chances," she said.

12

Lucinda dropped her estimated summer bread order, week by week, at Poppy's Convenience and then drove to Ruth to see the pastor's wife, Alma Worthy. She took the yardage of French cotton with the profusion of soft flowers for Alma to see. "It's beautiful," Alma whispered, and Lucinda told her it was for a summer dress, but Alma knew her well, read her as though psychic, which was why Lucinda wanted to talk to her.

Alma had a private room in the hospice wing at the hospital in Ruth. For the previous two years, though she'd been experiencing breathlessness, she wouldn't see a doctor. "Too busy with the orphans," she would shrug, going back to her e-mails and letters. A Quaker, she was a member of a group helping overseas orphanages. Though Pastor Fred Worthy of the Church of the Redeemer was on the fundamental side of Christianity, and she herself had been raised a Catholic, the variety of religious beliefs she lived with didn't faze her. She took to Neon Bar despite being the only Filipino person in the valley. "I'm a standout," she would say. "So special."

Lucinda lifted Alma's hand from the sheet and kissed the fingers.

"Nice place, eh?" Alma said, gesturing to the oxygen tank beside her bed and the room. "Unusual place for such a pretty fabric. Hmm?"

Lucinda ducked her head. "I'm afraid of making you tired."

"I have a minute to spare."

There were many stories she could tell – the patch of alarming weather they'd encountered on the flight down, the woman who'd brought along a pet parrot to a workshop in a house full of cats, the retreat at the Buddhist centre in Colorado where someone snored so loud it sounded like thunder. She raised her head. She said, "It was, in some ways, a difficult winter. Gabriel seems to have a new lady love." The words sounded to her plain but breezy, as though she was just trying them on. *Lady love.* "Her name is – well, we've always called her Idaho, from where she lives. She's tall. Beautiful." She paused. "Naturally." She cleared her throat again. "I'm sorry for bringing this up."

Alma shook her head, and Lucinda scooted her chair closer to the bed. She told the rest. Idaho had contacted them by e-mail, a long time ago, writing from a computer in her local library. Lucinda had sent a flyer, listing the names of the various workshops and where they would be, to her address, which was a post-office box. Then Idaho showed up unexpectedly on the last day of a four-day workshop, near the end of that season – fourteen months ago, March. "That's a while," Lucinda said, interrupting herself. "I mean – she's not exactly *new*, is she?

The . . . situations . . . don't usually last so long." Alma was watching closely. "I think you may be too nice a person to hear this," Lucinda said.

The remark caused Alma to cover her mouth.

Idaho had come to two workshops and then stopped, so if Lucinda thought anything was going on (which she hadn't) that would have been the end of it. Her husband treated her badly, Lucinda knew that, and she appeared to have been hit, or beaten, the time she came through the back door of the house with cherrywood floors; Lucinda recalled the floors clearly. She and some of the participants were in the kitchen, drinking tea and eating apples – the workshop was in Washington State, apples such a big thing – taking a break from the work. She herself was ladling kukicha tea when there was a brief knock on the back door. No one moved. There was another tap and then the door pushed open and a woman stepped inside, looking distraught. The door she came through had old-fashioned curtains on the window, madras tied in the middle, Lucinda recalled that fact too. The woman didn't make eye contact with anyone and she didn't speak. She stood as though she had taken the last step she was capable of taking.

They had been doing hands-on treatments in the living room, and so the massage tables were set up. Lucinda led Idaho into the living room and helped her to lie down and others adjusted the pillow for her neck. The bruise on her right cheek was a hot-looking reddish purple and there was a streak of blood on her chin, which a young woman dabbed using a dampened paper towel. Idaho started crying, tears running along her temples to the pillow, the tenderness of the woman's touch apparently moving to her. The hostess went to the other end of the house to get Gabriel.

Lucinda placed the palms of her hands carefully on Idaho's body, softly touching here and there, the others watching, bringing tissues, their eyes moist with empathy. Lucinda thought she detected panic around the heart chakra, a fluttering like bird wings, as though Idaho was trapped in her body and wanted out – "Out of her life altogether is what I picked up clearly," Lucinda said to Alma. "It seemed to me she'd come close to suicide, closer than most." Then she'd stopped crying. Under Lucinda's hands a coldness grew.

"A demon," Alma said.

Lucinda bowed her head, a pattern from childhood, to call up the verse: " 'For we wrestle not against flesh and blood but' – how does it go? – 'against powers, against the rulers of the darkness in the world.' "

Alma nodded.

"I was relieved and grateful, let me tell you, when Gabriel came in and took over. Feeling that deathly coolness under my hands was frightening. He told her to let the suffering go. To direct it into the earth. The earth could hold it, he said. She began watching him, you could tell she was analyzing whether she could trust him, and there was a frantic thing going on at the back of her eyes. And the thing is, she did it. What he asked. She let the pain go – its leaving was palpable – we all felt it – but then something went wrong. It had *hooked* her and she went after it, went deep, like a dive, following it. And then she was gone. No breathing, nothing, not a breath left in her body."

Gabriel had flipped her onto her stomach as easily as if she'd been a pancake. And then he placed the third finger of his right hand below the tailbone, into the vulnerable indentation near the anus, sliding his other hand under her belly, a move she'd never seen him do before. He said, "Breathe." But not in an ordinary speaking voice. He was commanding her: "Breathe. Breathe now." He told her that she was not going to get out of this life so easily. That she had met her demon – "I think he did use the word *demon*," Lucinda said, nodding at Alma – and that she had to deal with it. His voice vibrated with a fiery quality, melting the chill holding the body. His voice must have penetrated her unconscious, because they heard a boom like the sound barrier being broken. And Idaho was back. Breathing. Flushed and breathing.

Alma sighed. "The Lord works in wondrous ways."

Alma could take a stock phrase and apply it in such a way that compelled Lucinda to view a situation from a different angle. "Indeed," she said. "People drifted away afterwards. A little stunned or just distancing themselves from the experience, giving themselves time to take it in. Not long after, they were back in the kitchen, eating – the sandwiches in the refrigerator, cookies, the fudge someone had brought, the cheese and crackers, they just ate until everything was gone. Someone remarked that on the table Idaho had looked like a corpse, and it was true, I'd thought so too. Another said he'd heard the snapping sound in his own breast bone, it had been that resonant." Lucinda stopped. "When Idaho was still on the table, I noticed that strands of her hair – she has beautiful dark hair – were stuck to her wet cheeks. I tucked the hair behind her ears. Then I stepped back and Gabriel took over."

Alma nodded, a look of sorrow on her face.

"Would you like some water?" Lucinda said then and brought a glass over to bed. Alma put her lips on the straw and sucked. Lucinda set the glass on the tray and glanced toward the outside window, listening. An ambulance was wailing up the hill, coming their way. She turned to Alma. "Maybe that was my mistake," she said. "The stepping back."

When Milee finished cleaning the rollers – he had done rather a lousy job, Lucinda told him – he would have to scrape the floor where he'd dripped paint, though people in a summer kitchen usually didn't mind that sort of thing. Lucinda was talking a lot to herself, Mory thought. She sent them in his truck to the farm – the hippie farm, Milee called it – for her herb order. They parked outside and waited for the man who ran the greenhouse, who was finishing his lunch.

Milee said, "Why'd you come back?"

Mory lowered her eyes.

"Did you know your dad's sick?"

"Yes." She began to tap her thumbs together in her lap. "I know now, but I didn't."

"Didn't?"

"Know."

"After what he did to you, I don't know how you can be funny. Can be bunny. Honey. Runny, funny bunny," he said, rhyming. He stopped. "What, what he did to you – frickin' bastard –"

Mory put a finger to her lips.

"Depraved. Depraved is the word. The word for – for – for." He hit his palm with his fist. She had seen him do that movement before – fist, hit. He said, "Worse than my mum even. She was not a nice person either, you know that, right? I'm not pretending she was, but your dad is worse. Depraved. Do you know what that word means? Depraved? A person who deserves a fate worse than death. And your mum, I can't say about her. But he's the worst. I saw things when you were little."

"He isn't the worst," she said. Her thumbs tapped.

He watched her thumbs a minute. "When we first met? On the road? I was about nine? You were running away. After I met you, I used to go up there. I would ride my bike up and walk the trail to your cabin. I could hide and no one could spot me. I could live on grass like a grass-eating mammal."

"That would be a jeeter," Mory said.

"Okay, so I was a jeeter. A grass-eating jeeter."

"That's what they do. If you were a jeeter who ate bad people that would be something."

It took her a while to say this, but Milee listened, watching her closely. "I'm going up on a regular basis, ever since you came back. I want you to know. I'm watching them. I'm doing it for you. There's a bear watching too. I can feel him." He touched her hair, a quick touch. "My mum had dark hair like yours. But I don't miss her."

"She's not gone from you," Mory said.

He reached into the ashtray and brought out the butt end of a joint. Mory didn't toke any more, the smoke from others' joints was enough to make her mellow. Her parents used to grow maryjane, as they called it, in a field cleared out of the woods. They were doing fine until the police in planes started flying over, looking for grow operations. Then her papa dug another tunnel from the cabin and turned her play yard into a half-underground root cellar and they grew the maryjane under lights from generators, but they were noisy, and her mummy complained, "Did we cross a border and trek into the wilderness to listen to machinery?" For three months in the summer Papa dug all the way to Enterprise Creek and devised a system of electricity and the wilderness was quiet again, mostly.

She said, "It used to be a nice place." She was thinking of the flowerbeds and the apples from a tree that made the best strudel. Tears flooded and spilled.

He offered her a handkerchief. It was clean.

"Thank you," she said.

"Cry 'til they're all finished."

She shook her head no. "I know these tears. They are never done." She couldn't get her hands to wipe her face; they seemed dead. Milee cleaned her up with his handkerchief, pat, pat, spit.

Lucinda took the path through the fields down to the boat and went over to Poppy's Convenience & Gas and landed at the Neon Bar dock, a little flotsam of mossy logs and rusting ties, barely floating. She wore gumboots. A mallard pedalled by, and someone's brown-stained canoe was collecting water, its bleach-bottle bailer floating. In her pack she had presents for Willamina and Mary. Lucinda had been thinking about Willamina, who had worked at the Centre last summer. Her working for Lucinda had been a little sticky, Willamina being the daughter of a friend; Lucinda would find her sitting taking notes about something she'd thought of, or stopping what she was doing to launch into conversation – the ethical responsibility of the media was one topic – and to elicit Lucinda's opinions. She'd had to be coaxed back to work. Willamina had been in Toronto studying journalism, but this past year, Lucinda gathered, she'd become entangled with a man and skipped classes and then – nothing to do with him – her body had its own rebellion, and because she ignored her symptoms – for the man, Mary told Lucinda on the phone – the cysts grew and they had to be taken out along with everything else. Both ovaries, her uterus.

Lucinda sat at Mary's kitchen table over slices of pie, made from last year's huckleberries. They drank coffee from old-fashioned café-style cups that had heft and rounded handles. Mary and Poppy, both volunteers in the fire brigade, had been to a fire safety meeting in the Community Hall the night before, and Mary told her that the snowpack was not what it should have been again this past winter. She said, "It might look wet, but three inches down, the ground is dry. And, other news: Firebrands are not crazy people, like in the dictionary. Firebrands are flying cinders, embers that land on your shake roof and *poof*. And, believe it or not, the best way to save your boat is put it in the lake and pull the plug and sink it. When I heard that, I turned to the guys in the back and I said, 'Hey, boys, we got us a new cottage industry, eh? Draggin' boats out of the lake and hangin' 'em on the line to dry.'" She laughed. Lucinda felt at home, listening to Mary, sitting in the cozy kitchen, the familiar smells of dill and baking bread. She heard the muffled sounds of Poppy chatting with customers in the store at the front and bottles clinking; besides the bakery and deli, Poppy also ran Neon Bar's only liquor outlet.

When the conversation turned to Willamina, Mary lowered her voice and pointed a thumb upstairs. "Won't get out of bed. The nurse says she's fine. My daughter says her life is over. She wants to kill herself. She is a crazy person, crying all the time. If that bastard, Conrad, came here, I would slice his throat with a bread knife. Yeah, you bet. Bread knife. Hurts more that way." Lucinda saw that Mary's eyes were serious, weary even.

"I brought her a silk teddy with lace. Maybe not what she's in the mood for."

"You never know with my daughter. One minute sane, the next not so much. And how is His Lordship?"

Lucinda answered but said nothing of consequence, partly out of selfishness – she didn't want to get started about Gabriel – and partly because Mary seemed to have enough on her plate.

"And the hot flashes?"

"No, I won't take hormones, so you can stop right there." Lucinda smiled.

"All right, suffer then. Everybody around here, suffer, suffer. Who listens to me? A waste of all my wisdom. Come into the store before you go upstairs and give Willamina a talking-to. Poppy wants you to taste his new Montreal beef. Don't say it's too salty."

As they went through the beads hanging across the doorway, into the back of the store and down the short hall past the freezers, a commotion started out front. At first Lucinda couldn't identify whether someone was shouting just for fun or the racket meant a warning. On the road outside, the bell jingling on the door swinging behind them – Mary had started running – two young men, loggers wearing the typical short pants and suspenders, were looking up, their truck stopped at an angle. The air smelled of fresh-cut cedar logs. Lucinda stepped out off the concrete and shaded her eyes. There was Willamina outside her bedroom, on the porch roof, half in and half out the open window. She was wearing what Lucinda thought were fuzzy pink bunny slippers. Her nightgown was hitched up and showed her left leg almost to the panties. She was shouting, "You all go to hell! Leave me alone! I am not the cheerful type, Mama!"

The loggers were grinning, giving each other looks.

Mary narrowed her eyes at them, and they shuffled their feet.

Poppy, wiping his hands on the towel he wore around his waist, said to Willamina, "What do you think you are doing, my daughter, besides entertaining the neighbourhood?"

"I was planning a dramatic demise," Willamina shouted. "But what does it look like now? I am caught on a fucking nail!" She squirmed, trying to unhook the housecoat.

The front of her nightgown was streaked with brown and red; to Lucinda it looked like Willamina was hemorrhaging. She touched Mary's shoulder. "Is she all right? Is she bleeding?"

Mary shook her head, no, and called up, "You gobble those cherry-filled chocolates your auntie sent you?"

"Chocolate-covered cherries are revolting," Willamina shouted. "Think about it! Round balls, something gooey inside. More than you can say for me!"

"Tell me your sense will return," Mary said.

"Mama, Mama!" Willamina said, a shout of exasperation. "I give up, I give up! Tell everybody not to look."

"You out here, we looking," said Mary. "What you expect?"

"Close your eyes so I can get this damn thing off this goddamn nail. *Mama.*"

Mary turned to the small assembly in the road and raised her hands like a conductor of an orchestra. "Close your eyes," she said.

Poppy whispered to Lucinda, "I give her those slippers to make her felt better. No good they did."

When Willamina had extricated herself, she said, "I hope that gives you hicks something to talk about for a while! You, too, Jason," she added, pointing to one of the men.

"How you know him?" Mary said.

"Oh, Mama, how do you suppose? This hellhole is barely big enough for a dozen fleas!" She climbed back inside. She closed the window with a slam and drew the curtains.

Mary came over to them. "It's good you never had a child," she said to Lucinda. "They break your heart."

Everyone was milling around, including a couple of kids on bicycles who had just arrived. Mary said, "Thank you, thank you. If you know any eligible bachelors, send them over" – the sort of remark that made Willamina wild, Lucinda knew. The fellows hustled back into the truck, laughing, and honked once as they drove away.

The effect on her of Willamina's antic – Lucinda first thought of it as an antic – was a surprise. On the way back to the Centre she sped across the water, dodging bits of wood and other debris brought by the creeks. She was careless, nudged the hull of the little aluminum car topper too hard against their own dock. She tied up quickly, as though she had somewhere to be, and then, puzzled, one foot on the dock, the other on the thwart, she began to cry, something she had not done in a long time. She nearly lost her balance, almost fell, scraped her shin scrambling onto the dock on all fours. She lay face down on the warm wood and cried.

Doctors said you could not feel your uterus, except during the cramps of menstruation or childbirth. But Lucinda knew you could feel it as it lay inside you, barren.

When you love someone too much and feel yourself to be unworthy, you're blind when you shouldn't be and the headlights are coming straight at you and still you deny that there are dangers in your paradise. More was going on between Gabriel and Idaho than she'd admitted or been willing to face. She lay on the dock in the sun, a summery breeze flipping the leaves of the poplars overhead. The event in his life that she'd disregarded – that she'd let slip into history, as though the impact to him were over – was that he'd had a child once, he and a young woman named Suzanne. He and Suzanne had come to Neon Bar together from the east coast of the United States, bought land, started building the Centre with their Seventies' idealist, back-to-the-land friends, forsaking the city and the stock exchange and law. And then their baby, named Clara, toppled into a hole and fell asleep, so Lucinda was told, and someone, not looking and maybe high, threw dirt on her and after a while Suzanne started searching, her milk was leaking through her dress and they heard the sounds, couldn't think from where. On their hands and knees, Gabriel and the workers, all young, and Suzanne crawling, breasts dripping, listening for the child. Dug her up, except that creek water from an ill-fitted coupling had seeped into the hole and she had breathed into her tiny body rivulets of mud and didn't live long after, medical intervention making no difference, Gabriel flying her here and there. It was the dirt hitting her as it did, burying her, Lucinda thought, that killed the child, the psychological damage done to her, opened and trusting, being buried. Who knew. The boy who filled the hole had tried to kill himself by hanging a rope over a joist in the new barn, which Gabriel tore down, board by board by himself, using an axe and pry bar until it was demolished. Comfrey grew through the pile of weathered wood where it had been. Suzanne left after Clara died, they had been heading for a breakup, people said, and she was in the plane that exploded over Scotland. She imagined the curly-haired child waking, believing that she was still playing, yet not for long. Unable to see or breathe, cold water on her spine, the weight of the mud, something elemental in her knowing what being buried meant, so that she kept going back to it, the dying and death, despite her feeble resurrection.

In the little lock-box safe in the cedar chest at the foot of his bed, Gabriel kept a black-and-white picture. The photograph showed Suzanne frowning into the sun outside the tepee, holding the blond baby. He kept Clara's barrette too, carried it in the shrine box that went with him everywhere. A toddler's barrette was an innocent object, his child's a plastic mould of a little red bird.

She went up to the house. She put Bactine on her leg and covered it with a bandage. She went upstairs, to his bedroom – he was out in the garden – and shut the door behind her. She opened the cedar chest and picked up the barrette and held it in her hand and felt the bitter loss still in it.

13

Kathleen began to watch their house. She would stand at the smallest window in the cabin and pull aside the gingham curtains and peer at the house, waiting for something. She would imagine him looking out at her from the attic window that faced the cabin. Sometimes she saw his face, the moon quality of it, how dreamy he would look with his eyes closed, unlike the pragmatic man he was in the waking world.

The restlessness was located in the dry region of her heart, and the weather mirrored her feeling; outside, it thundered and yet did not rain, and the restlessness in her, like the earth's impatience during a drought, surfaced. She felt in her body such a yearning she thought her skin would weep. A finger, a hand, two hands; a torso, legs, soft belly, chest bone stretched against the length of her – she thought she would pass out with desire. She went onto the porch and watched the show, dark billows in the wide swath of sky, flashes of lightning so electric they remained in her retina after they were gone. Longing rose from the parched ground.

She went inside and lay her warm jacket on the bed. She got out the second blanket, a heavy cotton quilt. She lay roasting in the bed under the blanket and the pile of stuff just to feel the weight of something pressing on her skin. She was in the middle of nowhere, withdrawn from the challenges of life, from subways and work and the careworn faces of others. Alone in this cabin at the edge of the woods: a woman too young to be a widow, too old to be alone, beside herself, aching. It wasn't sex she needed, her feelings weren't sexual; orgasm she didn't consider. She needed nothing she could do for herself. What she longed for was sweet touching, caresses and rubs and the breath-taking weight of the other body sinking momentarily into hers; hair and smells and texture and sweat.

She struggled out of bed. It seemed obscene to indulge this craving. She put her hands in her hair and pulled it.

In the morning, Kathleen and Davida at the breakfast table, Boris having already left, Kathleen was putting her arms out straight and taking stock of her hands, trying to connect them to her body. Sometime in the night they seemed to have become disengaged or disconnected, because when she awoke she couldn't identify her limbs as her own. Davida asked her what she was doing. "You are staring at your hands," she said again, able to repeat herself without impatience.

"Am I?"

Davida pressed her hand briefly over Kathleen's and then went upstairs to get dressed for her day. Kathleen put the cup down and followed. From the bottom of the stairs she called, "Can I borrow your truck?"

"May I," Davida said.

Kathleen heard drawers shutting and the squeak of the pocket door. "Okay. May I borrow your truck?" She went back into the kitchen and poured half a cup of coffee and stood holding it.

"The vehicle isn't paid for," Davida said, gliding into the room, handing Kathleen the keys.

Kathleen first drove up the lake, past the small landholdings and farms, and then the road narrowed even more. Occasionally the views out over the lake from the roller coaster of a road were stunning but she was distracted; she drove, concentrating on the curves and turns. Eventually she turned off onto gravel and then onto pavement again and passed a bakery and convenience store and kept on until she came to the faded sign for the Centre for Light Awareness. She drove in and parked under a Lombardy poplar and rolled down the window and listened. The silence felt like a pause in the world's hand-wringing.

She didn't get out of the car, didn't know how to begin were she to knock on the door. She wanted something venturesome and bold, so she tore back to Ruth, driving fast, weaving the curves like someone who knew the road. The lake lay flat and hot on her left, the trees alongside the road dusty and wilting. She decided to find the wagon trail to the claim on the ridge behind the cabin she was staying in, if there was a trail, which, she reasoned, there must be. Blasting would have been out of the question for the modest amount of good ore her miner had managed to extract, and while a strong man on his own could get to and from the site, as her miner, and Boris, had done, a loaded wagon couldn't; to bring out the treasure, there would have to be a road of some kind coming in from behind. From up there she expected to see the shake roof of the cabin itself and the ambling path that her feet had made through the field to the house. She would have the view of the far shore and the bay where they'd had the picnic. And she would see what the miner saw – the trickle of the creek shimmering, partly hidden by the height of the grass, meandering across the field to the point where it entered a pipe and went under the road. On the other side, she knew, it became a waterfall – on an exploratory walk she had stood in its mist – before emptying into the lake.

She stopped by the government office and bought a topo-graphical map of the local area. She went to the beach and spread the map out on a picnic table. She found what was probably Davida and Boris's land and the faint *x* marking the claim. There did seem to be a road of some kind, a track or trail, anyway, that wound along the contours of the ridge, that went almost to the mine. She could park and walk the rest of the way. It would seem that to get to the trail, she should first take the highway and, at the second junction, turn south.

With this idea in mind, she drove westward on the two-lane highway for a mile or so and then turned left onto a logging road that crossed a creek. The creek was low, boulders like bones rising out of it, dead branches piled along the banks. The road was basically sculpted ruts, gravel mixed with dirt and rocks that had worked their way loose. The wheels of the SUV climbed over these obstacles like a moon explorer, one tire at a time. She climbed into the light and came to a fork. She held her foot to the brake while she thought about which way to go.

Both roads were hardly bigger than trails and both were overgrown with tansy and knapweed and obviously unused for a long time. As she was pondering what to do, the rear tires slipped, and the sudden, stiff backward movement scared her. Her foot was tense on the brake as she shifted into first – she should have been in four-wheel drive but didn't know how to set it – and she decided to take the lower road. For a short stretch the choice was calming and then the overgrown road began to gain altitude – she heard the grass brushing the undercarriage – and she continued on because she didn't know what else to do. The road, cut out of the steep slope, was growing narrower. She climbed and turned the wheel sharply left and turned it sharply to the right. The switchbacks were harrowing; for seconds she saw only the hood of the car and beyond it a sky that was smoke-filled. The road was so overgrown it was nearly impossible to tell exactly where it was, but to the right, on the passenger side, were trees and then, too soon, the tops of trees, descending, the slope they grew on steep. Once, she glanced into the rear-view mirror, a mistake. The road behind her was so vertical it seemed to drop away.

She came to a level spot and stopped. She set the brake but held fast to the steering wheel, just in case the whole road had an impulse to disintegrate. The car was hot and she was wet, in a sweat of anxiety. She stepped carefully down from the vehicle, so as not to dislodge anything; even her breathing seemed a potential factor. She was scared to shut the car door in case the reverberation upset the balance. She stood in the open door, close to the wheel. She removed her wet shirt and tentatively flapped it a few times to air it out. Then, knees trembling, she said to the car, "Don't go anywhere," and took a step back and then another forward and walked up the road a dozen paces. She did not see any reason ever in life for a person to think that being this isolated – view or no view – was a desirable thing. Up ahead, beyond where she stood, there appeared to be a widening in the road and, excited but controlling her excitement, she walked back to the car and carefully climbed back in and then crept forward until there was a small shoulder. Feeling almost saved she felt herself becoming foolishly brave and thought farther along there might be an even wider section, a turnaround possibly. She went up until she came to a rock fall that even the high clearance vehicle couldn't get past. She got out and threw a few rocks out of the way and pushed at two big boulders but couldn't budge them. She shouted in exasperation. A raven answered. Very carefully she backed down and eased onto the shoulder. She held her breath, expecting the sound of road crumbling, rocks on the bank coming loose and smacking each other in freefall. She jockeyed forwards and backwards, her arms aching with turning the wheel as she braked and lurched another inch and paused and muttered prayers.

When she was turned around, she set the parking brake, and keeping a hand on the wheel, frowned at the map that had been sliding around on the passenger seat. It was not making much sense. With her free hand she flipped it one way and another. Its heavy paper, new and crackling, unnerved her. She was unsure which way was north. The map was a maze of thin lines encircling each other informing someone who knew how to read it about terrain. To her just then it was unreadable – pale greens, slightly darker greens, the spirals more like art than information, an occasional blue thread indicating where a creek should be.

She thought about the Toronto apartment. It seemed sheltered compared to this, and she wanted to be there, in the living room with the shiny wood floors, the view through the balcony windows of tame, leafy deciduous trees, used to city life, used to living in a protected park, used to providing shade. The lostness she'd felt in those rooms seemed indulgent, certainly notional compared to the immediate physical reality of her being lost now.

Discouraged and yet expectant of finding the right road, she bumped along down the mountain, stopping every so often to peer, perplexed, at the map. The sky was changing again.

Wisps of cloud gathered in the space beyond the hood, between the rows of tall, thin, crowded trees on either side of whichever road this was. A raven landed on a boulder in front of her. His squawking muffled the engine. She hoped for rain, she was so overheated. She had no water to drink. She drove on past a clear-cut, the land naked and raped. She drove past a burned woods, dead trunks rising to the sky. Then she turned a strange corner in her mind, and images began to slip in: Grandfather came to her, sang through her throat. She entered the country of the Mossmen Standing, and River began to accompany her. She was comforted by River's presence because River would know the way to the ancient mossy woods. In the middle of what was a peculiar rhapsody, something large scraped the underbelly of the vehicle and caught. She jolted to a stop and peered out the windows. On her side, way, far down, there was a steep wooded ravine and, on the passenger side, the mountain continued its march to the sky. She put the car in first and rocked until the branch underneath came loose.

Once again she had taken something that belonged to someone else and was wrecking it. She thought for sure she'd scratched the paint at least; the transmission was smelling overheated. And it was becoming obvious that the longer she fussed with the map, the more lost she became. She began to hate the stiff, crinkling sound of it and crumpled it rudely and shoved it toward the floor. If she were to become thirsty, she didn't have water; hungry, not even a chocolate bar. She couldn't change a tire either, if it came to it. She did not make good soup. Her list of inadequacies marched past. The crust that had been the surface of this road relaxed into dust. The truck settled.

She sat still, the sun blazing on the roof, in a state she understood to be psychic disarray, in which one lets go of the idea of being anywhere. A story began talking to her as though a voice had been waiting for a susceptible consciousness to happen along. "Sometimes it takes three to make a baby. Stone Man did not like to sleep with women. He invited his friend Middleman to join him in marriage to Soft-as-Butter. In the front seat of a Pontiac convertible, Middleman began the act of lovemaking to Soft-as-Butter, while in the back seat Stone Man prepared himself . . ." The story was raunchy and possibly disgusting, imaginatively ribald as well as unlikely, and it excited her, the idea of the two men and the one woman, mouths and semen. She put her hand on her lower belly where a spasm of pleasure that didn't feel like pleasure uncoiled. She found a packet of tissues in the glove compartment and blew her nose.

She slid from the seat and slogged ahead a quarter-mile or so, where she found the road had withered, as though it had lost its purpose, misplaced its original estimation of itself – I am a road; had let itself parch and become overrun with the dried mats and weavings of green she now was used to seeing in B.C. but could not remember the names of, common or otherwise. Her mind was going, that much seemed evident. She stood in the heat and prickly thistles and something rustled nearby and she did not care what it was; her brain was an empty cauldron, a sensory organ that had once shared its life with her and kept her distracted with busy nattering and arcane comments. She stood, the heat baking her scalp, her feet aching, tied into knots of anxiety from the miles of painstaking braking and accelerating; and her hands hurt too, from all their work at the wheel. She had had it.

A deep, concentrated aroma of earth and moss, ardent and exotic, arrived in a drift of air. She looked at the weeds, seed-filled tips bristling lightly against her knees – not them, too dry – but she smelled it, the dense, primeval stink of some wonderful thing that she had not experienced before. Her brain kicked in, and she looked around, the muscles in her neck loosening. She stood taller, and as she did, she saw it, a way in, a trail. She was on the brink of the end, she thought, having thoughts again, and followed the track. She tripped over an underground root and seemed to tumble into a different sort of woods entirely, damp and cool, the trees widely spaced and large enough for giants to enjoy. Regaining her feet, she thought that brontosaurus would be at home here, the oversized unwieldy vegetarian sinking into plates of sea-green leaves the size of a human head.

Old men disguised as mammoth trees thinking long, thinking hard about the ways of this diverse earth, their branches draped in aged moss, ragged and striking as horses' tails in winter. Ten men holding hands – assuming you could find ten men willing to hold hands, she thought, a smidgeon of her self returning – ten men holding hands could not encircle the trunk of one of these cedar trees. Could not capture it, surround it, contain it. Had not, so far, logged it.

She laughed. A gulp of gratitude at the discovery of something primal, aboriginal, untouched, preserved – something saved. A laugh, a small gasp of sound hardly heard in the silence, she supposed after she'd recovered from it. The trees were between four hundred and eight hundred years old, something in that range, she'd heard – she couldn't say and didn't need to, which was a relief since these days she was supposed to know everything, decide everything. She was weak from effort the moment her eyes opened, reluctantly and in dread, as she lay in the apartment on the single-sized mattress she'd dragged in its plastic wrapper from the service elevator and upon which she'd slept, night after night all the long winter, moving the mattress from room to room, liberating without realizing it the space she lived in, releasing the rooms from the approach they had taken when James was alive, undoing the way they looked and their very functions, when it was James and her, James and Kathleen, a couple.

She thought of the cot-sized mattress waiting in the cabin. Not wide enough for two to sleep on and turn in the night, brush up against each other, pull knees up, kiss a shoulder, its owner unaware. She stood in the moist stillness, in oak fern and devil's club and trees covered in lichens and fungi, ochre and orange and banded in black, trees thriving from the nutrients exchanged with their companions.

She walked a little trail a Parks Canada person had been paid to clear, a tender, delicate trail so narrow in places it was one foot in front of the other. The trail glided over a hump of root and skirted a stream that still – despite the heat outside this grotto – rippled and trickled. The trail became so narrow that at one point she wondered if she could step across the water, onto the next part of the trail. She wondered about older people, she wondered about women with arthritis, about whether they would be able to continue on, whether the threadlike trail would stop them and make them turn back. She hoped that would not be the case at the same time she hoped that this old-growth forest – she knew it for what it was – would not ever have to become entirely accessible. She bent back to see the tops of the trees. Truly immersed in a mossy greenness, she saw very little sky. She broke out bawling. James was here, looking after her, he was around her, aglow inside her; he was making a point of showing her this new world.

Boris poured himself a glass of ice water with lemon, holding off having the first martini until six. Davida was still at work. He said, "You got lost? How'd you get out of it?"

She told him some of the story. That she had waited a while in the car. And when a grouse ran across the road, she took it as a sign and slowly backed down, guiding herself through the side mirror, pretending she knew the road by heart. Until then, of course, more had been going on, including talking aloud, passionately pleading about one thing or another, behaviour she didn't confess to Boris. She came down the mountain a different way than she had gone up; she hadn't recognized anything, and she didn't know how it happened. She told him parts of the Indian story that had come to her. He listened.

"A *Pontiac convertible?*"

"Yes."

"Don't you think that was improbable? In B.C., in this area?"

"I didn't make it up."

"You didn't tell me the whole thing."

"I am not going to tell you the whole thing. I don't even think in those words."

"What words?"

"I'm not going to say them and you know it. Bad ones."

"Oh, *bad ones.*"

She began to blush.

"Maybe you should. Think in those words." He gave her a scrutinizing look as though probing her, considering something. His eyebrows were dark and bushy. She said nothing. "I am full of loose, crazy stories, your term," he said smoothly as though there hadn't been a pause. "It adds a certain zing to life." He grinned and lifted his glass of water. From the mountain, she had gone straight back to the cabin, anticipating its claustrophobic safety, and smelled dust and walked in circles around the room and then she'd gone over to the house to sit in the kitchen, holding the rooster salt shaker, until Boris came home.

It was a Saturday, and Boris and Davida wanted Kathleen to go with them to the Frances Hill, to see the place. He was dropping Davida off for the morning because he needed the Toyota for some errands. They drove into Ruth, through the old section and across the bridge into the new. The Frances Hill was on a bluff overlooking the town and had a wide view of the lake. "The view is wasted on most of them," Boris said as they parked in his reserved space. Davida poked his arm. Their spells of playfulness surprised Kathleen.

Kathleen didn't like the smell of institutions (though she suspected she should get used to it because she would, at the rate she was going, end up in one). The building was all stucco and efficiency, a thin layer of charm in the foyer in the form of big baskets of dried flowers on platforms. It smelled like a hospital. "It's old person's pee," Davida said, her finger to her lips. "It gets everywhere." They strode across the foyer, nodding at the people in wheelchairs set around the edge of what was called the common area. They went into Davida's office.

Boris said, "Many of our residents have lived their whole life in Ruth. Ruth and the surrounding area. You have to respect them for it. Not long ago they were shipped out when they needed nursing care. Now they can stay right here where everybody knows them." He touched Kathleen's elbow and guided her to a chair. Davida was already at her computer, frowning as she pecked.

"Hi-speed Internet," Boris said. "It took a lot of lobbying."

"And we know the guy who gets the credit. Oh, all right," Davida said, with a cursory glance in his direction. "Everybody knows the residents and remembers who they were in the community. The Frances Hill allows a continuous flow of life." She shot Kathleen a look Kathleen couldn't interpret.

"Continuous flow right to the grave," Boris said, and Davida said, "Oh, give it up," and he walked around to peck her cheek. "See you later, baby."

"I am not anyone's baby."

"Baby, baby, ba-by," he said.

"Oh, give it up," Davida said again.

Back in the car, Kathleen wasn't sure how to behave. She said she thought maybe he and Davida needed some time alone together, but Boris said no. He seemed intent on taking her house-hunting. "Now, now, she and I talked about it," he said when Kathleen protested it was too much trouble. "She thinks it's the thing to do. She's concerned about you. Should she be?" He took his eyes off the road. They were startlingly bright.

"Maybe," Kathleen said. Her voice sounded husky, for a moment making her, she thought, sound interesting.

They briefly viewed two new houses and then climbed and wound around and drove along a small dead-end street with a willow tree and a graceful blue spruce and lilac bushes everywhere and poppies still bright orange and floppy. Boris stopped in front of a Victorian house that needed sanding and paint. "Owner was a Sonemayer, an old maid," he said. "Early family to the area, but they've pretty much disappeared." The house was perfectly placed on a big lot on the steep uphill side of the road. They got out of the car. Across the road and down a distance was Cedar Hideaway, a place with cabins for rent, a few RV spots, Boris said. He said, "Clarence Harker never made much out of what he had."

"Not everyone is in your league." Kathleen sounded so much like Davida she had to laugh. She turned herself around to see the scene from all angles. From the sloping front yard there was a satisfying view of the lake and the pilings with the light on top, for boats, beyond the tip of the beach. Up the slope under a blue spruce she noticed a bench of some kind, nearly hidden from view due to mugwort and nettly things and determined shoots from what looked like a felled plum tree. She walked up the slope to inspect it, saw that it had an ironwork back with initials in small, intricate letters forged into it – E & S.

"She had love once," Kathleen said, thinking of the long-ago woman, the "old maid," as Boris had crudely put it. She didn't speak loud enough for Boris to hear, and then her attention was diverted by an incongruous truck parked in front of the garage, and she went over to it.

"A food truck," Boris said, coming to stand beside her. "It'll be out of here soon." He was so close she heard him swallow.

The house had two second-floor dormers, one on either side. It was pale green and the window trim was pink and the inner casement red, and that would not do – already she was revamping. She smiled to herself and continued up the concrete steps that plowed through overgrown weeds to the veranda, Boris following. They walked along the length of the veranda, peering through the tall windows into high-ceilinged rooms, toward the huge yard in the back, and from there they stepped into a shady garden flush with lupines – pinks and purples filling the eye. She turned to Boris, enchanted.

"It's a good deal." He shrugged, and she laughed. He looked like such an appealing boy to her.

He took her back to town and to Ruth Realty and introduced her to a crony of his. They moved into the privacy of the man's office. She filled out the papers and put in a mid-range offer just to see what would happen. She was feeling bubbly and full of daring.

They went to his office at the high school ostensibly to collect another box of his things, because he was leaving the district. He'd been an interim principal – an interminable interim, he said – when the district had needed someone with his experience. A bronzed lamp caught her eye, the base an art deco figure of a scantily clad woman, a leafy vine winding round her body, her arm reaching toward the light. "I'm surprised," she said, thinking of how the boys must have loved being lectured to in this room. Boris gestured toward a seat. He sat opposite, within touching distance, his legs crossed, his hands folded under his chin. He stared frankly, so that she became uncomfortable. The toe of his shoe poked hers. He tilted his head, considering her. "You're very shy. I didn't know that about you."

"There's not a lot to know about me."

He took a breath and surveyed the room as though it was new to him. Her eyes followed his gaze and furtively took him in. She said, "I – I've become totally incompetent. I can't seem to function dependably. Maybe I'm like a light bulb, one that flickers, you know, almost burnt out."

"We probably shouldn't be alone together," he said.

A thrill ran through her. She could not meet his gaze. Irresistibly, coquettishly, she asked, "Why not?"

"You're very attractive."

She hesitated. "Heavier than I used to be."

"Sadness has softened you."

Her hands lay open in her lap. A tear fell onto her palm and spread. He rose from the chair and stood so that she couldn't help but notice the fly of his jeans. The rivets, the seam. She lowered her gaze to the well-used heavy-duty boots he wore. He patted her back. His pat was awkward and she shifted and stood up out of the chair, at the same time stepping forward so that she could face him. She wondered how many other girls had felt taken advantage of in this room, had been made uneasy, had felt the sexual tension. She was certainly feeling it, *and* she was thinking of herself as a *girl*. In an effort to shake off the mood that was becoming murkier and murkier, she said lightly, "Let's get out of here." Suddenly she thought maybe she was the only one involved in the fantasy, just she herself out on a limb feeling seductive and tantalized. She thought her face had a stricken look. Reassuring her, he took her hand, and she liked the rough feel of it. They manoeuvred through the door into the corridor. The floor there was buffed and shone. "Why are school floors always shiny?" she asked, foolishly, taking back her hand.

He led the way to the car. They drove over the bridge and home in silence. She felt she had done something wrong and she wanted to apologize but she didn't know what for. "Are you all right?" she asked him. They were parked in the driveway beside the house.

"Please kiss me, Kathleen," he said. And she did.

Then they had dinner, the three of them. They laughed. Davida had her headache and went to bed early. He brought his tongue forward so that the tip parted her lips. She allowed the tip of hers to touch his. Their lips were warm; they stood in the embrace for a time. Her tongue spread her own lips farther, and his, and began to explore, advancing to the root. He was very restrained. Had he moved she might have jumped him, but the man did not move; he held himself in check and in so doing created such a suspense of longing in her she thought she would burst with joy.

He slowly inhaled as though to breathe her in, and continued pressing her along the length of his body. Boris was a tall, big man, and in order to keep their connection, her head was tilted backwards, her throat arched. Their breathing seemed noisy to her, as they, holding themselves together, held themselves back.

He had come across the field, stepped onto the porch as though he didn't see her sitting in the dark, her feet on the railing, a glass of warm wine in her hand. He slipped inside. The screen door closed quietly. She was wearing a faded plaid flannel shirt of his that Davida had loaned her. You could smell smoke in the air. The burnt moon was high overhead. The bare peaks of the mountains glowed unearthly pink. She took a step herself and followed him in, set her glass down carefully on the little table just inside the door.

14

It was becoming the summer of the drought, and catastrophic fires raged in the interior. The skies were colourful until you realized it was fire causing the apparent sunset, fire creating an eerie end-of-the-world glow that reflected onto your own skin. As the fires started and stopped and shifted, the bears were restless and wandered where they shouldn't wander so that no one knew where a bear, or a fire, would pop up next – 874 fires in the province that July, they were hearing on the radio – winds spreading the smoke and the smell and fooling you into thinking danger was closer than it was. Or farther away. Back-country wildfire, by its nature, was elusive. You were outside it, saw only its flags in the sky, until you woke to the crackle of it in your own backyard. DC-7s, lumbering as bumblebees, dropped showers of red chemicals way back where you couldn't see, and Type II Bell helicopters towing orange Bambi buckets full of lake water disappeared and reappeared. The sky was often red and bits of grainy ash fell on the picnic tables under the hemlocks at Cedar Hideaway. In 1980 the Harkers had bought the place from Clarence's father's cousin. Extra lots came with the purchase and they thought lake access wouldn't be as important as it turned out to be. The camp was built around the old two-storey cabin from the turn of the century. The logs listed naturally to the south, like the place wanted the sun. Inside, the door frames were more flexible than door frames were generally given credit for, but they got used to it. The house – never referred to as a cabin – had a long covered area added to the back, where the firewood was piled for themselves, along with half a cord of smaller wood, available to the guests. They kept the cabin chimneys clean, so guests could have a little fire inside when it rained or on cold spring mornings.

The sooty air and road closures were not good for the tourist business. In Ruth there was a water-usage ban and the grass – in the case of Cedar Hideaway, mown weeds – went brown. The trees looked miserable and tucked in on themselves; leaves drooped. Then the town council changed their minds about the water ban because the whole of Ruth seemed too dry and tinder-ready. Bet Harker heard at the Chamber of Commerce summer potluck that council got to thinking they were inviting trouble by saving water. All it would take, someone pointed out, was one fiery cinder hurtling through the sky for the whole place to erupt. So on the hill the sprinklers started whirling and some put makeshift deals on their shake and shingle roofs, comical contraptions constructed out of wood, legs on either side of the spine as though the sprinklers were riding the houses like horses. At Cedar Hideaway, the Harkers didn't bother – the main house and the five cabins were covered in inexpensive tar paper with a red gritty surface, mostly hidden by the tall firs and the rangy poplars. Jay and Jerry, the twins, did some raking, pulling out the understory, brushy material the fellow who gave a talk on fire prevention called a buildup of fuel on the forest floor. He was a fire ecologist brought in by the Community Forest, and Bethany Jane – who wanted to be called BJ, over her mother's dead body – made her mum go to the meeting while she herself took notes. The fire ecologist had the view that the forests were just fuel for fire, unlike the tourists, Bet noted later, who thought what the area had was pretty.

During that same hot July, Drake Marshall, who owned a logging truck, drowned in a boating accident. Bet went over to Dolly's – they had known each other a long time – with her casserole of ham and scalloped potatoes, and she supposed afterwards, she'd gone with a sanctimonious attitude. Dolly had the look of someone nearly drowned herself, someone who any minute would come up gasping and have to face the fact that her impetuous man would no longer be raising hell and giving her something to complain about in the vegetable aisle of the IGA when the friends happened to run into each other on a Tuesday. Or Saturday morning, Dolly Marshall's habits as irregular as Bet's own.

While in the kitchen, the potholders showing grease stains and burns, there was the usual gossip – the young people who owned the handicrafts store were splitting up; a fifteen-year-old swallowed a bottle of Tylenols in a suicide attempt; Sam at the Zoo Café had developed diabetes. "Everything coming undone," Bet said, intending to be sympathetic to the mood in the house. "We are each tested mightily," a voice rejoined, the tone oracular, and Bet saw the minister of the community church seated at the head of the dining-room table, the polyester lace tablecloth pushed aside, his sleeves rolled up, taking notes for the memorial service. The family was talking to him one at a time – among them, Dolly's oldest boy just arrived from Prince Rupert – while he considered their words and what they had to add. "Only the mountains abide," he said and took his time cleaning his glasses on his sleeve, so that Dolly's daughter, Colleen, the same age as Bethany Jane, could pull herself together. She was having trouble speaking, sobbing into her brother's kerchief held with both fists, a woman from the church holding her up. Before Drake's accident, Bet had been feeling sorry for Dolly, and a little smug, because Colleen was pregnant. Due soon. Hadn't graduated with her class. The mountains outside the curtained windows were wreathed in an unhealthy haze.

Drake had been on the mountain, doing a bit of logging on his lease lot. Because it was hot, he must have decided to take the boat out, have a beer on the lake, jump in for a swim. They found the boat churning its crippled stem in the gravel on the far shore. Strange how that was: the boat leaving the man. No rules or laws, and no amount of certification was going to stop freak accidents, so someone suggested.

"But there was the beer," Bet piped up. They had found an empty case of beer in the boat, the bottles strewn on the bottom. Bet was holding a plastic glass of non-alcoholic punch, and as soon as the words were out of her mouth, she regretted them and peered crossly into the pinkish drink at the ragged, nearly sunk orange slice. The voices at her end of the room seemed to fall silent. Pissing hell, she thought – she'd sounded pious, a quality not usually associated with Bet Harker. The realization made her wince, place a hand over her eyes as though she couldn't be held responsible for her remark due to a terrible headache, which she figured she deserved as a result of someone smacking her hard with a baseball bat. "It was so hot that day, it was understandable," she murmured, trying to appear regretful rather than simply mean. Remorseful, at least. She'd spoken coldheartedly as though this death and the causes for it had nothing to do with the people she'd known her whole life.

As for Clarence, she was careless about him and why shouldn't she have been? They had their hands full running Cedar Hideaway and there were the kids being teenagers with their inevitable ideas. His left hand had begun to tremble the odd time and she thought it was a muscle spasm. He had been roofing the old shed, set at an angle so that it was hard to get at. And because he was a drinker, you expected a drinker to shake; he wasn't getting any younger. He was following his usual routines, nipping from the "secret" mickey he kept in one pocket or another, or tucked in the woodpile, on a shelf in the workshop or outside the kitchen door behind Bethany Jane's wild mint.

The morning Bet found out that her daughter had a secret life, the alarm on Clarence's side of the bed went off at 6:30, the usual time in the summer. He had an old ticking Timex with a ringer that jangled them awake. When the alarm rang, he reached over, pushed the button on the back of the clock, sighed. Turned his head her way, smiled, being careful not to open his mouth because he had bear-bait breath in the morning, the smile his way of starting the day as he'd been taught by his mother. (Her boys were raised to be grateful for everything, Bet liked to say, and that included finding a woman willing to share their beds.) He stretched his thin, nearly hairless legs, stretched his neck down to his sternum, groaned, rose slowly, jiggled himself into motion, went to the can, did his business, horked into the sink, brushed his teeth. Pulled on the oldest jeans he could find, on the floor at his side of the bed, did up the belt Bet insisted he wear so he'd be half presentable. With that gear and a plaid shirt he'd salvaged from the rag bag when she wasn't looking, he headed downstairs to the kitchen. Most of the year, except for the peak of summer, he started the woodstove with newspapers people left behind in the cabins, kindling and wood he'd cut and stacked in the hamper the night before. Meanwhile, she lay staring at the water-stained ceiling, vaguely wanting to do something about it for the thousandth time, and listened to the familiar sounds that started a day. Distant doors banging and a dog yapping.

Bethany Jane would rise before the boys, pad into the kitchen barefooted no matter the season, put the kettle on for tea, head back to her room. Bet would haul herself up, knowing damn well the girl would get involved staring in the mirror for zits or practising intimidating expressions or fall into a tizzy about what to wear, and make it down to the kitchen after the kettle had gone dry. After rescuing the kettle, Bet would stir the instant decaf into Clarence's mug and into her own and Bethany Jane would come along, wrinkle her nose at the jar of Maxwell House, make her Earl Grey tea. Then Bet would call the boys, holed up in the loft, she knew, like barely tamed animals or pack rats that you might find endearing if they had been with you long enough. Jerry and Jay were growing from the angled runts they had been a year ago into big, beefy boys. They had unruly, stick-up hair, Slovak hair she called it, after Clarence's mother's side of the family. The way Bet told the story, Clarence's grandmother was from Belgrade or some such place, worked in the Savoy Hotel that burned down in the Ruth fire of 1919. In the early days beds in the three-storey hotel were used in three shifts, eight hours each, and everybody had to rotate out so "the chinaman" could bring in clean sheets and towels. Jersey Harker, a member of the ragtag crew who drilled mines into mountainsides and cut every easy tree in order to build the first shanties, found her at the Savoy. The day he noticed her, she was hanging sheets on the line, a stolid, strong young woman; he knew a worker when he saw one. She was too young to know the difference between a good man and a weak one with high-minded intentions. Jersey Harker was a goofy-looking twit, stringy-necked and grubby. He resembled her Clarence in his younger days.

That morning she heaved herself out of bed reluctantly, dismayed that her bones ached despite the heat. Maybe, she thought, some of us aged young, something about the way our minds went at things, hardly giving us a break. She bent to massage her thick calves – fibrous they were these days, tough as chunks of wood – and wiggled her toes to get the kinks out.

In the kitchen, Bethany Jane poured tea. "I saw Auntie Nan yesterday," she said, dropping her little bomb.

Auntie Nan. To her daughter Bet said carefully, "Where did you see her?"

"She stopped in at the office to see Mrs. Malenko. Um, *Ms. Adrianna*, she wants to be called. I think they're friends." Bethany Jane was working at the retirement home that summer, organizing group sings and changing beds, saving money for school.

Bet no longer saw Auntie Nan, Nan Carmichael, which was hard to fathom in a way, the two of them having been friends since they were kids in school. Bethany Jane and the boys used to play with the Carmichael girls; the kids in the two families had grown up side by side. Bet felt a twinge of remorse, not about what had gone on two years before between her and the woman who had been her best friend, but more about her own attitude that, in retrospect, had been jampacked with moral rectitude. Her closeness to Nan was over so completely that it was as though Nan had moved to a foreign place where they didn't have phones, if there were such places any more.

"She's not a monster," Bethany Jane said.

"Oh, probably not." Bet opened the fridge and took out the bacon. While her friendship with Nan had ended, her relationship had not, odd as she thought that was. Thoughts of her old friend turned up, in the way Nan herself used to do, into everyday life.

"You should give up righteousness," said Bethany Jane, ever helpful. Bet threw a warning glower her way. She knew her girl didn't know the whole story; she'd pieced things together, Bet supposed, and got the essential part wrong, or so Bet believed. She never talked to Bethany Jane about it because some things weren't meant to be a child's business – what she had seen Larry Carmichael doing with Nan's oldest daughter, a girl not his own, Bethany Jane's age.

Bethany Jane's elbow brushed her mum's arm as she turned on the faucet to rinse her cup. Of slender build, Bethany Jane had a round, cute face, attributes she didn't inherit from her, as Bet would be the first to say. Bethany Jane went on, "It's only decent." She could be stubborn, and that trait, Bet thought, she did inherit.

She turned on the burner and pondered the idea of righteousness. Better than thou, she supposed that was an apt description of her own attitude of late. She hadn't been to church since the kids were baptized and routinely didn't answer the door when Jehovah's Witnesses knocked. Turning down the heat so the bacon would cook through, she thought that maybe righteousness and churchliness didn't necessarily go together.

"You're burning the bacon," Bethany Jane said, drinking a glass of hot water, part of her morning bowel health regimen. "You shouldn't be feeding that to the boys, anyway; bacon is full of nitrates and nitrites. It clogs arteries."

"Um." They always had bacon on Sunday; it was a family tradition. Bet figured she could afford to ignore the jibes, because Bethany Jane would be leaving for university soon enough and she would miss her. She poured the grease into the jar that stayed in the freezer until Clarence went to the dump; bears loved bacon grease as much as she did.

Clarence came moseying in, wanting another cup of coffee, followed by the boys. He sat at the head of the table, his long legs straddling the chair. The boys didn't bother with good morning, it would be too much to ask. Bet kept a fond eye on them. For a few minutes there was a racket, them pushing their chairs around. They both sat down. Then they both jumped up. For boys you had to threaten with a stick to get to do anything, they were always moving. In elementary school the teachers had called them busy. Now they'd switched to ADD – attention deficit disorder, some such thing. One of the teachers even said that her boys were "victims of ADD." Bet had laughed and was sorry afterwards. Better the teacher was on their side, whatever the reason.

"But we can make it from scratch," said Jerry, continuing a conversation started somewhere else. He snatched a strip of bacon from the paper towel.

"You can't be making a vertical broiler from scratch," said Jay, opening the fridge.

"Vertical broiler?" That was Bet, cracking eggs and wondering where the boys were in the most recent saga of their efforts to make enough money for the getaway from home. Their current plan was to drive around the country to fairs and the like, selling Greek fast food out of a truck. "Set the table," she said.

Plates clattered down from the cupboard. "Gy-ro truck," said

Clarence, shaking his head. A space showed between his front teeth when he smiled, which he was doing.

"*Euro* trailer," said Jay, correcting his dad's pronunciation. "The rig is called a trailer. G-y-r-o. Euro trailer. It's pronounced that way because it's Greek. That's foreign, Mum."

Bet thought she hadn't seen the twins so enthusiastic since they learned to aim in the bowl.

"Yeah, right. And the dude is paying us to fix it up." Jerry took a twenty-dollar bill out of his pocket to prove it, and then quickly stuffed it back as though his mum might nick it.

The "dude" was Eunice Sonemayer's nephew. Their neighbour Eunice had died, a very old lady, a few years ago. Her house was across the road and higher up the hill, with a view of the lake that you didn't get from Cedar Hideaway. It was a Victorian with roses and iris and poppies growing wild in the yard. Maurice, the nephew, had fixed it and sold it – some woman from Toronto paying more money for it than Bet thought it fair any one person should have – because he and his wife were based on the coast, near Richmond. They were food vendors who travelled around the country to fairs and exhibitions. Because the local grads had organized a fair with a real Ferris wheel and all the trimmings, the gyro truck had come to the celebration. Bet said, "Remind me again why he's willing to get rid of it?"

"Make sure to criticize everything, Mum," said Bethany Jane, slipping out of her chair and patting her mouth with a napkin. "I have to go. Going to be late."

"Yeah," said Jerry. "Don't wanna keep *the boyfriend* waiting."

The remark made Bet's ears perk up. "Where are you going?"

Bethany Jane was wearing a skimpy top that showed her belly and shorts. Her brown hair was long and straight and shiny. She turned back into the kitchen to give her mum a wide-eyed look, one of those mocking expressions Bet had noticed on half-hour comedy shows on TV. Like nothing is really serious. She said, "We're hanging out at Scott's Beach, Mum. Where else?"

"Put a long shirt over that top. Don't be walking around like that." Her voice might have sounded harsher than she intended. For some reason, something struck Bethany Jane as being funny. She laughed.

"Mum, listen," Jerry said, giving Bethany Jane a chance to skip out. The screen door slammed. "We can make megabucks." He was the one with what was called a lazy eye. It drifted when he concentrated, and sometimes Bet was grateful he wasn't much good at it. But now he had that look. "We'll sell a thousand a day. We'll go to the States, make American dollars, charge $7.50 a gyro. Do you know how much that is? In one day?"

Jay had a yellow-lined notepad and his school calculator out. "That's $7,500 a day, Mum, think about that. U.S. dollars. You know how you've always said somebody got to look after you –"

"– somebody *has* to look after you –"

"– right, right, in your old age?"

They looked across the table at each other, raised their palms for a high-five.

"Uh-huh," she said. "You don't even have your drivers' licences, am I right?" She could have bit her tongue. Initiative was initiative. Apparently the truck needed new hoses, new connectors, plumbing altogether, and if Maurice was paying the boys to help, she should be happy.

They finished and tore out of the kitchen – off to their job – leaving their plates on the table. Clarence always said she was too skeptical for anybody's good. "Twinkle in their eye," he said.

"Twinkle?"

His hand holding a plate paused. "Beg pardon?"

"You said twinkle. You said the boys had a twinkle in their eye. What's that supposed to mean?"

"Oh." He scraped the plate with a knife. "I did?"

For a second he seemed confused, then he gave her a wink, and continued rinsing the plates and stacking them.

He hadn't winked at her in years. Nor cleared and stacked for that matter. Her mind, however, wasn't on him, involved in replaying what Jerry had said. *Boyfriend? What boyfriend?*

So there it was, the secret that would reveal her to be a fool. Bet prided herself on ordinariness. She liked to think that nothing about her or her family was special – Bethany Jane did get a local scholarship for college, the first in Harker history, so Bet told everyone – but all in all, for years the family had given nobody reason to talk. No one gossiped about them that she'd heard about, and she probably would have heard. What they might have kept secret was out in the open: Clarence was a drinker, a quiet drinker. He was known to hang out at the Legion with others like him. Bethany Jane was their star – she on the school stage in June in a new lavender dress, Clarence mopping his brow, his way of showing emotion, so Bet joked. The twins, sixteen that summer, would always get by, and, as she said, with enough nagging they might turn out to be useful. She counted on her family's overall averageness the way some people counted on what they considered their uniqueness to separate them from the herd. Bet Harker considered herself to *be* the herd. Her modest ambitions kept her safe, she thought, from disappointment.

All season she'd been proud, and it was pride that took a swing and knocked her flat.

15

From the porch Lucinda watched Fred Worthy walking very slowly across the field, wearing, she knew, his favourite Scots cap. She could hear Mory mowing in the flat area above the house. Cottonwood puffs lazily floated in the air. She watched Fred pause, dab his nose with his handkerchief; everyone she'd talked to was having allergies this year. She listened to the sweet song of a yellow warbler as it made its rounds marking territory. It moved through the deciduous trees, the birch and alder, behind Fred, and flew past her to take its favourite perch on a branch of a tree in the old pear orchard and sing again. The robins in the field – they the most companionable of birds, she thought – seemed satisfied with things, feeding little ones, keeping an eye on you and flying erratically to the nest so you wouldn't know where their treasures were. Lucinda waved at Fred and he saw her and waved back. He reminded her of Fred MacMurray, the actor in old movies; he had the same pleasantly bemused expression and the gangly frame. Her upbringing had produced in her resistance to admonitions regarding behaviour, but Fred didn't make her hackles rise; they got along very well. He'd come to British Columbia after the Vietnam War, bringing aspects of his Tennessee childhood, the basic Christian injunctions, the physical hardship and the freedom with it – minus the rifles – to build his church. He believed his flock benefited from clear instruction.

"I apologize for my knee," he said when they were seated on the porch in their usual chairs. "I have been diligent in putting Bengay on it and taking Aspirin and it will flex but not easily bend. I will be unable to perform my duty as umpire of the slo-pitch game at the picnic." He was talking about their summer picnic. After years, some families still wouldn't come to the Centre for the food and the ball game – the hippie place, they said – but would go to the rummage sale and desserts at the church, on the adjoining land. Still, a few middle-aged women would take a dare and stop by the Centre and poke into the kitchen to inspect it for dirt and stashes of pot. ("That's what they think is going on in here anyway," she told Gabriel. "I'm thinking a few dried oregano leaves behind the breadbox would be fun for them to find." Gabriel, however, said it was cruel to mislead people.)

Fred tapped his knee. "A mistake in the design," he added. "I have spoken with our Maker on the matter, but please don't spread it around. Some would think it frivolous of me." He'd needed a walk and couldn't stay; he was on his way to see Alma. He'd heard that Lucinda had visited her. He said, " 'Her sun is gone down while it was yet day.' Jeremiah 15:9."

" 'The wife of thy bosom.' Deuteronomy. I think."

"Deuteronomy 13.6. And thank you."

Lucinda believed in turning points in life, that everything held together, interconnected and interdependent, based on the moment of a choice. She was thinking along these lines, about the love between Alma and Fred, when BB came running up, a cottage-cheese carton in his hands. "Look! Look! Worm, wormy, worm!" He had a drop of sweat moving down his forehead. His hair, as he leaned forward so Lucinda could see inside the carton, smelled of crushed peppermint and bedclothes. Lucinda saw a neat little pile of dirt upon which sat a lustrous fat earthworm.

"Nice worm, eh?" she said to Fred, expecting Fred, who was so good with children, to join in about what a fine worm it was. He wasn't paying attention. He was studying the child. Lucinda said, "BB, you should say hello to my guest."

"Like dancing?" BB said to the worm. Then he grinned at Lucinda and gambolled down the steps. She watched him a moment, as he broke into his uncoordinated run, holding the carton high, holding it carefully. She was thinking that Fred had grown much older over the winter, that he was less responsive, and because she made this judgment about him, she spoke kindly. "New arrivals – Mory Zimmerman, from the coast, here this summer. That's her boy, BB."

"Oh, I know. I didn't know that was his name. Oh, dear, forgive me."

Wariness rose in her. She took her time before speaking. "Yes?"

"Her name was Morla, originally. Marked resemblance. Indeed that is the child."

Within her body, between heart and belly, Lucinda detected a warning that she didn't want any more information. But of course she did; she was curious, she did want to know more and she was not smart enough to scatter off that porch and run away as fast as the wind. She was determined to put herself, detail by detail, through the whole story, and later, she would reflect that she was the type of person to spare herself no pain. The lawn mower choked and stopped. She had shown Mory how to uncap the sparkplug before reaching into the chute to remove wads of grass plugging it. She heard no cries for help.

"Oh, dear, I shouldn't have spoken," Fred said.

"That's all right," Lucinda said. Wishing to be another sort of person, one who interrupted, changed subjects.

"You don't recall the family? Up where the Silver and Enterprise come together?" He shaded his eyes with the palm of his hand and looked at the far mountains already cloaked in haze from the heat. "You really should know," he said gently. "Someone is bound to say something. At the picnic." A warm breeze ruffled the thatch of his too-long hair, and she watched it move, his hair the colour of lead pipe at the crown. "She – Mory – she's the *Zimmerman* girl. Surely you remember."

Wishing to be a person who would say goodbye for now and flee into bulrushes at the head of the lake, flow with a few female deer cooling off their rounded bellies, trot up the trail with them, into the high rock meadows where there might be early paintbrush or wild sunflowers or sweet mallow to nibble.

The lawn mower coughed to life again and then she was back, relieved that Mory was all right, relieved that she not been rude to Fred. A grey squirrel began protesting, and the air suddenly filled with the aroma of lilacs, as if the heat had liberated their fragrance. "You were here then," Fred murmured helpfully.

The man was dogged, Lucinda thought, and then – the story surfaced, despite her evasions. The older, reclusive parents. *Zimmerman*. She spoke: "Was the daughter mentally slow?"

"Yes. Smart in some ways, though."

Lucinda circled the information, approaching slowly. There had been a scandal, everyone talked about it privately, among themselves, because what had happened was too terrible. Then the knowledge broke through her resistance: Mory was the girl who had the baby. *The father.*

Fred said, "And may the Lord forgive me. I was aware of the family up there and didn't see it coming. You remember. The Populakis family helped her. Took her in and arranged for her to stay with their relatives near the coast. She'd come to them, you see. They had to bear the brunt of the father raging on their doorstep, but they held their ground. I believe they did the right thing. I didn't think that poor girl would set foot in this valley again."

They sat watching a robin bounce across the grass. Fred pushed his hat farther back and rose stiffly, with a little groan. Lucinda stood and they shook hands, oddly formal, as though they were sealing a pact. He patted her cheek and said, ruefully, "Welcome home." But it wasn't Fred that Lucinda was thinking about, nor was it Mory or her child. She didn't know exactly what was niggling at her. She felt heartsick.

She watched Fred from the porch until he was a dot at the far side of the field, her anxiety growing so rapidly that it felt like improperly swallowed food stuck in her throat. She heard Gabriel in the kitchen, the refrigerator door opening. Her instinct was to turn to him with all this news, but something held her back, some piece she had not put together.

Feelings loosening and bubbling in her chest, she ran toward the garden. She stumbled on an auntie rock – a trail marker – one she knew about, and she halted, out of breath, her toe throbbing, and then ran more, unable by the time she reached the tool shed to pinpoint what she was personally in such an uproar about, what she was so *enraged* about. She took the digging fork from its hook and swung through the gate into the garden. At the far end were some odd butternut/acorn cross that she hadn't got round to composting last year, nearly gourds now. She lifted the fork and hit the biggest faded orange one hard. She went along and split their heads, one, two, three. They were surprisingly mucky inside. She broke into the deeper dirt and flung dried out wads of roots to the side, all the time her thoughts racing.

The scandal at the Zimmermans had been around the valley. The girl, hardly a teenager, and the father – rumours and whispers, the collective shaking of heads. Who could say what had happened? But everyone tried to explain it. A girl that age might have had a secret boyfriend. Maybe the old man did it, eh, but he was drunk that one time. *Temptation is hard to resist*, she'd overheard a man say. *Way off up there, after all. The man is only human.*

A clod of dirt, caught on a tine, hit her in the face. Tears sprang to her eyes, but she thought she didn't deserve to cry, because she hadn't had the courage to rebut the disgusting remark when she'd heard it.

Nothing at the Zimmermans could be proven, anyway, and no one from the valley seemed to know what to do, not she herself or Gabriel. For some reason, they hadn't directly addressed it. What was the point? The girl left, and Oscar and Frieda Zimmerman disappeared under the radar. In the end, it seemed there was nothing to be done about a girl raised in the bush, living remotely, alone with her parents, a girl too naive to fathom predation. What other word for it?

Lucinda stood in the cavity of dirt and roots she'd ripped up and amongst the slaughtered pumpkins and wiped her fingers across her eyes and cheeks. The sun was so hot. *Predation.* Old men and their daughters, heaven preserve us, she thought. She knew from experience about old men and their daughters. She was an only child of an older couple – not molested, nothing like that – but she'd always known who it was that

Mother lived to please. Who ran the show. Whose life they really were living. From the time she was little, she had been taught. She had been *in training*.

She let go of the fork. It fell out of her hand and landed like a seesaw, one end striking the ground and bouncing and the other end landing with a quiver. For a second the digging fork seemed to have a life of its own – and then, overcome with fury again, she lunged for it, caught herself inanely grappling with the smooth, worn handle as though it were something live and struggling with her, aching for a fight. She dropped the handle, and it lay inert on the earth, conquered. She looked at it. No winning possible now. She had exhausted herself and could no longer crowd out the thoughts that were in her mind. She let herself go and in they came, the pictures. Blunt, crude, thinking in images about what went on in the Zimmerman cabin. She pictured a small, closed room, imagined where the father might be sitting, where the mother might be sitting, where the child might be sitting. A pretty little girl. She saw the three who might well have felt they were the last survivors in the world, moving around each other intimately, going through the day. Cooking, eating, pissing, shitting, cleaning, gardening, clearing. Always in the bush, clearing, keeping the forest back. Changing places among themselves, like dancers: now two in the kitchen doing dishes and now two there and now two – what went on between the father and his daughter too awful to think about. But she saw it. She took the fork back to the tool shed and hung the poor thing on its hook and started toward the house. There was so much to tell Gabriel.

Halfway, she lost her breath and had to stop. She had missed the essential point. The essential detail she'd missed was Gabriel. Gabriel had not confided in her, had not said so much as a word to her about Mory or the boy, though she had gone on about BB – saying he was "off" – developmentally challenged – all the right words – remarking, more than once, about what a strange child he was. Gabriel had kept his silence, withheld his confidence. He knew Mory and the child from the word go. *He had recognized the name.*

He was finishing a bowl of cereal, and he looked up, chewing, seemingly innocent of her approach, which she knew he was not; he had certainly felt the storm of her energy coming at him. He was behaving peaceably to calm her down. She knew him.

"Yes?" The expression was familiar, one with which she was intimate – he was waiting for her to get to the point. He put his spoon down. It clinked on the saucer.

"You knew about Mory, didn't you?" Her voice was more strident than she intended.

"Yes."

She hated it when he pulled that ingenuous trick of admitting the truth so easily. "Oh, for goodness sake," she said, lowering her voice into the proximate range of reasonableness. "Why didn't you tell me?"

He lifted the cloth napkin – it was red – and patted his mouth. He folded the napkin in half and then into half again. He studied her before he spoke. "What difference would it have made? She needed a place to stay. What would you recommend, that she go home, back up there?"

"I don't *recommend* anything around here. That isn't the issue. The issue is, you didn't tell me."

"Why do you care?"

"I care because I'm supposed to be – supposed to be –"

"– and you're good at it," he said. He smiled.

He wanted her to quit; he was trying to charm her; she knew his games. "Do you see? Do you see what you just did? Made light of the situation. I need to understand why you didn't confide in me about who Mory was. That's it. That's the issue."

"Do you now have a better idea about who Mory is?" He spread his fingers toward her, palm up, pulling a number, she thought, in her very own kitchen. Treating her like a client or *anyone*. She recognized the gesture for what it was – a technique. Part of the package of apparent artlessness, the package designed to assure you that he wouldn't moderate your feelings or judge the rationalizations you had marshalled in your defence.

Lucinda felt struck.

"Do you?" he said and she wasn't sure at that moment what he was talking about. Whether he was talking about Mory or if he'd picked up her feeling.

"You thought I couldn't handle it?" She snapped the hem of her skirt. Flecks of dirt fell onto the floor. She squinted at it, annoyed, and went on for an extra moment to stare at it, grateful in a way to have a break from the intensity of his eyes. She looked up. "You have to be everything to everybody, don't you, and I am just – well, what am I?" Suddenly her vision was blurry, and she couldn't see him. Instead, she saw BB – his odd eyes, his smallish head. "It's horrible, it's awful!"

"You see?"

She was rebuked by his gentle tone. He added, as though understanding what she hadn't said, "It's not his fault, Luce."

But Lucinda knew what Gabriel didn't. Mory and BB's story was no longer the point.

He told her only: "I have urgent business." He did not take her hands from the kitchen knife she was using and hold them while he told her that lie. She acted as though she didn't hear. She was busily chopping celery and didn't look up. She didn't follow his MG up to the airstrip, didn't watch him park it in the hangar, didn't watch him caress the flanks of the plane during the preflight walkaround, didn't watch while he forgot to lock the hangar as he always did. She did listen to the plane climbing overhead but did not search for, or expect, the dipped-wing greeting. She heard the sound of his disappearing in the southern sky. She took a breath and sent Mory and Milee over to the community hall to borrow the tables for the picnic, just as she would normally.

Then she was the hostess for the picnic and was glad there had been an early shower to freshen the air that was heavy with lilacs. She had to take an antihistamine, they were so strong. Mary was not there, up until dawn sewing the bright red slo-pitch shirts for Poppy's Convenience Boys, because that summer the team would be playing other teams throughout the valley. Young people living in the woods – the next generation of hippies – came for the first time, stayed separate, off near the creek, in a ragged, domestic circle, smoking their rolled cigarettes, playing music, mandolin and banjo, the girls in East Indian patterned skirts over black tights nursing round, half-naked babies, the young men tanned and dreadlocked. Among them would be the "woofers," willing young people from around the world who worked for room and board on organic farms, to learn the skills. Over there, off the porch, a couple of local loggers, in baseball caps, watched the barbecue, where, beneath the smoke, wieners and valley-made bratwurst sizzled. Fred Worthy, of course, was at the church seeing to the rummage sale and the rest of it. She put Milee in charge of "chicken shit bingo," the money collected going toward the new slo-pitch shirts. A little gang, including BB on the edge of their circle, waited for the caged Banty to make her move. The cardboard the little hen stood on was divided into numbered squares and if you'd bet on the square she chose, you won.

Lucinda watched the scene. More pickups were arriving with chairs and dogs and kids in the back. The event could have been idyllic – the sedges and bracken adding texture to the colourful field, the children running – except for the stone in her heart.

About his absence, she said the usual: "He had sudden busi-ness. You know how it is with that man." She said, "Someone having an emergency. You know how he is."

And she kept her mouth shut until they had gone home, and at the end of the day, her face was sore from all that smiling.

16

After his mum died in the spring, Milee Logan had taken over the big bedroom – hers, his mum's – in the long single-wide trailer, yet even with new yard-sale sheets on the bed the room wasn't restful and in it he couldn't relax. All summer he'd been trying for peace, yet his mother had not left him alone. The burden of her weighed on his back as though she were draped over him, her knotty fingers digging into his throat. Her clinging caused his Adam's apple to ache so that he could barely swallow. Despite his methodical cleaning, the trailer smelled of her, he could not eliminate the smell of her. After Pastor Worthy had said what he had to say at the cemetery in May – her properly buried – he had come home and scrubbed every surface and nook and cranny, erasing her powders, her creams, her smears of lipstick on the cupboard doors in the bathroom. Her hand had shaken toward the end; she dropped things. He had col-lected her knitting supplies – the unfinished orange and purple toques – and bagged them and put them in the shed. One last time she'd come home from the hospital. Held his arm trudg-ing slowly up the track. Stepped on the stones he'd embedded in the slope to help her reach the door. Winded, her breathing grew raspy and it went on and on and didn't stop being nerve-wrackingly noisy until it was all over. He'd done everything she expected of him, and more: ironed her blouses, ironed her sheets. Though in her last days she was a bag of bones and though he was very, very obedient, he stayed scared of her.

At Thanksgiving, he'd cooked a turkey, cut it into tiny bites for her loose teeth, mashed and mashed the potatoes; at Christmas he'd made a roast and soft biscuits. She told him that she was a bad mother, had almost bought him a tricycle from the Sears catalogue to make up for it. She said the words laughing, she was drinking rye whisky, she had minuscule snakes of red veins on her nose and her skin was jaundiced. You couldn't see the jaundice under all the makeup she slathered on, the line of her jaw always visible and the demarcation between the clown face and the ghastly skinny, pale, tendoned neck. He had helped her, dabbing the makeup onto her face with his handkerchiefs, having to boil them in vinegar and bleach to get the goo off, the goo as well as the unholy smell of her. Cirrhosis of the liver, the end quick.

To start the cleansing of his territory, he'd driven her mattress – sickening brown-edged stains reminders of his parents' careless drunken nights – to the dump. Sometimes someone was beyond the gate collecting money and sometimes they weren't. That day no one was, and the lock was gone again. You just had to pull the gate a bit to get the truck through, which he did. Back home, he dug the hole in the yard – the overgrown land between the trailer and the mountain – and hauled everything over to the pit, including her sheets that he'd shredded, sobbing, and splattered a little kerosene for good measure, struck the match. The moment the birch combusted – for one brief moment – he had experienced relief.

Afterwards, however, there'd been mistakes to ruminate over. The first mistake he made might have been looking into the hole and sniffing the unclean air. He should not have inhaled the air nor noticed the spiky heel of a shoe. He pretended he hadn't done either of those things, yet he sweated from more than heat while shovelling the dirt and roots and rocks over the baking pile. Then he'd gone inside, muscles burning. Had come inside and washed his hands, opened a few beer, chugged them back, tossed the caps onto the carpet, sprawled on the davenport, listened to his breathing. No one pointed at the beer caps. No one said, Pick them up. He waited, heart tense, the muscle along his chest wall quivering. He thought she would show up. When he looked out the smudged window behind the davenport, beyond the torn shade (the shade torn by her clawing hand trying to get his attention while he was reworking the stepping stones to suit her better), he saw the smoke wreathing around the trailer and didn't think twice – knew it was her ghost trying to get in. Believing it was possible for her to come after him from the grave – the mistake perhaps there, in that belief – had caused him to shove a different thought into his head: The dead do not come back. He said it out loud thirty-seven times and then lost count: "The dead do not come back."

Yet still he'd worried. He had not considered the roots he'd slashed through while digging the hole. The roots might be burning. Fire had a reputation: it could brood underground and strike overnight, turning the whole of the visible green world into fuel, nothing but fuel for fire. He went out, dug into the hole again, was halfway down when he did see smoke, a snakelike tendril working its tender way through the crush of her stuff, taking its time, following the whiff of air from above, moving through air pockets in the dirt, slowly growing in intensity. He ran the hose until the pit was a pool of blackened dirt, wet ash, mysterious, greasy substances floating to the surface. He left the water trickling. He went inside, opened another beer.

He had watched the clock, periodically glancing at the photograph of her beside a piano that hung on the wall above the space heater. The picture was taken during her lounge-singing days, as she described her "singing" career, though everyone knew the "lounge" was the old Ruth Pub, a place so beer-soaked his dad said you hardly needed a sip to get started, just breathe the air. He lay sprawled on the davenport for three hours, keeping an eye on the clock, unsure why. His stomach growled and he didn't move a muscle toward making a pot of spaghetti he could live on most of the week, which had been his plan when he left the cemetery, before Pastor Worthy had embarrassed him by grabbing him in a hug. Men didn't do that. He had struggled free and then began breathing too hard while the other part, the voice that wouldn't shut up, laughed at him for being such a dork. It used words like that, the other voice. He wasn't a dork. He got his hand out of his pocket in time, handed over the twenty dollars Estelee had loaned him to give to the pastor. She said that was the thing to do. It was just him and Estelee and Pastor Worthy, the three of them at the cemetery, and he had done all right, honoured her wishes to the end, the pastor told him so. He sat on the davenport and for three hours he did not feel better. His heart refused to feel eased. Maybe, the other voice suggested, she would leave in eight more hours. The voice said, Maybe the dead need you for just that long.

He had gone along with it, he'd had hopes.

The voice was lying.

After dark he'd crept back to the hole, wearing his gumboots – half the yard a slimy puddle, slick with mud, the hose still on – and placed his hands together as Pastor Worthy had done and he had prayed that she would stay away; he did not want to give kisses or bedtime pets any longer. He'd stood in the yard in the remnants of smoke, his heart beating like the rhythm of a running drum.

Mory was stirring the fire in the pit of the tepee when Milee got there. The smoke must have worked its way out to the night and he followed it in, smelling BB's hot dogs that she'd boiled.

He was skittery as an animal in a cage. She watched his shadow shifting on the canvas as he muttered to himself and moved toward her or away from her. Finally he said, "Up at the cabin there's grizzly tracks. Stacks, tracks, lacks." He stopped and pounded his palm with his fist. "Grizzly tracks, grizzly. Long nails, closer together than black bear tracks." He sat back on his heels.

She knew which cabin he meant.

He laughed. "I waited and what do you know? Patchy old bastard, went right for the bait. Left flank chewed. Not recent. Some old wound. Big sucker, hump like a dump truck." He cocked his head at her. A lock of his hair fell over one eye. He brushed it away. "I went right up to him and asked a question. About you."

"Bears don't talk," she said.

"Me and that old bear, we know things," he said, crossing two fingers and shaking them with emphasis. "So that old bear sure did talk. That old bear said your dad *kissed* you."

She looked across the tepee at BB asleep on his foamie. He was curled up with his back to them. "It happened," she said.

"It's disgusting. *That.*"

"It's not," she said. "You would like it."

"I hate him," Milee's other voice said. "He's despicable, he's depraved."

She had been noticing him taking peeks at her chest. She moved her body sideways, toward where he was crouched down. She said, "You can kiss me if you want to."

"Shit, no."

She put her finger against her lips.

He shifted so that he was a few inches farther from her.

"You want to."

"No." His face began to redden. "No. No kissing. Shit – no, no kissing."

"You like girls?"

"Sure, I like girls, you think I'm a wimp? I dated plenty of girls. Mum always wore nail polish and she had red lipstick. She said look for a fun girl like *her. But you like girls, you do want to kiss them –*" His tone had changed as he talked about kissing. Then in his normal voice he said, "I don't like them, I hate them, I hate titties. *Hooters. Yum, hooters.*"

He was talking to someone, Mory thought, that she had not met. Someone not yet in the tepee. She noticed that he was hard and trying not to be. She shook her head so that her hair flew around to get his attention. The movement startled him into quiet. "You could. It's okay with me."

She heard a groan.

"Everybody likes it," she said. "And BB is asleep."

She didn't hear his answer. She said, "I'm not supposed to. They said."

She undid a buckle of her overalls. The fire was between them and he turned his head to see her.

"Look here," she said.

She adjusted her clothes so that she held the tip of her breast on her palm and ran her fingers over the dark nipple, the length of BB's little finger when he was a baby. "Everybody likes it," she said.

He groaned again. "I hate your dad. He is a frickin' bastard." He sounded out of breath. Then again he said, "Ow."

She did not like clenched teeth and swear words. She didn't want to think about her papa, either. She tucked her breast away. "Now I know I won't. Too bad for you. You go now."

He made a growling sound and the flap of the tepee shivered when he left. She watched a lick of fire make dancing shadows. Despite the heat, her bones felt cold.

Some time passed. She heard crashing around in the bush outside and knew it was him and not a bear; a bear would have been quieter. The flap lifted and his head appeared. He said, "Knock, knock." He said, "I've been thinking. Please, just for a minute."

She'd moved BB onto her lap. He slept with his mouth open and breathy snores came from him. Mory noticed again the situation Milee was in and pointed to the cushion on the other side of the dying fire. "Go over there and lie down." She eased BB on to the blanket next to her knee, and when Milee was settled, she stood up. "Use a towel," she said and worked the clasp of her buckle loose again. This time she didn't hold the breast, she let it show itself. She let the overalls drop and pulled down her panties. She stood in the light there was.

"Don't look," he said.

She closed her eyes.

"Oh," he moaned and then she heard some other noises and, "Oh, Jesus," and then he was quiet.

She pulled up her underpants, tucked in her blouse, buckled the overalls, sat cross-legged again. She lifted BB back onto her lap. She thought that she and Milee could be friends now. She thought about her papa. He had tried to teach her music. They had a piano for a while, but he became fed up with it; he wanted to compose for the piano, but the piano didn't co-operate. Mummy had some problems during that time, the cabin was filled by the sound of vomiting and silences. Papa always played music, on cassette tapes or for real, violins and crashing cymbals, he tried to teach her, his sticky beard smelling bad in her neck. His waving arms made the music loud or quiet. She learned to carefully dust and polish the violin he never played and the cello that he did. He played the cello when the snow wouldn't stop, and there was the soupy smell of the cabin. She could smell Milee now, his sweat moving around inside the tepee. They put her in the root cellar when she was disobedient. It was supposed to improve her mind. She heard herself crying down there.

"I used you. I used you. Like everybody does. Because of *him*. I fucked you in the worst way, in my mind. More action than the real thing."

He was sitting up again.

"You did and you didn't," she said.

"Fuck, fuck, fuck. Um, juicy. You were juicy. That's the word."

BB stirred. She patted his head. She said to Milee, "I don't like bad talk. And you never were with anybody."

He blinked. She could see him reddening even from her distance. The fire made a little pop. After a minute, he said, "I pretended the whole time. I had it up. Nothing happened. I hoped it might work with you because you are so good at it," he said. He blurted, "I hated my mum."

"*No, you didn't,*" his other voice said.

Mory interrupted the beginning of Milee's conversation with himself. "You will have to leave now. I need to get some sleep."

"Was I talking to myself? Just now?"

"There's somebody else you talk to."

He frowned in thought. "Yes." His voice began to rise in excitement. "The other one knows everything. Is it a girl? Can you tell? Maybe I have my long eyelashes *for her*."

"Maybe another boy. But tell her she has to be quiet now. There's work to be done in the morning."

"I'm sorry. About, you know. Not being able to come."

"Men can't help trying. It means you are a real man."

"I'll wash the towel and bring it back. It might have drips on it."

"Thank you."

"Um, I tried once with a girl but I, um, couldn't do it. It was nice of you, though. Thank you. I get carried away and I don't know who wants what or who I am sometimes."

And Mory said, "My life is the same."

17

Lucinda walked into Gabriel's perfect bedroom. It was sparely furnished, in a Japanese style. He had a low-lying platform bed on which was a three-quarter mattress, the sheets specially ordered to fit the odd size, one perfect pillow in the centre in plum and a quilt in Japanese silk, the colour of plum blush, which shivered and slid like someone breathing if you were lying under it and restless. She started the search. Messages from a woman. New objects. Scraps of bills. A draft of a love letter. She lifted his meditation cushions and looked under them, and peered under a low, lacquered table upon which rested a bowl filled with sand from the western shore of the lake. A perfect, oval river rock was placed in the centre. She opened and closed each of the drawers in the ironwood desk that had belonged to his family. On the desk were pens and an Oriental brush holder and bottles of ink and sheets of rice paper, because he painted peonies and cherry blossoms and bamboo, the leaves like the evanescence of fireworks restrained upon the page, the joints of the bamboo requiring deft, double flicks of the brush. He painted as a form of meditation. When he finished, he folded the paper and tucked it into a small wastebasket on a lacquered stand. But there was nothing in the small wastebasket either. The room, in fact, was cool and withdrawn, as though he hadn't been in it for a long time.

Slipping off her shoes, she padded across and settled onto the bed, sank into it, her nose in his pillow rooting for the smell of hair and skin, sweat and bleach. The leftover scent was patchouli. She thought of his body, she was obsessed by the fineness of his body, its wonderful smell. She used to kiss the perspiration on his forehead and the beads broke against her lips. Outside the wind started, a blowy wind, and a bundle of bothered branches brushed against the window. She always liked wind in the valley, the way it cleared the clouds from their entanglement with the mountains.

Lying on her side, she ran her hand over the outside of her thigh, along the bone and the skin and muscle sagging toward the mattress, the thickness of the thigh bone that held on to the soft flesh prompting her to picture her whole body when she was very old, its slackened tissue loosening from the bone liked well-done chicken meat. She ran her palm along the edge of her hip and thigh, pressed the bone, pinched the flesh. Even back then, he'd had one crease on his little Buddha belly. When they first met, he said, "You live in your body like a guest." The introductions weren't completed and he knew so much about her; she'd been amazed. She touched two fingers to her breasts, caressed her nipples, ran her hand down her belly to her pubic hair, searched into the vulva and its sleek, eager folds. Gabriel's cock was silky and smelled sweet, his balls tidy bundles she nibbled and played with fitting into her mouth. His hairs were fine, his whole body smelled better than honey cake. She knew the shape of him inside her, how his cock thrusted, how she opened. She loved his penis more than anyone's. Afterwards, she rolled off herself, her mouth dry.

The phone rang and she answered.

"We're in the motel," he said. He meant the one in Sandpoint, Idaho.

So he was in *their* motel, the cheap one on the strip outside the city. Sheets limp with repeated washings, and the TV with only four channels, despite the HBO sign out front. Oldies stations on the radio.

"Luce?"

"Not now." Not that name now. He had taken that woman *there*. They'd had fun there, good sex. Peace and privacy.

"Other factors are in play."

Factors? She started back-pedalling. "Did you take two rooms?"

"Excuse me?"

"Oh, never mind. Idaho won't like the motel. It's not very nice."

"What? I thought you liked it." He sounded truly concerned.

"I do, I do." The habit of reassurance rising naturally. Rose patterns on the bedspread, snagged all over as though there'd been cats.

"I need to tell you some things. I couldn't leave her on her own, Luce. The husband's kicked her out. He's a brute, a monster. She's an emotional mess. There's *an unborn infant* to consider. Is anyone on the kitchen extension? Can you talk?"

The pillows, those awful ones, compact and flattened, but four more stored on the top shelf of the pocket-door closet as compensation. "Why don't you take women to nicer places? There's that lovely renovated hotel downtown that has the cool bar." *Infant?*

His tongue clicked against his teeth. "Lucinda. It's unbelievable," he said. "Unbelievable."

What could be unbelievable? Then her mind quit the inventory and began reeling. *Oh, for God's sake. It's his.*

Of course, in a Murphy's Law sort of way, the carpet layers she'd been expecting arrived. She heard banging on the door. He said, "This isn't a good time, I guess," and then he said goodbye and hung up.

After the carpet layers had gone, she vacuumed the Berber and put the foamies and pillows back in the loft and swept the whole downstairs, every nook and cranny, leaving not so much as a shred of the old carpet they'd dragged out or a particle of visible dust. She fired up the old heavy upright vacuum from the hall closet and became lost in its deafening roar, her hand vibrating. She vacuumed and vacuumed. She snagged fringe from a throw rug and the odour of burned rubber stank up the room. Let the whole house go up in smoke, she said to herself, then whiffed burned rubber mixed with fried wire. She happened to glance down the hall toward the kitchen. The threshold was lit by a stream of sunlight. The sight was beautiful, should have been heartening, she wanted to cry but didn't.

The hangar for Gabriel's Skyhawk was the size of a big garage, and it was warm inside, like an oven, and had an industrious aroma of oil and gas, with an underlay of dry dirt. The sheen of tools on his pegboards appeared as her eyes adjusted. The tools were mostly new and mostly unused; the right tool a handyman did not make, she used to tease, though he did keep his toys – the plane, the 1973 MG – clean and polished. She opened the car door and slipped inside. The bucket seat exuded complex aromas of fine leather and held her snugly, on the firm side, an English approach to the rump. The red leather seat was cracked where his right thigh rested against the ridge, the stitching along it cream-coloured. The instrument panel was similar to the one in the plane, old-fashioned and straightforward, round gauges, black background. She placed her hand on the gear shift. The ball of leather fit her palm. She sat in the angled position he sat in, his left elbow on the shoulder of the door, his right hand on the gear.

She felt saddened, as though her heart would rend, split asunder. She had loved this place, the steady presence of the peaceable mountains, she had loved the dramatic weather, the always-changing sky; she had loved the land thoroughly and well. And she knew him, and her knowing him so deeply and so well should count for something. Her nose tingled as though it wanted to cry on its own. The orifices in her head watered, yet emotion was blocked: she could not let herself go.

He likes us tall so that we have to stoop to pay attention. Let him never come back.

Oh, she did not mean it – such blasphemy! – though for one second she saw his plane losing altitude, vanishing into ether or cloud. Oh, she didn't mean it, she did not.

She stepped out of the car, closed the door carefully, walked out of the hangar, and locked it. She moved into the sunlight, into the midst of spaciousness granted by the widening of the valley, a small figure on an airstrip in the middle of nowhere and everywhere, in the very centre of who she thought she was and would always be. In the suburbs of Houston and the ranchos outside San Diego, she'd say to those gathered that it was the shape-shifting of the mountains at home that she missed. They seemed willing to understand shape-shifting – Gabriel's groups foresaw shamanistic-style outcomes – and the changing contours were part of it. A mountain you had been regarding for years one day changed shape because of light, the exact angle of a particular ray revealing a new bump, a hollow, an avalanche chute unseen before. You didn't know what your eyes would see when next you looked upwards. But really, sometimes what she missed when they went south to those open, hot lands were trips to the dump. From where she stood, she could see the dump road, a curve of it disappearing into the bush. Sometimes she would have to honk to get a bear out of the pit so she could empty the back of the pickup. She valued the respect between her and the bears, a black bear, say – a yearling – as they both went about their business, at a distance that was judicious as well as considerate.

It was lost. The land, the place, the man.

If she could beat that woman from Idaho to a pulp and chew the gristle and spit it out wad by wad, she would – the whole lovely length of her, so grateful, so trapped, so willing. About her, they had said – she and Gabriel – they had said that Idaho was out of the woods – "thou hast touched me and I have been translated into thy peace." Out of the woods, they'd said. Meaning she couldn't be wholly bad. Meaning that most humans were not found in a clearing.

Except that she herself was in a clearing, in the vacant strip of gravel and dust, the place where the plane should be. She took a step – kick kick touch turn turn – and raising her arms, she danced across the dirt, flung up her skirt, and bowed to the sky gods. She pointed her foot and posed. She inhaled, stretched her arms and legs, pulled her leaden centre out of its rib cage, breathed out, held the pose, muscles straining, little finger arched the way she was taught in toddler ballet. She held the position. Waiting. Sweat and sudden heat, water from her scalp dribbled onto her forehead and down the base of her neck. She felt so sorry for herself that she had to laugh and then she vanished, for a while, flew to pieces.

She found her grandmother's Bible in a storage box and sat in the fireplace room reading it. She read the whole day. She saw herself as dead: "The harvest is past, the summer is ended, and we are not saved." Jeremiah 8:20. She listened for the sound of his plane, feeling dread, the Centre about to be invaded. She became involved in paperwork – digging out the original agreement, in which she'd signed away her right to anything he'd had before he met her, and it included the land but not the Centre itself or her right to half of what they had created together. How that might work, she couldn't fathom; the Centre was Gabriel. The phone rang and rang but she didn't answer it. And then one time she did.

He said, "She's emotionally unstable."

Lucinda groped for words, came up with none.

"Are you there? Can you hear me?"

"Yes. Of course."

He sighed, as though comforted, and her heart, that loyal beast, went out to him. He said, "He's hurt her and she's not doing well. She's been in hospital. There's a restraining order. It's messy, Lucinda."

"What do you want?"

"I need your help," he said.

And she thought, Yes, of course he needs my help.

They hovered liked kites over a field, and then Idaho said something in the background and Lucinda eased the phone down on its cradle.

The night was hot and smoky. Lucinda stood in the dark kitchen peering through windows that might at one time have been Nell Sonemayer's, windows that she had found under a veranda of an old house in Ruth. It had been a yard-sale Saturday, during the period when she was collecting things. She had found a few torn pages from what might have been a diary, tucked under one mildewed edge of the window frame, a little of the past disappearing into the soil of the present, most of the words smeared beyond recognition. *Among those dead of typhoid was Sarah Linn Sonemayer, aged two months.*

Outside, BB was whirling on the grass, the gibbous moon sliced into golden sections because of the trees. *The moon making him crazy.* Most of the Centre's clients believed that the moon had powers – or they wanted to believe it did – the stars too, and birth order and blood type, and numerology and thrown bamboo sticks and tarot cards. In this situation, watching a bare-legged boy dancing in the hot night, they would say to themselves: The phase of the moon.

Mory was stretched out on the picnic table on her back, her legs swinging. She was wearing a short-sleeved T-shirt, arms spread wide. Her breasts had slipped toward her armpits, as though they were taking a break from each other. The moon cast its light precisely upon the centre of her chest. The space between Mory's ribs glowed a delicate teal colour. Close up she smelled salty and buttery and spicy, like a fresh-cut weed.

Lucinda left a jacket on the table in case either of them got cold and went into the living room and pulled out two of the massage tables from the storage closet and set them up. She lay on one and stared at a patch of ceiling and then lay on another and stared there. The ceiling in places had cobwebs and it was all she could do not to jump up and get a dust mop to deal with them. She pictured Idaho distraught, and it was easy to picture her distraught, troubled, upset. She might be the type of woman who was always distraught, who thrived on it, a statement that might be unfair. Lucinda wasn't in the mood for fair. She couldn't imagine Idaho in her kitchen, sitting at the table. Nor could she imagine the three of them together in the house, the two of them across the table from her, yet if they showed up, she would have steaming soup ready, she knew herself to be like that. She needed distance.

She slipped off the table and landed on her feet. She took off her shirt and batted at the cobweb and got it. In the office she went on-line and found the phone number for the motel. She went into his bedroom and sat on his bed and called from there. It was easy to get their room number; she said she was his sister. She felt clear; for a long time she'd been expecting Idaho – her coming belonged to the natural order of things. He answered, and Lucinda said, "Don't bring her here. Don't you dare bring her here." Then she hung up.

18

Lenore was heading north, having told Larry and Nan that she'd had a calling to go to the Centre for Light Awareness, to see a man named Gabriel. It was urgent that she get out of their house, taking with her the shreds of pride she had remaining. The girls,

Nan and Larry's three younger girls, had come home from summer camp, trooping through the basement lugging their gear, complaining of mosquito bites. Soon Nan had the three bathrooms full of bathing girls and the washer and dryer ran for six hours. Then she'd accelerated into overdrive and started worrying about Tilex. Lenore was to wipe the shower stall in the downstairs bathroom with Tilex every time she used it and dry it with a soft rag. Nan said to her, "Now that the girls are home safe, I have been worrying about those tiles and hoped you, too, are giving them a thought, but I see you haven't, and that" – rolling her eyes heavenward – "is disappointing. I might have to do a little *reconsidering* myself." She was referring to the tea set again.

Lenore took her cue: Exit, stage left.

And going to the Centre for Light Awareness was a calling in a way; she had called the Centre and a woman answered and listened to Lenore blathering – Lenore saw herself as having descended to a deeper level of distraction, that of babbler and food-hoarder – and then the woman said, abruptly, "Can you cook?" and Lenore replied (thinking of her cookbooks and recipes and the chef-quality knives that she'd stolen from Jack), "You're darn right I can cook!" She told Nan and Larry, however, that the calling had come in the form of a dream and they would know, naturally, how powerful dreams could be (though secretly she didn't think they were the sort of people to have dreams). She said to them, "I might be able to help. Stranger things have happened." Larry laughed, a mean sort of snicker, Lenore thought, and Nan did her usual, of late, which was to look tired and dismissive at the same time. Just as well she'd not told the truth, in case she didn't get the job as cook, a distinct possibility given her recent run of bad luck. Driving, she was preoccupied with ransacking her memory for vegetarian recipes, it dawning on her that she was more of a specialist in the cooking of meat.

She drove past an osprey nest on a piling, the long-winged bird cruising in circles above it. She turned to glance at the nest, which was a mistake, she realized instantly, for in the next moment, turning her attention back to the road, she glimpsed something darting across and she pounded the brake and the car slid and once again she came to a standstill in the wrong place. She practically cried out, "Am I trapped in a bloody time warp?" This time the Honda was angled sideways, nose toward the cliff edge; over the hood Lenore saw only sky and water, not a calming view. She huffed and puffed with exasperation. She knew the local stories, cars flying off the road, landing in trees, the drivers mangled; cars slipping over the edge, drivers drowned.

It had been a fox – bushy tail, pointed nose – reddish in colour.

She heard tapping. Someone wearing a ring was pecking at the glass and calling.

"Oh!" Lenore said. She rolled down her window. "I've been lost in thought. I'm – I saw a fox!"

"You have to get off the road," the woman said. She had a very big nose, and Lenore could not help but look at it. "Yes, I know," the woman said, acknowledging Lenore's stare, "but if a logging truck came over that rise, you would be toast. I almost hit you myself."

"I'm going to Neon Bar!" Lenore was speaking too loudly, she knew.

"It's Neon Bar or bust on this road. Put on the brake. Does your emergency brake work? Open the door slowly, step out, don't slam the door."

Once again, she was saved by an expert.

The woman eased carefully into the driver's seat, leaving the door open, and edged backwards, then gave the wheel a firm yank and drove to a shoulder where there was a van that must have been hers.

"My name is Estelee Chapman. I am Neon Bar's answer to FedEx."

"Oh, well, I'm Lenore Carmichael and I'm having an emotional breakdown, I think, in general I think I am."

"You're going to the Centre, aren't you?"

"Yes!" Lenore said. "How did you know?"

"Some things are just as obvious as the nose on my face, eh?"

Lenore could tell a false "eh" over the real Canadian sentence-finisher. "You're not Canadian," she said.

"Montana. But I try. Oh, by the way, Fox is a good sign. They like that sort of thinking at the Centre."

Lenore was thrilled. She felt like she already belonged. "A sign of what?"

"They're wily and clever. Know when to be seen. Or not."

"Oh, that's me," Lenore said. "Me to a *t*!"

Lenore was wearing the new pink jacket and the leopard pants. The woman glanced down at Lenore's outfit and smiled, and the lump on the end of her nose looked even bigger, and that sight made Lenore feel better. She had met someone, she thought, who understood a certain kind of suffering.

She followed the *E. Chapman, Unlimited* van all the way through Neon Bar to the gate of the Centre, where, after waving goodbye, she drove in and parked under a Lombardy poplar and, there, lost her nerve.

The place was more rustic than she'd assumed, having built an image in her mind of an architectural testament that you might see in the pages of a glossy magazine; she'd assumed, also, that the grounds would be manicured in order to be soothing to the overheated brains and wandering souls who gathered at a place promising, by its very name, to bring enlightened awareness. She could see one end of a house – big, rambling, a little off balance, as though it had been added on to – *where was an architect when you needed one?* – and a sloping field spiked with bare dandelion heads and spent lilacs, some of the bushes as big as trees, and bracken marching everywhere. Even horses wouldn't eat bracken, Lenore knew. She began preparing herself for the interview: "No, I will not use baby bracken in the cooking. Baby bracken aren't the same as fiddlehead ferns and are poisonous."

Her mind was dithering. She sat in the car, thought consoling thoughts: Be still. Shut up now. She noticed the other cars parked near hers. A mini-van, a beat-up pickup, a BMW that was mud-splattered, a Land Rover. The first two she expected – country people had lots of things to haul – but found the second two intimidating. Their owners could be in there, meditating, cellphones off. But, on the other hand, they might be hungry. She reached under the seat, unrolled the towel, found the spatula, thought of it as her sword.

She worked her way through the dry grass to the house and rang the cowbell hanging from a hook beside the door. "Hello, hello, toodle-oo, anybody home?" All around her lay forest and possibly deer ticks and certainly mosquitoes. A wind came up, hot against her face.

An interior door opened and a woman spoke from behind the screen. "May I help you?" Lenore stepped back to get a better look. Tall, willowy, auburn hair pulled back. One of those intimidating women.

Lenore said, "I'm here."

"You've come to see Gabriel?"

"I could use his help, I suppose," said Lenore. "Things have not been great lately. I – I'm divorcing my husband. I think I'm going to be forced into it."

"I'm sorry to hear that. But the man you've come to see, Gabriel, isn't here. It's better for us if people make an appointment, as you can appreciate. Gabriel isn't here just now."

"I do have an appointment, of a sort. All the signs have led me to him. Just now I saw a fox on the road."

"Yes, Fox is informative."

"The person who helped me said you'd understand. She said I was needed."

"Estelee said you were needed?"

"I might have invented that part," said Lenore. "Lying seems to be second nature these days. But I did see a fox, and, um, Estelee said it meant something. And, as you see, I have this spatula," she continued, "and I am applying for the position of cook."

"Well. Well, Fox, yes. Fox is excellent." She opened the screen and came onto the porch. "I'm Lucinda. People know me as Lucinda Markovice. Gabriel's name." The hand that took Lenore's was firm and strong, slightly dry and used to work. The woman wasn't as young as Lenore had assumed. The corners of her mouth had deep, downward creases, and she was dressed in an unflattering, long hippie-style skirt and a vest. She said, "I just had the idea about a cook the moment you called. I've had things on my mind. But it's propitious that you're here. We must welcome whatever is given. It's our unwritten policy. Gabriel has many unwritten policies. He's away."

Lucinda sounded annoyed or angry or pissed off, Lenore couldn't decide which, and Lenore herself was bewildered and disappointed – where was the healer she so desperately needed? – and also tired. She excused herself and eased into the rocking chair on the porch. "Do you have anything bubbling on the stove? I'm famished."

"I'm getting ready for the rush," Lucinda said. She gave Lenore a look that Lenore interpreted as assessment – would she be able to help, was she the sort of person who could get things done?

"I can cook when I'm not starving."

"Oh, yes." Lucinda went inside and after some noise from the kitchen – a kettle clanging on the stove – came back carrying a small teapot, a jar of honey, a spoon, and a stack of Oreo cookies on a tray. She placed the tray on the table beside Lenore.

Lenore pointed to the Oreos. "They're not as yummers as they used to be, eh? But thank you anyway. I'm ravenous." She moved fast and crammed a cookie into her mouth before she thought of anything else inane to say.

"Are you any good in the garden?"

Lenore glanced up from pouring her tea, cookie crumbs escaping from the corners of her mouth into her lap. "No," she said, crunching. "I never want to have a garden again." She was recalling how thoroughly she'd tried to entertain herself while Jack was hiking and kayaking. So many seasons her garden was pummelled by weather or burned out from the sun as fierce as the rain, tormented by wind ripping the hardiest squash blossoms off their stems. "No," she said again.

"Do you use herbs in your cooking?"

"I can. Sure. Bring 'em on," Lenore said.

"Oh, dear." Lucinda went inside, the screen door banging shut behind her. "Oh, I should fix that," she said. Lenore licked the inside of an Oreo, the white part, that, in her opinion, consisted of more shortening than cream these days. "Too bad," she said to a black cat that had appeared from under the porch. "You wouldn't have liked it anyway."

Where would she stay if she couldn't stay here? From the house came silence. She hoped something would happen, anything. It didn't matter what at this point, so long as she had a place to sleep that was not a motel room with particles of strangers' dead skin flaked onto everything. The idea of staying in that motel again – meaning she was heading back to the coast – made her woozy. Something had to open to let her in. She couldn't tolerate being alone in the Judith Lake Valley much longer.

Her stomach was rumbling. She was enormously hungry, so hungry it felt like starving, despite the cookies. What if Lucinda had gone out another door? What if the sun set and there was still no sound from the house and she was still outside waiting?

A flock of pine siskins began scolding and sissing, somewhere high in the trees.

She stood up, careful of the tray, and opened the door with one hand and her elbow and went inside. She manoeuvred through the mudroom and into the kitchen and there she heard crying, and she could hardly believe it. The crying was real, the woman was quietly crying. She was leaning against the refrigerator, her hand over her face.

Lenore set the tray on the counter. She let the cup and spoon rattle. She said, "I really can cook."

"Frankly, I don't know what to tell you," Lucinda said. "Everything is so up in the air." She laughed ruefully. "Literally. You have no idea."

"No, I don't," Lenore said. "But have you got anything to eat in that big refrigerator? You look like you could use a bite yourself."

Lucinda stepped away from the refrigerator and went on with what she'd apparently been doing when Lenore arrived. She began sweeping. Lenore, meanwhile, had her head in the refrigerator. There was leftover potato salad. She pulled back the tops of two of the containers and sniffed. Dubious. This woman did need help. There were eggs, however, and eggs lasted forever so she had the beginnings of an omelet. She found a green pepper, not too far gone, and an onion. She turned to Lucinda. "Have you got any tarragon or parmesan? Not the packaged kind, freshly grated is what we need."

The sweeping ceased. "All in heaven, preserve us. I can't be thinking about tarragon and cheese! Here's the situation: He took the plane and left." She stared into the refrigerator, over Lenore's head. "He just took the plane and left."

"He has a plane?"

"Oh, for God's sake," said Lucinda. "You don't know him. He has a plane, he has cars. Women after him, everything." The broom clattered onto the floor as she ran from the kitchen.

Lenore located butter in the freezer in the mudroom – enough butter to last forever, she thought, gluttonously pleased. A door somewhere in the house slammed, a car started up, and when the sound vanished down the road, she was aware of being alone in the silence of the kitchen. The black cat shoved its face through the partly open door. "Do you have a name?" The cat scuttled through the kitchen and hid under the table. Lenore said, "Why is everybody always leaving me?"

Down the hill somewhere the sound of an axe. On the lake, the buzz of a motorboat. Other people knowing what they were doing.

"I hate people and their secrets," Lenore said to the cat.

19

When Clarence disappeared as he usually did after breakfast, Bet Harker did what she had begun doing lately, which was to rush through the necessary chores and drive down to the beach to spy on the young people, always on the lookout for Bethany Jane. She lurked behind the rows of spindly shrubs out of sight, and swung her gaze from one end of Scott's Beach to the other. Near the point, the young mothers with little kids were parked for the day, and teenagers were clumped at the other end, near the creek. She watched a raven work the beach, listened to the kids shouting across the water to each other as they paddled around, close enough to the mothers to hear them laughing, wondering if Oliver, the blond lab, was trying to drown his owner or save her. Dolly's daughter, Colleen, was among them, lying on her back, her hands on her mound. They were a picture – the five women, girls really, nine kids, two umbrellas, one dog, fluorescent-coloured noodles and tubes, the babies in pale pink hats.

She moved along the trail toward the creek, keeping a safe distance. But among the young people splashing each other or lying around baking or smoking cigarettes, not one was Bethany Jane. Of course, there were other beaches, and other places, kids could go to, woodsy and pebbly, not so exposed, on the other side of the bridge. She drove across the bridge and then pulled over to reconsider, not believing she would be able to find Bethany Jane or wanting to. She tapped a finger on the steering wheel. She decided to make a Greek dinner, the Greekest dinner she could pull off, to compensate for her lack of enthusiasm about the gyro project. The only way to keep kids on your side, she'd learned, was to play into their hand. And the way to do that was by falling into their various traps. The boys had tasted the cucumber goop, the stuff you put on the meat and wrapped into the pita, only once and that was at the grad fair, when Maurice's Greek fast food had been an attraction. Bethany Jane had since investigated the sauce, visiting Maurice at Eunice's and going on-line, and found out that the commercial brand was loaded with monosodium glutamate, which she was against. She was against most additives, period. Food colours. Sodium something-or-other. The pita bread itself barely passed her inspection. *Organic* was a big word around the house.

She went home and finished the laundry, sprayed a set of sheets with Niagara starch and folded them, and ran a rolling pin along the creases, a useful trick. She made the bed in the cabin where, if she was lucky, a couple would show up to keep their reservation, smoke haze or no haze. Her plan was to make a batch of cucumber sauce – tzatziki – yogurt and cucumbers, anyway – and put it in a gallon jug to see how long a jug of it would last in the fridge. She knew she was stooping low: using the recipe from Bethany Jane's *Broccoli Forest* cookbook because she hoped Bethany Jane would be pleasantly caught off guard; she wanted the girl to confide in her. Bet didn't want her to be on a woodsy beach. Or in the woods. Or in a boy's deserted house, his parents away. Or worse – with an older boy, a man, a person with an obvious kind of experience.

She set out for the new health food store, to do what she could. She'd been only once before, with Dolly; they joked that they were going for the free rice crackers. She parked and went inside, thinking organic for Bethany Jane, quantity for the boys. Her plan was to prepare shish-kebabs that could be drenched in sauce and barbecued. The shish-kebabs weren't *real*, the boys would groan, but as good as they were going to get.

She crossed the bridge to the newer part of town, called by a real estate office "Water's Edge" – basically a tourist theme park, Bet thought – fake antique lampposts and a little filigree here and there. The turn-of-the-century assayer's office – a small house bought from Joe Dicolakis, him buying rounds in the Legion, grinning ear to ear, so Clarence said – was painted a rosy white with salmon trim. It sat beside a pub calling itself a saloon. The saloon was blue-grey with tan trim. Then there was an insurance office, and their colours leaned toward lavender. Too bad, she thought, she didn't own stock in paint. The store, called WildFoods, was a chain in from Calgary. Developers had a way of taking something real and making it appear fake, which she guessed everybody liked these days, there being so much of it.

The vegetables were organic and cost the world, she saw, higher per pound than meat, adding and subtracting in her head, and the bottom line of the cucumber project didn't look promising. Organic yogurt was through the roof. She wandered a bit. Didn't recognize half the stuff in the freezer section: brownish lumps – tempeh – tofu of various textures, meatless enchiladas. In the vitamin section, she passed a few bright-eyed young people talking about protein powders and carbs. The display of vitamins in the Wild label, white and red and blue, were supposedly discounted. She squinted at the vitamin C, turned the bottle over, stared at the price. Perhaps what she was seeing was the date, but no. A young woman with streaks of blue in her hair and a nose ring bounced up. "Can I help you with anything?" She scanned Bet up and down, and then she smiled. "We have these really cool weight-loss products now, no phen-fen. They work like for real, my mum is totally into it."

"Oh," Bet said. "Well, perhaps some other time. I'm in a bit of a rush." Who were these new people? She had no idea what the girl's name was or who she was related to. Swerving into the sundries aisle, she nearly bumped into another shopper. "Oh, sorry," she said, pulling her cart back. The woman had on sunglasses with rhinestones and wore a dress with huge orange sunflowers bursting out over it.

"It's cool. No problem." The woman's hand fluttered up to her hair as though she had enough to tidy – Bet thought it was a bit sparse – and then her head began tilting from side to side as though she was the Queen of Ruth riding on her float at a FallFest parade. She apologized: "It's the drugs that make me move like this. They have these lovely drugs up at the Frances Hill. I need them. Without them, I imagine past lives and children I never had, but it turns out I was right. I did have one child. They took him from me." She peered into the middle distance. "I'm doing it again. This incessant chattering. Do you know the Frances Hill?"

Bet looked again at the woman, so different from anyone else in town. This was Maryrose Malenko, related to Boris in some way – a sister, a sister-in-law, someone too young to be legitimately staying at a retirement home. Probably rent-free. Boris Malenko was an asshole of the first water on Bet Harker's list. And she didn't use the A-word lightly.

"Yakov's mother," Maryrose said. "Yakov Malenko." The name didn't ring a bell. "I was right, yes I was," she went on. "They tried to convince me that he was dead, but it turns out he wasn't." She leaned closer. Her breath hinted of menthol cigarettes. "Drugs are a good thing." Her eyes were very blue and way too steady for comfort, Bet thought, and she nodded quickly and picked up some organic shampoo in a bright green bottle and put it down, picked up a conditioner, frowned, put it down, and began moving steadily along, picking up speed as she neared the door, waved at the blue-haired clerk, made gestures that were meaningless, walked out with nothing in hand. Maybe they'd think she left her purse in the car, maybe she remembered an appointment, maybe the forgetfulness of advanced middle age was setting in. Then she sat in the truck and caught her breath. Maryrose Malenko came out of the store also and stood on the sidewalk, glancing fretfully up and down the street. Bet hunkered low.

She considered going back in and buying the cucumbers, but instead put the truck in gear and went over to the IGA and bought a box of sprayed specials from California at half the price. Home, she hauled in the groceries, one bag and box at a time, slid them onto the counter beside the sink. Clarence was sitting at the table, fixing his suspenders with pliers. He didn't get up to help; with the exception of the dishes on rare occasions he wasn't that kind of man. When the rest was in, on the floor beside the dishwasher that someday she hoped might resurrect itself from a slumbering state of disrepair, she asked him, "You ever hear Bethany Jane mention somebody named Yakov?"

She began washing the cucumbers. While waiting for his answer, she reviewed the state of affairs at Cedar Hideaway. They were secluded but not isolated, which in her opinion was what most people liked about the place. They had four families in the cabins, including three middle-aged couples. The RV hookup wasn't popular; no cable, no lake view, but there were two sets of older folks camped side by side playing a lot of cards. This was making for a quiet, dependable July. Clarence didn't seem to have heard the question, so she asked it again, louder. He gave her a look as though he was as daft as the woman in the sunflower dress. Clarence was never a great talker, so she let it go. He went back to his pliers.

"Yakov, eh?" he said after a bit. "Yuh, heard of the kid. Working at the Zoo."

For a while Sam and Marge over at the Zoo Café had their ambitions, hoping the Germans would come, or when that didn't pan out, the Japanese would come, some foreign group to build fancy chateaus and ski lifts in the neighbourhood. Naturally she was sorry about Sam's diabetes, but had always thought those two didn't care about the environment, as Bethany Jane would put it; they were childless and in their sixties, and already'd had the beauty of the place. She turned to Clarence. "How do you know who's working at the Zoo?" She moved over to the table to ask him, but now, for sure, he was not talking. His head was on a placemat and he was lightly snoring.

"Jack-off! Jack-off!" said Jerry.

"*Smooth*," said Jay. "Jack-off, Yak-off!" Uproarious laughter.

"Jack-off, Yak-off!"

"*Ew, Bethany Jane, gimme a squeeze.*"

They were in the tool shed. At first she couldn't see anything, though she smelled them, their week-old oily hair mixed with male adolescent hormones she wasn't in the mood to think about. Hearing her, they leapt to their feet. A pail clanked. Jerry said, "Ow!" and held his head.

"What is this shouting about?" She probably sounded seventy years old and cranky.

"Nothing." Of course that was Jerry who couldn't lie his way out of a paper bag or keep his mouth shut when he ought to.

Bet picked him to hone in on. She smiled. "Jerry." She just had to say his name in that motherly way she had.

"Bethany Jane's boyfriend," he blurted. Jerry could never work for an intelligence agency. Jay kicked him.

That did it. She put together something quick for Clarence and the boys to eat. As she was driving over to the Zoo, hoping to see this boyfriend, an image of a cartoon came to mind.

Crusader Rabbit, the one with the cape and big teeth, from the old cartoon shows. She felt a bit like he looked – foolish. The girl was nearly eighteen, after all, but Bet had a lot riding on her – university, for one thing. The secrecy bothered her more than anything. It wasn't like Bethany Jane to have secrets – she was the sort of girl who let you know everything on her mind whether you wanted the information or not.

She wound down Sam Hill Road and parked under a tree toward the rear of the Zoo parking lot but near enough to see who was coming and going. People glanced in her direction and she nodded in that clipped manner folks from Alberta have. The Alberta nod is like the dip of a hat, two fingers touching the brim, the cowboy way. She sat in the warm evening and wondered if she was making a mistake. But the Plymouth, Clarence's old car, was there. Then she spotted him. The tall young man with the stand-up hair had to be the one. How she knew, from the assorted groups of young people that were coming and going, that this boy was the one she couldn't say, but he had to be. He had a nose ring. Her heart fell. This was not good. He had a ring in his ear too. Her heart sank further. Bethany Jane must be serious, she thought. Pissing hell.

He'd come out from the kitchen, apparently to light a cigarette. Not a normal cigarette, she saw from the quick way he inhaled. He moved over to the darker side of the building, around behind the fence that screened the trash cans. She climbed down from the truck, strode across the macadam, walking like a narc on one of Clarence's TV shows. She could hear giggling and stepped behind the fence. There they were. The boy turned toward her, shielding Bethany Jane, taking his time as though nothing anyone could do would make him afraid. "Am I busted?" He said it lightly as though Bet might be amused. She was not. Bethany Jane peeked out behind his shoulder, the cigarette in her hand.

"Bethany Jane," she said, trying to keep her voice firm though she felt herself wavering, wooziness rising in her stomach. She spoke up. "Get in the truck. It's time to come home."

Bethany Jane passed the joint to the boy. "No. It's fine, Mum, really. I'll be home later." Her voice floated and to Bet it sounded wrong.

"I have to get back to the kitchen," the boy said, exhaling smoke. He pressed the burning end of the joint between his thumb and first finger. When he was satisfied it was out, he put it in his shirt pocket. His arm went round Bethany Jane, and he quickly drew her in. Then he kissed her full on the mouth. And then he addressed Bet. He said, presenting his hand, "You must be Mrs. Harker. Bethany Jane has said wonderful things about you." If this were an ordinary situation, she would have been thrilled to meet a young man so well spoken, so polite. A kid with the trappings of respect. But the situation was not ordinary and she didn't take his outstretched hand. He said, "I'm Yakov Malenko. This is not a great way for us to meet." He was waiting. She gave in and shook. Nose ring, earring, gummed-up hair, all these he had, but also manners and good teeth.

"Go on with your mum," he said. "I'm way behind on the dishes. Won't get free 'til really late. Let it go tonight, chill."

"Easy for you to say." Bethany Jane flounced in annoyance. He grinned at her and turned to include Bet. His manner with her, Bet thought, was too familiar. He had made his claim on Bethany Jane through the kiss in front of her and he was also making the assumption that they were equals, conspirators. He was a smooth talker, for sure.

"Please," she said to her daughter, "get in the truck with me. We'll pick up the Plymouth tomorrow, eh?"

"I'm perfectly capable of driving." She put her hand on a hip. Bet saw that her eyes did not look like she was perfectly capable of driving.

Yakov Malenko said, "Do the right thing, Betsy. You're blasted, baby. Enjoy it. Be safe."

He called her baby. He called her Betsy. His tone was a lover's tone. Bet wanted to throttle him.

Bet went back and waited in the truck, engine on, played around with adjusting the fans and air conditioning and peeked at the kids once or twice. They were tucked into each other like people who had been together for a while, his arms firmly wrapped around her petite body. A tinge of resentment or regret or some other complicated feeling niggled at Bet's heart. Envy, she thought, might be part of it; it was a lifetime since she'd been claimed like that by anyone, and the physical yearning that spiked through her was hollow but still painful and made her feel ashamed. A shard of something hard lodged in her heart, heavy as stone. She turned on the fans full blast until the cab was filled with cold and she was surrounded by thrashing air and noise. Chastened, goosebumped, she turned it off. Yakov came over with Bethany Jane, opened the door for her. "Nice to meet you, Mrs. Harker. The circumstances weren't the best." He smiled. He shut the door and then hit it with the palm of his hand, like you do when moving an animal out.

"You're grounded for life." She hit her foot hard on the pedal and took the switchbacks up to the main highway. She meant the remark to be flippant, but didn't mean for Bethany Jane to laugh as she did.

"Mum, really. I'm nearly eighteen. Girls are supposed to have a boyfriend at my age."

"What would I have to do to make you take this seriously? Wait until you come down, when the marijuana you're on does whatever?" She got so involved in the possibilities of the what-evers that she missed the turn toward home and was driving into Ruth itself. Street lights began appearing. "I mean, there's diseases and lack of judgment when you're smoking." Somewhere, she thought, there must be a kernel of sense in what she was struggling to say. She swerved left, toward the water, and followed the road around the bay to the new wharf. Music was playing and kids were clustered on benches. A gull perched on a piling was keeping an eye out for a wayward French fry. A younger kid was showing off some skateboard tricks. There had been some debate on the council, and Bet had signed a petition to allow the young people this recreation zone, away from the residential neighbourhoods, some place for them to go on summer evenings.

She parked at a little distance and turned off the engine, then decided to change her tack completely. "Do you want an ice-cream cone?" Bethany Jane used to love licorice ice cream.

"God, no. I ate enough crap today, a bag of vinegar chips, not even organic."

"It's illegal for him to have sex with you, you know. You're underage."

"Mummy. Just come off it, will you? Let's just get home, I need to sleep."

"Are you using protection?"

"Mummy, please. I'm a big girl, trust me."

They sat in silence, and Bet watched a couple of boys play-fighting and a girl bent over laughing, and watched the others in their small, skulking groups, smoking. All the while Bethany Jane didn't so much as glance her way, didn't try to explain anything. She had the coolness of a young woman who, by keeping her face turned slightly away, revealed that she was used to being looked at and admired and wasn't her mum's shy girl any longer, the one who, when noticed for more than a minute, used to giggle and blush. Bethany Jane's unflinching silence was more revealing than anything she might have said. Bet started the truck and drove home and parked in the usual place. Bethany Jane jumped out and ran inside, careful not to let the screen door bang in case her dad was asleep. Bet sat for a while and listened to the trees shivering in the heated wind. She smelled smoke in the air. She envied Dolly. Regarding her daughter at least, Dolly knew what her loss was.

Days later, the stone remained stuck in Bet's heart, sharp and heavy. It hurt where it was lodged, and she chided herself for not being more adaptable – sex was sex, Bethany Jane was the right age – yet she had turned enough pages in her daughter's psychology text to know about psychopaths, people who were nice as pie to your face and crazy on their own time. Yakov, she imagined, could be one of them. She went to the desk in Bethany Jane's room and peeked at the correspondence course assignment – Bethany getting a jump on university. It wasn't finished, due yesterday. She went downstairs, poured two mugs of cold tea. Bethany Jane was outside at the picnic table fooling dreamily with her hair. Bet went out and handed an iced tea to her and said, "Education is the most important thing you'll ever get." Her own hands, at the moment, were black from distributing lumps of charcoal to the firepits with the warning that there were to be no flames, just nice light and a backwoods feeling. Because of the ban, no wood fires were allowed, as though, she'd remarked to one of the guests, a wood fire would excite the trees into doing something they would ultimately regret. Bethany Jane had changed into jeans. Bet sat on a chair that needed mending. The moon was coming up half full.

Bethany Jane glanced at her, seemed to be considering the remark. "That's debatable." She had put some kind of gel in her hair so that it appeared to need washing. She was curling pieces around her finger.

"Why debatable?" Since when did a kid say *debatable* when her mum was making pronouncements?

"*Love*, Mum. Love is more important than education."

"Bethany Jane Harker, I didn't know you had turned into such a silly."

"There is nothing silly about love, Mum. Don't you remember how it was with you and dad?"

Whatever she once might have felt for Clarence was a vague memory. What she knew about Clarence now was that he was a putterer, a scavenger, a doodler, a man who wrote his accomplishments in abbreviations, on a little notepad with a stubby pencil. "Window, washes." "Shov. #4 roof" "Sharpt lawn mower." Informing her of his progress at Cedar Hideaway. And she knew well that toward the end of an afternoon of a typical day, Clarence would begin to lose himself, a restlessness overtaking him that no promise of a video after supper or a game of cribbage could do a thing about. Depending on a rhythm she never got the hang of, some evenings he would be drunker than others, a mysterious chemistry in his body or in his mind. But despite his moseying, meandering ways, he did get the jobs done in his own time and often with a special touch. He would carve a design into a moulding, as though anybody was going to notice, or spend days carving little animals – squirrels, raccoons – into the porch railings when there were other things that demanded doing. With the two of them, that's what it was, Bet thought, her grousing at him for his time-wasting habits one minute and leading him up to bed the next, his jacket smelling of smoke and booze from the Legion, of grass stains, truck grease, sweat, the ring around the collar so embedded in that old green jacket you wouldn't want to touch it with a ten-foot pole.

Bethany Jane was watching her closely, but Bet couldn't look her in the eye. Bethany Jane loved her dad, and one thing Bet did know was that she wanted more for her daughter than she had managed to get for herself. She said, as carefully as she could, "Are you suggesting that education doesn't make a difference to anybody's life?"

"Basically. Education yes, but school, no. You're talking about school."

Bet sat back, folded her arms across her chest. "And I suppose running a place like this because you have no degree would be just fine."

"So? What's the problem?"

"The problem? Do you think your dad or I ever went to school?"

"Going to school and living a good life aren't the same. Aren't synonymous, I mean."

Bet gave her daughter an unfriendly, sidelong look and Bethany Jane gave her one back and said, "In Mexico there are people doing some good in the world, teaching people to grow food without chemicals."

Bethany Jane always was a girl with projects. What did Bet expect? The girl had culled the Ruth Archives in the basement of the government building and for a whole summer called the junk at Cedar Hideaway "historical artifacts."

"I've always been interested in small-scale farming," Bethany Jane said, as though anyone needed reminding. When she was thirteen, she had an idea for what she termed a "hobby farm" that she'd read about in one of her endless piles of back-to-the-land magazines. She saved up her babysitting money, built a pen of stooks and wire, bought five turkeys. What a sight, Bet recalled, those five scraggly white-feathered scaly-necked things going at each other over random grievances and poor Bethany Jane rushing in, kicking dirt at them to unhinge the bill of one from the neck of another. She traded some babysitting time for half a dozen rabbit cages and filled them with bunnies and then when Clarence started in with rabbit stew recipes, she couldn't go through with the slaughtering aspect of having meat rabbits.

"Remember the chickens? How people liked the organic eggs?"

She kept the chickens out behind where the horse, Buttercup, used to live and the eggs were nice, Bet remembered, the yolks full and orange because Bethany Jane fed them oyster shell or some such thing. She sold half a dozen eggs at a time to guests who found fresh food memorable, a comment, Bet supposed, on the state of things in cities. "Whatever happened to that last turkey? Didn't it go over to the Zoo?"

Clarence was just walking up, where he had been keeping himself company in the tool shed, him and a mickey he had hidden there, Bet figured. "Into somebody's stew, I'd say."

"Dad!" Bethany Jane said, but Bet heard the fondness for him in her voice. "You understand, don't you, Dad?"

"Sure do," Clarence said.

"Would you mind?" Bet kicked her leg out and missed him.

"What?" He was wiping his hands on a well-washed piece of flannel.

"Look at us with our dirty hands," she said to Bethany Jane, exasperated at last and showing her hands and nodding at Clarence's. "My point exactly."

"I don't think there's shame in knowing how to do things," Bethany Jane said. "I think hands that work are a matter of pride."

"I'm talking about the value of education."

"I know nothing about that." Clarence grinned.

"No surprise to me." Bet raised her mug, one of a lightweight set she'd got for nearly nothing at someone's yard sale, and Bethany Jane raised hers back. "You know how far a person gets without education, is what I'm trying to say. Nowhere. Kind of like us." She made a point of saying it clearly, for Clarence's benefit, and then she cocked her head at her daughter. "Me and *Dad*." The mug came loose from her hand and fell to the gravel. Clarence fixed his eyes on it and then moved them up, onto her. Bethany Jane stood, picked up the mug, shook her head in mock despair. She kissed her dad on the cheek and took the car keys from him.

"What's eating you?" he said to Bet, after Bethany Jane had driven away.

"I am" – she almost said "fed up" but wasn't in the mood for humour – "nothing is eating me. I am fine and dandy. Where does she get such ideas? What is this business about Mexico? But I suppose you already know." She gave him the benefit of a good, steady glare. By the bashful turn of his head, she gathered that he did already know. She swooped the mug from the table and dropped it again. The cheap ceramic that it was made of broke into six or seven pieces, no real loss.

Opening the back door, Dolly announced, "The air conditioning is making a strange noise," and then she and Bet, Bet stepping inside, stood listening. The Marshalls were one of the few people in Ruth who bothered with air conditioning; bouts of extremely hot weather weren't the usual sort of problem the area tended to have, but Drake, a logger all his life, had been proud of what he could provide. Bet knew something about their spending; there was a time when Dolly had acted conceited and the women at the hospital auxiliary mentioned it among themselves, so Bet had heard. Dolly wasn't crying just then, though an intensity was going on in her that had made Bet expect tears; she felt teary herself.

Dolly plugged in the kettle and sat down at the kitchen table. In a drawer Bet found bags of spicy almond tea, and she put two bags in a teapot. "I'm not mechanical," she said, "though I will say the noise is high-pitched and damn annoying. I recommend you turn it off."

"I must be doing something wrong."

"Maybe not."

"*He* would have known what to do."

Bet said, "Clarence sure wouldn't."

Dolly was still a moment, her eyes wide, and then they had a laugh. Bet asked her about Maryrose Malenko and if she'd heard of Yakov. Dolly said she had, through Colleen. "He's just visiting for the summer. The kids think he's Boris's son and that Maryrose is one of the ex-wives. It's a tad racy." The conversation went back and forth as they drank the tea. Dolly said, "Let me show you the cutest baby stuff." She led Bet through the cool house and into what had been a guest room. There was a crib and a changing table and one of the walls was freshly painted blue. A border of trucks ran around the ceiling. "Look." She held up a tiny blue terrycloth stretch suit.

Bet touched it. "I'm sorry about Colleen. Maybe I never told you that."

Dolly had a scar under her eye that turned white when she was angry. It was white now. She folded up the little suit and put it back in the box it had come in. Her anger came as a surprise to Bet because they'd always talked about their girls going on to college; they had certainly assumed, that unlike the rest of local rabble, they were raising high-school graduates. Dolly said, winding up a music box, "She can always go back to school." The melody was "Somewhere Over the Rainbow."

Bet was out the door soon enough, yammering apologies, and coming into the driveway she turned too sharp a right and the tires scattered some of the gravel the boys had recently put down at the entrance, and that gave her one more thing to be sorry about. She sat in the truck for a minute but not long enough, she thought later, because then she backed out and drove over to the Frances Hill to see Maryrose Malenko.

No one was in the lobby, and she slid through the heavy doors and walked quickly through the lobby, past fake flowers in big vases, a modest try at refinement; she felt out of place in her sleeveless flower-print shirt and pedal pushers. She read the note on the bulletin board that listed names and rooms. The air was cool; more air conditioning. Maybe, she thought, she and Clarence were living in the past.

The hall was empty; it must have been naptime. Bet tiptoed down the corridor and tapped on a door. She could hear the television on inside. The door was flung open. "Good to see you!" Maryrose cried.

Bet was startled. She sputtered out her name.

"Oh, I've been expecting you. Come inside. Bethany Jane said you might want to have a chat. Such an intelligent girl. The children told me about their plan. More power to them, I say." Bet looked at the TV, thinking that some people left it on when they had company, invited or otherwise. You'd see them cast longing looks at their program, wishing you would leave. Maryrose turned it off, though, and asked if Bet wanted tea, but Bet declined and sat as she was bidden in a stuffed chair with a pattern of big blue and purple flowers. Maryrose seated herself on the loveseat in the same bright pattern. She patted a cushion and said, "It's a cheery print. It's important to stay cheery, at least on the surface."

"The kids have a plan?"

As Maryrose evaded her question and began to theorize about the return of her long-lost son, the earth began to shift – Bet was in a nuthouse. Maryrose was sure that Yakov was her true son who had been taken from her, stolen, when he was a baby. "Madeleine did it," she said and clacked her teeth together a few times. "Madeleine is Boris's sister, a horrible person. Boris was in on it, he's in on everything," and that part, because of dealings Bet had had with him in the past, she could believe.

"And what is their plan?"

"What plan?"

In the last while, Bet understood that two people she had talked to couldn't keep a thought from the beginning of a sentence to the end. Maybe conspiracy theories were right; maybe east-west planes were showering chemicals on the valley as they flew over. She sat forward, pressing her palms together, and said to Maryrose, one mother to another, "You said the kids had a plan."

"Oh, yes! Isn't it wonderful about young people, always thinking of others. You see," she said, picking up a pair of glasses with thick lenses from the coffee table and putting them on, "young people are always thinking of others. Yakov, you see, was raised in Mexico by people who weren't Mexican. His Spanish isn't very good, which is what gave it away." Her eyes were as big as saucers.

Bet slapped her knees, as though suddenly remembering an appointment, and stood. "He seems like a well-brought-up boy," she said, for something to say.

Maryrose stood also and began fiddling with her glasses, moving them up and down her nose. "It's the drugs. Another perseveration, they call it. You can't stop doing something once you start. Or you don't want to stop. Sometimes my hand starts writing words in the air and experimenting with different formations of the letters. Should a *d* start at the top or the bottom? This can be problematical: top or bottom, open or closed circle? Has that ever happened to you?"

"I can't say it has," Bet said and backed out, shutting the door behind her, hurrying along the dark hall.

Home, she pulled the chair to the desk in the office, sat gaping at the computer that she didn't know how to use except for e-mail and that was only because Bethany Jane had taught her. Out of the blue, she missed her lost friend, Nan. She would be the one to talk to. Who could she e-mail, what would she say?

She e-mailed Bethany Jane: What plan? Then pressed *Send*. No doubt, she sighed, another mistake in a day nearly perfect with them.

She threw out the cucumbers, already growing mould around their necks. What had she expected? They'd come on a truck from California. She wondered if bears, driven by fire on the other side of the mountain, fire that couldn't be seen except for a rising plume of deep grey smoke, would mosey down to Cedar

Hideaway for mushy cucumbers. She wondered if there was a ratty old bear nearby that desperate.

Bethany Jane came home after dinner. The boys were out, down to the wharf for the evening, they'd said. Bethany Jane sauntered through the door as though on a visit, as though her real life wasn't within these walls. She went to her room. Bet finished the dishes, she hung up the towel to dry on a knob of a cupboard, debated whether to go after her. Bethany Jane came back to the kitchen, carrying a backpack. "How could you be so cruel?" she said.

Bet grabbed the wet dishtowel; she always felt safer with a dishtowel in her hands or over her shoulder. She said, "Did you get my e-mail?" There were too many sins to sort through to know which one Bethany Jane was talking about.

Bethany Jane glared. She had that haughty teenaged attitude that reduced her mum to jelly. "What? What?" Bet found herself sounding like Clarence.

"*Dolly. Colleen.* It's a *baby.* A baby is coming. That is not a bad thing. It is never a bad thing when a baby is coming."

Bet thought she understood, narrowed her eyes. "Are you pregnant?"

Bethany Jane gave her a look Bet was sorry to get from a daughter of hers. "You are so beyond the beyond," she said. And Bet knew she was toast.

Around 2:00 a.m. Bet pulled a sweatshirt over her nightgown and shoved her feet into the rundown slippers the boys had bought from the Sears catalogue last Christmas. She climbed the stairs to the attic, the house holding the heat. Jerry, by the open window, snored a little already. She surveyed their big bodies, neither wearing pyjama tops but probably shorts because they were still shy, hadn't reached the age where men are confident, no matter what they look like. Even Clarence seemed oblivious to his stick-ugliness, in her view, and that sort of obliviousness seemed like a very masculine trait. She liked watching him undress, that was a fact. What kind of thoughts were these? she wondered and went downstairs into the living room and stood gazing at the old furniture, the small TV next to the fireplace. She could tell you every item in every drawer and could tell you how much money they'd made and how much they'd lost this year and last and where those brocade pillows on the corduroy davenport came from. The room was silent, but Bet knew that it would burst with life in the morning, and she thought that the living that went on here was important somehow, and she thought it mattered. Their children mattered – not that she and Clarence had been overjoyed to discover a baby on the way – but she and Clarence had become purposeful because of them. Bet went and stood outside the closed door of Bethany Jane's room. Bet wondered what was the matter with her. She couldn't make herself do the next obvious thing. She didn't ease open the door; she couldn't stand knowing. She pictured Bethany Jane safely in her childhood bed, breathing to her dreams. Bethany Jane had always been a girl with dreams.

"So where is she?" Bet demanded of Clarence as soon as the alarm shattered his sleep and he'd turned it off and lay back and opened his eyes. She had been lying in wait. Bethany Jane was, after all, a daddy's girl. There were no sounds of an electric kettle in the kitchen, though she didn't need anything so domestic to guess that her daughter had not come home last night.

Clarence scrambled out of bed. Any other time she might have laughed at the sight. He had nothing to say. He dressed quickly, tightened his belt. He glanced at her long enough to shrug.

"This is your *daughter*. What's wrong with you?" Speaking, Bet gritted her teeth and then winced at the sudden pain in her knees from flinging herself out of bed too fast. "Pissing hell!" The pain forced her to straighten up slowly.

"Leave the girl alone," Clarence said and ducked into the bathroom. He shut the door. She heard it lock.

For a minute she glared at nothing much, then pulled on a shirt and hobbled into the hall and goaded herself do what she didn't want to – she opened the door to Bethany Jane's room. Her bed was still made. Of course it was still made. She sank against the doorjamb, thought of all the things she could protect her daughter from and the one thing she couldn't: a boy. Girls never learned. Women either, for that matter.

Clarence tried to pass her in the hall, but she stepped in front of him so he couldn't get by. His breath smelled like peppermint. She flicked a spot of toothpaste from his bottom lip and then tapped an angry finger against his bony chest. "She stayed out all night! What's wrong with you? Why aren't you at least worried?"

She was leaning into him so hard her finger hurt. He escaped by turning sideways, and his quick movement made her lose her balance. She heard him catch his breath, but she wasn't paying attention otherwise. Instead, she went into Bethany Jane's room and mussed up the pillow and pulled the sheet and blankets loose. The boys didn't have to know that their sister hadn't come home. Though, likely, everyone already knew – the boys, Clarence, half the town – and it was only *her* left out of the loop. She appreciated the possibility of how true it was, and at the same time realized, for sure, that Clarence was in on it, a co-conspirator.

He was in the kitchen, their favourite mugs already side by side on the counter. The water was near boiling. The cupboard door was open to where the coffee was kept. His hand was reaching up to grab the jar, but his fingers couldn't seem to get it. She saw his arm go up once and then again and then his fingers seized and couldn't move farther, couldn't grasp the

Maxwell House and bring it down. He had a puzzled expression on his face. His hand seemed useless. He must have heard her gasp because he turned and the turning caused him to stagger. And then he stumbled into the table, bumping it. Uncertain of what she was seeing, she simply stared, and then stepped forward, arms raised, just in time to catch him. The weight of his body nearly took her breath away. He was heavier than she'd thought such a skinny man could be, and she half-stepped forward, lifting them both up, holding them both upright, and then her heart began to make her deaf and dumb and blind against whatever was wrong.

Clarence was in the hospital for three days. They didn't keep him long and Bet couldn't say as she blamed them. He was irascible when he woke up and was muttering swear words he had never used. The doctor said it was normal and actually a good sign. She walked back and forth along the road in front of Cedar Hideaway, staying close to home as she tended to do anyway, the lonely feeling more settled, though more inevitable, like a permanent weight of something invisible on her shoulders. It could take a few weeks or a few months for him to recover. The staff wouldn't make predictions. Even in the short term, she knew she was going to miss his mischief – him in front of the TV midday, or sneaking a last beer from the small fridge he kept in the shed, and the other small, domestic doings she used to complain to herself about, walking this road.

The air smelled of turpentine, not a good sign in the mountains: it meant that the trees were ready to go. It could be that kind of summer. A blaze started by a cigarette butt tossed by a careless tourist or started by a spear of lightning during a dry summer storm, or started by an arson nut overexcited by the endless coverage of the fires on TV, the roaring from somewhere else moving into the Judith Lake mountains, over the crest and into the valley and into what was the Harker neighbourhood, that edgy place where forest meets weeds.

20

By nightfall Lenore had discovered, room by careful room – Lucinda had not come back – that the Centre was bigger than she'd thought. There were several levels, including a spacious loft, obviously where people slept because of the stacks of foam mattresses and cushions. The loft had a small kitchen – microwave, refrigerator, farmhouse table, stools and benches. Downstairs, off the summer kitchen was a cozy room with a fireplace and its own private toilet. She liked that. Down half a flight, a long hall with rooms on either side. Storage rooms, some of them, the laundry room, then a serene bedroom she hesitated to step into, then the office, and the one that must have been Lucinda's: antique walnut furniture, kilim rugs on the floor, a Degas dancer print torn from a magazine tacked inside the closet.

Next to Lucinda's was an empty room, which Lenore decided was perfect for her. She felt like Goldilocks. She was glad to have found a bed to sleep in that didn't belong to her husband or to her brother. Inspecting the closet of her new room, she didn't understand why people would spend their money – she'd already been in the office and perused the brochures – a lot of money for a *workshop* – why people would spend money for such a shabby room, the walls drywalled on one side, painted tongue-and-groove on the other, a narrow closet, two shelves in back painted butterscotch. Rustic, unrefined. For the price, she herself would have chosen a hotel on the beach in Cancun. She continued her inspection, and at the end of the hall found the all-important

bathroom, behind the landing, and the toilet – she checked –
flushed. There were ferns growing in big pots under the skylight.
She swallowed her sleeping pill and locked the bedroom door
and slipped between the thin covers, sorry she'd left the duvet
behind. They were probably cuddled under it, Jack and the
nature girl.

Everything was shaking. She tried to sit up but something heavy
was lying on her chest. Cat-sized, a heavy cat. It didn't have the
warm weight of a cat, nor was it the hand of Jack, aroused, reaching for her in the dark. This sensation was unpleasant, extremely
unpleasant, and cold, clammy. She knew she had to struggle
against it, and she did. She willed herself to get up. But her body
stayed on its back, hands at rest inside the sheet. The straining
didn't result in movement; she must be paralyzed, her consciousness disconnected from her body, arms and legs disengaged. The
winds howled inside her room. The winds slipped inside her head
through her ears. No way to stop them. They swirled, bickering.
Her head pounded. A muscle inside her belly jumped. She began
to whimper, a sound she recognized. She wakened clutching the
sheets, holding on to keep herself from falling out of bed.

She untangled herself from the covers, glad to have survived
the blast to her psyche, and crept to the window. Something had
bumped against the house. The ground under the gnarled pear
orchard was damp and gleaming. The trees cast shadows, the
moon was so bright. Maybe she had awakened just to see the cool
night beauty. Her breath created steam on the windowpane. She
drew circles on the glass. Back in bed, covers to her chin, her belly
rumbled. Too many tablets of Herbal Cleanser.

She heard – felt – the sound again, the jarring impression of
an object, person, or creature actually crumpling its weight
against the house. The brush crackled. Unmistakable. She
crossed to the window. Definitely something there.

She dressed quickly. Now there were noises coming from the
kitchen level. Should she go down and check or not? On TV

crime shows, the victim (usually a woman who hadn't watched enough TV, in her opinion) went to investigate, her curiosity the very reason she was murdered in the first place. Lenore understood the temptation to investigate, however; a person just had to know what was going on.

Back against the wall in the hallway, Lenore wavered outside the door to the kitchen, a chill pickling her skin. She counted to seven and made her move – reached in and flicked on the light. Someone was banging on the door, and she heard muffled shrieks as from a wounded animal.

"What in the world?" She strode across the kitchen and flung open the door. BB was standing there, hysterical, his mother by his side mumbling apologies. Her hitchhikers!

"You scared me to pieces!"

BB barked something unintelligible and lunged inside. "Worm, wormie, worm," he cried, holding up an empty cottage-cheese container.

Mory spoke sorrowfully. "Bear around our place. Means bad for the bear."

Lenore realized she meant the bear would be shot.

"Big growls!" said BB. He scooted through the mudroom and into a corner in the kitchen, his back against the flour bins. He snuffled and moaned, hiding his head in his arms.

The boy gave Lenore the shivers – he sounded like something you didn't want to meet in the dark. She was unsure what to do. Mory seemed exhausted. Lenore sat down at the table to think. From a seated position she felt more in control; it reminded her of the classroom at the end of the day, the sound of her voice reading aloud a chapter before the bell rang. She said, "We need a fire in the stove." She nodded toward Mory. It was quiet except for the child's snuffling. The girl began crumpling newspapers and then she put in the kindling, struck a match. Lenore watched. The child stopped crying. After a while, the fire crackled. Mory explained, "There was a bear at the tepee. Sniffing around. BB running after it. Funny guy." She patted his head. "Why would you chase a bear," Lenore said to BB. "Are you stupid?"

"Not stupid. Very brave."

The boy slid his eyes to his mother. He appeared enraptured by her comment. Lenore shook her head. Why did some children love their mothers and some didn't? She saw his knees, their bleeding scabs, and at his feet and their long toes and their square nails. "There's blood. He needs a Band-Aid."

"BB likes Band-Aids."

"Some in the medicine chest in the bathroom. Help yourself." As soon as she spoke the words *help yourself*, she pictured herself as a hostess sharing largess with less fortunate guests. "Take as many as you like. Well, one or two," she amended as though the Band-Aids came from her own hard-earned supply.

Over the next days, she boiled the stewing chickens she'd found in the freezer. She chopped every salvageable vegetable and made chicken stock. She repacked the chicken pieces into the freezer and did the same for the stock. She had worked her way to the bottom of the freezer, to the last chicken, freezer-burned, when she came to a mental crash. Where was she? What was she doing? Who were the strangers in the tepee, who were they really? She went to bed. She took the soft duvet from Lucinda's bed and took it to her nun's cell room. And lay under it and realized that what was becoming most difficult in losing Jack was losing sex, for Jack was always, always dutiful and his lovemaking was metronomic, dependable, and uninspiring – his rhythm and his cool, determined, daily need a habit she was used to. He would rise on his arms, prod her breasts a few times each, tweaking the nipples, and enter, move within her, hold himself at arm's length, and watch them both heaving until she felt him enlarge and he grunted and bowed his head, counting the spasms, the "pumps" as he called them – eight pumps tonight, he'd pant in her ear. And she would already have come, like clockwork herself, oblivious to him: it wasn't he, particularly, who mattered, it was his erect organ, veined and hard and big and wide, and exactly the right size. How could this be, that what they had in common was a penis, a vagina, a tight, familiar fit? Not sexy, just sex.

Something faintly, distinctly dental about their sex life – both of them relieved and livelier afterwards, though it wasn't a barrel of fun. In articles downloaded from the Web she'd read that good sex prolonged life. When Jack switched his loyalties, she began bringing herself to orgasm. Sadness dulled her afterward, something she'd never experienced after the most banal sex with Jack. She wondered if she loved him. If missing sex, after nearly thirty years of marriage, was what it came down to.

She couldn't help herself – she got out of bed and went into the office. She turned on a table lamp and tapped the computer awake and reread Lucinda's personal e-mails from someone named Lukas Chirplean. Lukas had bought a ranch in southeastern Arizona, a place called Arivaca. He had written to her often, he had described the details of Arivaca and the dance moves he was practising. He had written, "The ranch house is very cowboy. I want you to see it, the possibilities. I loved the dancing with you. Why aren't you answering back?" Lenore was moved every time she read this particular message. Imagine someone wanting to hear from you. Wanting to share with you, someone's breath wanting to warm your cheek. Imagine *dancing*.

She went back to bed and thought about Jack. She stirred to noises from the outside that she couldn't identify. She heard gustings of wind, and the heat wouldn't let up, and she could not get comfortable. The phone was ringing. It rang and rang. She woke in the dark, forgetting where she was. She sat up quickly and bumped her elbow on the bedside table. She reached for the phone, but there wasn't a phone in her room. Grappling for the light switch, she made her way into the hall and was breathless by the time she found the office. She picked up the phone. "Hello?" The man's voice said hello, and she couldn't speak immediately, her throat was parched, and the voice said, "This isn't Lucinda," and after a pause the voice said, "Are you there? Did I wake you?" and Lenore said, "I think so." The line was quiet.

The voice said, "How are you doing?" Lenore said she was fine. "I'm glad," he said, sounding pleased. "Have you heard from Lucinda recently?" Lenore hadn't, truthfully, since Lucinda left in the BMW, mentioning Phoenix.

"I know who you are," Lenore said, feeling proud as a bright child. "When she left she told me to tell you that she was can-celling what she could for this month – you know, July – but that in August you and I are on our own." Lenore found herself thrilled to think of being on her own with Gabriel. There was something thrilling about his voice. She said, "I ate too much dinner. Chicken out the wazoo. I'm bloated. I don't know what I was thinking." And the voice said, "Yes."

The line was quiet. She pressed the phone to her ear. "I'm in the office," she said. There were the desktop computer and neatly stacked files. The voice said, "She phoned, telling me she was leaving, but I hoped she'd be back by now."

Lenore reached for the swivel chair and sat. "I don't know her, so I can't say."

"Did she tell you about our situation?"

Lenore didn't know whether acting in the know would be useful. If you acted as though you knew things, people might tell you more, get into the details. To confess ignorance could get you nowhere.

"She might have," Lenore said.

She heard him laugh, a light, easy laugh.

"Okay, okay. I lied. I'm hiding a lot lately. I mean lying."

"Yes."

"I sometimes forget where I am. I was bashing around in the hall. I heard the phone ringing. It seemed important to get the phone."

"To answer it."

"Yes. As though I was dreaming and this was going to be the message."

"Have you a question in mind?"

"I don't know what I'm doing here."

"You're in the right place even if it doesn't make sense just yet. Are you healthy? Are you having a physical concern?"

"Everybody does." She felt defensive and sat forward in the chair, placed her feet on the carpet. "Okay. Bowels," she said.

"Unfinished business, would you say?" He laughed again and the sound of it was genial and friendly, like listening to a shell at the beach, and she relaxed back in the chair. She had to suppress a nervous giggle. He said, "Are you finding everything?"

Lenore sat forward. "Yes. She left me lists everywhere." She pressed the phone to her cheek.

"Lists. Yes. And – I knew she had a friend. It's Phoenix, isn't it? Then Arivaca. My guess is Arivaca."

Goosebumps sprang up along her arms. "I may not be supposed to tell you."

"Don't worry. You won't be struck by lightning."

Her goosebumps subsided. The voice said, "Sorry I woke you. When you talk to Lucinda, would you tell her I'm thinking of her? I've tried phoning her cell, but it's off. I'm sending a cheque to you in partial thanks. You can cash it at Poppy's. And your name is?"

Lenore told him, feeling like she was standing up in front of the class, ready to show something marvellous just discovered. *I am Fox.*

"Ah. You're related to Larry Carmichael."

Lenore flushed; he was the first person to make the family connection. She said, "I'm good at cooking. Everything is okay here." She picked up the cheque Lucinda had left her, along with a corporate credit card. Should she mention them?

Before the thought was half out of her brain, he said, "Go ahead and cash the one in your hand. Please. We appreciate your holding the fort."

She felt a little sting of reprimand. She retaliated. She blurted – and she would think later how cruel it was to tell him what she did. She blurted, "She was wearing a wedding band when she left."

How did she expect him to respond?

No words came, and why would they? Silence.

She heard him breathing. "Hello?" she said.

"Slippery elm," he said, "may help you. I have to hang up now." His tone was regretful.

"Bye for now," she said. He had already hung up. "Bye for now" promised something, a continued relationship. She hoped she hadn't blown it with Gabriel.

She listened to the dial tone, placed the phone in the cradle. What made her so mean? For it was sheer malice that had made her mention the wedding band that she had noticed when Lucinda brought her the cookies, the Oreos. The band looked new, like an experiment. Lenore had been unconscious, as she usually was, thinking first of herself – she knew these things – and yet she'd noticed, because she was a person who noticed things, even though her responses tended to be clumsy. And she'd gone and said it, about the wedding band. Hitting a target she didn't know was there, forcing an issue that wasn't being discussed, the tension inside her – her knowing – forcing the truth forward. A self-interested way to look at what she'd done, but how else do you live with yourself?

She brought the computer out of sleeping. "Bye for now," she said. The screen came on. She clicked the menu bar, went directly to the e-mail program, and opened the Inbox and scrolled through messages. People inquiring about the Centre, requesting information, asking about the cost, wanting to tell Gabriel their latest breakthrough, their phone number on the bottom, asking him to please call when he had the chance, adding "best to you also." They knew Lucinda was reading the mail and they didn't like her, did they, Lenore thought, pleased for some reason. That meanness surfacing. An inner shark, a black hole, the animus, a shadow, the Other, the evil twin, the – she ran out of words. She looked at the last e-mail, glad everyone detested Lucinda. It was good to know someone else was disliked.

She became aware of herself holding everything together – holding back the bush, holding down the dark side of her own mind, holding in her tummy; she could hardly breathe due to the responsibility of organizing the place, keeping Mory and BB and a strange young man named Milee Logan working – the three of them, she often thought, could be characters in a southern movie. She had to supervise them every second, she had to reorganize the cupboards, gather supplies, oversee the garden work, answer e-mail, and explain to at least a few irate people who phoned what little she knew about "the situation," trying not to say the obvious: "He's not here. I don't know when to expect him. Come along if you like or don't. Up to you. Me, I'm up to my neck. *Hasta luego.*"

There were other moods she fell into. She reread the e-mail from the fellow named Lukas; she invented physical entanglements between Lucinda and Lukas and stopped when she realized the Lukas-body she had created resembled Jack's. The silence and the wind – it was supposed to be nice in July, Mary Populakis had told her – the wind blowing through the treetops made her worry more: trees falling on the house. She jumped at ordinary noises, the cat thumping off the table when she came into the kitchen – "Bad cat!" – and then, in the next moment, the fact of the cat running from her brought tears to her eyes.

She wrung her hands and walked in circles. Something was not right, the air felt crackly, helicopters appeared, thunderously loud, and then disappeared.

Taking a shower, her skin began to prickle; she knew she was not alone. She felt – more physical than thinking, she clearly *felt* – someone spying on her. She pulled back the curtain and peered out the fogged window and caught a glimpse of someone running away, and certainly the sound she heard was a whoop of laughter that she could only describe as wild. Perhaps this – the spying – was the reason for her unease.

On the porch, barefoot and wrapped in a robe, she spotted him: BB, standing in the weeds at the edge of the woods, his finger up his nose. He took his finger out of his left nostril and asked a question, in language she could barely understand. He asked if she liked something. About worms.

"What? Worms?" It was preposterous that he was asking about worms when he had been *spying*.

His finger went into the second nostril. The digging began.

"Your mother would not want you to do that," Lenore said, her voice rising to a shout. "Mothers know best!"

The finger came out of his nose. He stared at his pants. He laughed – a high-pitched sort of laugh that gave her the creeps – and ran off. Something must be wrong. Even bad. His jeans were unzipped. She was sure they were unzipped.

One minute she was involved in something completely ordinary and in the next she was slipping into paranoia or the mild beginnings of it, like a purple loosestrife hiding undetected amongst the other, wanted plants. Her mind was like that, hiding things. She was in the side yard, hanging her panties and slacks on the clothesline when, from the bushes, she heard a high voice twittering, "Like dancing? Bow-wow." She couldn't tell where the voice was coming from, and she should have let it go at that.

The brush rustled. *The ferret-faced child*, her mind thought. *Up to something. Spying again.*

Insects bit and beetles lurked. She pressed on to the tepee. She had to get there, didn't know why. Yes, she was followed. An extra thud she heard – her own heartbeat or his? She tried to dispel the menace by saying, very slowly and clownishly, "Is that a bear?" Nothing answered, no one answered; the sound she was bothered by no doubt her heart throbbing in her ears. How foolish to have called out in the middle of the day: *"Is that a bear?"* As though a bear would answer.

"Bow-wow, bow-wow," she heard.

Guess who.

Children – she had a cunning storytelling style; she'd entertained them, made them laugh. They loved the way she told stories, using her arms in large, dramatic movements, her body recoiling or lunging, her high and low voices. "Hello, little boy." She let her voice wring out the word *boy*, thrillingly, like the witch in Hansel and Gretel. No answer. "Are you a tasty little boy?" She cackled; well done, she thought. Where was the applause? Silence. Nothing.

Was she talking to *herself*? She peered around furtively, aware of panic out the corner of her eye, almost visible. There was the cat staring at her from the undergrowth. Lenore's face grew hot. Everything shamed her, even *a cat*.

By the time she came to the clearing and the tepee, her nose was clammy. A dog's nose. Noticing the temperature of her nose caused her to feel melodramatic. Animal-like and larger than life. Swerving into a strange, euphoric mood, she opened the tent flap and let herself stagger through and drop to the cushions, where she came to rest. She stretched out. Stretched her arms and legs, sighed. She was in the woods, the real woods, in a tepee, a real tepee. "Having an adventure!" she said. "Ha, ha!" Hollow. No substance. Just the gnaw of panic.

Under her left shoulder lay something lumpy. She lifted the cushion and found BB's stuffed animal. The little sheep smelled of stale milk. She held it out to get a good look at it. Its eyes did not match. The beady golden one was intact, probably the original, and there was one small button eye, blue plastic, one that Mory must have sewed on, her work because the stitching was childlike. More stitching on the tail at the rear end. Lenore breathed deeply, holding the sheepie-sheep – she thought of it as the "sheepie-sheep," remembering when that other child was having a birthday at the restaurant and Elmo was a present to another child. "You have your sheepie-sheep," Mory had said, a mother's voice reminding the child to be grateful for what he had.

While she was studying BB's sheep, another stuffed animal came to mind. She had almost forgotten about a white dog with brown and black spots. Gary's was a doggie. His crib companion and the thing he dragged everywhere, even as a big boy of four – he wouldn't go into a grocery store if the doggie couldn't sit next to him in the cart. The doggie led a charmed life. Until the summer Gary was turning five and he took it to the beach and it nearly drowned – what a calamity! The screaming – the wailing – that came from the child stumbling up the sand because of a stuffed animal tumbling in the surf: "He dwownding, he dwownding!" All the long ride home he cried and cried and held his wet doggie tight. At home, he would not let her wash the salt and sand out of it. She had intended to use the gentle cycle, cold water with Woolite, but no matter what she said to him, he kept wailing and grabbing for his doggie – as though she hadn't been the one to save it from drowning in the first place. He simply wouldn't listen. And she was fed up. She'd thrown the damn thing in the trash compactor and that had been that.

Now, in the tepee, she heard a noise, and the scritch-scratch – a stick, claws, fingernails? – against the canvas caused the walls of the tepee to flutter. She could almost make out the child's narrow shape. "Let's not do that," she said. "Why don't you come in? I know a story that you'll like. Boys always like my stories."

More scratching, and then the canvas fluttered faster. Unsettling. "Don't do that," she said, speaking louder and sitting up. "Stop it right now." Perhaps she'd got it wrong – perhaps it wasn't the boy causing the wind and the creaking; perhaps he wasn't out there and something else was: No mere child causing this havoc. She heard a raspy "bow-wow." Then a gruff "heh-heh-heh."

The flapping subsided and the boy's head, a little head, poked inside, his mouth grinning at her so widely it showed his flat, peglike teeth. His eyes caught hers, flickered to her stomach where his sheep lay. When it registered with him what she had, his eyes widened and he began crying, "Sheepie-sheep!"

"Shush now." She meant to say it sweetly. But he wouldn't stop shrieking. He tripped over his feet, coming at her. He crawled toward her, hand reaching. A feral, unclean odour emanated from him, an odour she didn't want to think about: boys doing their disgusting things. "Stop that. Stop that this instant!"

He dropped face forward onto the cushions, howling.

"Stop that crying now!"

The clamour of the child's crying was familiar; she began to shake and her hands grappled for something to hold. She raised the sheepie-sheep in front of her eyes and she pulled off its tail and she picked out its eyes and tossed it into the firepit, into the ashes. She was so dizzy she could hardly sit up. She heard the howling of the boy in the tepee and she heard another wailing also. Not her own or the boy's. *Gary's.*

And then she blacked out or almost blacked out. In any event, she wished she had. Because she had torn the eyes off of a poor boy's only toy. And the crying – his, Gary's, Larry's when he'd been shamed by their mother. All these boys weeping in her head, their unhappiness pouring into her – she could not move fast enough to get away.

She heard the tentative knock and opened the door. Mory and BB were standing on the porch holding hands, much as they had been when she'd first noticed them beside the highway. "He has words to say to you," the girl said.

"He does, does he?" She still sounded like the wicked witch of the west. "That would be nice," she said, trying harder.

"I spy," the boy said.

"Spying on you." *'Pi on you.* Mory said. She shook the hand that was holding his.

Prompting, Lenore thought.

"It was bad," he said. "I'm sorry."

Lenore exhaled. What a lot of effort had gone to ordering this series of little speeches. "Okay," she said. "It *is* bad to spy on people and I'm glad you know that now." She felt a nudge. *Oh.* "I-uh, I'm sorry too, about the sheepie-sheep. I'm, uh, sure we can fix it." She put out her hand. Mory let go of BB's hand and he raised it to shake with Lenore, who was not looking forward to the touch of those slimy, germ-ridden, nose-picking fingers, but she had come this far and there was no turning back. She took his hand, a dry, small-boned hand, the hand of a simple boy and not a monster.

She had moved beyond snooping and into cleaning. Though she could see that the house was well maintained overall, there were housecleaning specialties that Lenore could bring to the situation. She was grateful for the kneepads she found under the backseat of the Honda when she'd cleaned it out – she'd unpacked everything, she'd vacuumed, she'd polished the seats –

because the kneepads meant she could crawl around and clean spider fuzz balls from every baseboard in the rambling house. There were a great number of spider messes in corners and behind legs of furniture, spiders leaving pitted little remainders of themselves stuck into the floors. What spiders were up to when they left those messes she didn't know, but that, she thought, wasn't her business. Her knees ached and she wasn't the most agile person she'd ever met, but the work was good because it was methodical and allowed her time to think without sinking into despair, for the fact was, she was realizing, she had lost Gary's baby album. Deliberately misplaced it, as though her child was insignificant or unworthy, someone of no consequence, someone who did not matter. He was her *son*, and she had deliberately disavowed her whole life as a parent, depriving him of his right to a mother, at least a family past, a history. Because by now – at the fireplace, digging out the dust from the crevices of stones – she'd discovered that Gary's baby album wasn't among the things she had with her. She knew that their family pictures – his family pictures, his heritage when she came down to it, was in Number Eleven.

She listened to her laboured breathing. Through her breathing she heard Gary, crying – again! – in his room a long time ago. Had Jack pounded on the door and told him to cut it out? Because boys don't cry? He had, and she'd stayed in the living room pretending to read a book written for teachers about working with children with learning disabilities. It hadn't occurred to her that anything she was doing – or not doing, those nights when Jack was yelling and Gary cried – would make Gary have a learning problem, a growing-up problem, a drug problem. What had she been thinking?

She was keeping the peace like any good wife.

By the time she was in the pantry, removing cans and jars, wiping down every shelf, she recalled the entire contents of Number Eleven – two cans of artichoke hearts, two bottles of avocado oil, rolled inside the best pillowcases. And the Limoges. Yes. She hadn't wanted to give Nan anything. She had always resented Nan. Lively, slender: two excellent reasons right there to begrudge her sister-in-law. She'd probably chosen that suitcase subconsciously, knowing.

Then, finished with the bottom shelf, she rose and felt a twinge from the ribs she'd bruised in the mishap on the Trans-Canada. She remembered the sweet size of Gary's little hand, how he had trusted her. A brief time – he'd had to learn distrust in a hurry, raised by Lenore and Jack.

"You have some unfinished business," Gabriel said.

"Don't we all," said Lenore. She hadn't meant anything by it. She counted on hearing his voice, talking to him.

There was a pause, then a sigh. A rueful laugh. "Yes."

The sigh stayed in her ears. She felt a buzz of excitement.

He said, "Do you have children?"

She thought hard. A thunderous silence arose in the room and took it over. "Oh, my Lord, that's it!" she said. She shouted.

He said, "Bye for now," and she said, "Bye for now," and then she dialed Vancouver.

Gary picked up the phone. "'Lo."

"It's me. Mum."

"So?"

"Some of your, uh, problems may be my fault. Mine. I think you need help. Now, don't interrupt. Your dad's to blame too, for sure. Look at your life. What are you doing with yourself? Don't answer right away. I am not blaming you. Listen, I need your help."

She waited but he didn't reply, which made her think that her needing his help might not be the right tack. "You have choices," she said. "I need help here, a good cook. Or – and, well, Uncle Larry needs somebody in the store. A – a younger presence.

Somebody with background, a little panache, eh? Ruth is growing. He's got the building supply end of things sewed up, but he wants to open a kitchen department, bring in a line of good quality kitchen products. I'm telling you, Uncle Larry was asking about you." She was out of breath from all the lying. He didn't hang up on her.

"Yeah?"

"Yeah," she said. "Totally. He'll give you a call. And, uh, go down to the corner and pick up a big container of powdered slippery elm from the health-food store."

Her hand over her heart, she hung up and leaned back a moment.

Then she picked up the phone again and dialed Larry at the store. "I have to talk to you," she said.

He grunted. He sounded wary. "I'm coming into town," she said.

An hour later she stood outside Larry's glassed-in office, Larry himself on the phone, the door open. He beckoned her in. As he talked, she looked around the store. Two of the clerks she remembered from high school. Unchanged except paunchy, a condition she could identify with. Larry gestured with his fingers that the man on the other end was blabbing away. He said into the phone, "I'll get another supplier." He winked at her. A beefy man should not wink, Lenore thought. She decided not to wait, because he would hold court so she could watch; they'd always competed for attention. Of course she had no intention of actually leaving, but he wouldn't know that. She was on the sidewalk before he caught up with her. "The guy was a big wholesaler. *American*," Larry said, as though that was reason enough for his behaviour. "Now, before you say anything, just think back to when you were thirteen."

She thought back. She had locked herself in her bedroom, angry at their mother. She had vowed never, not ever, to be rude to people, the way their mother was. She had used Larry as a witness.

She gave her brother a look. It was terrible that the person who knew you better than anyone in the world was the type of person who kowtowed to Americans. Boys, she thought suddenly, have a hard life.

"We need to talk," she said.

He looked around as though everyone passing, nodding to him, would want to know what it was they were saying, would want to know what Larry Carmichael was up to. Something tragic about a man like that, she thought. To need to feel so important. Then she was taken by surprise, propelled around the back of the building, half-lifted off her feet. They entered what looked to her like a bunker.

"Sorry," Larry said, when they were seated on a padded glider, a footstool in front. There was a fake palm tree in a corner. "This is my private space. They don't bug me in here." They were behind the building, where the trucks waited. They could hear the noise of men talking, loading blocks and patio spacers.

She narrowed her eyes shrewdly. "You're hounded to death, aren't you," she said. The question was a gamble.

"You don't know the half of it."

She put her feet up. Larry put his beside hers. Their feet were similar in shape, rounded, sturdy. "This is nice," she said. "I like a little noise in the background, a blue sky overhead."

"As long as the noise is making money, isn't your wife whining."

"Yeah. *Women*," said Lenore. She shifted her feet, left over right. "I might as well get to the point. Gary needs to get out of Vancouver, out of that damn condo. He needs a job. Some guidance and discipline. This is important. And. You can open a kitchen wares department. Ruth is changing. Everybody is looking for Italian-made stainless-steel strainers, trust me, I know this sort of thing."

"I have other things on the go just now. With the wife." He took off his Carmichael Building Supply ball cap and flipped it in his fingers.

"He's your only nephew. The only boy in the family."

His foot tapped.

She was thinking about what she could use on Larry when she clearly heard Gary's words: "I'm not moving, if that's what you think!" He had made such a sad assumption. She felt it wrench at her heart. "We all do things we're sorry for," she said. Then a memory surfaced – Nan mentioning she'd been occupied by other things when Mother died. Karen, the oldest girl. At boarding school. Why would you send a girl away? Pregnant? On drugs? How many other people in the Judith Lake Valley had girls away at school? Ha!

She went for it. "Why did you send Karen to boarding school?"

If he hadn't gone pale before her eyes, she wouldn't have believed it possible. She was itching to ask, to pry, to inveigle out of him the secret she now knew he had. But it was imperative that she control herself, keep focused.

"Okay," Larry said. He cleared his throat. His cheeks had gone pink.

Shame? Embarrassment? What had Karen done? "And he'll need a plane ticket. He doesn't have a car."

Larry agreed again. "I could use somebody in the store, sure. There's a room in the back. Yeah, sure."

Though she longed to know what she didn't, she understood that when you were on a winning streak, you didn't quit. She said, "One more thing. There's a suitcase in the woods – don't ask questions. I need your help in retrieving it. I'll explain later. Tell Nan you need to spend some time with your sister. We could get there and back in a day" – even now she didn't want to think about the bedspread in the motel – "and it would be fun, hanging out with you, talking." She saw the look on Larry's face and amended her sentence. "Just shooting the breeze, nothing important. I, um, listen. I promise I will not pry into your life if you don't pry into mine."

He rubbed a big soft hand over his nose and mouth and flipped the cap back on his head.

She said, "There's treasure in the suitcase, and if you present it to your loving wife, she will be grateful. I can't presuppose in what form the gratitude will take." She raised her eyebrows. She could imagine his confusion. She felt a little confused herself. She looked at the bags under his eyes, at his gaze avoiding hers. She felt light-headed, as though some good-fairy house-keeper had entered her and was cleaning out the unsavoury corners of her nature. She said, "An inukshuk knows where the suitcase is." She stood up. She looked again at her brother. "I love you," she said. "I promise, no prying." He stood then and they shook hands.

Though Gary would bring some slippery elm, because Gary was reliable in that sort of way, and Larry was on the phone to Vancouver that very second, she picked up 200 grams of the stuff at WildFoods. The clerk with blue hair told her to put the powder in a blender and then chug it down with water or juice. But do it fast; it expanded. Back at the Centre, Lenore did those things.

She had to get to the toilet.

She turned to flush and looked down. She stared. The matter that floated in the bowl was shaped into a mucus-laden, knotted braid, purple-veined, here a spot of bright blood, there a swatch of burnt gold. The strangest, oddest excrement in the world –

something that had been so entwined into the literal entrails of her being. The polyps all neatly packaged, released. Free from her body. She pushed the handle.

Ann-Marie arrived, bringing her chihuahua and nine people who had vowed on the plane out to become macrobiotic because a woman who had recovered from a particularly virulent form of cancer in their group convinced them the diet would benefit them all. Busy with towels and bedding, Lenore had begged Estelee to drive into Ruth and buy up all the tofu from WildFoods and a fifty-pound bag of organic brown rice, and then Milee Logan hauled it to the house by pulling it on a tarp, along with all the bags of turnips, miso, onions, seaweed, salted plums, and barley sugar Estelee could find. Lenore then downloaded recipes for the macrobiots, as she called them, from the Internet while the group was sorting themselves out in the loft, doing a lot of shrieking in the manner of strangers determined to be magnanimous toward each other, determined to have a good time.

Ann-Marie did not want to sleep communally, any more than Lenore herself would have under the circumstances, not interested in farting in the night or garbled dreams or snoring. In a group that size, women or not, someone would snore and the others would joke about it and that would be the first bonding experience. Ann-Marie cornered her in the kitchen. "I must have my own space," she said in a stage whisper.

Her eyes bugged out like the eyes of the chihuahua in her arms. Lenore made a decision and took a firm step back. "We don't offer separate rooms. You received Lucinda's e-mails."

"I work with angels, you see. I need candles and crystals and intense solitude to do my work. My work is in the subtle realm of the supernatural. Intensely, intimately spiritual."

The woman was so lunatic, so zealous, coupled with the shivering chihuahua, that Lenore buckled. She gave the psychologist her room and moved into Lucinda's, which had a better bed. She made a big pot of brown rice and cut up tofu and fried it in sesame oil and then dripped tamari on the works. She knew they would eat brown rice. That night, while they were still jet-lagged, she gathered them around the farmhouse table in the loft. After Ann-Marie said the grace, during which she called on all the higher powers for good to come in and join them, Lenore, at the head of the table, waited an appropriate moment and then stood. She took her time, delayed speaking until they quieted, noticing her. She was uncertain of what to say, but she knew from having worked with children that first you had to get their attention. These people were from Cincinnati. "Watch out for bears," she said.

The little gasps and inhalations fluttering from one person to another around the table was satisfying. She was on the right track.

"You're in *Canada*," she said, letting the fact sink in – snow, blizzards, Mounties, whatever they thought they knew.

"The wilderness," she said, opening her arms dramatically, gesturing to the windows out of which were trees, nothing but trees and mountains and sky. They craned their necks, they turned on the benches to look.

They began murmuring among themselves, recalling the drive from the airport, the endless miles of wilderness they'd passed through in the van pushing northward.

Lenore recounted a "bear kitchen" story, in which a bear gathered garbage bags and deposited them in a shed to sort through later. Bears do not keep tidy kitchens, she said. She told them to look at the marks on the shed beside the trail and they would see bear claw marks, grizzly bear claws, she said (though not sure if they were claw marks she thought they could be.) They were lucky they didn't eat bacon, she said, because bears love bacon. And if they went walking, they were to wear a bear bell on their ankles – kept on the porch table for their use –

Lucinda had planned for everything – don't go if menstruating because male bears might be driven crazy. Eyebrows shot up. As she spoke about bears – she'd heard some of the stories from Milee Logan and some from Mary Populakis – she added a few flourishes of her own; she began to feel part of a lineage of sorts. After that, organizing them into cooking teams and cleanup teams was a cinch.

She knew what to do next. She went into the office and woke up Lucinda's computer. She clicked her way to Toys 'R' Us and ordered an Elmo. She used Lucinda's post-office box and, for convenience, her credit card too, because Lenore knew herself to be the kind of person who could, in the end, figure out everything. The Elmo was on its way.

21

A heart could break any number of times, and one time it caught Kathleen toothbrush in hand, her body engaged in habit, performing a small, necessary task, when she stopped moving, just like that. In the unexpected quiet caused by her immobility – no slippered feet sliding on the parquet, no water running – she began to notice a stirring, like something tearing, starting in behind her right breast and moving across her chest to the pulsing tissue behind the left; she felt movement, a silent slipping, as though sutures that had been sewn tight, back there in the dark, were coming undone. Some doom impending, on its way, moving in, taking over, alongside it a pulse-racing concept: James died. Her ears closed up, as when moving upwards too rapidly in an elevator in a skyscraper, or on a plane descending too fast, and they began to ring, two tonal sounds, one after the other. She shook her head but the ringing remained. She stood in a void, as if she were without a self, in a weightless, spacious, gaping nothing. Her ears popped. Because it was true and would always be so, the loss of James a fact engraved, literally, in stone and no hope for otherwise despite her efforts, there was no end to time to be endured. What to do with herself, anyway?

After she'd fled, ashamed, from Ruth – Davida had discovered Boris missing from their bed the night he was in the cabin with Kathleen – she had tried to erase Boris from her mind, but a passing thought of him as she bustled along a Toronto street thrilled her, the cascade of sensation washing the length of her body and splashing up again, exhilarating and restorative as though he was the secret source of life. Aware of him, she managed the trek through her days; she managed to get by. She began the task of sorting James's many things, she worked with clients, she had lunch with friends, everyone said she was doing so well. Then one evening she drank half a bottle of pinot noir and telephoned Boris. He wasn't home. The next evening, she drank the other half of the bottle and phoned him again. It became a focus, the drinking of wine, the phoning of Boris. He was never home. She had not left messages, in case Davida was there. She had no way of knowing what had happened between them. She had Googled Boris, sitting at James's big desk that the movers had delivered because she'd burbled, Yes, send it over, to a colleague from his office over the phone, but she had forgot how big the desk actually was and had had to phone a friend to help move the bedroom furniture out of the master bedroom – move out his dresser, his chest – in order to fit in the desk that she then put her computer on – a new one, one that James had never seen, one that he didn't know anything about, nor hardly did she; she'd bought new shower curtains too and bed linens – she put the new computer on his desk, and when the movers were gone and her friend was gone she'd sat at the desk and cried buckets because then she knew – how dense can you be? – she knew for a fact that James was not hiding in his office. Her entrenched hopefulness was difficult to explain to people in their rational minds, her constant, almost-cheerful checking in places where someone might not have thought to look, where he might yet turn up. As long as James's desk and file cabinet were at the office, it was possible – how you surmised these things was uncanny – that he also was there, involved in a project beyond their grasp, intensely busy. When his office furniture showed up at the apartment, where he was supposed to be living with her – and yet he was nowhere around to claim it – well, was that a hostile message or wasn't it? A person could lose patience. She had a lot to tell him by then. She had begun to further unravel, to lose her exterior equanimity, as the signs of James's ongoing intention to remain absent continued to gather like crows at sunset.

The trees in the park beside the building began to lose their summer sheen. The fountain sounded exhausted instead of refreshing. There were scurries of wind that scattered a few early leaves onto the ground. There was no future for her in Toronto. She sat in the dark at James's desk and Googled Boris and at least knew where *he* was – mentioned on nearly every Ruth-related site, and she knew his phone number and heard his voice on the voice mail and she knew the look of the town where Boris was, alive and somewhere.

At the end of August, she rented a car at the airport that, being compact and white, stuck out like a sore thumb when she parked it two hours later among the vans and pickups at the WildFoods store in Ruth. She locked the car, as usual, and then brought her bag of organic carrots back to it and automatically punched the keypad and heard the car beep. Out here, watched by the massive mountains, the rented car piping up made her feel ridiculous. She drove up a hill she remembered driving up with Boris, in the fragrant rosiness of June – she had since been along the road a hundred times in her mind – to the old house now hers, steering around a large shaggy black dog (once she'd ascertained it wasn't dead) lying in the middle of the road. She'd braked, opened the car door, and then it had looked up. She drove around to the back of the house, the house smaller than she recalled it, and parked in the alley behind the fence. It was growing dark and she was buzzing as though she'd run the whole distance. Coming back west was a spur-of-the-moment idea; for days she had been to and from her apartment's storage locker, hauling files and boxes up to the apartment, sorting through James's letters and mementos. He seemed to have saved everything, including intellectual mush notes to past sweethearts. She had found some of the lines disconcertingly familiar.

She couldn't get the ancient gate to open – wired shut by a snarl impossible to sort out – and she got back in the car and drove around to the front of the house the long way, she would learn later, around the dog again, and parked awkwardly; the road seemed to have an upward slant that she hadn't noticed that magical day with Boris, and there was a pothole that she tried not to set a wheel in. Gathering some things, she heard a sound overhead and a raven came into view beating the air, flying so hard, the heavy air working against its powerful wings, the resolute whoosh, whoosh as if its keeping itself aloft – keeping going – was a struggle. All the letters to Davida, unanswered, her heartsickness a vacuum where friendship had been – *Oh, what have I done to you?* she had written. And had not received a single word, which, no doubt, was warranted. Who could say what really went on between a couple?

She glanced up the slope at the ironwork bench, a patch of mushrooms working their way toward it on stretch of alien green grass, the rest brown. The sight of the hidden bench with its initials E & S did not cheer her – so much mugwort and, now she saw, thistles to grapple with, in order to free it from its tangles. She left the heavier luggage in the car and went with her bag of carrots and overnight bag up the concrete steps and across the cement path, weeds growing through the cracks, and onto the porch.

Someone from the real estate office was supposed to have sent someone to clean; she'd phoned to arrange it, but the first glimpse inside did not bode well. There was a layer of dust on the floor and dead flies on the windowsills, and over there, one split, yellowed shade half drawn, and when she stepped inside, the overall odour was musty with an underlying taint of mildew; no Mr. Clean had darkened this door. She followed the long hallway toward the kitchen, where the situation was worse. The kitchen smelled of something awful, something sprouting, rotten or dead or both. She stood a moment under the overhead fixture, the light not working, turning words around in her head: something awfully dead, something dead-awful.

The bag of carrots thunking on the counter made her realize another fact: she didn't have a juicer. The only reason she had acquired two pounds of carrots in the first place was to make a healthful juice because she'd thought, driving north, ears ringing, that she needed the vitamin A, the beta carotene, and whatever else carrots had going for them. She had started thinking of carrots and the juice as the Dash 7 veered and bumbled over the mountains from Calgary, air disappearing from beneath the wing and the subsequent queasy, breath-stopping downward jolts causing tense looks between her and the fourteen-year-old seated beside her. It had not helped that they had seen flames in the back country, flames on the mountains and rising streamers of hot blue smoke. She'd put on a good face because by then she knew that her row-mate was travelling by plane for the first time – he had tried to tip the flight attendant for the orange juice – here, he said, this is for you, reaching across Kathleen holding a loonie with a confidence that neither she nor the attendant had the heart to destroy – oh, you just keep that now, lad, the flight attendant had said. You'll need it.

Thinking of the naive, well-meaning boy on his first flight and of the useless carrots that she had so purposefully, stupidly bought, the green ends shooting out of the 100%-recycled paper bag with a sort of hopefulness – green! organic! you'll be fine! – the whole gamut of recent events ganged up on her and tears threatened. Once, she had been captivated by the house – in this dull light so badly in need of renovation! so shabby! – mesmerized by it, mesmerized by a romantic bench with a view and a few gloriously old apple trees and Boris. The contagious buoyant charm of Boris.

She would carry on and make the best of things. She tugged open a painted wood drawer, looking for a vegetable peeler, and found only a few plastic knives. She pulled a carrot out of the bag and turned on the faucet – the water worked – and washed it and began to eat it, unpeeled. The carrots had worked their way into her plan; they represented her new beginning. She would eat right, exercise, start fixing up the house – paint, paper, whatever – then, who knew? She had allowed three weeks for the future to let itself be known – Boris – then she would head back and close up the apartment, send furniture west, start her new life in the mountains far away from where she and James had lived together, far from anything they'd identified as being theirs as a couple but not so far that he couldn't find her if he was passing by and wanted to stop in. He would recognize Ruth; he knew the place, he'd liked it.

She tried the next drawer and it was wedged, as well. You had to wiggle it to get it shut and even then it went in crooked. No drawer runners. She opened the cupboard under the sink, looking for cleaning supplies. There was half a bottle containing something a malignant green and some rags, moulded into rigid shapes. She closed the cupboard door and bit into the carrot and chewed with renewed determination but then, because it was cold in the house, despite the frantic heat, an unlived-in cold, and was already darkening outside and the wind was rising, and the smell terrible, she began to cry and as she did half-chewed carrot pieces slipped out of her mouth onto the floor.

Outside, she heard a *woof*, a single *woof* sound. It startled her into closing her mouth. She listened. But there was nothing further.

Being tired made her feel cold. She looked for a thermostat and turned it past 25°C, put her hand on a baseboard heater in the dining room, hoping. It didn't exert itself even to creak. How could a house be so chilled when it had been so hot all summer? She lifted the phone. Of course not. How had she thought her new life would begin, when she hadn't even considered electricity? She went outside and stood on the porch, intending to get her suit-cases from the car. She had packed three or four cans of chicken broth for emergencies; one of those things you do feeling perfectly sensible. She had not packed a can opener. She'd once seen a movie where a fellow with cases of canned food was dropped off by plane in the Far North, and he had no can opener either. She thought he ended up catching and eating rodents, maybe mice. She was thinking about eating mice herself when she looked up and saw light beginning to leak into the sky from behind the mountains. The haze had lifted, exposing darkness and a few stars, and across the lake – she could see a glimmer on the water caused by lights from the town – the mountains were regrouping, coming forward against a backdrop of brightening aqua blues. There was one peak – she couldn't remember its name – more pointed than the others and behind it she recognized that the glow wasn't caused by northern lights but from the rising moon.

If her stomach hadn't growled, she would have pondered the sight for a while, but her mind went into auto pilot and she remembered the can of sardines she'd packed at the last minute. And she had a mini of cabernet sauvignon in her carry-on bag for use in emergencies. Her spirits rose.

She started the car and looked at the clock. It was late enough, Eastern time, for her to be really hungry. Sardines and carrots?

There were alternatives. She could drive back into town and hope for an open café. She should do that, she could. She turned off the car and watched her breath making steamy puffs on the windshield. She touched the glass with a finger; smeary.

The road was dark, there were no street lights in this neighbourhood, she saw, and she was so weary she might drive herself into circles and not find her way back. Sardines and carrots it would be, despite how desperate the combination sounded. She took a bag inside and trudged up the stairs, into the big bedroom at the front of the house. She had imagined that the bed would be made; she had pictured a candle in a brushed nickel holder ready to be lit. But of course there was not even a bed in the room, nor were there linens, there was only linoleum, in greys and lilacs, worn thin and torn in places, nailed to the floorboards.

She opened the closet and found a foam mattress, rolled and tied. She was practically giddy at the discovery – that, and the room smelling cleanly of dust and maybe, maybe she was inventing the next sensation, old roses. Galvanized, she went through the rooms upstairs, into every closet and cubbyhole. She located a cotton comforter that must have belonged to a child, or was made by a child, the pinks and blues in the patchwork faded, the stitches holding it together loose and big. It was something to put over her legs, however; it would be warming. She unwrapped the foam mattress and tried to press it flat, but nothing doing. Only when she used a corner of her suitcase to hold one side and lay upon it did it give in a little and begin to settle.

This would be a long night. She took clothing out of the suitcase and lay pieces on the mattress to make her bed softer, and then she went outside to get the second suitcase and the moon was higher and brighter than before – the clear white globe of a summer moon – and the second suitcase was heavier and there was that sound again, that *woof* that stopped her in her tracks and made her breathing audible and then she thought of bears. Davida and Boris had told her bear stories; according to them, Ruth was a haven for bears, spring, summer, and fall. Bears were hungry in general, always fattening up for winter, even she knew that. Her limbs were paralyzed as she stood halfway up the final set of steps toward the safety of the veranda and its porch, almost to the house but not there yet. *Woof.*

Dog.

It was the big, curly-haired black dog that had been lying in the road. In the glare of moonlight she saw the wide set of its friendly eyes in a big face, its tail flapping. "Oh, dog," she said, letting go of the suitcase. "Oh, it's you, dog," she said. It smelled like a dog in need of a bath, but it smelled better than whatever was in the kitchen.

She sat in the dining room on the one chair, wearing her jacket, and ate the sardines, extra-small ones packed in olive oil, holding the can under her chin. She ate another carrot for good measure. She went upstairs to get ready for bed. She glanced out the small window of the upstairs bathroom into the shadows of the woods behind, the moon silhouetting trees against the sky.

In the morning the yard from the dormer looked faded, like the grass had run out of colour, everything pale in the throes of a summer of unforgivable dehydration; she'd watched the B.C. fires on the news. A helicopter startled her, whanging its blades overhead. The sapling maple leaves outside the kitchen window were yellow, a grave and disheartening yellow, an early death knell for the season, the colour hard to look at. Beyond the sapling were a few sunflowers, volunteers, she supposed, brown and hung over, looking hard done by. The house, however, remained cool; it seemed to have sucked in all the moisture.

There was no time to waste; she needed electricity and a phone. She washed her face and ran a brush through her hair and walked down to Cedar Hideaway and wended her way along the treed path, past vacant camper spots, past three small cabins. At Cedar Hideaway, they would be used to tourists and questions and they would know who she should talk to about the power and where to find everything. The owners had lived in the area a long time; Boris, she remembered, had said so himself. She knocked on the door that said "Office" with a notepad beside it nestled in a dusty cedar house, an unsharpened pencil hanging from a string.

The door opened and a rumpled woman with bright eyes, apparently not surprised to see a stranger so early in the day, said, "You must be in Eunice's place. I heard you were coming." *I heard you were coming.* The words darted through Kathleen's mind and in the next instant she understood that Bet Harker – the woman introduced herself as Bet – would know about Davida and Boris Malenko – everyone knew Boris, even she knew that – and with the realization that *someone would know something* she felt calmer than she had in days and days, possibly in weeks, and then she felt elated – unsuitably, inappropriately elated. She introduced herself and was invited in and they walked through a small office that had a bowl of wrapped candies on the counter and into the sitting room where Bet introduced the man in the wheelchair as her husband. "Hardly miss him working around the place," she said, raising her voice. The man looked up, tossed his head in reply. Bet invited Kathleen to stay for tea, and Kathleen accepted, and sat in the kitchen while Bet wheeled Clarence in and parked the chair at the head of the table.

Bet said to Clarence, raising her voice again, "You'll soon be doing this yourself. I am worn out from being your servant."

"Yuh, you are," he said. "Make that one fuckin' clear-cut."

"He tangles words a bit but always did, eh?" Bet said to Kathleen, then turned to Clarence. "You! Watch your language." She turned her attention to the making of the tea and set out the brown betty teapot and the bags of Red Rose ready for the boiling water. She set out cups and spoons and retrieved a cut lemon from the refrigerator and a carton of half-and-half and took out a bag of digestive biscuits, and while she did all this, she told Kathleen what had happened to Clarence that summer: "It was a stroke, though not so serious as it looks. Two weeks ago he was walking and all but's had surgery on his knee that got worse when his brain was damaged. *Yes, it's damaged all right,*" she said to Clarence, "because you keep *swearing.* As though I didn't have enough trouble with *teenaged boys.* Oh, hell," she said, pouring the sputtering water from the electric kettle into the teapot. "Soon as his knee picks up, it's back to the shed with him so I can get some peace."

Clarence was smiling and nodding affably.

"You see how he likes the attention," Bet said, squinting at him. "They're all alike, men. They just can't get enough."

Clarence chuckled.

Kathleen, observing them, felt like an intruder. The banter between them seemed clumsy – she didn't believe that they had always, throughout their marriage, talked to each other in the jolly, upbeat manner she was hearing. She stirred sugar into her tea. Bet sat down and Kathleen heard her sigh. "Must be hard," Kathleen said to be polite, clucking her tongue.

"Harder for you."

The comment took Kathleen by surprise, and part of the surprise was the tears that sprang to her eyes. How could someone she hadn't met before know anything about her? Who besides Boris and Davida knew about James? And then she thought of her phone call about the cleaning and the realtor or someone in WildFoods store – who knew – and she supposed that was the way it was here in Ruth, which was why, in fact, she was in her neighbour's kitchen in the first place, to get news and information.

"Ah, now," Bet said.

"It just catches me, odd times," Kathleen said, speaking of the weeping, unexpected and out of the blue.

"Fella's here, all righty," said Clarence.

"What are you on about now?" Bet walked past him and into the other room, bringing back a box of tissues that she placed on the table. Kathleen pulled one and patted her cheeks and blew her nose.

"See him clear as day," Clarence said. "A fella. Has a beard. A hat."

"He's not been the same," Bet said to Kathleen.

"A red-haired fella."

He was talking about her own red-haired fella, she knew. She had almost been expecting James, she had been thinking he would get in touch with her, he would know that she was pressing toward an unknown edge, know that she was behaving outrageously, dishonourably, compelled by nothing decent or virtuous or moral, compelled by a rush in her body, its breathlessness, its insatiable desire, its running toward union.

Coinciding with her perception that James was nearby, the atmosphere in the kitchen became charged with an energy that definitely wasn't ordinary. The hairs on her arms stood on end, and her scalp prickled. Anything was possible, of course, and she believed that the scrim between this world and the next, invisible to her, could thin to transparency; she believed in the ethereal, she believed in the possibility. She'd seen a program on A&E, about ancient Roman pottery, and the camera had zoomed in on the relief on a small vase that the narrator pointed out depicted a dead soldier returning home to say goodbye to his wife. The couple were facing each other, the widow's gaze downward, not seeing him. His hand clasped hers firmly, but her fingers weren't folded to return the pressure, because she was unsure, Kathleen had thought at the time, whether she was touching anything or conjuring it, invoking it through her melancholy, though on the vase she had gone so far as to extend her hand, just in case. Kathleen thought, *Just in case*, and she put out her own hand, palm up, and waited.

Clarence was peering beyond her, over her shoulder, toward the window above the sink. She turned her body in the chair to look, expecting a shimmer or glow, but she saw nothing unusual, just fading flowered curtains and the range with a frying pan on a burner. She looked back at Clarence, her hand still out, and saw his expression open as a child who was too naive and trusting to know that he might fear whatever he was seeing. She wasn't startled either, as a warmth that felt gentle moved along her right side. Across the table Bet started to say something and then didn't. The kettle fussed a little, cooling down.

"Over there."

Her palm suddenly burned.

"Gone now," Clarence said and smiled at Kathleen and winked a blue eye. It was just what James used to do – look at her fondly like that, then deliberately wink and smile. Kathleen thanked him and felt the kitchen return to normal – three people at a table, sharing a simple tea – and wondered about forgiveness, if James would forgive her for what she was up to, and she wondered if where he was, forgiveness even mattered.

"Well," Bet said, still standing. She was looking around the room, at the ceiling.

"I guess," said Kathleen and poured a dollop of half-and-half into her cup.

The refrigerator grumbled. Clarence's head drooped.

"Falls asleep in the middle of a sentence like an old man. Now seeing things." Bet took her chair at the table.

"At least you have him."

"True." She looked comically dubious and Kathleen sipped her drink and smiled. She said, "My husband's name is – was James. I often feel him around, as though he's looking after me, in a way. I assume he knows things, that he's aware of me. I don't visit the cemetery or talk out loud, I don't mean that. It's – well, I came to get some information, to tell you the truth. I – I wanted to ask about Boris. Malenko. You must know him."

"Money-grubbing bastard."

"Well, yes, aside from that," said Kathleen, leaning forward.

She drove into town with instructions from Bet and found a manager at work in the cinder-block hydro office. He said it was company policy to do a credit check before hooking the house up, but if he didn't do it today, she would have to wait a week. She showed him her credit card. She said, "Here, it's good." He looked at her and then toward the window. He rubbed a hand over his chin and looked at her again. "You can put that away now," he said. "Harry at Ruth Reality sold you the place?"

She tried to remember if the man's name was Harry. "Tall? Smooth-skinned, sort of bald?"

The man nodded. "You'll be set this afternoon," he said and let her use his phone to get her telephone service going. She drove into the old part of town and went into a small hardware store. She walked up to the counter, and said to a man with a pleasant face, wearing glasses, "There are mice in my house, I found one dead in a cupboard."

"Whereabouts are you?"

She started to explain how to get to the house, unsure how the information was relevant. "Oh," he said, after a moment of her struggling with directions. "The Sonemayer place. I suppose that would be yours now, eh?"

Kathleen nodded. "They said they would clean, but it wasn't done, so it was a mess when I got in yesterday."

The man looked straight at her and said nothing. He turned to another customer, an older man browsing the sale shelves. "This lady has mice. What do you recommend?"

"The mice in Eunice's house would expect something fancy, like havarti, would be my bet."

"Oh, no," a woman said, carrying a pack of light bulbs. "Peanut butter. They're not particular. Jiffy works."

The man at the counter looked again at Kathleen. "I myself use good old Canadian cheddar, the oranger the better." He went away for a moment and came back with three traps, which he set before her. "These will do the trick."

"I don't know how to set a trap."

"You don't say?" The older man at the sale shelves stepped back as though to get a better look at someone who didn't know this obvious thing.

The man behind the counter gave him a smile and turned back to Kathleen and looked at her over the rim of his glasses. "Harkers have boys. Down the street. Go see them."

"Are they good workers?"

The man looked at her the way he had before, solemn. Then he raised his eyebrows. "You could get a cat, I suppose, eh?"

"I guess," Kathleen eventually said, laughing lightly with the others.

She went down the street with her mousetraps and into the real estate office. It was lunch hour evidently, Harry wasn't in; he'd gone home. Kathleen was told by a young woman at a computer that she could wait or come back later, though the man had several appointments in the afternoon. She herself was making up for a late morning. "The thing is," Kathleen said, "I'm in the Sonemayer house. You may know it."

"Yes," the girl said.

"He was going to get someone to come over and clean before I arrived and it wasn't done."

"Oh," the girl said, cheeks reddening. She sat back and crossed her arms. She swivelled her chair and came to a halt at an angle from Kathleen. "Diane was going to do it, but her little boy was sick, they called her from the babysitter's, some flu going round. She tried to get Marlene, but she wasn't available, working for the home care the way she does. It was her day off, she had to get her own place looked after. She has teenagers."

"Oh," Kathleen said. "Well, it was awkward coming into the house for the first time after a long flight and all the rest. You can imagine. There was a dead mouse in the kitchen. It was bad."

"They do smell, especially in the heat," said the girl agreeably, swivelling back to her keyboard. "Set a trap with cheddar. Don't bother with the American cheese, especially the slices. It isn't real and they know it. Mum says they're smart."

The whole time Kathleen was running her errands – engaged, busy – her heart beat capriciously, in a pitch of controlled excitement: she might see him at any moment, he might come down the street toward her, he might drive past, he might be sitting in the café where she intended to have a big green salad with dressing on the side and a glass of milk for the calcium. He might be shopping in the grocery store, the small one in the old part of town where she was planning to go for cleaning supplies and breakfast supplies and B.C. wine and two kinds of cheese and peanut butter, he might be buying potatoes, she knew he liked potatoes, Davida had made potato pancakes with sour cream on top one morning and he had complimented her on their flavour and texture. At the thought of Davida, her heart picked up its pace, but there was nothing exhilarating about it, a prompting of obscure angst and a twinge of bleakness. Davida had moved out of the house. She and Boris had a separation agreement; Bet Harker had said that Davida had been so angry that she went to a local barrister instead of one in Tucker, two hours away, and the news – not the lawyer's fault, Bet added; the woman working in the office at the time liked a drink or two at the pub and had talked and then was fired – anyway, word had got around that Boris was unfaithful but, then, everyone knew he always had been.

"He is? He was?" Kathleen hadn't meant to speak out loud on the street. Yet the news of his repeated unfaithfulness hardly mattered when she first heard it and it hardly mattered now, because four steps farther along, five steps, six: she might see him, he might come around the next corner, walk toward her, lift his hand in greeting, he might come close and touch her hand, place his palm on her cheek.

In the morning she went to look out the window in the north dormer and saw a puzzling sight, a trail of powder or dust or a weird growth meandering across the dew-bright yard below. Strange. She could not think what would have popped up overnight in the grass, something that looked mealy, like Red River cereal, fallen from the sky in an uneven pattern. She wondered, next, if these were fairy mushrooms or a message or a code from a passing star. She stood a moment, blinking, then went down and found her leather ankle boots – she needed to get some more suitable footwear – and put them on and crept outside. She followed the trail across the road and down a lane she hadn't noticed before, to where it started at the open door of a shed, a derelict Volkswagen in it, and then followed the erratic trail back up, her breath vapour ahead of her, onto her own rise and into the yard, around the side of the house, past an apple tree – the apples smallish and unripe – and through the long rustling grass, around a stack of wood in a falling-down cradle, around a wild rose bush wearing dried-up rosehips, and into a bed of struggling cosmos, small in size and fading in colour, and then the grain – for it was grain, she had rubbed a sample between her fingers – continued into the bush behind her place.

She was considering going farther, but at her feet was a pile of brown animal poop, not dog, the sheer size stopping her in her tracks. She knew what dog looked like. The pile was definitely fresh but didn't smell, and it had been deposited by something large. Her aloneness gaped; it occurred to her that while she thought of Eunice Sonemayer's property as hers, the fact was it had been uninhabited for a long time and had gone back to nature, and from the woods behind it anything could come strolling out, she herself the newcomer. She turned toward the house; she spun and waded, splashed through the high grass, clambered onto the back porch.

There was a knock on the door. Two big boys stood on the front porch, hanging their heads shyly. The one called Jay said, "We heard you needed mousetraps looked after."

"Oh, yes," said Kathleen. "I do. I was telling your mother. And I was just screwing up my nerve to give them another try. I snapped my finger once, and I have all this cheese and peanut butter – everybody had different ideas – what do you think? Do they like cheese or peanut butter? Havarti? Cheddar?"

The boys looked at each other and hung their heads lower, confused, probably, by her chatter. "Oh. Hey. Come in," she said, "please."

When the traps were set she led them around to the side of the house to look at the trail of grain still visible in the grass. The one boy, Jay, broke into a grin. "Old Warren was mighty" – she thought he was going to say "pissed off" but he changed his mind, his brother frowning disapproval – "p.o-ed about the loss of all that chicken feed."

"Door left open," said the other boy, the first she'd heard him speak.

"Pardon?"

"Mechanic working on the Volkswagen."

"Left the door open."

Kathleen waited, her hands open, for the finish. The boys looked at each other. "Bear," Jerry said, speaking, she thought, with slight emphasis as though she weren't quite bright.

Afterwards, she went to the general mercantile and bought a lined Dickies-brand plaid shirt with snaps. She bought a pair of gumboots, a size too big but that's all they had. From there she drove out to Boris's and quietly, holding her breath, hoped to see his Subaru, but there were no vehicles she recognized in the driveway, though there was one she didn't, and the house itself looked closed down. She drove slowly back to her own house – what had she done, buying a house on a whim? – and went in and continued scrubbing. Someone from the telephone company came by and added a phone jack for the bedroom upstairs. When he had gone, she lifted the phone, and overcome by reassurance – the sense of power and connection granted by a trusty dial tone – she phoned Boris and thought the words: "I'm here and I want to see you." But she couldn't say them and listened to the silence on the line instead and, hanging up, lay as still as possible on the makeshift bed.

22

Bet found out easily enough that Bethany Jane had spent the night with Yakov in the cabin at the back of Boris Malenko's land, where the boy – Boris's bastard son, his nephew, some distant relation – rumours were rife – had been staying. Everything was loose this year, nothing quite holding its place, Bet thought, except for her. And she was holding. It turned out that Bethany Jane had gone to Mexico with the Malenko kid, taken a bus headed to someplace called Jalisco, and had promised, through the letter she left for Clarence that Bet found under her pillow – Bet had *mussed* it, not *lifted* it – that she would write when they were settled. She didn't know about her dad's condition, and maybe, from Bet's point of view, that was just as well. The girl had something to get out of her system. She and the boy – Yakov seemed to Bet like a joke of a name – were planning to work on an organic farm under the supervision of a group from New York who were encouraging the Indians in the area to stop using the sprays so available on their crops. They would be living in a group house. There was a name for what they were doing, but Bet couldn't keep it straight. The volunteer part she could understand. The cause she could understand, almost, but she leaned toward the idea that food growing reliably every year, organic or not, was better than no food. But the fact that even in Ruth there was an organic foods-and-such store meant the world was changing, and she was no doubt the one out of touch.

Clarence was sleeping. The dishes were done. The boys were working up the road. She climbed into the cab of her truck and sat a while listening to her own breathing until she knew what she needed to do. Two years of anger and silence were enough. Water under a bridge, at this point. The girls – Bethany Jane and Karen – close childhood friends, separated by what Bet had seen and how she'd acted afterwards, the girls women now, moving on to make the mistakes that women inevitably did. And even when she'd heard that Nan had had breast cancer, she'd not sent so much as a card.

Righteousness. She was so full of it. She started the car and drove south of town, needing to see Nan. Back then, every time Bet went over to the old house, in town where they used to live, to explain, Nan slammed the door, and Bet had gathered her pride and given up. Then the Carmichaels built the new house and moved farther out. The trouble began while on a boating weekend, up the lake, when Bet had come upon Larry kissing Karen, their oldest daughter, who was sixteen at the time. Nothing fatherly about the kiss. Karen wasn't biologically his – an indiscretion he never forgave Nan for – which may have made his behaviour remotely acceptable in Nan's mind. So Bet supposed, and she'd had time to give it sufficient study; maybe that was how Nan had excused him. As though she *owed* him because of her original infidelity – getting pregnant with Karen in the first place – and now they were even. They'd sent Karen away to a boarding school in Calgary. Where Bet blew it, she'd always supposed, was going to Boris Malenko, acting principal at the high school their girls were attending, to ask for advice. For that she should have had her head examined.

Turning into the Carmichaels' driveway, her palms were in a sweat. The driveway was so long she couldn't see the house, and the distance made her hesitate; there could be a trap up ahead, and she might not be able to get back out. She parked outside, walked around the gate. The pine needles were dry underfoot, some of the trees brown; pine beetle or some other damn infestation, she thought. It was hard to keep up with all the disasters.

Nan was in the flower garden, tucked into a butterfly chair, one of those well-cushioned, wide-winged ones you could sink into. She was facing away from the driveway, toward the water, but from Bet's distance Nan seemed physically small.

"Hello?" Nan had heard her and Bet stopped moving forward and said, "It's Bet." Unsure Nan would recognize her voice, it had been so long since she'd heard it. "I'm sorry," Bet said, stepping around the chair so Nan could see her. Nan had her chin propped by one fine manicured finger.

"I've come to talk."

Nan raised an eyebrow, the gesture dripping skepticism, a gift Bet thought Nan had begun developing in high school.

"I'm sorry I went to Boris. There I was out of line."

"What are you prattling about?"

"Back then. With Karen."

"I don't have time for this," Nan said.

Back then Bet had assumed Nan would move mountains to do the right thing, but she'd chosen to defend Larry by her silence. Recklessly, Bet had raced down to the school to talk to Boris about what a person should do in a case of child abuse. To think that she had believed for one second that Boris Malenko, of all people, would be a beacon of decency just proved she had been in deep water. One thing led to another.

Karen hadn't come back to Ruth to graduate with her class. Nothing else surfaced.

Bet took a breath. "I might've kept my mouth shut, not gone to Boris, but it wouldn't have been true to my nature." She waited for Nan to laugh, but she didn't even blink. Bet went on: "In other news, Bethany Jane isn't going to university. Not this fall anyway. She's on her way to Mexico to do good works. A three-month stint." The tone of her voice sounded either cynical or bitter, she couldn't decide. "She gave up her scholarship," she added.

Nan's lip curled, as if to let Bet know that if it was her pity she was after, she wasn't going to get it. Nan laughed, a bark of sound. "All four hundred dollars," she said.

Okay. All right. So she knew about the scholarship. It was the old Nan, always one up on you, a reserved meanness that kept the other person a little off balance. Still, Bet began to explain: "Well, there was only" – and then stopped. She was about to pull a Jerry, rationalizing when it would be wiser not to speak, she was about to go too far, to point out that none of Nan's girls even made the honour roll, that only twenty-two kids in the whole graduating class had been chosen for a scholarship in the first place. "I've not forgotten you," she said and moved so that her torso shielded Nan's eyes from the bright light reflecting off the lake.

Nan said, "I'm sorry. I'm not myself. They want to do more tests. And Larry has gone off with his sister overnight. Just when – well." Nan gave her one of those bare, down-to-the-bone glares that Bet would come to recognize over the next months, a look that resulted from a person having nothing to hide and no strength to try. Nan said, "And I've never forgiven you. For not trusting me to handle it. Which I did."

Bet went across the lawn and found a high-backed green plastic chair and set it near but not too near and faced the lake also. A wide-brimmed straw hat with flowers on its rim lay at

Nan's feet. Bet reached for it and handed it to her. Nan settled
the hat on her head at the angle that was perfect for her graceful neck.

"Clarence had a stroke. A little one. He's supposed to recover.
At least to where he started."

Nan covered her mouth. She might have been laughing, but
Bet wasn't sure. They had always teased around about Clarence.

Nan nodded. "I know." Then she said, "Life." This time
there was a little laugh. Her shoulders were moving. She wiped
her eyes with a handkerchief that had been tucked at the side
of the chair.

"I'm not here to completely apologize," Bet warned her. "In
case you thought I was."

Nan's eyes caught Bet in their beam. "Wouldn't be you," she
said, straight-faced.

Then Bet laughed and then she wept as a child does, with no
second thoughts.

At home she finished making the beds in the cabins and went
inside and made tunafish sandwiches from one of Bethany Jane's
cans of albacore in water. She poured out the water, added
canola oil and mayonnaise, enough so the bread wouldn't stick
to the roof of your mouth when you chewed it. She left out the
fine-cut celery so Clarence wouldn't choke on it, and spread
the tuna on white bread, the soft white bread that Bethany Jane
detested. On her own sandwich she added a slice of dill pickle
and extra pepper. She carried the two plates upstairs to the
bedroom. Clarence was dozing or pretending to doze. "I'm here.
And when the boys get home, we're going to haul Bethany Jane's
bed into the living room so you can keep track of what's going
on. Cooler down there too. Be more a part of things."

An eyebrow moved, his lips chewed on themselves for a
moment. She set the sandwiches on the dresser and waited,

looking at him. He had aged. The eyebrow twitch was apparently the only response she was going to get. She knew every wrinkle in Clarence's face as well as she knew the back of her own hand. He did look old. She lay down on the bed next to him. As to whether he'd heard her – maybe he did, maybe he didn't. Maybe he didn't need to; maybe through the years she'd said quite enough. You couldn't tell with her Clarence; he'd always kept her guessing. "Ah, love," she said, and then did the unordinary, placed her hand over his heart.

23

Willamina was supposed to be helping Mory pile rocks from the outdoor picnic area Lenore was constructing – if somebody tripped and cut their hand on a broken glass, for example, the Centre could get sued, she said. Willamina was wearing a cardigan that had belonged to her granny, Ja-Ja, a lilac stitched on the pocket, though it was hot out. BB had on a pair of sunglasses that made him look comical, but no one laughed in front of him. Willamina was angry as Mory thought maybe she was meant to be, since she was angry so often. But she supposed it was good that Willamina was out of bed, though the noise from the firefighting planes and helicopters passing back and forth over the ridge was pissing her off.

"Men and their machines," Willamina said as another helicopter rose from the lake and climbed above them, its bright-orange Bambi bucket suspended from a cable, filled with water, swinging overhead. Willamina covered her ears. When it had flown over the ridge, she said, "Men! Did that or did that not look like a big orange testicle dangling from the sky?" She shouted, "Bastards!" Mory noticed that Willamina's eyes were deep brown and close set and that her chin stuck out a bit. Willamina picked up a rock and hurled it so far it whacked a fencepost. "Ow," she said. Then she ran her fingers through her hair, dark and curly like her mother's. "I'm going to cut it off. I'm going to look butch by the time I'm done with this hair."

"Too bad."

"Oh, good Christ, everything is too bad. There has to be a way out of this fucking place. No offence." Then she stomped home.

Milee said, "This land grows rocks. Everybody knows this as a fact." Which was why, he explained, they were putting more rocks in the wheelbarrows and unloading them onto the rock piles. Last year he and other helpers collected rocks from the garden and the year before that and here they were, back again. Not the same ones, different ones. "Glacial till," he told her, "is the word. And it is always on the move, in secret nooks and crannies underground. The rocks will continue to surface forever. They will keep turning up like *the truth*." He looked at her. "You're chicken, aren't you? Like you would frickin' hate him and you're scared to."

Mory was used to him trying to get her stirred her up, but she was tired of it and tired of working. She sank onto her knees. He pulled her unresisting to her feet and folded her over his shoulder. She let her legs flop and her long arms dangle across his back. She let her neck go loose. He walked along the path from the garden, her hair flouncing against the nape of his neck as he carried her up and down and around the trail.

She had not been carried since her papa last carried her to the root cellar as he did sometimes when she needed it. Or else he carried her to the woods and laid her down on his wool plaid coat and read a book to her that had many very good words she couldn't understand, his voice going along nicely and deep like the music he played on the cello, the strings pulsing like her heart at her wrists when he held her hand and looked into her with that expression he had, and Mummy's voice calling from somewhere, and his moist nose hairs she crossed her eyes to focus on. And him saying, Look at that bird, look at those tracks, look at this moss, carrying her around his neck, holding her legs, her fingers holding tight to his long greying hair, the feel of him laughing beneath her body, the smell of the fresh, clean woods.

Outside the tepee Milee set her on her feet and placed his hands on her shoulders. "I could carry you anywhere," he said. It was not his voice but the voice of the other, who was always surer than he. He cleared his throat and came to himself and began to talk fast, so the other wouldn't have a chance to come in. He said, "Can you walk now? Should I carry you to bed? Are you fine now? Can you walk?"

"Yes. Be quiet."

He blinked at her.

"You're talking," she said. "You don't want to."

"It's true. Good thing, bad thing, it depends. When you think about it. It could be a blessing or a –"

"Think some other time," Mory said.

Willamina came back and found Mory in the tepee. She'd cut her hair. "Just before I was stripped of the good stuff, I applied for the Army Public Relations Officer training program, just so you know. I haven't told anybody. I sent the application Priority Post. If I am accepted I will have to do another year of school on my own – this time in *Vancouver* – thank God! – and next year I, Willamina Populakis, plan to be in Saint-Jean, Québec, for the thirteen-week Basic Officer Training Course. That's my news. As for you," she said to Mory, raising her voice another notch, "you are running out of time. This whole hellhole of a place could burn down tomorrow. You have to go see him, take BB, show him what he did." Then she whirled around, still wearing her granny's sweater.

Mory waited for Milee to show up the next day for work and when he did, she told him, "I give up. I'll go."

"I have to warn you. He stinks. The bastard stinks to high heaven."

"He always did," said Mory.

In the afternoon they left BB with Willamina. It took fifteen minutes bouncing along a dusty, rutted dirt road to get to the turnoff to the cabin. Just seeing the turnoff reached up and throttled her breath.

He said, "I'll go in with you."

Mory shook her head. He didn't ask again, and they sat in the truck and looked through the windshield. Ahead was the road and a few weathered fenceposts and then the road turned north again. Milee rolled down his window. They listened to Enterprise Creek.

When she was ready, he led her down the path, staying close to the trees so as not to be detected. They passed patches of thimble berries and a rusted roll of barbed wire. They climbed over a rotting tree and walked around an anthill and a dried-up spring. The cabin came into view, the roof overgrown with moss, the logs with lichen on them.

"Don't faint," he said.

The cats found them and rubbed their legs.

"Papa is allergic to cats," Mory said, remembering that he used to try to kill the cats with Mummy's slingshot.

Her mother once told her that her papa was a man who couldn't stand isolation. Mummy had spoken slowly, petting her face. It was why he does what he does, she explained. He would rather hate himself than be alone with his feelings. She saw it in her mind, Papa snuffling against her, her mummy with worry on her face. They had come out of the bedroom. He looked at Mory in a certain way. "Don't cry," Mummy said to her. Helping. "Look at me, look at me, look at me," Papa said, holding it, looking at himself, his face rosy and gleaming. Turning so that Mummy had to look too. "Open your eyes, Frieda," he said. "You must look at me. The rules." Mummy went behind him, hands on his shoulders, closing her eyes not to see. Mory's hands on his chest with the hairs, spread on his lap, facing him, the rules. Her eyes on Mummy's closed eyes. Always so quiet in the cabin, but somehow thick with old sounds and struggling and the smells of wool and wood and the chicken soup smell of the bodies.

Milee said, "This is the scat I've been telling you about."

The scat was big, round, and honey-coloured with seeds in it. "I wish a bear would help me," she said and then she started walking toward the cabin. A car in the driveway was covered with dirt and dust and had a flat tire. At the door, she said, "Mummy, Mummy."

The smell came back as the door opened, the root-cellar smell of rotten pears, damp alfalfa, potatoes, mould. Something rotten.

"Let me in. I want to see him."

Frieda casually stepped back from the door as though her daughter lived just down the road. Boxes were everywhere and the smell thick as bad pudding and pots and pans on top of stools to keep them off the floor and the sound of a pipe dripping, the grunting. Open cans of Campbell's chicken noodle soup and tomato soup and white rice grains solid to the floor. There were cats, thin, weasly cats watching her.

Frieda fluttered her hands. "Oh, oh, oh." She was laughing, showing her few teeth, and she said, "Oh, I can make you some tea!" Then a spiteful look crossed her face and she said, "We don't have any water for tea, you won't get any."

Mory pushed through the soiled bed linens on the floor and the books and magazines, toward the bed where her papa lay, his rheumy eyes trying to see her. He was a very old man, his face bones and his beard hardly growing and what was, was grey. His milky sight couldn't see her. His blanket was covered with food bits. The chewed-up nipple on a baby bottle lay beside his hip, his hands trembling up to greet her.

"Don't," she said, keeping her distance.

More tears fell. His ribs under the covers moved.

Through the window Mory saw Milee spying. Her mother could not see him; Mory knew she should be wearing her glasses. That was how it was: whoever was dying got the attention.

"I can make you a scrambled egg," Frieda offered. "They are so nourishing."

"No, thank you," Mory said. "But thank you." She looked around the cabin, at the furniture crowded together and the boxes and stacks of books falling and the notes and pens in coffee cans and the musical instruments propped in corners and the telescope facing into the hall by mistake and no one noticing, no one left with sight enough to see the sky, and the violin hanging on the wall, cracked and dried out as a coconut in a grocery store bin. She sat herself on the edge of the bed, out of reach of his hands. His lashes had disappeared in the crusts growing on his lids.

She was thinking of the nights on the deck, the telescope pointing here and there, her papa pointing look, moons, he would say, bending, steadying, fiddling, fixing, look he would say, holding her up to the eyepiece. "Oh, child," he would laugh. "Maybe you are just too young."

She said now, "I'm back."

She gave him time to speak. He was always in a hurry to speak.

"He can't hear you," Frieda said. "I don't think he hears any more. I believe his hearing has been deeply affected by his affliction," she said.

Mory leaned closer to her papa's lips.

He wanted to talk. His tongue was like a hungry turtle.

"Babble, babble," Frieda said. "Some days I just say babble, babble all day long and he seems happy. Does he seem happy?"

She heard her mother shuffling closer, and her heart started beating with the fluttering fearfulness of a child's heart. "No," she said. "No," she said. Then the room went dark and she smelled poop and pee and she was thrown outside, her clothes ruined and bruises on her from their anger. She had laughed in the grass, her face in the gravel on the path to the earth-covered greenhouse. Then her papa came and gently picked her up and bathed her in the laundry tub and she did not faint and let herself ruin the water because of her loose bowels. Her papa used to say, "You are a hard girl to love, but I do and I always will. You will always be my lover girl," he would say, "and I won't let anyone touch you, ever. You can count on your papa."

"Do not touch me, do not come closer." She was speaking to her mother.

Her papa's hand started feeling around for her. She moved in, close enough for him to touch. His hand had scabs and sores on it and the skin had brown patches. She leaned her body closer so that her breasts were within his reach. His hand found one like a baby would. His hand didn't feel like much of anything on her body, like a leaf or a feather. She looked at him. There were globs of yellow tears in the corners of his eyes.

She shifted her body slightly so that if Mummy wanted to see Papa's hand, she could.

Then Frieda Zimmerman sat down on the rocking chair, the only chair not piled with newspapers. She folded her hands in her lap. She closed her eyes.

Heat, fires, Oscar Zimmerman: Milee suspected he was as frazzled as the bear he was scouting, up at the cabin. And now new scat in his yard, an unsettling turn of events, because he *recognized* it. As though the bear knew where he lived. Wound tightly through the scat was desperation grass – thick, reedy, indigestible. Roots or a tuber of some kind. No black bear had the claws to dig deep enough for *tubers*. Disturbing things had begun to happen inside the trailer too. Aspirin fell off the kitchen counter in the night. Beer caps spun out of his fingers.

Seeing the old man had caused Mory to cry all the way home. He was sorry he'd made her go. She would not take BB up there, she decided not to show them BB, she would never show them BB because he was the one good thing she had got out of living in that smelly cabin. But when she was finished weeping and talking, he could tell she was tired, like a little body done in by the weight of the crimes against it. The old man dying his decaying death but *not dying*.

Milee drove back. You could hear the two creeks, too loud for this time of year, the glaciers themselves melting, global warming, the drought. He parked off the road, as he usually did, in a copse of ash and poplar, the poplar a useless tree, he thought, no good for building or burning for winter warmth, hid the truck in a spot where it couldn't be seen by anyone casually passing, anyone going farther north where the gold mines used to be. Salted gold mines, bringing in excitement and hotels, faking out the suckers. He liked those parts of the old stories – greedy bastards being faked out by guys in the woods. He walked in, stepped around rusting cars, wound carefully past unmended fences, carrying another sack of smelly garbage he'd been saving. He placed it outside the cabin's back door. Then he moved away and sat quietly on his favourite boulder, hidden in behind the trees, and watched the back door of the cabin and listened to the thundering creeks. The bear was nearby; he could feel its little beady eyes peering from the thick brush. He had known bears who could steal a sack of garbage in the time it took you to get something out of the truck. A watchful bear could scoot down the mountain like a shot and nab what it needed. But this bear was different. Vigilant. More cunning. It could steal his offering even while he was watching. The next thing he knew, he would be blinking and the bag would be gone. *Vanished.* It had happened before; the bear, he thought, was speeding up. The size of the bunghole dropping the scat *in both places now* was the old one, the bastard he'd glimpsed, as wily and careful as he himself was becoming. He fixed his eyes on the garbage bag and waited.

Mory Zimmerman had been running away the day he first met her, a day when he'd stolen change from his mother. He was nine years old, chewing on a Snickers outside of Poppy's, waiting for his mother to wake up and check her purse – had he put her lipstick back under the hanky instead of nestling it on top as she kept it? She would not stop to think that being punchy with drink meant she shouldn't drive. She did not do one-and-one makes two. She would come after him. She hated him. She made no bones about it.

The growing apprehension had caused his balls to twitch, those little nubbins she teased him about, stirring in the dark of his underwear. Standing against the store, his back to the warm siding, close enough to the door to escape inside should he see the tornado of dust trailing her and the sway-ride of the car with its loose steering careening toward him from the direction of the trailer, he reached down with his free hand and poked impatiently at his jeans to make the tickle stop.

Then he spied the figure on the road, coming toward him from the north, a girl in a dress, moving with determination.

He folded the candy-bar wrapper carefully around the last big bite and tucked the bar into his back pocket and ran diagonally across the road under the post-and-rail fence where the black cattle lived. He ran across the field, his intention to hide at the far side behind the row of trees that bordered the gully, parallel to the road. He watched her.

Her hands reached into her scalp and picked something out and dropped it. She shook her head from side to side and her hair that had been confined by a rubber band sprang loose into an exuberant mass, like something alive. He wanted to touch it. He stepped out of hiding. "Where did you come from?"

She looked up, her face in a halo of dark frizz. Her eyes were small, set apart, blue. They looked at him without comprehension or fear. She was taller than he, bony, wearing a dress too small for her with a sash drooping in the back.

"Follow me," he'd said. They crouched together in the shade of the trees, and he knew exactly what he wanted. Her hair was soft as an animal's fur. Then he gave her the last bite and soon her breath smelled of his Snickers – peanuts and sugar and caramel. He'd reached out and picked a piece of peanut from between her two front teeth. She'd let him do it.

When he was a little boy, he thought he would marry her. They would hold hands. He did not want to kiss girls. He could not stand lipsticked mouths. He did not want to be a boy. He had never wanted to be a boy.

He heard a sound, a snuffling in his ear. The air smelled putrid. He blinked and looked at the back door. *The bag of garbage, gone again.* He either was lost in thought or the other in him – the straight-talking one – had come to the fore, had seen the bear and not let him see it. Anxiety popped in a rush of blood in his chest. The evidence was mounting that something was not right here with this bear. *Show yourself.*

He didn't know why he was cleaning out the shed; he'd come home and started. He hauled out rusted axes, shovels with loose handles, snarls of wire, broken-down sawhorses. He shoved old clothing and mouldy rags and yellowed newspapers and plastic plant containers into orange garbage bags and took them to the dump and threw the bags over the fence. He came back, found wooden boxes stacked in the back of the shed, and filled them with his dad's busted tools and pieces of galvanized pipe and rusted fruit cocktail cans of nails of no use to anybody. He got tired of thinking what to do with some things – tire rims, buckets that might come in handy, cardboard boxes and hoses that leaked – and tossed them out the door. With much of the junk strewn around the yard, the inside of the shed smelled like dry cedar. Warm wood and something sweet but not fresh like jelly on bread. He dragged his mother's overstuffed chair into the sunlight. You could tell mice had been living in it, the stuffing was sticking out. It was so hot he had no sweat left and his headache was like a brick lodged inside his skull. He started drinking beer. After another hour he was still drinking but hadn't had a piss; that hot. He felt restive again, as though he were being watched.

He sat in his mother's chair and studied the bear trail, a recent scat nearby. He'd always let them come. Hadn't put up a fence, as some would have, electric or wood; hadn't called the animal control to bring their trap, hadn't shot them. They ambled down the trail, passed through his yard, crossed the highway, loped on into Neon Bar, scouted the fields and incidental orchards. They were picky about fruit, ate the ripened pears first, then made do until the plums were ready. He ate a bag of chips. He popped open a can of beer, kept an eye out for what would appear next. *Show yourself.*

Waiting for the apples to ripen frayed their tempers, he could identify with that. Moody they were then. Waiting for anything to start or end was an ordeal. Worn out from foraging in the heat, not stuffed enough, grouchy with fly bites, eyes bloodshot – not enough rain, not enough sugar in the fruit. And circling back, checking every tree in your territory, heaving yourself up, stepping out on a branch, reaching toward the very last pear near the top, the wanting of the pear making your mouth water, the cracking of the branch giving way a signal of pain to follow and you, dumbfounded, thumping to the ground, lying on your back in the moonlight.

He had seen the way the old man had grabbed at her, the way the old woman closed her eyes. He crushed the empty can, threw it into the bush.

He did not sleep, his skull tight with pressure, his nose runny, his eyes dried out from the heat and ash in the air. The next day he worked more on the shed, swept it, had just started collecting the junk from the yard to throw out back when the air suddenly turned hotter, and there was distinctive rustling of leaves and twigs and the hairs on his scalp bristled. The sound grew, and the wind blew up fast as the back of his dad's hand – wham.

He heard a boom and fell forward onto his knees. He held his hands over the back of his neck and rolled in order to see what was going on, to see what was coming. The trees climbing the mountain seemed alive – leaves spinning, the tops twirling, loud snapping from under the ground. A ferocious noise hurt his ears. He rolled onto his back, saw high, streaky wisps of cloud. A garbage bag, torn on a side, billowed and scampered a few feet toward him. Tools propped against the shed fell, their clatter adding to the pandemonium.

He scrambled to his feet, scuttled across the yard and up the stairs to the house, a hot wind blowing his face. He had to pull hard from the inside to click shut the aluminum screen door. The trailer shuddered and creaked. He lurched into the bathroom, reconnoitered the situation from the window. The lake was frothing with whitecaps big as some houses. He slid the window shut and locked it. Still the sound was everywhere. He covered his ears, made for the big bedroom, crept onto the bed, face

down. The bedroom door whisked shut. Wham. *Him.* It all had
something to do with him.

The crashing roar of a helicopter brought him back. He may
have been sleeping or just gone. The other voice often took him
places that he couldn't remember having been, could make
him do or say things that later he had to wriggle out of – bad
things. Dirty things. Hands slapped, bum spanked – half the
time he didn't know why.

His upper lip was perspiring; he was sweaty all over. He
pushed himself up on his elbows. The windows weren't rattling,
but the reverberating sound was still there. A helicopter. Directly
overhead. Zeroing in on some poor bastard running in an alley
in a police movie.

He was in no movie. What he was cringing from was a Forestry
copter and that meant the fire had come home. The whop-whop-
whop of the blades made it impossible to hear anything else – not
the other voice, not his heart, not his earlier panicky snivelling.
He slipped on sandals and made his way outside, around to the
road side of the trailer where he could view the mountains across
the head of the lake. Good-sized plumes of smoke, all right, no
doubt caused by lightning igniting a tree. One tree, two trees,
three trees, more. Dry lightning – thunder, lightning, no rain –
that explained what he'd experienced in the yard. Heat, wind, a
cloudless storm, perfect for starting fires.

He went to a coffee can he kept in a certain place and found
a joint. He went back to the yard and sat uneasily in the aluminum chair and lit up. He inhaled deeply. Though he knew the
noise was from a helicopter, he remained afraid, fear shooting
from his heart to his gut. He said, "My frickin' bear don't
scare." He spoke aloud, using language he normally did not
approve of. "Frickin'. Frickin' shit. Frickin' stickin' lickin'

shit." Hearing his voice erupting so suddenly sent adrenalin roaring in and the words in his head began to speed up. A cascade of rhymes came to him unbidden and his shoulders twitched and his chin jerked to the right. The unfear of bears, the no damn diddly piddly widdly unfear-reality of bears, cares, wares – "Shut up, shut up," he said, wanting the spirit of the bear, wanting what he had. Wanting the fearlessnesslessness fearno-fearness-queerness, beerness of the bear.

He sprang to his feet, propelled by a fact that he'd missed, a fact that finally had wormed its way into his head. He *was* being watched. *He* was the one being spied on. The old grizzly was scouting *him*. The grizzly was supposed to be back on the avalanche slopes with his big griddle cake face in the cow parsnip or his stinky, hidelike snout in a nest of wasps, but the bastard wasn't. *He was here.*

Heat rose, filling Milee's head until he thought he might explode. He leapt down the track to the truck, having no thoughts that he knew of. He began to speed up as he drove along the north road and parked in his customary place. Walked in. Later he remembered walking in. He saw the cabin, crept round it. All as usual. There was the scat he expected, scat he recognized. *His bear* had a mean glint in its eye. A figure darkened the doorway of the cabin. He recognized it too, wearing a long dress and a soiled apron with apples painted on it.

Show yourself. He didn't hide. He stood upright. Raised his claws.

The ravens were shrieking in the pass. They'd been shrieking for quite a while. His knuckles hurt as he knelt by the creek, his hands in the water and dirty bits trailing downstream. His chest ached. He had screamed the whole time. Until he'd stumbled to the creek and nearly lost his balance when kneeling, he hadn't known where the sound was coming from. He had come upon the grizzly and it had growled, a sound so deep his vocal cords felt torn.

24

Estelee Chapman's porch was crowded with broken-down chairs and a chaise with holes chewed out of the foam cushions, and the main room of the log house had enough stuff to open a second-hand store, but Milee's favourite was a collection of kerosene lanterns in good condition but dusty. Coming in, he went over to the shelves and picked up the one with the base of heavy pink glass and laid his open palm on the curve of the chimney, a pot-belly style with knobby edging, as he did every Sunday morning when he got himself together to come to her place. She was open on Sunday mornings, as she put it, told everyone it was a breakfast service. The log house smelled of griddle cakes that she'd prepared on an electric griddle found at the dump, so heavy to lift that it made her wrist think twice, so she said. Decor in her kitchen consisted of two shelves of canning supplies, a flour sifter, one jar of pears in sulfurous syrup undisturbed since 1984, according to the label, and numerous empty bottles of Log Cabin syrup set out on a Coca-Cola tray.

He preferred the Sunday breakfast in the winter when it was often just Estelee and him and they could play rummy all afternoon. Today, however, he could hear several voices – Lenore's and Estelee's at first and then there was Willamina, with her new, overriding tone, telling everyone about the Brunel Mountain Park fire. The fire – he'd heard about it too – had burned fairly hard and though supposedly was contained, had erupted again, probably arson. "Horseback lightning," Willamina was explaining to Lenore as he came in. "The name for arson in the

Caribou," she added. "Some guy looking for the work." She was at the counter, her hair cut short, on one of the vinyl-topped stools in a curve around the bar. Estelee had salvaged the Victorian wood bar from a hotel renovation in Ruth. Milee took the stool farthest from Willamina, not keen on her loud voice. In high school he and Willamina had taken walks along the lake and sometimes his voices started talking and she let them, interested in everything he had to say. "I like the smart one," she'd told him. Milee sat next to Bethany Jane, a shy girl he'd seen at Willamina's.

Estelee went round to pour Milee a coffee, adding sugar the way he liked it. He spooned out some of Estelee's huckleberry jam-syrup onto a steaming griddle cake. People gave Estelee huckleberries and raspberries in exchange for picking up mail and other things for them in Ruth. She made the best whole-berry syrup he'd ever tasted.

"Mountain Park is ranked a 4. I checked it on-line." Willamina stopped slicing a griddle cake into squares and grinning, bragged some more about what she knew. "Rank 4 has smoke grey to black. The smoke from a Rank 5 is black to copper. Cool, eh?"

"Nowadays," Estelee said, "Forestry will fly in Subway sandwiches rather than have someone local cook. They've taken all the mystery out of fire," she added. She explained to Lenore that even though Mountain Park was in the Judith Lake Valley regional district, no one locally was getting the benefit from it. In the past, with a big-project fire like that one, Forestry rented the community hall and there was work for locals. Today, a big-project fire only hired people who'd been certified – "given new fancy names like security and warehousing and expediters," she said, "the folks needed to drive gear and supplies back and forth." They would hire a certified cooking crew – "whatever the heck that means," she said – to guarantee seven thousand calories a day to the men on the line, roasts and potatoes and gravy and bacon and eggs. All they could eat.

Milee sipped his coffee. Nothing like when his dad was home from a fire, handing him Hershey bars, face rosy from the heat and hard work. In those days a man could be tagged for a firefighting crew if he happened to be in the pub at the wrong time. Spot the fire warden come through the door, and all the guys with fresh pints who didn't want to man the line better run – because if you didn't, you'd be heading up a washboard logging road in the back of someone's pickup, your lunch of sandwiches, thickly sliced cheese and piles of ham, already made and wrapped in wax paper. His dad would come home smelling of smoke, a few beer under his belt and cheerful. Good pay, real good pay. Now everything was contracted out, and the contractors required training. You had to take the basic course and learn fire lingo – "fire suppression." You had to learn about water pumps and the staging area and interface problems. You had to deal with fire behaviour specialists with their computers and people standing around with cellphones. Milee had lasted two days at FierceFire, the contractor outfit in Tucker and then they said – the fellow made him nervous, burly and big, hair on his chest curling out of his cotton undershirt – "This isn't your line of work, Logan. I am saving you from a whole lot of progressive discipline."

Willamina turned to Lenore. "The guys on the line wear these orange suits. Maybe lightning doesn't like orange. Hey. Did you hear about those two people?" She was thinking about the big deal CBC News had made about the two people in the next valley getting hit. The man and a woman were on the beach, wet after a swim. The man suffered heart arrhythmia and a wad of the woman's hair fell out into her open hand. Willamina, hearing that, had patted her own hair, feeling a bit sorry she'd chopped it off so heartlessly. Last night she and Bethany Jane – BJ – had gone for an overnight of camping in Sawmill Bay and made promises to their mothers that they would not take the kayak that they'd tied to the roof of the car into the middle of the lake, "lightning having a preference," Willamina quipped to BJ, "for open water." They chose a spot on a protected knoll under just the right number of trees to be able to see the sky through, and while driving a stake for the tent, Willamina said, "Mom told me the lightning stories three times, for luck. And, like, 'What's so special about you, that lightning wouldn't strike you?' She is so determined to make it really clear that I am *so* not special." She'd rolled her eyes.

"Ah, but you're special to me," BJ said in a high twittering voice, which had made them both laugh. Then they'd got a bit stoned on local pot, and Willamina made BJ drink some maple syrup to get her blood sugar back on track and she'd recommended she sip maple syrup every day, she'd told her maple syrup was essential to her getting better, getting rid of the parasites, and waxed into a rhapsody about maple syrup, the most Canadian of all exports (besides trees and water). She'd been feeling really fine. At the end of her soliloquy she saw the first stars of the night and a loon warbled. She'd lifted her plastic cup of Kahlua for a toast. "Thank you," she'd said. "Thank you God, thank you God, thank you God." It was a little embarrassing to recall the next day when you were being looked to as an *expert* on things of real significance.

Bethany Jane slid her eyes to Willamina, who was back on topic again, talking about fires. She herself would like to be like Willamina, the sort of girl who knew what she was doing with her life. She had tried not to be sorry for what she had done – running off with someone completely insincere, practically a womanizer – but she was, indeed, so sorry she could hardly bear the writhing guilt in the pit of her chest. Because of her dad having the stroke. Her mum alone with him, besides heart-broken and humiliated by her daughter. Now her mum was looking into taking the postal clerk exam, figuring the best money was at the school, the hospital, the liquor store, or the post office. And at the post office she'd know exactly totally everything going on in the whole valley. Bethany Jane had made that remark to Willamina and been sorry afterwards. Bethany Jane knew her behaviour had hit her mum hard. The scholarship. Giving it back. The donations people made for her. The whole town had worked on bringing her up and she had behaved selfishly. "Oh." She spoke out loud. Flagyl was helping but the parasites were not gone. "Excuse me." She ran outside and up the slope to the outhouse.

Willamina explained, "She just got back from Mexico."

It occurred to Lenore that Bethany Jane would be reliable in a way, she had to concede, that Gary, perhaps, was not; he'd already disappointed her by failing to show up for Larry, due to a "gig." They were talking about Estelee's new rooster, who couldn't tell night from day, when Lenore said, "Wouldn't be looking for a temporary job, would she?"

"Bethany Jane? As a matter of fact she is," said Willamina. "She's lost weight but she's strong *and* smart. She needs to get out of the house. But don't tell her I said so."

"There's a fire in the Natalie Valley, I heard."

"Yep. Timber Creek. Interface fire, worst kind. Oh, you *will* need Bethany Jane's help with that bunch. Residents on evac alert."

Bethany Jane came back in and took her seat. "You already sound Army."

"Sixteen, they said. Old people, some kids –"

"They've been up there since the seventies," said Estelee. "Inbred like rabbits, I suppose."

"I like rabbits," Lenore said, suddenly wishing to share last night's experience. The Unitarians had turned out to be more interesting than she'd thought, besides their willingness to try macrobiotic food. She looked at the others looking at her, Estelee's spatula midway between the griddle and Lenore's plate. "Right." Estelee smoothly kept the pancake moving and added, "Draft dodgers, leftover from the Vietnam War."

"Rabbits are a Centre for Light Awareness thing," Lenore said, then found she couldn't say another word. What had happened had been a mystical and, it seemed, private experience. She'd also been levitated by the Unitarians but did not want to mention that, either, didn't want to be laughed at – You? Levitated? Lord, they must have been weightlifters – though she didn't think the people at Estelee's would respond in that way. She'd learned about the deeper meaning of rabbits when the group explained that being anxious and upset about your life wasn't necessarily a bad thing. Rabbit energy could be good. In fact, if she thought about it, she'd come a long way, despite her fears. She'd done the hardest thing already – taken a chance, set out, given in, let go. She didn't need to be wily and hidden as a fox, she could stand in plain sight and let herself be swallowed by whatever came along, including the future itself.

Lenore had been skeptical until she'd felt the sneakiness of the fox leave her heart and a brave little rabbit take its place. She said, "Rabbits are scared, but there's more to them. They mean change. Transformation."

"Ah, you've discovered the New Age have you?" Estelee smiled and put on a second pot of coffee.

Lenore felt blood creep up her cheeks.

"Something to it, I always say," said Estelee, though in truth she knew no one had heard her say anything of the kind.

Willamina licked her fingers. "Milee Logan, listen up.

Incoming bulletin with your name on it: the Centre will need more frequent garbage runs and food *procurement* and all the other activities to do with feeding and housing sixteen or so people. Oh, hey. I'm required to take French. It's the *Canadian* Army, after all. I have a little French but not enough."

The phone rang and Estelee raised her eyebrows, as if to say, "On Sunday morning?" She went into the main room to take it.

For months it seemed Milee's heart had run at high speed. It hurt to have a heart scared – as a rabbit's, he saw – a heart that bounded and skittered, felt chased. He had listened to what Lenore had to say because though he'd felt like Rabbit, he'd not understood the real meaning. Too much had been going on all at once: people sick or dying or dead, smoke from the east and those words – *oppression*, *ignorance* – the words used by the other voice. All summer he couldn't keep up with himself, couldn't get himself quiet, did not know what oppression meant, knew more about ignorance. The words came to nothing if fear was what you were left with. Already he wasn't feeling the anxiety in the same sharp, breathless way. He had been, he thought, transformed.

Estelee stood listening hard in the dim light of the low log ceiling. She was gesturing to them to be quiet, and she exclaimed more than once, "Oh, my God. Oh, my God," her hand placed over her heart. Bethany Jane crossed the room and stood next to her, while Milee, behind the bar, poured another cup of coffee. He added quite a bit of sugar this time. In a stage whisper directed at the kitchen, Estelee relayed the news. She clasped Bethany Jane's arm and said, "The Zimmermans. Old couple in the bush," directing her explanation toward Lenore, a comment that caused Lenore to put down her fork. "Both of them. Apparently a bear. Grizzly. The cabin is a mess." And then she said something else into the phone and hung up. "That was Mary, at the store. She's concerned about Mory. She's on her way over to the Centre."

"A grizzly? Really?" Lenore couldn't help herself.

"Those poor people," Bethany Jane said, following Estelee back to the kitchen.

"Let's face it, they weren't anybody's favourites," said Willamina.

"Are they dead?"

"Yes, they are dead," Estelee said to Lenore, at the same time giving Willamina a reproachful glance.

Willamina shrugged. "I mean, it's only the truth."

"Were they mauled? Blood, guts, everything? A *bear*?"

"We are talking about *human lives* here," said Bethany Jane.

"Young males on their own," Estelee pointed out, "no longer cubs, can become rogues. Likely to do anything. So I've read. My God. Oh, dear." She unplugged the coffee pot and the griddle and started for the door. Bethany Jane collected plates and put them in the sink.

Lenore took that last bite and said, "Oh. Of course. I should get back."

Estelee plucked her keys from the forged square-nail she used as a hook. "That poor girl."

Willamina slid off the stool and turned to Milee, still behind the bar. "Hey, Logan, stay and clean up, will you?" She slipped on her backpack and hurried to catch up with the others. At the door she said, "I've heard about some fairly bizarre things, but not here in Neon Bar, eh?"

On the trail to the vehicles, the women agreed that it was the time of year when the accidents happened, the meetings between humans and bears, summer sorting itself out.

On the third day after the news, Milee took BB for an ice cream at Poppy's – the last one of summer, he said – and BB's little hand was sticky from strawberry, his favourite. They walked together to the tepee. Mory was lying down, covered with the blanket though it was hot. A mob of crows were cawing. BB picked up his Elmo and went outside.

Milee sat across from her, on the other side of the firepit. He wrapped his arms around his knees and closed his eyes. The intensity of the heat building up inside the tepee was all right, he liked warmth and small places. When he opened his eyes her face was as he recalled first seeing it – the wide-set, blue eyes upon him, no fear and no questions.

"I am offering you the trailer," he said. It was the other creating just the right words. It wanted to keep talking, explaining everything, to make sure she understood what he meant and all the details leading up to his decision to speak. He did not let that voice keep on talking. He stopped it by closing his lips and shifting his body, causing some squirming. His shoulders twitched, but he kept his lips together and then the voice gave up, for the moment.

She ducked her head half under the blanket. "I think you are a jeeter," she said. "A grass-eating jeeter."

He did not want to answer everything, nor play. He had to get this off his chest; he persevered in what he needed to do. "I fixed up the shed," he said. Now she was giving him a different look. "I'll be like a bear in a cave," he said. "You and BB take the trailer. You will please come."

He saw her as she had been that day, a girl on a road heading in his direction, looking for safety. The wrong that happened to her existed in the person of BB, a confusing but likable little guy. A person who shouldn't have been born, a person a lot like himself, a boy who would never be a man, who was a child but not carefree. Burdened. That was the point at which he and Mory came together: their meeting on the road that afternoon, each gnawing on themselves, each attempting escape. The chocolate, the shade, him reaching into his pocket, sharing what he had with her. He did not love her, he was not so naive.

25

Kathleen's first phone call was from Davida. "He doesn't want to see you," she said. "He's out of town anyway for another three days. So I hear."

At the sound of Davida's voice, Kathleen's yearning to talk to her hit with the wilfulness of a single-minded child. "Where are you?"

"What?"

"Where are you? I mean, can we talk, can we meet, how are you?" Davida responded by saying nothing.

Kathleen tried again: "I think I'm off the rails, lost on a darkening sea," she said, sounding all wrong, sounding like the old pattern, nothing contrite or appropriate.

"I pity you."

"I'm sorry, I'm so sorry. But I – but I came back."

"He doesn't know how to *love*, if that's what you're thinking, take it from me."

"I'm sorry about everything, I think I was –"

"Oh, shut up."

Kathleen waited for the connection to break but it didn't. Dog barked up the hill.

Davida said, "All right. I'll come over. I'll stay exactly twenty minutes, not one second more."

Kathleen put out her two ceramic mugs and a teapot, some Earl Grey in bags, and a box of lemon cookies. She'd found a wooden tray with handles in a crawl space upstairs. She ran out to a tree in the yard and gathered some hazelnuts in their sheaths and spread them around on the tray. Her plain black mugs were set off nicely.

She organized her buckets and teatree cleaning soaps and sandpaper and paint and the rented floor sander that had just about ripped her arms out when she'd tried it. Then she sat on a chesterfield she'd bought at a yard sale and looked out at the mountains and noticed the pine beetle damage. She'd read about pine beetle damage in the west in the *Globe and Mail* available at the drugstore. She shuffled through the fashion pages and the Weekend Section and tried to read columns by young women who used words like *slut*. She and Davida would have had a field day on the topic. Where was she?

Kathleen opened a bottle of gamay from the Okanagan. She drank half a glass. Davida did not arrive.

An hour later, Davida phoned and launched in. "I called to tell you that I'm not going to let you off the hook based on your loss, your mourning, your grieving, whatever excuses you've come up with to rationalize your behaviour. Being out of your mind or separated from your conscience, which you must have been and still are – well, that's just too bad, dear, because I will never forgive you. My – my situation has turned out very well, actually, but I will never forgive you."

"*This house has mice*," Kathleen wailed, but Davida had hung up.

She put away the tea things and returned to the bottle of gamay and had another glass, then drove back to Boris's, wearing her gumboots. She sat in the car, and looked at the dark house, waiting for some sign. She felt panic rising: She'd made a serious blunder and stepped into a parallel universe, and what she thought was true – what she had counted on as being true, that Boris secretly *wanted* her – was not true at all, a fantasy concocted by her feverish imagination, her neediness over-whelming reality. Sitting across the road from Boris's dark house, she began to hyperventilate and put her hands over her mouth and breathed into her palms. Then she grabbed her new flashlight and flung open the car door and ran clumsily in the gumboots across the road and onto the porch and peered inside the front room. Yes, she did recognize that black leather chair and the bronze sculpture of a hand on a side table – Davida's hand, Boris had had it commissioned by a local artist, he had made a big deal about it to get on her good side, he'd said, laughing, the "her" being Davida, and Davida glowering.

She went round back and noticed a light in the cabin, and while she knew they rented it sometimes, she wondered if Boris was hiding out there, his aversion to her so extreme. She could creep across the dark field and find out. She hesitated. No. Boris Malenko was not a man to hide from anyone, especially, she realized, a woman. She cupped her hands and looked in through the mudroom door, and there were things she recognized – his plaid work jacket hanging on the hook and his gumboots, much like hers, set side by side. She looked a long time, longingly she might say if she had anybody to say it to, the longing misplaced, mysterious, practically predatory.

She then decided she did not believe a word Davida had said about Boris. She started the car and drove back through Ruth and up and down the streets and then had the idea that she needed to find Davida and drove through town and went north on a road where the white line seemed especially important, a ribbon unravelling through darkness, the road Davida had driven with her that afternoon, to see Davida's little horse in the field at Miriam's, getting along so well with Miriam's horse. She drove slowly, along the curves, in and out of a number of side roads that were slightly more than gravelled paths that wound down toward the lake.

The sky was one big dark cloud cover when at last she recognized the road to Miriam's, the shape and feel of it, and she went down, knowing that they would see her approaching if they were sitting on that side of the house or walking to the sheds, though that was unlikely at that time of night and in this weather; the two women were inside, having dinner. She could see smoke from a chimney; she pictured a hearth, a colourful carpet on the polished floor in front of the fire.

Remembering the day of the strange tea – birch-leaf tea – and what Davida had said about Boris – how useless he was, how boorish – and the way in which Miriam had responded, Kathleen pulled over and listened to the rain that began drumming on the roof of the car and could not grasp what she was trying to think of.

Davida had not confided in her. That much was clear. Hadn't confided in her about anything, even during the visit in June. Maybe she'd been too busy feeling sorry for her – over the year she'd listened to Kathleen rave on the phone for hours but had volunteered nothing about her own life. Selfless, in a way, except, Kathleen realized, she'd been eased out of Davida's emotional life, out of the intimate "inner circle" – not by God, not dropped by God as Davida had said on the boat, just by her, Davida herself. Kathleen took an inward breath and held it. Her eyes stung with tears. She'd been too self-absorbed to realize.

Then, exhaling, she proceeded slowly, slowly past the main shed toward the house until she could see into the cul-de-sac, and there, in her headlights, she spotted Davida's 4Runner. Just because Davida was staying at Miriam's didn't necessarily mean anything, it did not necessarily mean that Boris was entirely free. Yet there it rose, up through Kathleen's heart, a wash of exuberance at the thought of the field to him wide open.

The phone was ringing when she got home. Boris said, "I'm back," and she said, "I'm coming over."

"I warn you, I don't have much energy," he said. "It's been a helluva summer." He'd been bringing things in from the car; he set his duffel bag down. "It's been a long day." There was a leather satchel in the threshold between the kitchen and the mudroom, where they were. She could see the phone on its little table in the kitchen. He was wearing a fine-woven houndstooth jacket over a pair of jeans and his bronze belt buckle had a cowboy on it inside a large ring that read, *Yukon Centennial.*

"Nice to see you also," she said. "Why did you duck my calls?"

"I thought you might be crazy," he said.

She gave him a look.

"You seemed, what's the word, intense."

"To put it mildly."

"Yes. To put it mildly."

She nodded. She looked at the belt. Thought about the kind of man who would wear such a belt.

"Look," he said. "I needed time. It – it was all kind of sudden. Everything." His voice caught in his throat. "God, you look so good." He moved quickly, kissed her hard and, lifting her sweater, deftly undid her bra. He ran his warm, hard hands over her breasts, bent down to suckle briefly, looked into her face and saw what, obviously, he wanted to see because he said, "Undo your jeans. Turn around." He loosened his buckle. She heard the zip.

It was not what she expected.

"I've been thinking about doing that to you since you left," he said, catching his breath.

"Slight variation, but me too." She shivered. Her lips felt bruised. He left her and came back with tissues. She tucked them into her panties and zipped herself. "You didn't use protection. Did I just get HIV?"

"You make me wild," he said and placed his hand on her cheek. She closed her eyes and left his hand where it was, the thumb caressing her jawline. Then she reached up and twisted his fingers hard.

"I said, did I just get HIV?"

"No. Christ."

"You have quite the reputation. Don't deny it."

He frowned. "Yes. No. But I'm always careful." He took his fingers from her grasp and rubbed them. "I knew you'd be all right. I knew you and James were faithful to each other. I knew you would be safe."

"How do you know what I've been doing in Toronto all this time? Maybe I've been cruising a bit myself. How do you know *you* were safe?"

He stopped cinching his buckle. He looked stricken, his eyes assessing her in this new light. She smiled. "You really, really don't know," she said. She took a step nearer and narrowed her eyes.

He said, "I thought you – I thought you *missed* him."

"I do. Oh, I do. Yet here I am. Here you are."

"I thought you were still faithful."

"To who? Whom. To whom did you think I had an obligation to be faithful?"

"Well, James of course."

Boris looked to her like a boy caught in a white lie and she erupted into a little laugh. She waited for him to waver. He did not. "So," she said. "Boris Malenko, I have your number. But what about Davida? Was Davida faithful before you walked across the field to take advantage of me?"

"I didn't –"

"You did. Be quiet. But what about Davida?"

He lurched a step away and bent at the waist as though she'd kicked him. "Christ," he said, straightening up. "She's not interested in men, you must know that."

My situation has turned out very well.

"Oh. Right." Kathleen took another step closer.

"You didn't realize all the shit that was going on when you were here. We – we sheltered you, in a way. Because you – well."

He took a step sideways. He was now backed against the shelves that held jars of canning, plums and pears, so much domestic effort. "Listen. I don't want anything to do with a relationship. I don't trust women any more, you know what she's up to, and I certainly don't want another wife. And my damn daughter wants to stay in Winnipeg, which means I pay the school for her upkeep, fees, clothes, shit – oh, Christ. Enough. I have had it up to here with the demands of women."

"I get it," Kathleen murmured.

"It was awful after she left," he said. "She left messages for two entire days and if I answered, she hung up. I went out to get away from the phone ringing and when I came back, the box was full, the messages of her hate and how despicable she found me. And I couldn't blame her, I couldn't, and I blamed her anyway. It was all her fault. She didn't want a real man." He looked embarrassed. "You know what I mean. A man. She didn't want a man."

"Sshhh. You listen. You walked across that field and you took me. I wanted it. I wanted it as much as you did."

He inhaled sharply. He touched his groin.

"I don't want to be your wife," Kathleen said. "But I have to say this," she said, reaching for his Yukon Centennial buckle. "I love you. I have to tell you. I love you. I am in love with you."

They moved to the couch in his office and then they had to laugh and they moved upstairs to the bedroom and she hesitated, but only for a moment, before she let him lay her down upon his bed.

She woke up around five and watched him sleeping and then left and went home to shower and change and have her own coffee and breakfast. She ground the Oso Negro Deeply Organic beans and set up the Melitta filter on her favourite mug. A rooster crowed. A few small flies warmed themselves on the outside of the window. She waited for the kettle to boil and looked at the six-by-six section of kitchen floor she had sanded to see if she could do it, the brick-coloured acrylic paint gone in that patch, down to the wood underneath, which was fir, Bet said, because all the floors in the Victorian houses in Ruth were pine or fir. The Sonemayer house would be fir because the house, as Bet put it, was quality. Kathleen had started her list, room by room, of what was needed. What she wanted to accomplish would take years, but the house would be beautiful. And hers.

She sipped her coffee as she looked out at the mountains, the larch yellow; it seemed fall had arrived overnight. The black dog sat companionably on the other side of the long window. Bet Harker had told her the dog belonged to the drug dealer – Bet had said "drug dealer" without blinking – and because the dog wasn't looked after, she wandered and so was called simply Dog.

Boris telephoned. "Where'd you go, babe?"

She remembered how Davida fought off the term of endearment, "babe" and "baby." The word must remind him of the erotic side of a relationship, she thought, for Boris was deeply rooted in sex, despite his domestication – he had been married twice that Kathleen knew about. "Home," she said into the phone. "You were so . . . ummm . . . last night," she said and could not believe the words had come out of her mouth, her innocent mouth.

"Oh, babe," he said.

James would not believe her now. "Hot," she said and made her voice a whisper. And heard Boris laugh. She almost cracked up herself. But she felt good. Their exchange felt good.

He invited her to go with him up the lake, where he had business, he said, some property to see. She said yes, she would like that, and dressed in jeans and her flannel shirt. She did not know how far their relationship would go. It would be entirely different from what she and James had; Boris was a different man altogether, self-serving, self-focused. And here she was, a different woman, already manipulating Boris from the place where he lived – his sexuality. Their sexuality. Their mutual attraction.

They passed the road to Miriam's and neither of them looked down it, though Boris did come to a brief pause in the midst of his ramble about how Ruth's micro-minded town council was overlooking his offer to . . . she lost track of his thread, then picked it up again. He was trying to sell council, at a sizable discount that only he could provide, the portable fire suppression units, so they could resell to home owners. "What we need is fire-preparedness in every nook and cranny." And she knew a bit about this portable unit he wanted to sell council and everybody else, because they were pulling it behind another of his vehicles that seemed to turn up when he needed it – this one a Dodge Ram 4x4 with an open bed and a mounted tank of extra gas. The fire unit had one hundred feet of red, quarter-inch hose, two hundred feet of bright yellow rolled firehose mounted on the side, a motor, a water pump, and a five-gallon container of non-toxic biodegradable foam. She gathered a distributorship was in the works.

He had picked her up in the Subaru and then they'd driven to a rental property outside of town and switched vehicles. The unit was tucked into its own trailer beside a one-hundred-gallon water tank – empty, because Boris said it was wasteful to pay for gas to haul water when they could get water, hell, they could get water from any creek. His earnestness made her smile. How could she not smile at the man, a single-minded civic entrepreneur driving in the wilderness conveying a machine that looked like a cross between a turn-of-the-century big-wheeled cart and a tiny, shiny fire engine?

"I mean, it's damn shortsighted," he was saying now, "when we have a Canadian company making the things, and they need the business and we need the protection – how are you going to protect five thousand people spread out over more than a thousand hectares, unless you gear them up with these caddies, set 'em up with water tanks or, if they have a creek, teach 'em how to pump water? Hell, think of it this way: some lone-wolf hermit holed up in a crappy cabin could prevent a whole forest from burning because he's where he is and *prepared*."

A ray of sunlight shot through an opening in the cloud cover and shone into a bay on the far shore as Boris drove and talked. She watched as the ray of light moved along the shore. She thought of the women who had gone across the lake in their finery, in their hats and high boots. She remembered the photographs of the small boats that they had travelled in with men in suits and hats. She thought about how those women and men would have needed to trust each other; Judith Lake was miles across.

Her view was obstructed as they passed between trees on both sides of the road. Around the next bend the bare cliff provided a clear view of the bay again, and she thought she saw a figure on the beach, shadowed by the woods immediately behind, and she was reminded of her miner and of how much attention and reflection she had invested in that solitary, imagined man. She suspected, now, that what she was seeing – had seen, the road moved inland again – was just a tree struck dead by lightning.

Boris lay his hand on top of hers a moment. He gave it a squeeze.

They stopped in Neon Bar, across from a gas station and convenience store, a deli, a good one, he said, and he told her to wait in the vehicle. She knew, from his shifting eyes – Boris did have shifty eyes, it was part of his charm, she thought, he was so obvious, everything about him was so available, so accessible – that she couldn't go inside with him because the situation was delicate – of course it was – those people knew Davida. Everyone knew Davida, everyone knew the Frances Hill and would be asking, Who was this woman taking Davida's place? Soon enough they would learn that Davida Adrianna and Miriam Fauquier were starting a life, but for now, Kathleen expected she would have to wait through it.

At her window, with the affability of a waiter whose name you knew, Boris listed off for her the sandwiches available, from which she close roasted eggplant and tomato and Boris a salami with lettuce. He brought the food back and they ate in the truck, as though they were on a picnic, windows rolled up against the black flies. Then she waited while he showed the fire caddy to the couple who owned the deli, a middle-aged woman and a man of the same age, curious about her, whom she saw in the rear-view mirror. She thought about herself as a woman who should learn when to take a walk or when not to go with him in the first place; she was the "other" woman, and she waited to be stricken by shame, but it did not come – how rare it was to find love, even the physical semblance of it – and she smiled, in case they could see a reflection of her in the mirror or on the vehicle – in his eyes, she thought, they might see her reflection in his eyes – the pleasant-looking dark-haired couple.

Then he was back in the truck and they were driving through the open gate of the Centre for Light Awareness. "The deal is," Boris was saying as he parked, idling, adjacent to a white pickup. "I'm not here to buy the property, not to make an offer, nothing like that. Nothing threatening. It's only a rumour so far about the possibility of a sale. I personally would doubt it, but you never know. This guy is a weirdo, yeah, but smart as hell, comes from a great family. Loaded. So, the deal is, we're showing the caddy."

"I'm not supposed to hide?"

"Christ," he said. "Don't pull that female crap. It's a different deal here."

She remembered that Davida had taken a workshop at the Centre. That she'd said Gabriel was special in some way. "Why is he selling?"

"He's not. Not officially."

"Thinking of selling, then."

Boris turned off the engine and shifted toward her, placing his arm across the back of the seat. "You are a regular Miss Marple, eh?"

She wondered what crime had been committed on this spot to make Boris suggest one, and then she acknowledged to herself that she was being melodramatic, though it did intrigue her that Boris, who seemed to know everything, was, in fact, protective about what he knew.

"Sorry," she said. His right hand eased down to her shoulder and rested lightly, the tips of his fingers caressing her collarbone. Little electric shocks flew. He moved across and kissed her on the lips, then drew back. "It might be," he said, "that I do know there has been a dustup and that the sister of my pal Larry – he owns the building supply – was looking after things for them this summer but she's going up to cook for the heliskiers and a new woman has moved in, has a baby, but let me warn you – no, not fair. She might be all right. Mentally fragile, let's say. Something like that. Lucinda, who was Gabriel's partner, is off on another adventure – Jeez, enough." He gestured over his shoulder. "Okay?"

"I could wait in the car."

"Don't be self-effacing. It doesn't suit you."

His abrasiveness surprised her, caught her off guard. Thrilled her. The bully aspect of him related to the great sex thing they had. The connection was astonishing, she thought. Tears – those useless pity tears – rose in her throat. She swallowed them, held them back. "I want to know everything," she said, "like you," and opened the car door and stepped out.

Gabriel Markovice met them on the path and introduced himself to her. He was attractive, eyes that she supposed would be called piercing or riveting if they weren't so veiled; he seemed withdrawn, perhaps disappointed that a stranger had come and he couldn't rise to the occasion or didn't want to.

"Forgive me for my exhaustion," he said, shaking her hand. "The baby keeps me awake."

Kathleen's brows lifted, and she laughed for some reason – the ease and humour with which he made the statement – and he laughed as well and then she felt fine and liked the man and the place.

"What have you got there?" Gabriel said to Boris, and the two men walked over to the fire suppression unit and Boris pointed out its features while Kathleen wondered about the woman who was not mentioned and the baby who was mentioned – someone must have been watching the baby – and took in the view of the lake and the wedge of cottonwood and the wet promise of fall that rose through the bottom of her feet.

"First-rate parcel," Boris was saying. "A boom in retreat centres happening all over rural North America, no need to say the obvious. Cities such traffic jams, eh? Can picture a few cabins over there by the creek, eh? Individual fireplaces, the drill. My nephew has a bit of interest in this sort of thing."

Kathleen heard Boris fishing, his approach so obvious, so blunt that you almost didn't mind. She turned her gaze to Gabriel and saw he was transparent and had to blink to see the white tea towel over his arm again with baby spit-up on it and see him in his solid body. He looked at her. She felt light-headed. The air in Neon Bar, she thought, was rarefied.

After a few more exchanges, they said goodbye and shook hands again and Gabriel opened the car door for her and she slipped in, unsure of what had transpired between the two men, both seeming positive and matter of fact, and she decided to let it go, let it remain part of the general appeal of men, their essential mystery.

"It's a long story," Boris said, a few miles later. He was talking about other people, another situation. They had started back to Ruth when he'd suddenly pulled into a turnout partially hidden by brush. A wide, curving trail led uphill. He wanted her to go up to a trailer – she could just make out a patch of blue and white through the bush – and ask whoever was there if they had water, if they had heat, if they were keeping up the repairs. "Nose around," he'd said to her, and when she didn't budge, he began the cajoling, the "long-story" part, his resistance to explaining why he wouldn't, or couldn't, go up himself.

"I'm not elaborating on the details now," he said, "and may never, we'll see. The point is, everybody who's been in the valley a while shares a history, personal information, knowledge about each other, whatever you choose to call it. I can tell you things that would make your jaw drop and your hair curl." He grinned. "That was nicely put, eh?" She nodded.

He gave another of his expressive sighs, implying that she'd beaten him down, again, and Kathleen held her silence – realized that to deal with him she would remain inscrutable at times and she would need to live in her own house – and when she still didn't speak, he said, "All right, all right. The girl up there is staying with my – my tenant. She was in the hospital for a couple of weeks last month. Don't ask me how I know, I know. Pneumonia, let's put it that way. She's inherited a whack of property farther north, a knockout piece of land, that let me tell you would make a fine retreat if this other thing doesn't work out."

"You are so – calculating," Kathleen said.

"I am." He handed her a pair of fur-lined gloves. "Here. Soon as the sun's down, it's cool. Damp. Put these on." He shifted forward in the seat, sat back, cleared his throat. He didn't reach for her though her hand was available. She was glad that he didn't use her vulnerability to his touch to get his way. He said, "Are you in?" It was barely a question.

She bit her lip. He was thick-skinned, insensitive, possibly a real jerk. She thought a moment longer. He was diverting, he took her out of herself, she was attracted to his masculinity, his machinations, his secrets, his ongoing plots and schemes. He wanted her to be part of them. "Please," he said.

"Nice touch," she said. She knew he was manipulating her, knew he had manipulated her from the moment she'd first stayed in the cabin. She looked up at the trailer hidden in the bush and wondered what she would find there. She was willing to go see, she would go that far.

It was effortless to hop out of the car, trod up the staggered path – stones half-embedded, untrustworthy – onto the partially rotting wood porch to the door. She knocked. She could see a torn blind – the narrow ones that tended to crumple with one bash – and then the door opened and a thin young woman stood behind it, her hair shiny and voluminous around a small-ish head.

"Can I help you?"

Kathleen strained to understand the pronunciation and she smiled noncommittally and peered around the slight figure to have a quick look inside – landlord's orders. She could see a light on above the kitchen table and a child sitting doing something with crayons. "Well," she said, "I'm just here to make sure you have everything you need." The house smelled nice, like muffins.

"I do," said the young woman. "We are fine."

Kathleen inexplicably and suddenly believed it; she believed the words so completely in the moment in which they both stood that she experienced a surging in her heart, an intensity of feeling that caught her off guard. She wanted to pull open the screen door and grab the strange little person standing there and pull her close. There were dark circles under her eyes, she noticed them now though she'd missed them initially, taken aback by the appearance of such an extraordinary, ethereal being, one she had never expected to meet in the woods of the distant place called Neon Bar, a place she'd not imagined existed until she'd actually arrived. She felt breathless. "Well," she said again.

And suddenly it came to her, the way truths did. Sometimes you didn't arrive at forgiveness in the way you expected to, if you hoped for it at all. Absolution for an action or for an inaction – always the weighing regarding what you didn't do as well as what you did. And complicity, she thought. We are always complicit. She glanced down the road where Boris, out of sight, waited. She did not entirely believe that Boris's heart was in the right place, though James had presented it as a possibility so long ago. A saving grace for some people, James had said – more prescient than they'd realized at the time.

The young woman smiled and dipped her head shyly and as Kathleen made a move to leave, she slowly shut the door, and Kathleen was left to walk cautiously down the trail, placing her feet as you do in cross-country skiing, sideways and each parallel to the other. Forgiveness might not come in words but through a place, she thought, the gift of a place. Her house. Ruth itself. Judith Lake. She started along the curve and saw Boris out of the car, standing on her side, the passenger side, looking for her, looking anxious. He waved, relieved, she thought. She slowed, to make him wait, and then considered that this was not the time, nor was she in the mood, for games. She took the last steps toward him, her hands toasty in his big, soft gloves – he was rubbing his from the cold, his gestures dramatic, his gestures would always be dramatic.

Acknowledgments

With thanks to David Zieroth for steadfast counsel and editorial tenacity; my daughter, Robin Ballard, for finding the story at its early stages; Anna Warwick Sears and Lynn Sears for teaching me the way of root vegetables; Barney Gilmore and Lorraine Symmes for comments on the manuscript; and to dear old friends Roberta and Peter Huber, who through it all kept the home fires burning. A toast to good neighbours, past and present, for many forms of sustenance.

This book would never have been realized without the foresight of Denise Bukowski, my literary agent, and Ellen Seligman, publisher of fiction at M&S. I am grateful, also, to Jennifer Lambert for her editorial excellence.

The following publications were among those that provided me with a wealth of historical context: *Pioneer Families of Kaslo* and *Historical Kaslo*, both by the Kootenay Lake Historical Society, undated; *Kaslo – the first 100 years*, George McQuaig, Kaslo Senior Citizens Association, 1993; *Where the Lardeau River Flows*, Peter Chapman, Provincial Archives of Victoria, 1981; *Minnie Kane Livingstone in Kaslo*, edited by Wm. Leverett, unpublished.

Art Westerhaug, of the Ministry of Forests and Range, in Nelson, British Columbia, patiently explained to me the complexities of modern fire suppression. I am grateful to Art and many other British Columbians for helping me with details of life in the interior.